PRAISE FOR *THE WINDS OF*

"Sailing ships of the sky! Bradley P. Beaulieu's *Th[...]* energetic, swashbuckling novel with a distinctive[...] a plot filled with adventure, interesting charact[...] the kind of fantasy I like to read."

—Kevin J. Anderson, *New York Times* bestselling author
of *The Saga of Seven Suns*

"Elegantly crafted, refreshingly creative, *TWOK* offers a compelling tale of men and women fighting to protect their world. Politics, faith, betrayal, sacrifice, and of course supernatural mystery—it's all there, seamlessly combined in a tale driven by intelligent and passionate characters whose relationships and goals a reader can really care about. A great read!"

—C. S. Friedman, bestselling author of the
Coldfire and Magister trilogies

"…a page-turner with twists, turns and palpable danger…"

—Paul Genesse, author of *The Golden Cord*

"In *The Winds of Khalakovo* Beaulieu navigates through a web of complex characters… dukes, duchesses, lovers, and more, while building a rich and intricate world thick with intrigue. He plots the course of Nikandr Iaroslov Khalakovo, a prince laden with disease and courtly responsibilities, and deftly brings the tale to a satisfying end that leaves the reader hungry for the next installment. Beaulieu is a writer that bears watching. I look forward to his next novel."

—Jean Rabe, *USA Today* bestselling fantasy author

"Bradley P. Beaulieu is a welcome addition to the roster of new fantasy novelists. *The Winds of Khalakovo* is a sharp and original fantasy full of action, intrigue, romance, politics, mystery and magick, tons of magick. The boldly imagined new world and sharply drawn characters will pull you into *The Winds of Khalakovo* and won't let you go until the last page."

—Michael A. Stackpole, author of *I, Jedi*
and *At the Queen's Command*

"If Anton Chekhov had thought to stage *The Three Sisters* onboard a windship, with a mix of *Arabian Nights* and *Minority Report* thrown in for good measure, the result would have been Bradley Beaulieu's *The Winds of Khalakovo*—a startling combination of fantastic elements which seems at once both comfortably familiar and refreshingly new. It's a wild ride well worth taking, and an exceptional debut from an author who takes risks and consistently delivers."

—Gregory A. Wilson, author of *The Third Sign*

THE WINDS OF
KHALAKOVO

THE WINDS OF KHALAKOVO

BRADLEY P. BEAULIEU

NIGHT SHADE BOOKS
SAN FRANCISCO

First Edition

ISBN: 978-1-59780-218-5

Night Shade Books
Please visit us on the web at
http://www.nightshadebooks.com

For Joanne, who was with me every step of the way.

Thank you, dear friend, my lovely wife.
I couldn't have done it without you.

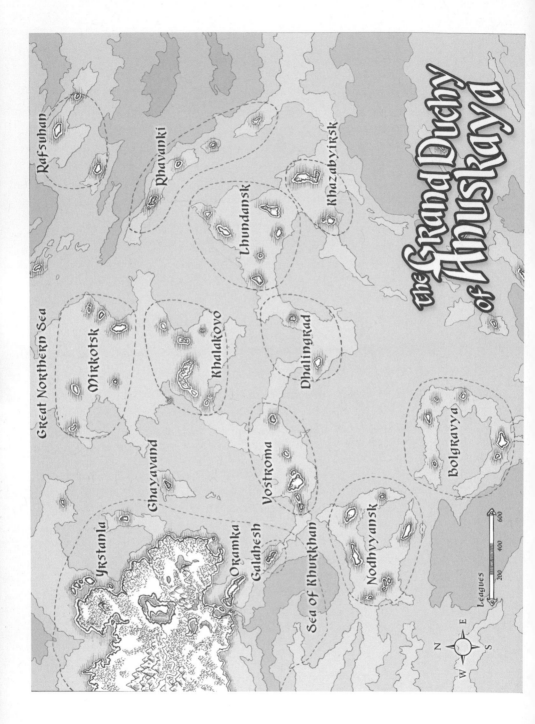

The Grand Duchy of Anuskaya

Great Northern Sea

Rafsuhan

Rhavanki

Lhundansk

Khazabyirsk

Mirkotsk

Khalakovo

Dhalingrad

Yrstanla

Ghayavand

Oramka

Galahesh

Vostroma

Sea of Khurkhan

Nodhvyansk

Bolgravya

Leagues
200 400 600

N
W E
S

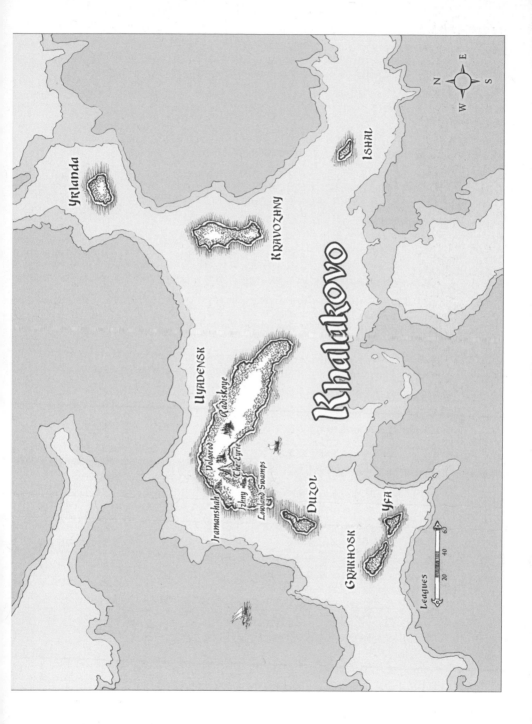

DRAMATIS PERSONÆ

Prince Nikandr Iaroslov Khalakovo
— youngest son of the Duke and Duchess of Khalakovo.
Princess Atiana Radieva Vostroma
— daughter of the Duke and Duchess of Vostroma. Nikandr's betrothed.
Rehada Ulan al Shineshka
— an Aramahn woman. Nikandr's lover in Volgorod.

THE DUCHY OF KHALAKOVO

The Duke and Duchess
    Duke Iaros Aleksov Khalakovo
    Duchess Saphia Mishkeva Khalakovo
Their children
    Prince Ranos Iaroslov Khalakovo — eldest son.
    Princess Victania Saphieva Khalakovo — only daughter, middle child.
Others
    Yvanna Antoneva Khalakovo — Ranos's wife.
    Gravlos Antinov — a shipwright. Oversaw the design and construction
        of the *Gorovna*.
    Isaak Ylafslov — the seneschal of Palotza Radiskoye.

THE DUCHY OF VOSTROMA

The Duke and Duchess
    Duke Zhabyn Olegov Vostroma
    Duchess Radia Anastasiyeva Vostroma
Their children
    Prince Borund Zhabynov Vostroma — eldest child and only son.
    Princess Mileva Radieva Vostroma — daughter, sister to Atiana.
    Princess Ishkyna Radieva Vostroma — daughter, sister to Atiana.
Others
    Katerina Vostroma — a Matra of Vostroma — Zhabyn's sister.
    Nataliya Iyaneva Bolgravya — wife of Borund.

THE DUCHY OF BOLGRAVYA

The Grand Duke and Duchess of Anuskaya
    Grand Duke Stasa Olegov Bolgravya
    Grand Duchess Alesya Zaveta Bolgravya
Their children
    Konstantin Stasayev Bolgravya — the first son.
    Grigory Stasayev Bolgravya — the fourth son.

THE ROYALTY OF THE OTHER DUCHIES

Duke Leonid Roaldov Dhalingrad
Duchess Iyana Klarieva Dhalingrad

Duke Yegor Nikolov Nodhvyansk
Duchess Kseniya Zoyeva Nodhvyansk

Duke Yevgeny Krazhnegov Mirkotsk
Duchess Polina Anayev Mirkotsk

Duke Andreyo Sergeyov Rhavanki
Duchess Ekaterina Margeva Rhavanki

Duke Heodor Yaroslov Lhudansk
Duchess Rosa Oriseva Lhudansk

Duke Aleg Ganevov Khazabyirsk
Duchess Zanaida Lariseva Khazabyirsk

THE ARAMAHN AND THE MAHARRAHT

Ashan Kida al Ahrumea — one of the arqesh (master of all disciplines)
  among the Aramahn.
Nasim an Ashan — an orphan boy with strange powers.
Jahalan Atman al Mitra — Nikandr's havaqiram (wind master).
Udra Amir al Rasa — Nikandr's dhosaqiram (master of the stuff of life).
Fahroz Bashar al Lilliah — a mahtar in the village of Iramanshah.
Soroush Wahad al Gatha — leader of the northern sect of the Maharraht.
Ahya Soroush al Rehada — deceased daughter of Rehada and Soroush.
  Died on the shores of Bolgravya.
Bersuq Wahad al Gatha — Soroush's brother and second in command.
Muwas Umar al Mariyah — a gifted jalaqiram.

PART I

CHAPTER 1

In a modest home in the center of Volgorod, Nikandr Iaroslov Khalakovo sat in a simple wooden chair, considering the woman sleeping on the bed nearby. Dawn was breaking, ivory light filtering in through the small round window fixed high into the opposite wall. His woolen cherkesska lay across his lap, ready for him to slip into. His boots were already on.

The rumpled bedcovers left half of Rehada's form uncovered. His eyes traced the curve of her shoulders, the soft valley of her spine, the arch at the small of her back. Her dark skin blended with the blanket and sheets—cocoa against crimson and cream. The air inside the room was chill, but Rehada would be warm, and he wanted nothing more than to slip beneath the covers, to return to her arms, however foolish it might be considering the family that had landed on the island the night before and the events of the coming day.

He gripped the arms of the chair, readying himself to head for the eyrie, when Rehada stirred. He paused, wondering what her mood would be now that the day had come.

She turned over, her dark eyes focusing on him slowly. When she spoke, her voice was hoarse. "Will you see her?"

Nikandr shook his head. "I doubt she will brave the weather."

Rehada paused. "Is she so frail?"

"Frail?" The hint of a smile touched his lips. "*Nyet.* The Vostromans are not frail. But I fear she looks upon this marriage in the same manner as I."

"And how is that?"

"Have I not told you?" he chided.

"Tell me again."

He stood and took a step toward the door. "As an unwelcome obligation."

She leaned on one elbow. The covers draped over her waist, accentuating the bow of her hip, the lines of her thighs. A mole marked her left breast,

1

just above the nipple. Anyone else might think there was little emotion inside her, but Nikandr knew the signs. She was hurt.

He glanced up at the window and the brightening sky. He could, perhaps, justify a short delay.

He was nearly ready to go to her when his stomach clenched. That painful, familiar feeling had returned, and it was all he could do to mask it from Rehada.

It was a scene they'd played out a handful of times already. She studied him, confused but unwilling to voice her concerns when he was so clearly unwilling to share. Words of explanation nearly slipped from his mouth, but as he'd done so many times before, he remained silent. This was not something he could share with her. Not yet.

"Go," she said, turning away from him and lying down. "And give your bride a kiss for me."

The pain was growing worse—perhaps a sign from the ancients. Either way, he was late.

He leaned down and kissed the top of her head, and though he left without another word, the scent of her jasmine hair haunted him throughout the cold and empty streets.

As his pony crested the snow-covered hill, Nikandr squinted from the reflection of the morning sun. The walrus tusk cartridges on the bandolier across his chest clacked as he shifted position in the saddle. Although the wind was brisk and bitter, it had been a long ride and he had long since grown accustomed to it.

The road ahead lay empty—a change from the previous hour, which had brought a score of wagons and coaches heading in the opposite direction toward Volgorod. He could not yet see the eyrie on its high cliff, but its presence could be felt. A dozen ships, waiting for their berth, held position among the burly white clouds. The ships bore goods or dignitaries, or both, in anticipation of the coming Council. Most would return home immediately in hopes of flying the circuit again before Council finished three weeks hence, but some—those whose homes were too distant or whose master's only purpose was to treat with the gathered royalty—would remain for the duration.

As Nikandr continued down the slope, a massive galleon belonging to the Duchy of Mirkotsk climbed and arced northward, passing high overhead. Four masts were affixed in each of the primary directions: starward, landward, seaward, and windward, sixteen in all. It was a large ship, difficult to pilot, but that was no excuse for the way it was heeling to its windward side. He cupped his hands to his mouth and called like a gull, wishing it safe journey. Moments later, several of the men hanging among the lower rigging waved.

Soon the eyrie came into view. It lay at the edge of the sea, affixed to a towering gray cliff that separated the dark waters from the steady rise of the hills beyond. From this distance the five long quays built into the face of the cliff looked like natural stone ledges, but he knew that each had been built painstakingly by Aramahn stone masons over the course of a decade. The quays each held twelve stout perches that were supported by graceful sweeps of stone as they extended outward from the cliff; they were used to moor, lade, and unlade the windships. The eyrie was—as troubling as it sometimes seemed—the heart of commerce for Khalakovo, the goods it brought the lifeblood. Windsmen and landsmen—hundreds of them—unladed the cargo and hauled it along the ramps leading up from the quays to the eyrie's grand courtyard—a cluster of offices, warehouses, and auction squares that stood on a wide plateau at the edge of the cliff.

A coach pulled by four ponies passed Nikandr on the road, the driver bowing his head as he passed. Nikandr waited for it to crest the hill behind him before retrieving a silver flask from inside his woolen cherkesska. After downing a healthy swallow of the bittersweet brew, he shoved the flask back into his coat. The warmth of the draught suffused his gut, doing its best to quell the feelings of unease that had been his constant companion over the last two months.

He kicked his pony into a trot and covered the last half-league quickly. Once inside the eyrie's courtyard, he steered his pony toward a handful of stone buildings near the first of the cannon emplacements. Wagon wheels clattered over the cobblestones as drivers maneuvered through the space. Gulls circled above, while below an auctioneer called out to a small crowd of men wearing fine wool coats. After giving his pony over to a stable boy, Nikandr entered the lobby of the administration office and found the eyrie master, Aleksei, among the orderly rows of desks on the far side of the brass-and-marble counter. Aleksei was inspecting a ledger while a younger man looked nervously on. When he finally pulled his nose from the ledger, and the man beside him nodded and ran off, Nikandr caught his eye with a wave of his hand.

Aleksei was a balding man with a trim black beard. He wore spectacles upon his nose and—despite the chill interior of the building—a sheen of sweat upon his brow. His expression upon recognizing Nikandr was a mixture of exasperation and relief, but then it turned to one of business-like seriousness as he pulled his spectacles from around his ears, bowed his head, and motioned Nikandr to join him in his office.

Nikandr stepped into the austere room and turned his gaze to the iron perch in the corner beyond Aleksei's impeccably neat desk. Resting on the perch was an impressive black rook with a golden band about its ankle. The band made it clear that this bird was a member of the palotza's rookery, a beast ready to serve Nikandr's mother, Saphia, should the need arise. Thankfully Nikandr could not feel her presence through the chalcedony soulstone around his neck, so he knew her attention was currently elsewhere.

Were there a choice, Nikandr would have held this conversation outside of his office, but he couldn't speak to Aleksei where there was any risk of being overheard—not about this—and he didn't wish to raise Aleksei's curiosity by calling him away from his normal duties.

"My Lord Prince…" Aleksei swept around to the front of his desk and set the ledger down, motioning to the polished leather chair across from him. "What might I do for Palotza Radiskoye."

"I know you're busy"—Nikandr's stomach gave a twinge as he took his seat—"so I won't keep you long."

Aleksei sat as well, smiling as pleasantly as he could manage. It was clear from his downward glances that he dearly wished he could look over his ledger. Nikandr knew from experience that this was a man used to doing three things at once, but it was a measure of Nikandr's stature that he would leave it untouched for fear of giving insult.

"The *Kroya*," Nikandr said.

"Ah!" He began to rifle through the documents piled neatly to the left of his desk before Nikandr had even finished speaking. From it he pulled a single sheet of paper and slid it across the desk. "Here it is, at last. I was going to send it with the noon pony."

It was a report from the master of Rhavanki's eyrie—a confirmation that the *Kroya*, one of Khalakovo's stoutest ships, had left nearly six weeks prior. When they had received word that the ship had not arrived on Khalakovo's shores, a search effort had been waged, but no remains had yet been found. All efforts would of course be made to find the missing ship, but the attacks of the Maharraht had been growing since the settling of winter, and it was possible that the ship now lay at the bottom of the sea or—worse—in the hands of the enemy. It was not the news Nikandr had been hoping to hear, but neither was it unexpected—he, along with everyone else in the palotza, had already assumed the worst.

"Very well," Nikandr said as he slipped the paper back onto the desk.

After filing the document back into the sheaf of papers in the same location as before, Aleksei shuffled them neatly together and regarded Nikandr. "If there's nothing else, My Lord?"

"Actually, there is," Nikandr said, pausing for effect. "There's been word, Aleksei, that you traffic in certain goods."

"Goods, My Lord?" Aleksei's face remained composed, but the skin along the top of his balding head flushed.

Nikandr leaned forward. "I'm not here in an official capacity, Aleksei."

Aleksei's eyes thinned and his eyebrows pulled together for one brief moment, but then he leaned back into his burgundy leather chair with a look of understanding. "Your sister?"

Nikandr nodded. "She has time yet, but the final stages approach."

"There are several unguents I might recommend, but—"

"I'm here for the grubs. You have two, do you not?"

Aleksei tried—and failed—to hide his surprise. "I-I do, but they are more effective in the early stages of the disease."

"Let me worry about that."

Aleksei sat higher in his chair. "My Lord, they're both spoken for."

"I'm sure you'll find more."

Aleksei looked defeated, but it was only an act. Nikandr knew how shrewd he was. And how greedy.

"I could make arrangements, but my patrons, the ones who were promised the grubs, will be arriving tomorrow. I can only imagine their anger."

"The price, Aleksei."

"Two-thousand."

Nikandr paused, allowing the figure to sit in the cool air between them. "They're worth eight-hundred. No more."

"A year ago, *da*, but times have changed. We have become more desperate."

"Twelve-hundred, Aleksei. That is all I will pay."

"My Lord—"

"And I'll ensure," Nikandr said, sitting back, "that my brother's men steer wide of the Master's office."

Aleksei looked around the office as if he had just considered what would happen were he to refuse Nikandr's offer.

"Of course, My Lord. They—They may not prove effective."

"A fact you share with all your patrons, I'm sure." Nikandr waited a polite moment for Aleksei to move, and then prompted him. "The grubs, Aleksei?"

He stood with no small amount of reluctance and moved to a set of shelves behind him. From the highest he slid aside a neat stack of books and retrieved a lacquered wooden box. After carefully setting it on his desk, he slid open the top and pulled out a glass vial filled with golden liquid and a fat, colorless grub the size of Nikandr's thumb. Nikandr stared, fighting to keep his disgust from showing—the thought of eating the thing was threatening to turn the unease in his stomach into all-out revolt.

As Aleksei—a sullen look upon his face—set the second vial carefully on the desk next to the first, Nikandr felt his mother's presence through his soulstone. A heartbeat later the rook in the corner of the room began flapping its wings and cawing loudly. Aleksei immediately swung himself around and bowed reverently. Nikandr stood and did the same as his mother's presence grew deep within his chest. He was painfully aware of the vials sitting within arm's reach, but he knew the worst thing he could do would be to draw attention to them, so he waited and prayed that she hadn't been privy to the conversation.

The rook shifted on its perch, and then spoke in a voice that was perfectly recognizable—in quality if not in tone—as his mother's. "Imagine my surprise, Nischka, when you were not in the courtyard at the appointed time."

"I can see you have business to attend to," Aleksei said as he scooped up his ledger and rushed out the door.

"You were to wait," Nikandr's mother said as the door rattled shut. "Do you care so little about decorum?"

"I have many things to attend to, Mother. My life doesn't revolve around ceremony."

The rook cawed and flapped its wings. "Things to attend to... What's done is done, Nischka. No matter how much sweat you've poured into that ship, it would be better if you left it to the Vostromas. There are more important things to worry about."

Nikandr bit his tongue. "Is there anything else?"

"She is a fine woman."

"As I've said many times."

"So many times that I wonder if you say it in your sleep, but I've never once believed your words. The Duchy needs this marriage, Nischka."

"A fact you've made me well aware of, but you can't expect me to love her simply because you say so."

The rook flapped its wings and cawed. "*Nyet*, but I can expect you to treat her family with more than formality. While they're here on the island, you will embrace them, and that starts with the launching of the *Gorovna*."

Nikandr stood. "Is that all, Mother?"

There was a pause as the rook gave him a baleful stare, but then it cawed and pecked at the iron perch, producing dull, metallic tings. "Go," it said. "Bid your farewells to your precious ship."

And with that the presence he felt in his soulstone fled. He waited for a few moments to be sure, the rook flapping its wings and hopping along the perch, showing none of the intelligence it had only moments ago, and then he retrieved the vials and tucked them inside his cherkesska.

After leaving several banknotes on Aleksei's desk, he left. He didn't see Aleksei among the throng of clerks occupying the outer office. No doubt the man had secreted himself away to take care of business without being bled by the likes of Nikandr.

He left the building and strode through the cobblestone courtyard, passing six wagons being loaded with grain from the Empire of Yrstanla, far to the west. The grain would be headed not to Radiskoye, but to the seaside, to Volgorod, where hundreds of starving families would be waiting for their weekly allotment. With the blight worse than it had ever been—fishing and hunting and farming yields all at record lows—grain was the only thing keeping the islands from collapsing under the weight of their own demands. The farming season was about to begin, though, and everyone was hopeful that this year would break the stranglehold the blight had taken on the islands.

Beyond the courtyard was a wide road—sheer cliffs to one side, a low stone wall to the other. He followed this to the highest of the quays, the one reserved for ships of state. The calls of the gulls came louder. A strengthening wind assaulted him as he strode past the large ships moored to the first several perches.

He stopped when he reached the fifth. There rested the *Gorovna*. *His* ship. The ship that would soon be given away to the Vostromas as part of the sweeping arrangements surrounding his marriage to Atiana.

His first instinct was to go aboard and complete his business with the grub, but he stopped himself. This was not the time to rush. He closed his eyes and inhaled, taking in the distinct odor of fresh wood that mixed with the smell of the ocean. He realized the fear that had been building within him since he'd left Rehada's home was gone. The only thing he could feel was a sense of pride at what he and so many others had accomplished. The ship might be transferring hands, but it would always bear his mark, and *he* would bear the mark of the ship as well. He had started a young man who knew the *wind*, but now... Now he knew *ships*, which was an entirely different thing. Helping design and build her had made him a better man, and for that, he was glad.

He strode along the edge of the perch, close enough that he could run his hand along the freshly painted surface of her hull. He loved the feel of it—the smooth landscape of the delicate grain, the knowledge that every small part of her was connected to the others. He sensed the very nature of the wood, its ability to provide lift—at least, he liked to *think* that he could. Such things were the domain of the Aramahn, but there was no one, not even the shipwright, who could claim a closer bond with this ship.

He stopped as he neared the windward mainmast and stared upward, taking her in in all her glory. Twelve masts, each cut from ancient specimens Nikandr had chosen himself. Five hundred trees had been felled to fill her frame. She bore thousands of yards of sail and rope. Fifty men would sail her, and she would live longer than Nikandr, longer than his sons if the fates were kind.

He took the gangplank up to the main deck. Even though the ship was lashed to the perch, it swayed with the wind. The surefootedness that had served him so well took over, his pace slowing, his steps widening ever so slightly. A handful of crewmen were aboard, making her shipshape. Several took note as he climbed the stairs up to the aftcastle, but they neither waved nor approached; they knew and respected his wish to be alone.

He made his way to the helm—the one piece of the ship he alone had crafted. The helm had three stout levers made from winter oak; he touched each of them in turn with a melancholy smile. It would be sad to see this ship go, but it would be an honor to pilot her on her first true voyage, even if it was brief.

Knowing that time was growing short, he pulled one of Aleksei's vials from inside his coat. He stared at it soberly, his stomach churning from the look of the thing. He had decided that this would be the place he would consume it. He was not overly superstitious, but there was a certain sense of rightness to doing this here. The grub and the poison contained within it was said to burn the wasting from those who consumed them. The only legal methods for treatment of the disease were to visit leechmen or licensed physics, but Nikandr knew that neither could do a thing to halt its progress. They'd done nothing for his sister, Victania, and they'd do nothing for him. And so, to his shame, he had resorted to the black market in hopes of smothering the disease before it had truly had a chance to take hold. So far, nothing had worked, but the effects of these grubs were legendary among the right circles. He prayed to the ancients it would work, not only for his sake, but for Victania's as well—the second would be hers if all went well.

The moment he unstoppered the vial, the air filled with the rancid scent of cod liver oil. His lips rose involuntarily as he grabbed the tail and pulled the white thing out. It dripped golden liquid back into the reservoir as he stared, thoughts of crunching down on its pale white skin running through his mind. He had never eaten a more repulsive thing than this. Ancients willing, he never would again.

Before he could think overly much about it, he stuffed it into his mouth whole and began chewing. The slick texture of the oil only made the bulbous grub seem that much more revolting. The cod liver oil was heavy, and it tasted like the fermented haddock that the people of Mirkotsk—though he'd never understood why—enjoyed so much. Things grew worse when the viscous interior of the grub, which tasted like rotted chestnuts, squirted free and inserted itself into the mix. He wished he could swallow the thing whole to be done with the chewing, but there was simply too much of it. Any attempt to swallow it now and he would launch his breakfast—what little he'd eaten of it—and the grub all over the deck. So he chewed and chewed and chewed, until finally he pierced the tail, where the poison was said to reside. A bitter, mineral taste spread throughout his mouth. The tip of his tongue went numb. He chewed even faster until finally he was able to get down the first mouthful.

Swallowing a part of it made things infinitely worse, for he was now fighting the urge to gag while simultaneously trying to force the bulk of it down. He swallowed, chewed more, swallowed again, as his stomach began to heave.

Then finally, all of it was down.

He leaned forward, holding on to his knees while breathing deeply. The scent of the deck was gone, as were the smells of the sea. All that remained was the bitter scent of the oil and weeks-old chestnuts.

The numbness on his tongue was growing worse, but he was able to stand and once again breathe with some small amount of ease.

But then his stomach reeled and he began heaving and gagging heavily. He turned and ran to the gunwale behind him. As he stood there, hands gripping in rigor, the contents of his stomach raged up his throat and coursed toward open sea.

CHAPTER 2

Nikandr spit to clear his mouth of the bits of undigested grub.

How desperate had he become? How blind?

The need to save himself, to save Victania, had grown stronger as various remedies had failed to help. He'd placed his faith in ever-more-obscure treatments until finally arriving here, at the belief that a worm taken from the desert to the south of the Great Empire would heal the wasting.

"Are you well, My Lord Prince?"

One of the deckhands. Nikandr waved him away. "Too much vodka, too little bread."

"Of course, My Lord."

Nikandr stared down at the waves as they broke upon the rocks, wondering—when the last stages of the disease had finally taken hold—if he would allow it to consume him or if he'd launch himself from the cliffs like so many of the seamen chose to do.

As he pulled the second vial from his coat and stared at the white grub within, a burst of anger boiled up inside him. He reared back and launched it as far as he could toward the sea and the tall pillars of rock below. It twirled downward, the sun catching the glass, making it glint under the morning sun, until finally it was lost from view.

In his mind he cataloged the broths, the salves, the unguents he had secretly purchased and tried. Other than the first few days after realizing he had the disease, he hadn't felt any sense of desperation—he'd felt like he would somehow find a solution, that it would reverse course—but now, with no avenues left except for the vicious blooding rituals employed by the people of the lowlands, despair was taking hold.

"Looking for your fortune?"

Nikandr turned and found Jahalan standing at the top of the aftcastle stairs. He was a tall man with a gaunt face and sharp, sunken eyes. Had Nikandr not known him for so long, he would have thought *he* had the wasting, but it was simply how he was built—that and the fact that he ate like a bird. He wore a circlet upon his brow that held an alabaster gem. The gem glowed softly from within—an indication that his bond to a spirit of the wind was active.

"I am," Nikandr replied, "but I always seem to be looking in the wrong place."

Jahalan raised his eyebrows and smiled. "That is the way of things, isn't it?" He looked around the ship, as if taking it in for the first time. "Are you ready, son of Iaros?"

Nikandr shrugged. "As ready as I can be."

Jahalan, perhaps sensing Nikandr's mood, took his leave and moved to the starward mainmast, the position from which he would use the spirit bound to him to guide the winds and take the ship on its short maiden voyage.

Udra, a wizened old woman, was already there. She wore a circlet as well, though it held not a stone of alabaster but an almond-shaped opal that gave off a radiance the sun could not completely account for. Aramahn like Udra used opals to bond with dhoshahezhan, spirits that allowed her to control the heft of the ship. Her eyes were closed in concentration, her hands pressed gently to the mast, preparing herself and the ship for the coming voyage. It was an insult, her refusal to give him greeting, but it was one he had grown accustomed to. Udra knew her work, and that was good enough for him.

The crew stopped what they were doing as a familiar sound rose above the din of the eyrie. It was the rhythm of wooden blocks being struck in rapid sequence. Nikandr strode down the gangplank to the perch as the eyrie turned its attention toward the sound.

A procession of lords—and more than a few ladies—made their way down the cobbled road from the courtyard and onto the highest of the quays. They were led by servants in fur robes holding korobochki—brightly painted blocks—that they struck soundly with rounded mallets. The landsmen made way, kneeling and bowing their heads as the procession passed.

When they reached the *Gorovna's* perch, Nikandr's father, Iaros Aleksov Khalakovo, was in the fore, and he was arm-in-arm with Duke Zhabyn Olegov Vostroma, the man who would soon become Nikandr's second father.

"And here he is," Father said. "As promised."

Nikandr embraced each of them in turn, kissing their cheeks as he did so. "Father… My Lord Duke… Welcome."

Zhabyn, with his sleepy eyes and an expression that made it clear he was not amused, took Nikandr in, glancing toward the ship. "Your father tells me you worked on the ship yourself."

"That is so," Nikandr said, pleased he would take note.

Zhabyn turned to Father as if Nikandr were no longer present. "It had best perform, Khalakovo, no less than the others."

Father smiled, pointedly ignoring Nikandr. "I have been assured that it will."

Zhabyn stared up at the ship, his emotionless eyes somehow critical. He walked past Nikandr and strode up to the deck as if it were already his. Father, sparing a flash of disapproval for Nikandr, followed.

Nikandr's sister, Victania, was speaking with Zhabyn's son. She was covered in several layers, but it was clear to anyone who cared to look that she was not well. Her cheeks were sunken, her lips colorless. She had applied powder to her face, but the hollows of her eyes were dark, and there was no hiding the jaundice in the whites of her eyes. She was well along in the wasting, a disease that had grown more rampant over the last decade. Other islands like Rhavanki had had it worse in recent years, but if father's physics were to be believed, Khalakovo seemed to be making up for lost time.

The disease struck randomly, with no apparent rhyme or reason. The peasants often thought that touch or breath caused it, but there had been too many cases of solitary souls contracting the disease, and a good many who came into contact with the afflicted but never became ill. It was looked upon as a sign of weakness by most, but in Victania Nikandr could see only strength. She was more active by half than most healthy women. She was doing her best to look beyond the disease, to do what she could with the time remaining to her.

As the gathered noblemen made their way to the deck, she broke away and pulled Nikandr aside. "It was not a wise choice you made this morning, Nischka. Zhabyn was ill pleased."

"So it seems."

"Borund as well. Mark me well, brother. You'd best see to it that your voyage is a pleasant one."

"You worry too much. I merely came early to ensure that all was well with the ship."

Borund, the heavily built son of Zhabyn, and one of Nikandr's closest friends growing up, was just now taking the gangplank. He, like his father, was ignoring Nikandr for the present, but that would soon pass. They hadn't seen one another in several years, but once they'd had a chance to talk their old habits would take over and they'd be playing jokes on one another as they'd always done.

"And what of last night? Their arrival?"

"The same."

Victania scoffed. "*Nyet*, brother. Today you said your goodbyes to the ship and last night you said goodbye to your whore."

"She's no whore, Tania."

"I don't begrudge you your fun, Nischka. Ancients know you'll have little enough of that once the chill of Vostroma's daughter falls across your bed. But you'd best be careful. Father wants no complications."

Nikandr suppressed his annoyance. "There will be no *complications*."

"My dear Nikandr," she said, glancing over her shoulder, "there already are."

Nikandr took in the crowd, wondering what she meant, but then he saw them. The three sisters. They were standing near the back, speaking with their Aunt Katerina. They wore billowing dresses, fur coats, and ermine caps, and though their tastes had grown apart in recent years, they were still dressed similarly enough to one another that a whole host of memories were dredged up from his childhood.

Katerina and two of the sisters—Mileva and Ishkyna—were staring up at the ship, but Atiana, Nikandr's fiancée, was staring at him. He stared back, uncomfortable under her gaze, and surprisingly, more than a little embarrassed. When they were young, he and Borund used to tease them mercilessly. Tying locks of their hair together at lessons. Stepping on the trains of their dresses. Dropping frogs into their soup when they weren't looking. They were childish things that boys did to girls—nothing to be ashamed of when both of them had outgrown their youth—but Nikandr remembered, and he had come to regret them.

He wondered if she felt the same. As they'd grown older, the sisters had become more and more vicious in their quest for revenge. Even after he and Borund had reached an age where they were looking well beyond the girls of Vostroma, they'd continued with renewed vigor, perhaps sensing the remaining time for balancing the scales was growing short. Once, at the beginning of Council, they'd put a dye in Nikandr's food that had colored his mouth black for a week—teeth, tongue, gums, and all. He still shivered at the thought of trying to painfully scrape the stuff off night after night, and though Zhabyn had reluctantly forced each of the girls to apologize, they hadn't bothered to tell him that scraping would have little effect and that in time it would wear off on its own. All three of them had made a point of catching Nikandr's eye and smiling—genuinely enough so that it wouldn't be considered taunting were they to be caught doing it but wide enough so that it was clear they were salting the very wound they had inflicted.

Without a word to the women near her, Atiana broke away and made a beeline toward him. She was now twenty years old—four years younger than Nikandr. The hair beneath her cap was powdered white, and she wore a subtle rouge upon her cheeks. They had always been pale-skinned, the sisters, and the rouge only served to draw attention to it, but he was surprised to see how much her face had filled in—her figure as well—since the last time he'd seen her three years before.

As she approached, Victania squeezed Nikandr's arm and made her way to the gangplank.

"You were missed last night, My Lord Prince," Atiana said. "This morning as well."

Her tone was self-righteous, and it grated. "Duty called, My Lady," Nikandr said, bowing deeply, "but fortunately we find ourselves here."

"A pity I won't be able to take the ship," she said, glancing up at the masts.

"There's nothing that would interest you, I'm afraid. She's as bare as they come."

Atiana raised one eyebrow. "Is that how you like them?"

Nikandr paused. "Is there a man that does not?"

A wry smile lit her face. "Perhaps you would grant me a tour."

"I wouldn't dream of robbing Gravlos of the pleasure."

"But you worked on her, did you not? Is it not *your* right as well?"

Nikandr waved at the ship offhandedly. "A ship is a ship."

She said nothing, and her face changed not at all, but she was weighing his words. She knew—knew how much he loved this ship. To speak of it in such a cavalier manner would speak volumes to someone like her, a woman who had always—despite what other faults she might have—been insufferably bright.

"I suppose you're right. There's much to do over the next few days. I doubt we'll see much of one another until the dance."

"Regrettably, that is most likely true."

She glanced toward the gangway at a call from her Aunt Katerina.

Nikandr took her hand in his and kissed it. "Until the dance?"

She fixed her gaze on her hand, which was still held in his. Then she pulled it away and met his eyes. "I look forward to it."

When they were growing up, the sisters had always had a subtle tone to their words. Sometimes it was Mileva, sometimes Ishkyna, and sometimes—though more rarely—it was Atiana. They would say something that sounded innocuous while in fact was steeped in meaning. Nikandr's ear had come to recognize this tone, for more often than not it was meant as a challenge. She was daring him to unravel the mystery, daring him further to prevent her from winning.

"I await with bated breath," Nikandr said.

The ceremony itself was short. A collective prayer for the *Gorovna's* safe passage, a song written and sung for the occasion by one of Volgorod's most famous troubadours, and for a select few a tour from the shipwright, Gravlos.

Then the gathering left—all except Borund, who was bidden by his father to judge the ship for its windworthiness. Gravlos was given the honor of launching her from the eyrie, but Nikandr soon took over and guided her eastward along the length of the island. It would be a short flight—out to open sea, a curve around the far end of the island, and back again. Enough time for Borund to assess her, enough time for a bit of celebration, and then a return to the shipyards for final fittings.

They were nearing an hour out to sea. The entire time Borund had looked as if he were at a funeral.

"Come," Nikandr said, trying to lighten the mood. "We'll give you a proper tour."

Borund, who was thankfully facing Nikandr and not Gravlos, rolled his eyes and spoke softly, "Can't we just share a drink in the kapitan's quarters, Nischka?"

"It will take but a moment," Nikandr replied under his breath.

"I've been on a hundred of these ships, Nikandr. I know what they're about."

Gravlos, who was eager to show off more of the ship than had been possible earlier, had come close enough to hear, and though he showed no disappointment on his face, his shoulders dropped, and the bow of his head he gave to Borund was longer than it needed to be. "Perhaps a turn at the helm, My Lord Prince…"

To Nikandr's horror, Borund declined this as well and began pacing the deck, spending more time examining the forward cannon mount than anything else.

Gravlos's face was red as he stared at Borund. Before Nikandr could say a word to him, he limped to the shroud running up along the mainmast and began yelling at the men to tighten the deadeyes. It wasn't much longer before Borund stepped up to the aftcastle with an exasperated expression on his face. "It does seem terribly slow going, doesn't it?"

"That's natural," Nikandr said, trying to hide his displeasure, "with only half her sails flying."

"*Da*, but we're also taking a rather circuitous route."

"Well then, perhaps I could arrange a skiff to take you back to Volgorod."

Borund exhaled noisily. "Nikandr, I know I'm being a boor, but until last night I had been on a ship for nearly a week, and the winds were not kind, believe me. The last thing I wish to do"—he glanced toward Gravlos and lowered his voice—"is spend one more minute on this ship than I need to."

Considering their history, Nikandr had hoped to bring Borund around to his way of thinking—to enjoy the day and the ship, to give honor to those that had spilled sweat and blood upon her decks—but now he saw that he would not. To him, this ship was nothing more than a row in his father's ledgers, and it set his blood to boiling.

"Your wish is my command, My Lord Prince." He called for the ship to come about.

Gravlos looked over severely, but Nikandr ignored him, and once Jahalan had sufficiently altered the winds, Nikandr steered the ship away from the lazy course he had set and flew straight for the shipyard, a course that would take them directly over the palotza.

Borund looked nervous when he realized what Nikandr was doing, but then he tipped his head back and laughed. "Well, that's one way to go about it."

Flying over the palotza was normally ill-advised, lest it be misinterpreted as an act of aggression, but the streltsi manning the palotza's cannons had been briefed—they knew who was piloting the ship and would be much more forgiving than usual.

Just as they were coming abreast of the palotza, the ship's master waved his hand over his head several times, the sign that danger had been spotted and that silence was required.

This was not a seasoned crew. It was a collection of old deck hands that Gravlos had put to work in the shipyard, but many of them had served in the staaya—the windborne wing of Khalakovo's military—or the merchant marine, and old habits die hard. Once the signal was picked up, it was passed silently to the landward and windward sides and finally below to the few who would be manning the seaward masts. The two gun emplacements—one fore and one aft—were manned with a crew of three men each.

Nikandr, his heartbeat quickening, waved Gravlos over to the helm and raised his hand in the signal for the crews to begin loading grapeshot. They complied, finishing in respectable time, as Nikandr sent another sign to the ship's acting master, calling for muskets.

The *Gorovna* was not complete and had been readied with only five muskets. They were removed from their locker by the master and four of them were passed out to the crewmen known to be good with the weapon. The fifth was handed to Nikandr.

He immediately pulled one of the walrus tusk cartridges filled with gunpowder from the bandolier across his chest and began loading the weapon. He finished well before the others and began scanning the ground below. It took him a moment to find it among the mottled patches of stone and snow—a skiff, nestled in a copse of scrub pine. Once he had found the ship, he found the men. Twenty paces away four of them kneeled at the edge of a tall cliff that ended hundreds of feet below in a forest of spruce. They appeared to be inspecting the ground, though for what reason Nikandr couldn't guess.

It was possible they were Aramahn like Jahalan and Udra, but their almond-shaped turbans and long beards and threadbare clothing made him think otherwise. Plus, the Aramahn knew that to come so close to the palotza without permission was to risk trial and possibly death. They had to be Maharraht, members of a group that had decades ago broken with the peace-loving ways of the Aramahn, dedicating their lives to driving the Grand Duchy from the islands and drowning them in the sea.

Nikandr sucked in breath as one of them leapt from the cliff. The man's descent quickened. He spread his arms wide, as if preparing for the cool embrace of the sea, not the singular end that would be granted by the earth and stone that lay below him.

Improbably, his descent slowed. His long robes were whipped harder than the speed of his fall could account for, and soon it was clear that the wind was carrying him like a gull on the upward drafts that blow along the cliffs. Like a feather on the breeze he was carried, arms held wide as many of the wind masters do. He soon regained the level where his comrades still stood, at which point he alighted to solid land as if stepping down from the mountain on high.

Nikandr coughed and pitched forward, supporting himself with one hand on the deck. A well had opened up inside him, a hole impossibly deep, impossibly black. It had coincided so closely with the man's leap that he couldn't help but think they were linked in some way, though how this could be he couldn't guess.

On the cliff below, the one who had leapt turned and pointed up toward the *Gorovna*.

"Come about," Nikandr called, "and bring her down by half!"

As one, the Maharraht bolted for the skiff.

"Jahalan, they have at least one havaqiram with them, probably two."

"I feel him," he replied, "but it is not just a havaqiram, son of Iaros. They have summoned a hezhan."

Nikandr turned. "That's not possible."

"I agree that it should not be, but they have done it."

Nikandr doubted him, but now was not the time for questioning; they needed to neutralize this threat before it could be brought to bear on the *Gorovna*—or worse, Radiskoye.

The skiff was airborne in less than a minute—the same time it took for the *Gorovna* to come about and close within striking distance.

"All fire!" Nikandr called.

The crack of four muskets rang out, followed a heartbeat later by the thunder of cannons. Bits of wood flew free from the stern of the skiff, and one of the Maharraht jerked sharply to his right, his shoulder and ribs a mass of red. One of the others helped him to the floor and immediately began binding his wounds while the other two steered the craft northward.

The clatter of four men reloading their muskets filled the air as Nikandr sighted carefully down the barrel of his musket. His mouth was watering, his throat swallowing reflexively. He took as deep a breath as he could manage and released it, slowly squeezing the trigger as the urge to curl into a ball grew markedly worse.

The pan flashed. The gun kicked into his shoulder.

The shot went wide. He'd been aiming for the man holding the sails, but it had struck the Maharraht tending to his wounded comrade. The man held his shoulder and stared up at the ship. Nikandr was close enough now that he could see the look of venom on the man's face.

The wind continued to blow. The sails began to luff, and the ship twisted with the force of the wind. Jahalan was trying to adjust when a gale blew across the landward bow. It was so fierce that the ship's nose was pushed upward and windward.

Nikandr blinked at nearby movement.

A heavy thud sounded next to him.

When he turned, he found a crewman lying on the deck, moaning and a river of red flowing out from underneath his head. The severe angle of the deck caused him to slide. Nikandr reached for him, but he was too far. He accelerated until Borund, holding tightly to a cleat, locked his meaty arm around the man's waist.

Then the wind reversed.

The ship tilted sharply forward. There were only sixteen sails in use, but they were full and round and near to bursting.

A crack resounded from the upper part of the ship. Like a spruce felled in the forest, the topmost portion of the foremast tilted and was thrown amongst the rigging astern it.

"Reef the sails, men!" Nikandr called above the roar of the wind.

The crew began lowering the sails as the wind intensified. It was so loud that most would no longer be able to hear Nikandr's commands.

The ship had now tilted to the point where the dozen men on deck, including Nikandr and Borund, were sliding toward the landward bulwarks. Nikandr landed well enough, but Borund cried out as the weight of the wounded man fell upon his ankle.

"Gravlos, right her!"

Gravlos fought hard against the controls, saying nothing as the ship tilted further and further.

CHAPTER 3

As the ship continued to rotate, the hull groaned. A crewman plummeted from the starward foremast and was caught in one of the windward shrouds. He screamed in pain, his left arm hanging uselessly above his head at an unnatural angle.

Gravlos, who had been forced to maneuver himself onto the cabinet that housed the helm's levers, was pulling frantically on the one that controlled the roll, but it was having no effect.

Suddenly Nikandr realized what was happening. "Gravlos, release the controls!"

Gravlos's eyes grew wide. "*Nyet*, My Lord!"

"Now, Gravlos!"

The ship had tilted nearly to the point where the starward masts were pointing toward the horizon.

Gravlos's eyes locked onto Nikandr, his face filled with fear. He swallowed and began pulling upward on the lever he had been working so hard to maneuver.

Nikandr stared in disbelief as the lever refused to budge. Gravlos wasn't going to be able to release it on his own. Nikandr slid along the bulwark until he was positioned directly below the helm. Borund, sensing his plan, leaned against the now-vertical deck and interlaced his hands. Once Nikandr had placed a foot into them, Borund heaved the lighter man upward.

Nikandr grabbed onto the helm and pulled hard on the lever along with Gravlos. They tried again and again, but it refused to budge. He feared it would *never* give, but then finally it came free with a hollow thud. They moved quickly and did the same to the other two.

For long moments the ship hung in the air, tilted on its side as the wind howled. Nikandr's heart beat madly. He had thought that freeing the ship's keels from the effects of the unpredictable aether would allow it to return to a state of equilibrium. Though the tilt was no longer getting worse, it wasn't getting better, either.

Several of the crew shouted warnings.

Nikandr looked up. His eyes widened, and his skin began to tingle.

Reeling among the sails was a vortex of wind and moisture. It looked like the waterspouts that sometimes came with spring weather, only smaller. Jahalan had said plainly that a havahezhan, a spirit of the wind, had been summoned, but Nikandr had never seen one with his own eyes.

"The dousing rods!" Nikandr called to the men.

He doubted anyone had heard him above the terrible roar caused by the hezhan, but even if they had, the rods would be nearly impossible to reach, stored as they were belowdecks.

The nausea that had struck him moments ago intensified, and then, like a dog hunting grouse among the bushes, the hezhan twisted closer and closer. The crew retreated, moving nimbly along the bulwarks and rigging. But then the hezhan seemed to find what it was looking for.

It headed straight for Nikandr.

Nikandr leapt from the helm down to the bulwarks in an attempt to evade the creature, but it was on him in moments.

The wind tore at his skin like hail, forcing him to bury his head between his arms. A deafening roar assaulted him. The breath was sucked from his lungs. Among the madness he saw, inside his shirt, his soulstone glowing bright white, though he had no time to wonder why this might be.

He fell to his knees and crawled along the bulwark, but the spirit hounded him. Stars danced behind his eyelids. His arms began to weaken.

And then he felt something thump against his chest.

The hole that had opened up inside him filled. The feeling of a yawning, bottomless pit vanished in a moment. The wind began to die. The sound faded, and eventually, he could breathe again. He retched several times, but thankfully nothing came up. It would have been understandable—to vomit after such a strange encounter—but he didn't care for the entire crew, plus Borund, to see him in that state; it would bring too many unwelcome questions.

Moments later he was finally able to stand. When he opened his eyes, a final gust buffeted him, and then all was calm. He scanned the rigging and sky for any telltale signs of the hezhan, but it was clear the creature was gone, and he could only thank the ancients that they had somehow watched over him.

He pulled out the heavy gold chain that held his soulstone, knowing now that it had been the source of the strange sensation against his chest. He stared at it, dumbfounded.

The stone was smoky and gray and somewhat transparent, whereas before it had been cloudy and white with a low radiance to it. He polished the surface against his coat, thinking it had become dirty. But he soon came to realize that the encounter with the hezhan had altered it, perhaps for good. Why had it shone so brightly when the hezhan had been close? Had the stone somehow destroyed the spirit? Had it been damaged while doing so?

Seeing Borund watching him, Nikandr kissed the stone as though he were thanking the ancients and stuffed it back inside his shirt.

The *Gorovna* eased back into balance as the breeze bore them southward like a seed upon the wind. The crew, seeming to realize the danger had passed all at once, cheered and whipped their woolen hats in circles over their heads. Even Borund appeared to be caught up in the emotion as he rushed forward and took Nikandr in a bear hug, lifting him from the deck.

"Let go of me, you big ox!"

"Ha ha!" Borund twirled him around several times before finally setting him back down. "How did you do it?" he asked with a grin as wide as the seas.

Nikandr could only shrug. "I don't know."

"You don't know?"

"That's what I said."

"Then you're the luckiest man I know, Nischka!" Borund picked Nikandr up and twirled him around again, laughing the whole time.

"Enough!" Nikandr said.

Borund set him down as the cheering finally began to subside.

"Set sails, men. Let's go home."

The crew did so, and though at first they did not sail smartly, the master soon brought them in line with his booming voice while Gravlos steered for the shipyard.

Nikandr, meanwhile, moved to the gunwale and scanned the island below for some small sign of the skiff. There could be no doubt that they had been Maharraht. What wasn't clear was the purpose behind their attack. The *Gorovna* might have represented a juicy prize had they been able to take it—even juicier with Nikandr and Borund aboard—but in attacking they had also announced their presence. Why settle for two princes when Council was upon them? Why not wait for the ships of the incoming dukes?

Nikandr continued searching for a long while—both for the answers to his questions and for the escaped men—but as he had feared, he found neither.

High within Palotza Radiskoye, the setting sun angled in through deeply recessed windows. It fell upon a tall black rook, which unlike the golden band around its ankle or the silver perch upon which it stood, seemed to absorb the light completely, making it black as night in the dying light of day. It did not preen nor move along its perch, but instead studied Nikandr with an intelligent gleam in its eye. It was Mother's favorite, Yrfa, the one she inhabited most often, though whether this was due to some form of affinity or because the bird happened to be the easiest to assume, he didn't know.

"You sensed nothing?" Nikandr asked.

"Nothing," the rook replied, "until the hezhan had entered this world." The words, though spoken through a primitive tool, had the cadence and inflection of his mother's voice.

A gold chain swung lazily from Nikandr's hand in time with the beating of his heart. Hanging from the end of the chain was his soulstone pendant—still darkened, an effect that had proved all too permanent. He pressed his fingers to his chest, recalling the sharp pressure as he was blacking out. "How could they have done such a thing?"

"There was a similar occurrence when I was still young to the ways of the aether. Four years into the Great Drought, a havahezhan crossed. It was two days after the equinox, and harvest was still in full celebration in Izhny. It headed straight for the festival grounds. It ripped three children limb from limb before vanishing."

Nikandr shivered, wondering if the hezhan had been about to do the same to him. He rubbed the smooth surface of the stone, barely able to sense the cracks. It had been given to him at birth; since his blooding day he had never been parted from it. It had held the tale of his life, his essence; now, he didn't know whether his legacy had been tarnished, or worse, wiped away altogether. Even damaged as it was, the stone would one day be placed in the family's mausoleum beneath the palotza. It was something he—like any member of a royal family—looked forward to leaving behind when he died. He had imagined it would be a grand stone, one that would outshine all of those around it, but now... Now he would be leaving behind a shadow, a silhouette, and it shamed him that he had allowed such a thing to happen.

There was one small consolation—he had feared that the stone and the abilities it granted had been permanently damaged, but when he had returned to Radiskoye he found that he could sense Saphia, his mother, and she in turn could sense him. He had no doubts, however, that when he traveled beyond a certain distance their mutual bond would attenuate and then vanish altogether.

"Why only children?" Nikandr asked.

"I cannot say. The hezhan are drawn to certain people, perhaps as they are drawn to the Aramahn. But that spirit, even though it had fully crossed, appeared dim to me, as if I were looking through a pane of dusty glass. The hezhan that crossed today, I saw it as bright as a full moon against the midnight sky."

"You were young then. Inexperienced."

The rook's head dipped and craned upward. "*Da*, but I do not think that was the cause. Things have been strange these last few years, Nischka. The fishing, the fields, the game—all struck by the blight longer and harder than we could have imagined. And at the same time the wasting grows worse. Perhaps this crossing is but another facet of the same jewel."

Nikandr stared levelly at the rook, wondering if she had guessed his mind. He suspected that the hezhan attacked him because of the disease. After all, there were others on the ship with soulstones. Why not them? He alone had the wasting, and his symptoms had intensified the moment the hezhan had been summoned. There must be some sort of connection. But he could not voice his concerns no matter how burning they might be. His shame at hiding the disease for so long was too great.

The door opened, and in stepped his father, Iaros. He wore an embroidered kaftan the color of emeralds that ran down to his ankles. The tips of his silk slippers poked out from beneath the hem. His beard hung down to his chest and, like his hair, had only a token amount of the brown color that had not long ago been dominant. His soulstone, glowing faintly beneath his beard, seemed mocking.

Father nodded in greeting and paced over to the perch, holding out one finger. The rook ran its beak along his finger several times, and then he smoothed down the rook's breast feathers.

These signs of affection were reserved for Mother; there were none for Nikandr as he stared down gravely. "The ship is in bad shape, Nischka."

"There was nothing I could have done."

"You could have stayed the course given to you."

"I told you—"

"*Da*, Borund requested that you shorten the tour, no doubt so you could go drinking in Volgorod. Council is being held on Khalakovo, if you'll recall, and the *Gorovna* is still our property until your wedding day."

"We might not have found the Maharraht."

"You confuse the relationship. It was *they* that found *you*."

"How could they have known?"

"Stop being so naïve, Nikandr. They have *spies*, here and everywhere else. The *Gorovna's* maiden voyage has been common knowledge in two duchies for more than a season. Now Gravlos tells me it will be weeks before repairs are completed."

"I don't think they were spies." Nikandr stood and looked out through the nearby windows to the cloudy sky beyond. To the west, less than a league away from where he stood, one of Khalakovo's most powerful warships, watching for the Maharraht, slid into a low bank of clouds and was lost from view. In the forest below, Jahalan was at the site of the hezhan's crossing, examining it for any evidence that might prove useful. "I think they chose the location for a particular reason."

"What reason might that be?"

Nikandr shrugged. "That's what I mean to find out." He pulled the necklace over his head and made to leave.

"Do not show that stone openly."

"Why?" Nikandr asked, disliking the way he had said *that stone*.

"Zhabyn is ready to bolt at the first sign of weakness. He's looking for excuses to demand more out of your wedding or to call it off. We can afford neither."

"I have always worn my stone openly."

"And there are plenty who don't. I trust you'll be able to explain it away to anyone bold enough to speak of it. Now go. Your mother and I have much to discuss."

Nikandr left, feeling like a boy dismissed from dinner. There was sense in his father's words, but when he tucked the pendant inside his shirt and felt the chain tickle his skin as it settled into place, the stone felt weighty, obscene, as if the sign of a coward had now been hung around his neck.

CHAPTER 4

The next day a bitterly cold snowstorm swept over the islands, leaving behind a cheerless sun and weather that drew warmth from the very marrow of the bones. Wind howled among the cobblestone streets of Old Volgorod, lifting the dusting of snow and creating whorls and eddies among the meager crowd that had gathered to watch the execution. Though many grumbled at the wind and biting snow, Rehada thought nothing of it; it matched perfectly the bitterness and resentment deep in her heart.

From this ancient circle where the gallows stood, the seven major streets of Volgorod fanned out like cracks in a frozen lake. Along one of these clattered a flatbed wagon pulled by two stout ponies. A soldier dressed in the uniform of the Posadnik's guard drove the wagon with a light hand, while another, holding onto the driver's seat for balance, stood in the bed, watching the three young men chained securely behind him.

As the wagon turned onto the empty street surrounding the circle, tack and chains jingling, the soldiers gave little or no notice to the crowd that had gathered. The boys, however, stared wide-eyed, their faces growing increasingly nervous, until finally the wagon pulled to a halt near the gallows. Standing on the stage were no less than a dozen armed streltsi. Such a show of force was abnormal, but Council was upon them, and apparently there had been some scuffle between the Landed and the Maharraht during the launching of a new trade ship. Rehada gave the story little credence, however; she had received no word that Maharraht would be coming to the island. More than likely it was a drunken brawl that had grown with the telling.

The driver climbed over the bench to join his comrade. They looked calm and collected in their long woolen cherkesskas. Even their woolen hats with tassels of gold lent them a look of austerity, as if a hanging were something that came as easily to them as polishing their black leather boots.

The crowd—most of them Landed peasants—pressed forward, but

Rehada stood her ground, studying the boys as they were led one by one from the rear of the wagon to the wooden platform where nooses swung lazily in the wind. The first two boys were scrawny, the sons of a peasant family that lived on the outskirts of the city. They wore simple leather shoes, roughspun trousers and patchwork coats. Socks with holes for fingers to poke through covered their hands. They fought to keep their balance as the streltsi forced them to their places at the gallows, and though they wore looks of remorse as the nooses were fit around their necks, to Rehada it seemed like an act; she doubted they harbored any feelings of true regret for the atrocity they had committed three days before. She didn't doubt they regretted *some* things—stealing into the home of one of the city's richer widows; killing her when they found her unexpectedly home; forcing the third boy, a boy she had come to love, to return with them in a lame attempt at blaming him for their crime—but she doubted very much that they regretted the actual killing or the life of the young man next to them that now stood forfeit.

They had been discovered by the nephew of the socialite widow while forcing the third boy, Malekh, back to the house. The Posadnik's men had been alerted, and in short order all three of them had been taken for murder. For days Rehada had felt responsible; Malekh had been heading to Izhny after delivering a message to her. Worse, it was a mostly innocuous warning that a man named Ashan might be coming to her island, that he might have a boy with him, and that she should send word immediately if he were discovered. It was doubly frustrating because she knew Ashan, an arqesh among her people—she knew the boy the note was referring to as well—and so of course she would have sent word immediately upon hearing of their presence on Khalakovo.

She stared at Malekh, who was just now being led to the third and final position of the gallows. This was no peasant. He was a boy that had begun training as her disciple, a boy his mother—the fates treat her kindly—should be proud of. He wore the garb of the Aramahn: a simple woven cap, inner robes dyed the deepest ocean blue, outer robes only a shade lighter. There was fear and uncertainty in his eyes, but nothing like the simpering of the two next to him. He was facing his death with, if not bravery, contemplation, and it served to raise her already high estimation of him, even in these last few moments of his life.

When the news of his hanging had arrived yesterday she had gone to the city jail to petition for his release, but because she was not his mother, or any other form of relative, they refused to allow her to speak with him, or to vouch for him to the magistrate. The Landed still did not understand that the wandering people were one. Blood mattered little to them, but it was all important to those that ruled the duchies, and so she'd been forced to leave before they'd asked too many questions about their relationship. It was risky enough coming to the hanging—few Aramahn attended such things, and those that did were often labeled as suspect, as Maharraht, either in mind or in deed—but she could not find it in herself to leave him here to face death on his own. Her presence, at the very least, was something she owed him.

The shorter and older of the two streltsi began reciting transgressions from the records of the court. As he did, the boy scanned the crowd and finally met her eyes.

And he smiled.

He *smiled*, as if to console *her*.

Pain and regret and anger coursed through her. She felt her hardened core crack and fragment, but she did not let those emotions show on her face. Neither did she return his smile, for that would be disingenuous. Instead, she held his gaze with a reassuring look upon her face. She had decided before she came that she would meet his eyes as long as he wished it. She would not turn away, even though the sight of him dangling like a crow from a farmer's belt would haunt her for the rest of her life.

Learn, she tried to say. *Learn, even in death, and you will be rewarded in the next life.*

The strelet finished by reading the judgment of the magistrate.

From the corners of her eyes, she saw the seven other Aramahn turn their backs on the gallows, not from any lack of courage, but in protest, as a sign of disapproval. She, however, refused to turn away no matter how much she might wish to do so.

The rest of the crowd had not brought rotten vegetables or mud, as she had seen happen so often in the cities of the Empire to the west, nor did they shout epithets. They merely watched in silent condemnation.

The plumes of breath from each of the boys came white upon the wind, but unlike the two next to him, Malekh's face had transformed into a look of confusion, as if the things he had been sure about only moments ago had been brought into doubt.

Go well, she wished him, nodding once.

The strelet, his reading now complete, stepped back. As soon as he had, the other soldier pulled a thick wooden lever. The doors beneath the boys fell away with the clatter of wood. The rope snapped taut, and all three of them bounced once before swinging awkwardly in the wind.

When they came to rest, the crowd began to disperse, but Rehada remained, watching her young man swing for long moments, storing the image deep within her heart so that she might retrieve it when it was needed most. So lost in this effort was she that when two ponies entered the circle from a nearby street, breaking her trance, she wasn't sure how much time had passed. Even then, she watched them from the corner of her eye and paid them little mind.

This was a mistake.

She should have noted their courtly dress, should have noticed the train of children following them, hoping for a coin or two. When she *did* look, she realized one of them was staring at her. Nikandr. The Prince upon the Hill.

Her face burned as she turned away and walked toward the nearest street. He had been on the far side of the circle, and the wind had been blustery. She was wearing clothes that he wouldn't be accustomed to seeing her wear. It was possible, just possible, that he hadn't recognized her.

But she knew in her heart that he had, and it made her anger burn even higher. To be found out by Nikandr because she had, in one of her few acts of compassion, come to bid a friend farewell, was galling, not because she and Nikandr had lain together, but because she had worked so hard to conceal her true self from him.

No matter. If he discovered she was Maharraht, she would welcome it. She was sick of hiding it in any case, especially from him.

She turned and headed up one of the curving streets that led uphill toward the Bluff, the section of Volgorod that held her home. The street, as far as she could see, was empty. The light of the sun angled in between the tall stone buildings, leaving much of her path in shadow.

She stopped when she saw someone sitting at the entryway to an alley.

He wore two sets of robes: a black inner robe that was wrapped by a wide belt of gray cloth and an outer robe that fell to the tops of his brown leather boots. It was his turban and beard, more than anything, that marked him as one of the Maharraht. His beard was cut long and square. The turban was almond-shaped and ragged; its tail hung down along the front of his chest like a sash of honor.

It was dangerous to dress this way on Khalakovo, one of the most powerful of the Duchies, and downright foolish to come into the city. These were the clothes worn—not exclusively, but most often—by the Maharraht, the sect of the Aramahn that were bent on the destruction of the Grand Duchy and their Landed ways.

Rehada approached, but then she stopped, gasping as she recognized him. He had a ruggedly handsome face and dark, commanding eyes. A ragged scar ran down from what was left of his ear to his neck and cheek. The upper part of the ear remained, and he wore a handful of golden earrings there.

This was Soroush, the leader of the Maharraht, and the father of her child.

He had always been a brazen man, but to come here when he was at such a disadvantage? Snow fell on his dark turban and the stone of jasper held within it. She knew the stone was useless—at least to Soroush—and she wondered if he wore it as a ploy or to remind himself of his past. Soroush was nothing if not steeped in the past.

She continued walking past him, and he stepped alongside her, the two of them falling into a pace that made it seem as if they had always been together. Still, there were feelings of anxiety and uncertainty welling up inside her. Had it been so long since she'd seen him that she could act this way? Had they fallen so far out of touch?

"You were told not to take a disciple," Soroush said.

"I have been here seven years, Soroush. Questions were being asked."

"Attachments, Rehada, are to be avoided."

She scoffed. "Have you come this far to chide me over my urge to teach?"

They walked in silence for a time, their footsteps scuffing the light dusting of snow. She did not look toward him, but she could picture the muscles along his jaw working, as they had always done when she'd tested his patience.

"We have lost the boy," Soroush said.

Then Rehada *did* look at him. His face was set in stone as he walked, refusing to return her gaze. "How?"

"I misjudged Ashan. He stole him away a month ago."

"Then we are lost."

"I do not believe so, not as long as Ashan is headed here to Khalakovo."

"Can you be so sure that he is?"

"The rift over Rhavanki has nearly closed, while the one here over Khalakovo is widening."

"That means nothing. If he suspects what you're about, he'll keep Nasim away."

"I don't think so. He believes that Nasim is the key to healing the rifts. He will bring Nasim here, and he will continue to study him. It is his only hope of unraveling his mysteries."

They came to a larger street. Though there was some traffic—some peasants with baskets, others with carts—Soroush continued on as if he hadn't noticed them. Rehada did so as well, so as not to draw attention.

"We cannot succeed without Nasim."

Soroush nodded. "We shall see, but there is much to do in any case. Two days ago we gathered the first of the stones, and there are still four more to find."

"You have learned so much?"

"We know how to find four, and the fifth may well indeed hinge upon Nasim."

They were heading across an old walking bridge now. No one was in sight, but Rehada still felt terribly exposed.

Soroush stopped at the foot of the bridge, just before the street resumed its upward trek. His face was resolute, his body like stone. It made Rehada cold inside to see him like this. "Three days from now, take the road to Iramanshah at midday. Release your spirit the day before you come."

Rehada was suddenly very aware of the beating of her heart. "What am I to do?"

"Can you not guess?" The expression upon Soroush's face was not one of fervor, as she might have guessed, but of lamentation. "You will find for us our second stone."

CHAPTER 5

Nikandr and Borund guided their ponies around the gallows where three young men hung from the ends of ropes. No doubt they had been taken for simple robbery, most likely for food. It was too common a scene in Volgorod of late. Ranos had taken a serious stance on such crimes—allow such things to go on, he'd said, and the city would devolve into chaos. And if Khalakovo's largest city fell prey to such things, the rest would soon follow.

One of the boys was Aramahn, something he took note of not for its rarity but for the boy's age. The Aramahn were, nearly to a fault, honest, and it seemed improbable that the boy had been caught stealing.

As they continued their way around the circle, Nikandr noticed a woman wearing black robes of mourning. She was a good distance away, and the wind was throwing the snow about, but he was sure it was Rehada. She seemed to notice him as well, for she immediately turned and strode down the nearest street and was lost from view moments later.

Had Borund's presence made her act that way? They had agreed not to advertise their relationship, but in the instant their eyes had met she hadn't seemed worried. She had seemed ashamed.

"How much longer?" Borund said irritably.

Nikandr glanced over, wondering if he'd seen. "If I didn't know better, I'd say you could no longer stand the cold, Bora."

"I can"—Borund sniffed—"when necessary."

"You were the one who insisted on joining me." Nikandr guided his pony onto a wide street that hugged the River Mordova on its final stretch toward the bay. As they passed a small graveyard, where chips of chalcedony marked the myriad of gravestones, the smell of the sea grew stronger.

Borund's frown deepened the creases on his brow, but beneath his bushy eyebrows his eyes twinkled. "That was when I thought we were visiting the shipyard. Had I known he was buried among the wharfs, I might not have been so hasty."

"Well, we're nearly there now." Nikandr nodded ahead, where the river emptied into the bay and the street turned onto the long, curving quay.

A large fishing ship was pulling in to berth—probably the first of the day. A sizable crowd was pressing in around it. He wondered if his brother in the Boyar's house knew how bad it was getting down here.

From a large boulevard several hundred yards further up, ten streltsi leading a large black wagon turned onto the quay and marched toward the ship. The soldiers wore fur hats and thick black cherkesskas buttoned high up their necks. Their muskets were slung over one shoulder while their tall berdische axes were held in readied hands. The desyatnik of the streltsi—a man whose hat was gray instead of black—shouted at the crowd, demanding room for the palotza. The wagon carried a handful of workmen in Radiskoye's livery and was adorned with the Khalakovo family seal: a sailfish arcing high above a turbulent sea. It pulled wide and then arced around until its rear was even with the gangway of the fishing ship.

The crowd made way for the streltsi and the wagon, but did so grudgingly. Many would go away hungry, Nikandr knew. There simply wasn't enough to go around. The fishing beds that had been so reliable in years past had gone dry; add to that the pitiful yield the crops were looking to have and one could easily predict outright famine this year.

Nikandr and Borund stopped short of the crowd and tied their ponies near a ramp leading up to the doors of an immense workshop. An ancient figurehead of a man gripping a hammer in one hand and a large pearl in the other hung above the doors, one of which was propped open. They found Gravlos within, walking alongside a fresh spar, a curl of wood falling free from the plane he was using to smooth the rounded but still-raw shape of it. His wooden leg thumped softly as he went. When he realized someone was standing in his doorway he stood and wiped his brow with the sleeve of his forearm. His face was severe, but he managed a kindly smile when he recognized them.

"Lose your way?" He set his plane on a nearby worktable, winking as he did so.

Nikandr's entire body tightened as something splashed to his left. Borund backed up as well, staring at a large tun that stood just inside the workshop doors. It was as tall as Nikandr's chest and was filled nearly to the top with water. Nikandr approached, but it was with a sickly sense of dread, like when he'd played find-me-if-you-can as a child late at night with Ranos and Victania in the dark and mysterious halls of Radiskoye. When he finally came close enough to look down into it, he saw something folded over, as if a random bolt of weathered canvas had been tossed into the tun and then forgotten. The canvas rippled, and Nikandr saw what looked to be a jaundiced eye.

"I bought it from a fisherman this morning." Gravlos picked up a stick that had been resting against the door and poked the thing. It rippled again, and an enormous jaw unfolded itself, revealing a triple row of thorn-sharp teeth. A thin tongue whiter than fresh-fallen snow slithered out and glowed momentarily.

Nikandr laughed from the sheer horror of the thing.

"The old sailors call them tarpfish," Gravlos continued. "It was caught off the coast of Duzol, only three leagues out to sea."

"Excluding Nikandr," Borund said with a distinct note of awe, "that is the ugliest thing I've ever seen."

Gravlos began poking the fish again. "Wait, it gets worse."

Only a moment later, the fish belched out a stream of shit-colored ink and began flapping around the tun. Water sprayed everywhere. All three men backed away, laughing and holding their sleeves against the fierce smell of rotted cabbage.

Nikandr couldn't help but think of the wasting, of the rot that was growing within *him*, but to laugh with Borund felt good. It felt like the days of old, and he wasn't about to feel sorry for himself at a time like this.

Borund pointed at it, still laughing. "What in the wide great seas made you buy such a thing?"

Gravlos nodded toward Nikandr. "You've not heard?"

Borund looked between Nikandr and Gravlos. "Heard what?"

Gravlos caught Nikandr's eye, waiting for permission. When Nikandr nodded, he said, "I thought My Lord Prince would want to see it. He's been flying around the islands, every spare moment he's had outside of our work on the *Gorovna*, searching for clues."

"Clues to what?"

"To the blight," Nikandr answered.

Borund chuckled, but stopped when he realized Nikandr was serious. "We should have asked for more ships if you have so many to go about."

"Easy words for you, Bora. Vostroma has not been hit so hard as Khalakovo."

"And Rhavanki is worse off than you."

"But that's all changing. Rhavanki's hauls have been better. Their first plantings look to be healthier than years past."

"This is my point, Nischka. Nature will do what it will. It matters not what attention you might pay to it."

This was a thought that came to Nikandr every day, but he refused to believe it. "Did you know that when herds of goats become sick, we have found hordes of black fleas on them?"

"Not surprising with diseased animals."

Nikandr shook his head. "When we take them in and wash them with vinegar, the goats become well again."

Borund laughed. "You should have told us. We could have brought you a herd."

"The potatoes," Nikandr continued, "if we discover mold in the roots, we know which fields should go untended. I can tell you by looking at a pack of wolves which are infected and how many days it will be before the pack devours them. If I watch the coast of an island for a day, I can tell by the flights of the gulls which shoals will yield the most herring."

"And by the time the ships get there, things will have changed."

"That isn't the point. We learn more all the time, and someday we hope to understand the blight. Perhaps the wasting as well."

Borund's expression turned to sadness. "Nischka, the news of your sister's illness was tragic, but do you really think you can unlock the secrets of her disease?"

Let's hope so, Nikandr thought. "I'll never know unless I try."

Borund shook his head. "The blight and the wasting are unpredictable workings of the world, and nothing you do will change that."

Suddenly the sounds of a grumbling crowd grew, making it clear the business of unlading the haul had gotten underway. It also made it clear that it was a smaller catch than the crowd had been hoping for—with so many visiting Khalakovo for Council, the palotza would need the ship's entire catch and most likely several more beyond it.

Gravlos's smile faded. He led them away from the doors toward the wooden ponies and workbenches. "It's been getting worse." He glanced meaningfully at Nikandr. "Not that I'm complaining. I know the people on the Hill have to eat as well. But some don't see it that way. They say too much is taken from the city, more than a fair share."

"Our share is what we take," Borund said before Nikandr could reply.

Gravlos dropped his gaze. "That's as may be, My Lord Prince, but there's enough grumbling stomachs to go about, of that I can assure you."

Borund opened his mouth to reply, but Nikandr raised his hand. "The blight isn't something we'll solve by talking, and we have other things to discuss."

Gravlos nodded and motioned them toward one of his workbenches, upon which sat a complicated mass of wood and iron. Six cylindrical sections of wood, each of which looked like they'd been sawed cleanly from a windship mast, were connected with an arrangement of iron levers and hinges. It looked like two logs laid across one another with a third skewering them both. A complicated mass of hinges at the very center allowed for free movement of each spar. Nikandr knew it was the *Gorovna's* rudder, the very same one he'd shown them on the ship two days earlier.

A healthy rudder, when fixed properly in the center of a ship, would align with the keels, and by using the levers at the helm, the rudders would divert the flow of the aether that ran along them, thus turning the ship in the desired direction. The key was not the outer casing of wood, but the obsidian core enclosed within it.

Nikandr could already see that something wasn't right. Lying on the table, just beneath one of the exposed pieces, was a pile of black powder and stone that looked to have been purposefully chipped away.

He bent over to inspect it. "Why did you do this?"

"Run your finger over the stone."

Nikandr had no more than touched one of the exposed faces than a section of it crumbled away, adding to the small pile.

Borund did the same to another section. "Was it inferior?"

Gravlos looked insulted. "*Nyet*, My Lord, it was not. I chose the blocks myself and inspected each section carefully after milling."

Borund seemed less than convinced. "Then what happened?"

Gravlos shrugged. "Rudder stone can crack, but that's after many years, and typically there are only a handful of fractures. Nothing like this."

The stone hanging from Nikandr's neck—hidden beneath his shirt—felt suddenly heavier. Clearly whatever had happened to the rudder had also affected his stone; at the very least they were loosely related. He nearly pulled it out to show Gravlos, to get his opinion, but his father's words felt like they made more sense now—Borund was an old friend, but he couldn't be trusted to keep word of it quiet—and so he left the stone where it was. "Could it have been the hezhan?"

"Perhaps." Gravlos ran one hand over his bald head and shrugged. "Who would know?"

Borund rubbed the obsidian powder between his fingers and stared intently at the sparkle that remained. "Were the keels damaged?"

"*Da*, which is why the repairs will take so—"

"We cannot accept a ship such as that, Nikandr."

"The damage did not travel far," Gravlos continued. "Less than the length of your hand. We'll be able to cut the keel and lengthen the rudder to—"

Gravlos was cut off by sounds from the crowd. Their grumbling had grown steadily during their conversation, but it had spiked considerably; men were shouting and several women could be heard screaming over them.

They moved quickly to the front of the workshop to see what was happening. No sooner had Gravlos pulled one of the doors open than the crowd pressed backward. A half-dozen people were forced onto the shallow ramp leading up to Gravlos's doors.

With his high vantage, Nikandr could see that the streltsi had fanned out around the royal wagon and were using their axes to ward off the crowd. Their breath, coming quickly, blew as smoke upon the cold breeze of the harbor.

"Back!" shouted the desyatnik.

"He stabbed me!" a man screamed. He was bent over, perhaps nursing his leg, but when he pointed to one of the soldiers, steam rose from his blood-coated hand.

Several women continued to shout, shaking their fingers right under the officer's nose. The crowd pressed in. More joined in, demanding that the rest of the fish be left alone.

It was then that Nikandr realized that there were only five crates on the wagon. *Five crates* from a ship that would have hauled four dozen only a few years ago.

"Best we stay inside, My Lords," Gravlos said as he began swinging the door closed.

As soon as he'd said the words, however, one of the streltsi fired his musket into the crowd. A young man with a barrel chest was propelled backward into the older man behind him, his face a look of shock and wonder.

"My son!" screamed the man holding the wounded one. It was a cry that brought the entire scene to a stunned silence.

And then the quay was madness.

CHAPTER 6

Peasants were a hard people, and they weren't accustomed to asking for handouts, but eventually the strain had become too great, and once it had, they became insistent. They had asked, then begged, then *demanded* that the city's Posadnik provide them relief.

With the farmers' fields stricken as they were, and the fishing so poor, the obvious choice was to buy food from the Empire, but the grain and rice from Yrstanla was by common agreement spread among *all* the Duchies. Little enough was rationed to each of the nine Duchies; it was cut again for each of Khalakovo's seven islands, and then again for each of the cities on those islands. Volgorod was Khalakovo's largest city by far, and so it got the lion's share, but still, the sacks went quickly as more and more families came for their dole.

The incoming aid—however inadequate it might be—stemmed the tide of discontent, but everyone knew that it would build again, however slowly. And now, here, as the peasants bore witness to the palotza's hording, Nikandr could feel their anger bubble up and boil over. They stared wide-eyed at the strelet who had fired his musket into the chest of one of their own. They shouted, demanding he set his weapon down and give himself over. Those further back joined in, then further still, the sound of it deafening as the entire crowd began pumping their fists at the sky, screaming for justice.

The meager perimeter the streltsi had managed to maintain collapsed. The desyatnik ordered his men to hold fire, but as the shouting intensified and the man wailed over his dying son, two more shots rang out. One of the streltsi tried to stab with his berdische, but it was grabbed by a pair of men and he was pulled viciously into the crowd.

"Halt!" Nikandr shouted. "By order of your Prince!" But no one heard him. He nearly drew his pistol, but rejected the idea when he realized that firing it would only serve to heighten the chaos.

"Nikandr, come!" Gravlos waited at the doors, motioning for Nikandr to get inside. "There's nothing we can do here!"

Behind Gravlos stood Borund, pistol in hand, eyeing the crowd warily.

Nikandr stood impotently as another strelet struggled to break away from two men who had grabbed his musket.

And then he turned to the weathered old tun.

"Help me!" he said to Borund and Gravlos as he pushed the left door open. He pulled at the edge of the tun, using all his weight, but it wouldn't budge. Even with Borund and Gravlos helping, it was clear it wouldn't tip over.

He ran into the workshop as another shot was fired and the excited commands of the desyatnik were cut short. He scanned the workbenches and the tools hanging on the walls behind them, knowing Gravlos had an axe but not sure where—

He spotted it on the far end of a long workbench. He grabbed it and sprinted back. The crowd was feeding on its own blood frenzy as he cocked the axe and swung with a heavy grunt. It cut deep, and a thin stream of water began leaking from the cut. He swung again and again, more water sluicing between the staves with each strike. On the sixth, three of the staves gave way, and water gushed out.

Along with the tarpfish

The deluge splashed into the crowd, surprising many. A moment later, the fish was carried down the ramp, flipping and flapping as it swung its great bat-like wings about. The talons at the end of its wings sunk deeply into an old woman's leg. She shouted in pain and fright as she staggered into two younger women. The fish hooked someone else with its other wing, and as the two separated from one another, the thing flipped, squirting brown ink. A moment later it was lost among a sea of legs.

"Back!" Nikandr shouted as he drew his flintlock pistol and fired it into the air. "Back, by order of the Duke!"

Borund followed suit. Finally some in the crowd recognized them while many more retreated from the putrid, writhing mass of skin and bone and teeth.

"Back!"

The crowd eyed him and the streltsi warily as the tarpfish flipped closer to the edge of the quay. Finally it fell into the water with a hollow splash.

It was with that one simple sound, from an animal few had ever seen, that the winds were released from the sail. Those at the edges of the crowd—the realization of what they'd done clear on their faces—retreated, and then ran. Soon the area was clear save for the wounded and the soldiers.

After reaching the Boyar's mansion in the center of Volgorod, they spoke briefly with Ranos, but he soon put them off to deal with the wounded streltsi as well as two women who claimed their husbands had been shot "without provocation."

"Wait here," Ranos said as he grabbed his coat of office and opened the door of the drawing room. "I'll be back as soon as I'm able, and then we'll go to the eyrie together."

Without waiting for a response he closed the door, leaving Nikandr and Borund in a room that held little to occupy their time. Ranos's wife—cold in her choice of decor—had left it without so much as a deck of cards. By the time they had finished their second mazer of vodka, it was clear Ranos had been delayed.

Nikandr set his ivory mazer down with a clack and stood. He could feel his nose and cheeks and ears flush from the alcohol. "Come, good Vostroma, and we shall see what the eyrie holds for us."

Borund, his rounded cheeks still red—more from the vodka than the cold—surveyed the room as if it were his last hope at warmth, but then he raised his lips in a wry smile and downed the last of his drink. "*Da*. Fuck Ranos."

Nikandr smiled. "Fuck Ranos."

Soon they were back on their ponies and headed uphill from the city along Eyrie Road, the wide, gravel trail that climbed up to the highlands and then west to the eyrie. After they passed the first rise, the wind picked up, and both of them buttoned their long cherkesskas up to their neck. As the trail led them above the expanse of Volgorod, they spotted the tall white cliffs of the eyrie and the great pillared rocks that withstood the churning green seas to the south of them.

Traffic along the road was high. Laden carts and wagons clattered toward Volgorod, while empty ones returned. Far ahead, a wagon had pulled onto the grass. Two men were changing the rear wagon wheel.

"Don't you think it's time we discussed my sister?" Borund asked as he pulled the collar of his coat up.

Nikandr stared at the men repairing the wagon as their ponies trotted onward. "I'm sorry the ship was damaged, Borund. I know it has caused difficulties with your father—"

"That's not what I mean, Nischka."

Nikandr didn't know what to say, not without causing insult.

Borund's thick eyebrows bunched together. "My sister is not so terrible."

"She was always the worst of them, Borund."

Borund laughed. "That may be true, but she's grown into a fine woman."

Perhaps, Nikandr thought, but the churning in his gut he got every time he thought about being married to her was still as strong as ever. Yet despite that, despite all his fears—founded or not—he would have buried his discontent and prepared for the wedding with diligence—if not passion—had it not been for the Aramahn woman he had seen near the gallows. Rehada. Had they come from slightly different places, he would have already asked for her hand in marriage. As it stood, however, such a thing was out of the question. Impossible. But it didn't stop his heart from yearning for such a thing, even more so with the knowledge that he had little time left.

"You're right," he told Borund. "She is a fine woman, and I'll love her as she deserves."

Borund laughed, though there was little humor in it. "That's small consolation coming from you, Nischka. You'd do well to love her better than that."

Nikandr bit off his reply, unsure what to say without lying outright or causing insult. He was saved by the approach of a galloping pony. It turned out to be Ranos. He looked cross, even from a distance.

"You were to wait," Ranos said as he pulled his roan pony to a stop. His cheeks were flush. He wore a belted woolen coat, similar to Nikandr's fitted cherkesska, but it didn't have the same ornamented cartridge pouches on the chest, and the cuffs, embroidered with golden thread, ran halfway up his forearm.

"You were busy," Nikandr said. "I thought we'd go ahead."

Ranos glanced at Borund, who was keeping his round face as straight as he could manage. "I was *busy*, as you say, dealing with your mess."

"*My* mess?"

"You could have done better than throwing a fish at them, Nischka, and I daresay you could have done it sooner."

Nikandr urged his pony forward, forcing Borund and Ranos to keep up. "Well, next time I'll just turn a blind eye, shall I?"

"Come, come," Borund said, reining his black pony between them. "Nikandr did well enough."

Nikandr frowned. *Well enough?*

"We're finally together," Borund continued, "and we're off to see the ships, *da?*"

Ranos looked between them, clearly displeased, but then he smoothed his wide moustache and visibly unwound. "I suppose you're right."

Ranos led the way down several switchbacks to the eyrie's third quay. The eyrie was alive around them: the clatter of carts, the bark of the clerks, the ever-present cry of the gulls both high among the ships and far below where they built their nests. The quays were just as busy as they had been the day of the *Gorovna's* launching, the only difference being that there were four times the number of streltsi standing guard among the warehouses and the quays. All five cannon emplacements were manned as well. Father was not willing to take any chances after what had happened to the *Gorovna*. The Maharraht would be foolish to attempt anything now, but in reality this show of force was as much for the landing dukes as it was for the protection of Khalakovo. With politics in play, they could ill afford to look weak.

They stopped at the first perch. The ship moored there was an ancient and wounded carrack. Ranos made a grand gesture of stopping and turning to Borund. "This," he said while giving Borund a short, polite bow, "is the first."

The ship's hull had dozens of battle scars from her decades of service. Nearly every mast had been repaired instead of replaced. Even the figurehead, a charging ram, was marred by several pockmarks from some ancient battle. Nikandr knew it wasn't a sign of neglect but a remembrance of the ship's first kapitan, who had died at that very spot on its maiden voyage. Borund, however, who had up until this point held an eager expression on his face, didn't know this, and so as he examined the carrack, his face became more and more splotchy. He opened his mouth to speak, but then closed it and swallowed heavily.

Nikandr clamped his jaw to keep himself from smiling.

"Old she may be," Ranos continued, "but she's stout, and once the new mainsail's complete, she'll be tip-top."

For years Nikandr and Borund had played jokes on one another. He would normally have played the role of instigator himself, but Borund had become too wary, so he'd enlisted Ranos, and from what he could tell it had been a wonderful choice. He was barely able to contain his amusement over his brother's straight face. He feared Borund would notice and sense the nature of this exchange, but Borund wasn't paying the least bit of attention. His eyes were locked on the ship, jaw clamped shut, a look of deep indignation on his face.

"Your father promised us stout ships…."

So grave was Borund's voice that Nikandr nearly confessed, but their time together had so far been very stiff, and he hoped that by breaking the ice, the old camaraderie between them would return. And so he strode to the edge of the perch and slapped the ship's hull. "Believe me, I served on her for six months. She's as stout as they come."

Borund peered up at the rigging. "She needs a season's worth of repairs before she'll cross the neck."

"A season's worth…" Nikandr shook his head. "A week at most. I tell you—"

"Ranos," Borund said, ignoring Nikandr. "My father made our position clear. We will not accept ships that are ready for pasture. Bad enough your brother allowed our prized ship to be damaged beyond repair, but now you try to pawn off the debris of your fleet as if we're Motherless beggars who'll take anything we're given."

Ranos's face hardened. "My brother saved your life, Bora."

Borund scoffed. "*Nyet*, Ranos. You had the right of it when you said Nikandr should have done something sooner. So it was on the quay, so it was on the *Gorovna*."

"Bora," Nikandr said, raising his hands. "This was in jest. Only in jest. This isn't one of the ships you'll be given."

Borund's face was pinched. He was tight in the shoulders and in his stance. Nikandr thought he would come down from the heights of anger, but if anything he grew angrier as he stabbed his finger at Nikandr's chest. "This is no time to joke. We are no longer children, you and I. We are men. I am a Prince of Vostroma, in line for my father's scepter, and you play a prank on me as if I'm your servant boy?"

Nikandr shook his head, confused. "We used to do this all the time."

"There are many things we used to do, Nikandr, none of which make the least bit of sense to continue, including your insulting refusal to accept the hand of my blood and bone as you should—with grace and humility."

Nikandr realized with those words how much Borund must have been holding back on their ride together from Volgorod. He had seemed, if not cheerful, at least jovial, something akin to what they had once shared together, but Nikandr realized now it had all been an act. Borund had become much more like his father than he ever would have guessed.

A piercing whistle tore through the cold morning wind, burning away the tension that hung between the three of them. There was a moment of silence as the entire eyrie turned its attention seaward.

An incoming ship—a twelve-masted barque—was listing to one side as it drifted toward the eyrie. Nikandr recognized it immediately as the *Kroya*, Father's missing ship that had weeks ago been presumed destroyed or taken by raiders. There was a momentary sense of relief, but that emotion was soon tempered by the signs of battle that became more apparent the closer it came.

CHAPTER 7

The eyrie master's loud voice bellowed, shouting for landsmen to run double-time to the eyrie's topmost level. Using bright red flags, a flagman waved signals, telling the ship which perch it should take.

Ranos turned meaningfully to Nikandr.

"I'll take care of it." With a quick turn to Borund, Nikandr snapped his heels and bowed his head. "Good day to you, Borund."

Borund did not reply as Nikandr left, and he was glad for it. As heated as the discussion had become, either one of them might say something they would come to regret.

Nikandr's anger faded as the wounded ship approached. As was proper for an approach to the eyrie, only two of her mainmasts—starward and sea-ward—had any sails to speak of; the sails along her windward and landward sides were tucked in completely. Two of the foremasts were shattered near the halfway point, and the forward rigging was stripped bare; most likely the crew had taken it down to begin repairs before reaching the eyrie. The hull below the bowsprit had sustained several holes the size of pumpkins and a landscape of pockmarks from grape shot. The forward cannon, which would have sat at the base of the bowsprit, was missing. The crew had most likely jettisoned it, for any loss in the delicate balance between the masts would cause severe instability, forcing the kapitan to reduce the metal onboard to an absolute minimum or risk losing control of the ship.

By the time Nikandr reached the uppermost quay—the one reserved for the ships of war—the *Kroya* was near. Standing amidships on the platform reserved for the wind master was a man Nikandr didn't recognize. He stood ahead of the starward mainmast, arms spread wide, eyes closed and face upturned. It was clear that there was no dhoshaqiram to control the heft of the ship. This qiram must be gifted, indeed—it was tricky, though not impossible, for the havaqiram to affect the ship's altitude by direct-ing the wind.

Crewmen stood at the gunwales, tossing bits of hardtack to the wind. Gray cliff gulls fought for it with piercing cries. When Nikandr had finally reached the perch, the eyrie master and his men were securing the ship. Two doors opened in the hull and gangplanks were maneuvered into place. One more was lowered from the upper deck, and from this a heavyset sailor lumbered down and shook forearms with the eyrie master.

Then he spied Nikandr.

Immediately he removed the ushanka from his balding head, held it to his breast, and took a knee two paces away from Nikandr.

Nikandr did not know this man well, but he tried to learn at the very least the kapitan, master, purser, and pilot on every one of his father's two-dozen ships. Mladosh used to be the *Kroya's* pilot, so he could only assume that the kapitan and master had both been wounded or killed.

"You may rise, Mladosh," Nikandr told him. "Tell me what happened."

He rose, but kept his gaze fixed on Nikandr's black, knee-length boots. "Maharraht, my lord. A clipper and two schooners set upon us a day out from Rhavanki."

Nikandr pulled Mladosh aside so the unlading of the hold could begin.

"My mother as my witness the day was clear," Mladosh continued. "Hardly a cloud in the sky, but before we knew it the sky had cast over and the clouds had swallowed us. That was when they struck." He pointed to the ship's bow. "Seven men died on the opening salvo. The kapitan took a sliver of wood through the neck, died before the surgeon could get him below."

On the deck, a dozen or so Aramahn gathered, smiling, kissing cheeks, and preparing to disembark. Like jewels among gravel, their loose, bright clothing and swarthy skin stood out against the weathered wood of the ship and the charcoal clothing of the crew.

"If it wasn't for that one," Mladosh said, pointing his thumb at the older Aramahn who had guided the ship to berth, "we'd've been lost."

As often as the Aramahn moved among the ships, Nikandr could not keep track of them, but he had personally recruited the qiram—an Aramahn wizard—for the *Kroya's* voyage. "Muqtada is dead?"

Mladosh nodded. "I pulled him from the Motherless hold. His name is Ashan Kida al Ahrumea. He was the only bonded wind master among them but by the ancestors was he strong!"

Motherless was the term most sailing men used for the Aramahn, referring to their penchant for constantly wandering the great ocean, rarely staying in one place for more than a season. They have no Motherland, the sailors would say; they come from nowhere, and that's where they'll go when they die.

Ashan had summoned enough wind to force the other ships away while

Mladosh ordered the crew to release the ship's hold of the ley lines that guided them southward along the Rhavanki archipelago. As Mladosh continued the tale, Nikandr studied Ashan, who was waiting for the last of the Aramahn to disembark. He wore inner robes of bright yellow; his outer robes were orange. Several layers of white cloth wrapped his shins and ankles. There was a calmness to his demeanor that transcended the placid disposition so many of the Landless possessed.

A circlet rested upon his brow, and an alabaster gem could be seen through his tousle of nutmeg-colored hair. The gem had an iridescent quality to it and a glow that told Nikandr that a hezhan, a spirit from beyond the aether, was bound to him. The bracelets at his wrists, however, gave Nikandr pause. One of them contained a large glowing opal, the other a stone of dull azurite. Three gems. *Three* spirits could this man commune with—and two of them at once! Such a thing was not unheard of, but it was rare. Mladosh and the rest of the crew were lucky, indeed, to have taken aboard a man such as this.

A young boy, perhaps ten or eleven years old, huddled close to Ashan. As carefree and confident as his guardian seemed to be, the boy was just the opposite. His arms were crossed tightly over his stomach. His gaze wandered the perch, the eyrie, even the bright white clouds, as if this were the last place on Erahm he wished to be. There was no circlet upon his brow, which was not strange in and of itself—most Aramahn never became proficient enough with spirits to bond with them. It only seemed strange that a man like Ashan would have a disciple with no abilities.

Ashan must have felt Nikandr's gaze. As he negotiated the plank, guiding the boy ahead of him, he smiled at Nikandr and nodded politely.

As a group, the Aramahn were ushered to one side of the perch by an immigration clerk. He took each of their names in a thick, leather-bound journal before allowing them to continue on. He questioned Ashan for some time, as he was clearly a qiram of some renown. He spent a good deal of effort on the boy as well but seemed to get nowhere—the boy ignored him entirely while hugging his gut and gritting his jaw and blinking as if he were staring into the sun. Each time the official asked him a question, Ashan would reply, perhaps making excuses.

Finally, his questioning complete, the official released them, at which point Nikandr dismissed Mladosh and fell into step alongside them. "I hear I have much to thank you for," Nikandr said.

Ashan waved as if it were nothing. "It was self-preservation, Nikandr, son of Iaros."

"Do I know you?"

"We have not met, but *I* know *you*, certainly."

"Well, Ashan, son of Kida and Ahrumea, we owe you much. Never let it be said that the Khalakovos leave debts unpaid."

Ashan picked up his pace. They were just short of the busy quays, where it would be more difficult to speak, so Nikandr took Ashan by the elbow and slowed him until he stopped.

"How may I repay you?"

"There is no need to repay me for saving lives"—Ashan smiled, showing a healthy grin full of crooked and yellowed teeth—"not the least of which was mine."

The boy was still using his rail-thin arms to hold himself about the waist. He looked so miserable that Nikandr found himself wishing there was something he could do for him.

Nikandr bent down and looked him in the eye. His stomach chose that moment to become queasy. Before he could manage it, a cough escaped him, but then he breathed deeper and forced the feelings down. "Are you well, boy?"

Nikandr expected him to shrink and shy away, but he didn't. If anything, he gained a certain sense of gravitas: the look of pain faded, and he began to stare into Nikandr's eyes with a singular focus that was wholly discomforting.

"As I explained to your official," Ashan said sharply, breaking the spell, "Nasim has been dumb since he was a young boy. He rarely speaks, even to me, and when he does it is with words that have no meaning."

Nikandr stood, ignoring those staring eyes. "No meaning to you or to him?"

"Indeed"—Ashan's smile brightened—"that is the question. I believe they have *profound* meaning to him, but he cannot communicate his thoughts. They come out sometimes over the course of days. I thought I was a patient man before coming to know him, but now, after learning to piece together one small thought over the course of weeks… The word has taken on new meaning."

"He looks like he's in pain."

Ashan smoothed the boy's hair. "He *is* in pain, but he doesn't complain, do you, Nasim?"

Nasim was staring at Nikandr's neck, and Nikandr realized that his expression was no longer one of wonder.

It was one of rapture.

Nikandr felt a tickling sensation in the center of his chest, just below the surface of the skin, and it took a presence of mind not to raise a hand and begin scratching it. Only as the boy began walking forward did Nikandr realize that it was his soulstone, hidden beneath coat and shirt, that had so caught Nasim's attention. With a completely innocent look on his face, Nasim reached for it.

A vision comes. A vision of a grand city. It spreads wide and low near a crescent bay, tall towers and massive domes bright beneath a golden sun. It seems whole, but the streets lay empty and barren—lifeless—as if it has long been abandoned.

An unreasonable anger came bubbling up from somewhere deep inside Nikandr; before he knew it, he had slapped the boy's hand away and shoved him backward. Immediately Ashan took Nasim by the shoulders and guided him to the nearby railing, whispering into his ear.

"My apologies," Ashan said over his shoulder. "He can be a curious boy."

"It is nothing," Nikandr said, shaking his head to clear away the sudden vision and the confusion it had left in its wake. "Please," he said, "there must be something I could offer. Gold…"

"What need have the Aramahn of gold?"

"Food, then, for Iramanshah if not for you."

Ashan shook his head. "There is little enough to go around. Nasim and I will do fine, as will Iramanshah."

"Access to our library. Gemstones. A discussion with our scholars. You have only to name the price."

Ashan smiled once more and herded the boy away from the railing and up the perch. "There is most certainly nothing"—Ashan nodded, reverently it seemed to Nikandr—"but I wish prosperous times upon you and your family." And then he turned and walked away.

Nikandr could have stopped him for the insult, but he didn't. They had been through enough, these two, and it was unseemly for him to badger them now.

And the boy… He was strangely compelling, and not simply because of their shared and inexplicable exchange. When one sees someone around whom the world revolves, one knows it, and the boy, even more than Ashan, was just such a person.

CHAPTER 8

The Bluff lay in darkness, but there was enough light coming from the windows of the three-story homes lining the street that Nikandr could make his way. When he arrived at his destination—a home nearly indistinguishable from the others—he glanced along the lengths of the empty, curving street before removing the silver flask from inside his coat and taking a healthy swallow of the bitter tonic. His stomach felt strangely healthy, but he wasn't about to take chances—not tonight. He took the steps up and knocked upon the door five times, a bitter wind pressing against his back.

He turned, holding the fur-lined collar of his coat tight against the gusting wind. Over the tops of the nearby homes the lights of Palotza Radiskoye could barely be seen on the mountain overlooking the city.

He knocked again, softer this time, wondering if he'd made a mistake, but just as he was about to walk away, the flickering light of a lantern shone through the thick, wavy glass of the door's high window. The door opened, and there stood Rehada Ulan al Shineshka, wearing a thick nightgown and a circlet that held a softly glowing gem of tourmaline. When he saw her face—how beautiful she looked in the golden light of the lantern—he nearly made his apologies and headed back toward Radiskoye. And yet, there was—as there always seemed to be—a beckoning luster in Rehada's dark eyes, even as tired as she must be, even dressed as she was.

Without a word being spoken, she stepped aside, allowing Nikandr to enter her home. They moved into a lush sitting room. A host of large pillows arcing around the hearth, and the air, beneath the faint smell of jasmine incense, was redolent of garlic and ginger.

From his coat Nikandr took a small leather bag filled with virgin gems and placed it on the mantel. Then he threw two logs from the cradle onto the remains of the evening's fire and began stoking the flames. Rehada did not acknowledge her payment as she moved to a silver cart topped with an ornate shisha. Normally they would have smoked tabbaq, the most common of the smoking leaves, but she chose instead a cedar box from the cabinet built into the base of the cart and retrieved several healthy pinches of dokha, a mixture of tabbaq, herbs, and fermented bark that came from Yrstanla's western coast. It was extremely rare among the islands, and for a moment Nikandr nearly refused her, but he knew enough to know that this was a privilege that Rehada bestowed upon precious few patrons.

Tonight was going to cost him, so he was willing to accept such a gift. He lay down on the pillows as Rehada stepped between him and the fire and placed the tray carrying the shisha on the carpeted floor. The slosh of liquid came from the base until it had settled, and then all was silence save for the faint whuffle of the burgeoning fire.

After lighting the dokha in the bowl at the top of the shisha, Rehada offered him one of the silk-covered smoking tubes. He accepted it and for a time simply breathed in the heady smell of honey and vanilla and hay, wondering how long it had taken and by what route it had traveled along the thousands of leagues from its point of origin to Volgorod. How many wagons had brought it from the curing house to the edges of the Yrstanlan Empire? How many hands had carried it on its way to Khalakovo? How many ships had borne it? How many lungs had tasted of the same harvest?

"You look thin," Rehada said, perhaps growing tired of the silence. She held two snifters of infused vodka, one of which she handed to Nikandr as she settled herself gracefully upon the nearby pillows.

"The work on the *Gorovna*..." Thankfully the wasting had given him a small reprieve—tonight he felt none of its effects.

"Ah, your other mistress."

Nikandr, ignoring her gibe, drew upon the tube and held his breath before slowly releasing the smoke up toward the ceiling. "That was you at the hanging, was it not?"

The silence lengthened as Rehada took the second tube in one hand. Anyone else would have sucked from the mouthpiece, but not Rehada. She placed the ivory mouthpiece gently against her lips and drew breath like one of the rare, languorous breezes of summer. Her hair, like many of the Landless women, was cut square across the brow, not propped up in some complicated nest like the women of royalty. She held her breath—a good deal longer than Nikandr had—before exhaling the smoke through full, pursed lips. "There are those I would say farewell to before they depart these shores."

Visions of the boy swinging in the wind next to the two peasants played within his mind. "Who was he?"

The space between Rehada's thin, arching eyebrows pinched, but she did not otherwise show her annoyance. "What does it matter who he was? I have witnessed the deaths of those who I've never met."

"If you had never met him, you wouldn't have acted like you did."

"What makes you so sure?"

"The look you gave me."

She regarded him levelly, the shisha tube held motionless near her mouth. "I knew that boy, but the look was not for him, nor was it for you."

Nikandr paused. "Borund?" He searched his memory for the few times they had discussed her past, but he was unable to remember what connection she might have with the Prince of Vostroma. "I don't understand…"

"Then perhaps your wife could explain it to you." She pulled on the shisha tube and released her breath, much more forcefully than she had the last time.

And suddenly he understood. Borund, as Rehada well knew, was Atiana's brother. Could it be she had been jealous? Or perhaps the juxtaposition of death and marriage had made her pause; she, like so many of her people, was always making emotional connections like that and contemplating them for days or weeks at a time.

"Now that she's come…" Rehada allowed herself another long pull before setting the mouthpiece aside. "Now that you're staring face-to-face with the prospect, will you marry her still?"

"There's little choice. She'll be my wife within the week whether I like it or not." Nikandr smiled. "Though I may have delayed it by a day or two."

"And how might you have done that?"

"I should be up at the palotza now, signing the wedding documents."

"You've said how prickly the Duke of Vostroma can be."

Nikandr nodded, and his smile widened. "*Da*, he can be that…"

Rehada regarded him, the firelight and the shadows accentuating the features of her face. "You aren't bound to her yet. You could go where you will."

At this Nikandr's smile faded. "You're not so naïve as that."

"If anyone is naïve, it is you. You tell me every time you come how much you love the wind. Surely you have enough money to buy a ship. You could take to the winds, travel the world…"

"I'm not Aramahn."

"Meaning what, that you cannot bear to be parted from your precious family?"

"I may voice displeasure from time to time, but they are my life. They are my love."

"If I had one rachma from every man that's spoken those words…"

"You'd what, take to the winds?"

"I've done my traveling. I've found my place."

Nikandr drew breath from the shisha as if it had somehow insulted him. "And I haven't?" he said while forcing the smoke from his lungs.

Rehada raised her brow and tilted her mouth in a quirky smile. "*You're the one running from your marriage.*"

"I'm not running," Nikandr said. Rehada was prodding him, but the effects of the smoke had already taken the edge from his anger and his feelings of being trapped on the Hill. Without willing it to, his mouth twisted into a smile that was a mirror image of hers. "Well, I suppose I *am* pulling at the tether a bit."

"Why do you never speak of her?" Rehada asked. "Tell me what she's like."

As he downed half of his vodka, the lemon-infused liquor searing his mouth, throat, and finally his stomach, he turned to Rehada and admired the graceful curve of her eyebrows, her long eyelashes and full lips. The orange tourmaline held in the circlet glowed ever so softly. He knew good and well the sort of hezhan that gem granted, and he couldn't wait for the heat of her to fill him, for the touch of her red hot skin, so unlike Atiana Vostroma's, which was certain to be white as bone and cold as winter's chill.

Rehada, perhaps feeling the effects of the smoke as well, smiled mischievously and poked Nikandr in the ribs with a slippered foot. "What is she *like*?"

Nikandr shrugged and leaned into the pillows, knowing he'd already smoked too much for his own good. Part of him wanted to answer Rehada's question—the part that always wanted to please her—but he didn't really know what Atiana was like. He couldn't remember a single time he'd spoken to her when she wasn't with Mileva and Ishkyna. He knew them only as a single, three-headed beast.

"You're impossible." Rehada threw the shisha tube aside and straddled him. Her muscled legs tightened against his waist as her long black hair fell across his chest. She didn't grind her pelvis like a dock whore would, nor did she lean in and kiss him, though her dark eyes spoke of the desire. Instead she smiled. With the low-burning fire lending her already dark skin a ruddy glow, she was breathtaking. She lowered herself, her breasts pressing against his chest, her cheek brushing his. "Tell me something about her," she said, her hot breath tickling his ear. She raised herself and regarded him. The gem upon her brow glowed brighter. Nikandr felt his loins and chest heat, and despite himself he began to harden. "Unless you'd rather return home to be alone with your thoughts."

"I didn't come to talk about my fiancée."

"Then why *did* you come?"

"To be with you."

She poked him in the center of his chest. "The truth…"

Despite himself, he laughed. "Is that so hard to believe?"

"I know your moods, Nikandr, better than she ever will."

He paused, wondering if she were right. "A man arrived on a ship today, one we thought lost to the Maharraht. His name is Ashan."

Surprisingly, Rehada stiffened. "Ashan?"

"Ashan Kida al Ahrumea. He arrived with a curious boy on one of my father's ships, a ship snatched from the jaws of the Maharraht."

Rehada stared down at him seriously, saying nothing.

Nikandr chuckled and threw his arms behind his head. "*Now* who's avoiding questions?"

"I should hold your answers hostage until I get mine."

"But you're not petty, like me."

"Few people are…" Before Nikandr could reply, she continued. "I met Ashan once, years ago."

"The kapitan of the *Kroya* said he was very powerful. He summoned the winds for days straight to save the ship."

She nodded. "He is arqesh."

Nikandr jerked back involuntarily. "He has mastered all five hezhan?"

Rehada stared down with a look that made it clear he had disappointed her. "He has also come to terms with this life and the one that has come before and the one that will come next. He has traveled the world and seen every one of its mysteries. Among all the islands, there are only six like Ashan."

"You're saying you would expect no less from a man like him?"

"I'm saying Ashan is closer to vashaqiram than I will ever be, and that I have no right to judge him."

Vashaqiram was the state of mind all Aramahn searched for. It was complete calm, understanding, forgiveness, and many more things Nikandr did not yet comprehend. It was why they roamed the world as they did, moving constantly from place to place.

Rehada had taken on a look of introspection, one he'd rarely seen from her. She often talked of having given up her quest of wandering the world, of having learned enough to be comfortable on Khalakovo. But he knew better. She too often became like this when faced with tales of travel to the other archipelagos or to the Motherland, Yrstanla.

Rehada's expression darkened. "Why do you come to me late at night to ask me of a wanderer?"

"I saw him only today, mere hours ago, and I wondered—"

She rolled off of him and set her glass of vodka aside. "There was a time when you came here for me…"

Nikandr stared, confused. "I only thought you might—"

"Your thoughts…" She stood, her face cross. "I see where your thoughts are, son of Iaros. They are not here, nor are they on an arqesh. They are on the Hill, a place you should be now." She glanced meaningfully at the entrance to her home, waiting for Nikandr to take her meaning.

"I would stay, Rehada."

"Your wife wouldn't think so well of that."

"She's not my wife."

"A point she, I fear, would beg to differ."

He nearly protested, but he had come here for solace, not to fight with a woman he paid for her company. He gathered his things and left without another word, but as Rehada shut the door behind him and the wind howled through the city streets, he found himself not just alone, but lonely—lonelier than he had ever been.

Nikandr treaded through the cavernous hallways of Radiskoye toward his room. The faint and familiar creaks of movement could be heard somewhere in the floors above—Radiskoye in slumber.

When he reached the second floor he paused, seeing light coming from beneath the door of his father's drawing room. He went to it and opened the door, finding Father seated in a padded armchair, one leg crossed over the other. He was holding the wooden bowl of an ivory-tipped pipe with a stem as long as his forearm. He puffed on it, staring into the dying embers in the nearby fireplace. He looked weary and old, words rarely leveled against him.

An oil painting of Nikandr's great-great-grandfather stared down from the mantel, his serious face cast with heavy shadows. Gold leaf decorated the room, especially along the wainscoting border and the carved wooden columns above the mantel. To say that it felt ostentatious, especially after the lush simplicity of Rehada's home, was an understatement, and to Nikandr it felt foreign and familiar, both.

Nikandr moved to his father's side, kissed his forehead, and took the empty chair.

When Father spoke, it was with a soft voice, contemplative. "Zhabyn came to me today. He was more than passing curious over the ways in which you mean to honor Atiana."

"Father?"

"He is concerned that his future son will be flying among the islands, chasing after meaningless pursuits."

Suddenly, Zhabyn's purpose became clear. The conversation he'd had with

Borund where he'd told him about his desire to understand the blight—he must have shared it with his father. "Borund doesn't understand."

"Neither, it seems, does his father."

"But you do," Nikandr said.

"I do, but we have seen few enough results."

"That will come."

"How soon, Nischka? This year? The next? Ten years?"

Nikandr wanted to laugh. He wouldn't be alive in ten years if he didn't find a cure for the wasting. "We knew it would take time."

"And by then the blight might have moved on, as it has done with Rhavanki."

"Can you deny that things are becoming worse, that the next time it returns it may well destroy us?"

"In truth, I know not. What I do know is that we have to protect our family now. This year. And to do that I had to seal your marriage."

Nikandr shook his head. "What do you mean?"

"Zhabyn and I signed the papers today."

His words were heavy, and it was clear there was more to the story than this. "And what might have changed Vostroma's mind so easily?"

For the first time, Father turned to Nikandr. The wiry beard framing the lower half of his face and running down his gold-threaded kaftan gave him a truculent look. "The *Malva* will be given to them."

"*My* ship?" The *Malva* was the ship he and Jahalan and Udra had been sailing the last two years to investigate the blight.

"*My* ship, Nischka, and I will do with it as I please."

"I have many things planned."

Father shook his head, his beard swaying back and forth over his kaftan. "*Nyet.* The *Malva* will be returned to us when the *Gorovna* is delivered to Vostroman shores, but when it does, you will no longer be given leave to go where you will. I need you to command a wing of the staaya. The Maharraht have become too bold."

Nikandr's stomach, which had been fine the entire day, chose that moment to wake itself from slumber. Like a yawning hole in the ground, nausea spread through Nikandr's gut and chest, but the feelings were nothing compared to the sense of foreboding over what might be lost. "I will not shirk my duty if that is what you ask of me, but please do not ignore what Jahalan and I have done."

"You have done well, Nischka, but the *Malva* is already his. You will sign your papers tomorrow, and then you will ensure that you spend more time with the Vostromas."

"There is little choice."

"And yet you found time to visit your woman in Volgorod, twice in the past week."

Nikandr stared up at his father, angry over being watched so. "Father, forgive me, but I will see whom I please."

Father smiled. "You are not your own man, Nischka. You have never been, and the sooner you get that into your head, the better off we'll all be." He stood, staring down at Nikandr. "In time, such things can be overlooked, but not now, and especially not during Council. All it will take is one more perceived insult—one more—and Zhabyn will take his contracts and grant them to another Duchy, no matter that it makes him poorer in the end."

He made his way to the door, his slippered feet falling against cold marble tile. In the fireplace, a pile of coals crumbled, sending the sparks flying upward.

"Mark my words." The door clicked open. "If I find that you've been visiting that Motherless whore again"—he stepped into the hall before turning, his expression so grim it made Nikandr cold—"she will not live to see another sunrise."

CHAPTER 9

Rehada lay on her pillows, the redolence of Nikandr's musky scent fading but still present. The embers in the nearby hearth crumbled, creating the faintest of sounds as sparks flew upward, and it reminded her of just how long she had been lying there, lamenting. She rose and threw three logs onto the nearly dead fire, lighting it with a simple summons of the spirit bound to her. She stared into the burgeoning flames, yearning for the freedom to be in Nikandr's arms, knowing that such a thing could never be.

As these emotions played themselves out she realized she had allowed herself more fantasies than she had been willing to admit. Years ago, when she had arranged for their first encounter, she had hated him just as much as she hated all the Landed, perhaps more. He had been childish and full of himself, but his time among the winds and the growing blight had somehow tempered him, and she had found him to be interested in the ways of the Aramahn, more than she would have guessed. It had never occurred to her that she would have feelings for him, but like ivy, growing slowly but steadily, he had found a way into her heart.

And she hated herself for it, even more so now that Soroush had returned. She felt weak, as if she'd *allowed* the vines to creep between the mortar of her resolve, until the wall she'd thought so impregnable years ago was ready to crumble before her very eyes. What was worse was the fact that—even knowing how weak it was—she was unsure whether she wanted to repair it. Soroush had ordered her to come two days hence, surely to work against the interests of the Grand Duchy—or at the very least of Radiskoye—and she would go, but she found herself, more and more often, wishing that the fates would resolve these disputes so that her people might move closer to their destiny. So that *she* might.

After removing her robe, folding it carefully, and setting it on the carpet nearby, she retrieved the small leather bag Nikandr had placed on the mantel. Inside were a dozen tourmaline stones—the price they had agreed upon long ago. The stones would keep her for a season, perhaps more, and though it was relieving to have her supply doubled, it was still galling to find herself at the mercy of the Landed, even though she was also in a position to use them.

She released her bonded suurahezhan, an act as simple as a sigh. Like most of the Aramahn gifted with the ability to commune with spirits, she could not keep them for weeks or months at a time. She needed to release her bond after several days or a week, lest it grow too hungry and begin feeding off of her unnaturally.

After removing the old stone and fixing a new one into the hinged setting of her circlet, she sat before the fire and opened her mind to Adhiya, the world beyond. She ran her hands over the fire, giving herself to the flame to lure a hezhan closer. For a long time, she felt nothing except pain as the flames licked her skin, but eventually she felt a keening, a yearning for life that she coaxed toward her. It took time—it always did—but eventually the suurahezhan came close enough for her to offer herself to it.

It readily agreed, allowing itself to be bonded so that it could taste life. Erahm was the place from which it had come, the place to which it would one day return; it thirsted for the stuff of life that it was otherwise deprived of. As the bond was forged, the flames in the fireplace lost their hold on her until they felt like little more than the kiss of the sun on a warm, windless day.

The ritual was complete, but she did not stand. There was still work to be done.

She created a bond between herself and the fire, allowed it to run the length of her body, allowed the heat to lick her thighs, her stomach, her breasts, her lips. It suffused her frame, some of it pooling in the place between her thighs at the mere remembrance of Nikandr. She grit her jaw, angry over her lack of will, and lay down close enough to the fire so that she could feel the heat not only through her tourmaline, but through her natural senses as well.

When her mind was once more clear, she placed her feet into the flames. "I give of myself," she said, "that I might be cleansed."

And with that she lay back and closed her eyes. At first, she felt only gentle warmth on the soles of her feet, but like the sun upon the obsidian shores of the north the heat built steadily, her link to the fire preventing her flesh from burning. It created a self-feeding cycle that made the pain more intense than if her feet *had* begun to burn.

Her body went rigid, but she forced herself to relax. She recalled all of the impure thoughts she'd had since her last cleansing a week before: joy when she'd heard of a fishing ship lost at sea, rapture when she'd learned of a small family that had succumbed to the famine, jealousy when an old friend had taken the wind for further shores.

Lust for a man she knew she could never have.

She shook the thoughts of him away and instead focused on the pain. It washed over her and intensified as she fed it with renewed energy, and though the heat climbed higher than the stars, she never screamed, never allowed it beyond her mortal frame. This was her penance, the cost of the decisions she had made during her life. Her only hope was that she could atone for them in later lives.

She would, she muttered through the veil of pain.

She would.

The pain became so intense it was all she could think of, and still she pushed herself to keep her feet in place, to allow them to burn longer.

She deserved every second of it.

She opened her eyes and drew her legs to her chest as a long moan escaped her lips and tears slipped along her cheeks. Flames the color of the ocean shallows flickered along her ankles and feet, and for long moments, she rode the crest of the wave, swallowing hard, coughing, fighting the urge to snuff the flames as the heat bore deeper and deeper beneath her skin. She would not relent so easily; she would take what it would give, purify as much of herself as she could.

Finally the heat and the pain faded. When her feet had cooled enough to set them back upon the carpet, she curled into a ball and began to sob.

She wished she could fly on the winds and visit distant shores. She wished, only for a moment, that she had been born of the Landed, so she could do as she wished, when she wished. This was yet another thought that she would pay dearly for the next time she placed her feet to the flames, but for now, for now, she cherished it like a jewel in the nest of a rook.

The village of Iramanshah contained a celestia—an open air dome supported by thick pillars of clay-colored stone. Concentric steps led down to a floor that was complicated by a vast collection of lines and circles—indicators of various constellations and their positions at certain, significant days of the year. Dozens of Aramahn men and women, scattered like seeds, stood or sat, speaking softly with one another, sharing their experiences, their loves, their fears. It was a thing that Rehada missed dearly, and for a time she simply stood and watched, wishing she could take part in their conversations. She recognized a man she had met years ago on her second crossing of Mirkotsk, and she realized that she couldn't remember his name. Had it been so long that she had begun to forget the names of those she'd met? And if she had forgotten him, what else might be lost to her? This was her history, her life…

She was pulled from her reverie by a golden voice.

Nearby, the seven mahtar—the village elders—were standing around a man with tousled brown hair. He wore an alabaster gem within the circlet upon his brow. On his wrists were tourmaline and opal, worked into beautiful golden bracelets, and though she could not see his ankles, she had no doubt there were two more gems: jasper and azurite.

This must be him, she thought. Ashan Kida al Ahrumea. As she stared—longer than she should have—one of the mahtar, a woman named Fahroz, noticed Rehada. She gave Rehada a look of disapproval while the others guided Ashan to an area free from prying ears.

"Have you reconsidered, then?" Fahroz said as she came near.

"Forgive me, but I have not."

She allowed her gaze to roam the celestia. "Then please, why have you come?"

"Am I forbidden to speak to my people?"

"Play what games you wish. You know you are not welcome in Iramanshah."

"Until I cross the fires for you."

Fahroz frowned, causing the heavy wrinkles around her forehead and mouth to deepen. "It is not for me that you would cross the fires, Rehada. It is for you, for the lives you have lived and the lives you have yet to live."

"Then perhaps I am here to contemplate."

One of the other mahtar called to Fahroz. She turned, waved, and then returned her attention to Rehada. "That, I doubt, but I hope in my heart it is true. Think on what I have said, Rehada. Come to me if your thoughts change."

"I will."

Fahroz joined the others in their low conversation with Ashan. Rehada felt conspicuous as she made her way down the steps to the floor and to a boy that was lying down, arms and legs spread wide, near the center. She should probably not have come, but after Soroush's sudden visit—and the news from Nikandr that Nasim had landed on the island—she could not help herself. This was a boy that held the hopes and dreams of the Maharraht in the palm of his hand, and she would know more of him, Soroush's permission or not.

Nasim was staring up at the underside of the dome, which was layered with a dark mosaic of the nighttime sky at winter solstice. As she neared, she could see that his eyes were moving from constellation to constellation. His eyes would thin, and he would mumble something as if he were conversing with the stars, and then he would move on, his eyes widening.

She sat cross-legged nearby, hoping he would take notice of her, and when he didn't she simply watched, curious how long it would continue.

"Can you hear me, Nasim?" she asked. "Are you there?"

Nothing.

She continued to speak to him, but in the end decided it was a fruitless tack. Soroush had been unable to speak with him reliably in the years that he'd held him. How could she in mere minutes hope to do any better?

Instead of trying, she closed her eyes and opened her mind to the suura-hezhan she had bound to her the night before. She let the world around her fade and bid the fire spirit to come. She could feel it on the far side of the aether, and as she communed with it, she asked it what lay nearby within the spirit world of Adhiya. But bonding with the hezhan was a wholly different thing from communicating with them, and it was not a skill with which she was particularly gifted. She tried for a long time, learning nothing.

She was startled by a tapping on her shoulder. Looking up, she realized that Ashan was standing over her.

Immediately she stood and bowed. Her heart was beating madly. "I am grateful our paths have crossed." She had hoped to speak with him on this foray into Iramanshah, but she had had no idea she would be so cowed by his presence. Again she regretted she had never met one of the arqesh while she had been on the path of peace. Why was it only now, when she had tied her fate to that of the Maharraht, that the fates decided she should meet one?

She would contemplate this later, and hopefully learn from it, but for now she pushed the thoughts away and gave all her concentration to the task at hand.

Ashan bowed his head, smiling a wide, crooked smile. "I am Ashan Kida al Ahrumea."

"My name is Rehada Ulan al Shineshka, and you are known to me."

"I see you have met my young charge, Nasim."

Rehada was surprised that he used his real name, but then again, he was arqesh, and would find it difficult to lie. Plus, no one on the island, except perhaps her, would know anything about Nasim. It was the unfortunate nature of the Aramahn and their ceaseless travels that so many of them were strangers to one another, even if they did have long memories.

"I can't say that I've truly met him," she replied. "He seems like a contemplative boy."

Ashan chuckled. "I've heard him called many things before, but contemplative hasn't been one of them."

"What would you call him, then?"

"I would call him lost."

"Lost."

"Lost within the confines of his mind, constantly trying to find his way out."

Rehada looked down at the boy and considered this. He continued to study the mosaics above. His lips moved, but she could hear no sound.

"And you're helping him to find it?"

He shrugged. "As I can, though the path has been difficult."

"If you've come to the island to learn, then perhaps I could help. I've been living here for nearly seven years."

Ashan smiled that same crooked smile, as if he knew something Rehada did not. She should be grateful for any words she spoke with such a man, but she had to admit that the gesture was starting to annoy her.

"What is it you find so amusing?"

"I am not amused, daughter of Shineshka, but surprised. Your mother, in all her years, never stopped in one place for more than a season."

"You knew her?"

"At one time I knew her well, though we lost touch shortly before you were born."

"How did you know her?"

He raised his eyebrows. "She came to me often, and we discussed the ways of the world. We traveled together for a time, but then she met your father, far on the northern edge of Yrstanla. It was a cold and barren place, and I suppose at the time she wished for warmth more than she did learning."

"She died, you know."

"I heard. May she return to us brighter than before."

Despite herself, Rehada smiled. She had left her mother when she was fifteen, nearly twelve years ago now, but she had always remembered her mother as a bright soul. It had been and was still a source of pride—one of the few that remained—coming from a woman such as her.

"You didn't answer my question," Rehada said as a new group of Aramahn entered the celestia and began seating themselves.

"I wasn't aware that you had asked one." That smile again.

"Would you like me to come, to guide Nasim around the island?"

He shook his head. "Were Nasim a boy of normal qualities, I would gladly accept, but unfortunately he is not. He would not hear you, and *you*, despite all your best intentions, would not hear *him*. Better if you leave him to me." He motioned with one hand toward the small crowd that had settled themselves. "If you care to, I'm giving a talk about my most recent travels."

It was a tempting thing, but as she had already been reminded, she was not welcome in Iramanshah, and there were those that she wished to steer wide of as much as she could.

"Thank you for the offer, but I had better be heading home." She bowed her head and turned to leave, but stopped as Ashan spoke.

"Rehada?"

She turned back to find him looking at her expectantly.

"*Yeh?*"

"I'm afraid you never answered *my* question."

She tried to smile as he had. "I wasn't aware that you had asked one."

He chuckled and bowed his head in kind. "What would your mother think if she saw her daughter staying in one place for so long?"

Rehada felt her face flush. Did he know? Did he know about her ties?

He could not, she decided. He was only casting a net, something the wise fish could easily avoid. She masked her discomfort by putting on a pleasant face. "I think, Ashan, son of Ahrumea, that she would be jealous."

"Jealous?"

"I know this island more intimately than she, more intimately than any of the islands she visited in her short life."

He stared for a long time, but then he reared back and laughed. "Perhaps you're right, Rehada. Perhaps she *would* be jealous."

Rehada turned and left to the sounds of his chuckling, not at all sure that he meant the words he had spoken. Perhaps, she thought, he was not half so bad at lying as she had guessed.

CHAPTER 10

The heat within the bath house stifled the breath. The air smelled of the hempen incense that had been sprinkled over the hot stones in the middle of the room. Nikandr lay on a padded table, naked, as a servant massaged his back and shoulders. The other men of Khalakovo were not present; only those from Vostroma had come, in order to learn more about the young man who would soon become part of their family.

When the massage was finished, they prepared for a jaunt in the snow. He left with the dozen other men through a door that led to a wide terrace overlooking the mountains and sea to the east.

He paused as the others left. He had been having trouble eating, and his ribs were gaunt. They had already seen him in the bath house, but it was dim there, and steamy. Outside it would be bright, his condition more evident. But, he realized, there was nothing to draw attention to a problem like trying to cover it up—act confident, his father had always told him, and they will believe it is true—so he caught up to the others quickly, stepping into the snow as if nothing at all were the matter.

After so long in the heat, the cold was invigorating. One by one, the men tossed their towels onto the nearby racks and slid onto the fresh blanket of snow that covered the shallow steps down to the lower level of the terrace. They slid, turning like penguins as they went. Young Edis took a running leap onto it, twisting and hollering as he went. Zhabyn took a more stately approach, catching himself carefully with his hands and then thrusting forward, sliding slowly down after the other men.

Without a word being spoken between them, Borund and Nikandr both took two loping steps and dove toward the terrace railing. For a split second Nikandr thought about ceding the lead, but if Borund sensed he was doing such a thing it would cause more damage than could possibly be mended, and so he launched himself with all his might, sliding and laughing as he went. They used their arms to continue the slide, moving closer and closer to the railing. He was clearly going to make it there first—Borund's belly had become too rounded for him to keep his speed up—but then Borund grabbed Nikandr's wrist and yanked him backward. The underhanded trick gave him enough momentum to reach the railing first, and when he did, he slapped it soundly and rolled onto his back, laughing all the while.

"You were always too skinny for your own good!"

Nikandr gave him a sour look and slapped the wooden railing, only then allowing himself to roll around in the snow, cooling skin that had spent the last hour building and storing the heat of the bathhouse. He got to his knees and looked over at Borund. "Fat will get you in the end, Bora."

Bora stood and turned so that his large, hairy backside was staring Nikandr in the face. "It already has, Nischka!"

The other men laughed as Nikandr grabbed a handful of snow and whipped it at Borund. Borund tiptoed away, howling and grabbing one cheek as the laughing increased.

"Enough," Zhabyn said as he approached.

There was an indulgent smile on Zhabyn's face, but no laughs, not from the Duke of Vostroma. There never were.

He held two towels. One of them he handed to Nikandr; the other he ran down his beard, which was flecked with snow and sweat. After scrubbing the back of his neck and his hairy chest, he wrapped it around his waist and waited until Nikandr had done the same.

"We haven't yet had a chance to talk, you and I."

"*Nyet*, My Lord Duke," Nikandr said, bowing his head, "something I've been hoping to remedy."

They had seen one another early this morning when Nikandr had finally signed the marriage documents, but they'd hardly spoken a dozen words to one another. Zhabyn had seemed furious, his face stern, his jaw set grimly, and Nikandr had been nervous to say anything for fear of angering Father or Zhabyn or both. The signing had finished with Zhabyn leaving the room with only a perfunctory nod to Father on his departure.

Thankfully he seemed to have cooled since then. He had greeted Nikandr in the bath cordially if not warmly, and now he was regarding Nikandr with something like acceptance. He motioned to the corner of the terrace, a place far from the other men. "This would seem like the perfect time, my young Prince."

They strode together and stood near the railing, both of them staring out across the island and the churning green seas below. There was little wind, but the cold was beginning to invade the soles of Nikandr's feet.

In the silence that followed, Nikandr found himself edgy and uncomfortable. When he was very young, he had been petrified of Zhabyn, and though those feelings had eventually been replaced with a mixture of awe and resentment, traces of that scared little boy had stubbornly remained. Even now, though he was a Prince, an heir to the scepter of Khalakovo, he felt inadequate standing before him.

He also recognized that it was time for these feelings to stop. Zhabyn had never been an overly kind man, but neither had he been cruel, and Nikandr vowed to right his unwarranted feelings; they were the remnants of his youth, nothing that should be allowed to taint the relationship with his second father.

"I am most sorry for yesterday, My Lord Duke. Much has happened over the last few days, and I will admit that my mind wasn't in the right place, but I tell you that it is now."

Zhabyn continued to stare out over the sea. "Five years from now who will remember such a thing?"

You will, Nikandr thought.

"I would speak with you of the *Gorovna*," he continued.

"I know the imposition the attack has created for you—"

Zhabyn shook his head, drops of water falling from his beard. "That matters little. I care more that the Maharraht have been found on Khalakovan shores. What do you think they were after?"

"The obvious answer would be the ship, to destroy it, or if they were very lucky to take it from us on its maiden voyage."

"And the answers that lie below the surface?"

"With Council upon us, one could assume that they hoped to catch nobility on the ship. But if it were that simple, why not wait until all the dukes had arrived? Why tip their hand?"

"Go on."

"There's Borund and myself... Perhaps it was one of us in particular."

Zhabyn nodded, as if he'd already been thinking along these lines. "Borund has told me that the hezhan seemed to hone in on you as soon as it reached the ship."

Nikandr hesitated, for he wasn't sure he wished to share this information, but the urge to reconcile with Zhabyn pushed him onward. "That same moment, just before it attacked, my soulstone glowed brighter."

Zhabyn stared at Nikandr's chest, though his stone was back in his rooms. "And what does the Matra have to say about that?"

"She is as confused as we are."

"That I doubt, my young Prince." He frowned, returning his attention to the sea. "Why? Why attack a prince?"

"Perhaps it was meant to be a signal of their power, to murder a prince on the very doorstep of Radiskoye. Yet I cannot shake the feeling that they didn't know about the ship, that they were interrupted in their true purpose."

"To summon a hezhan?"

Nikandr shrugged as the light wind died. The warmth of the sun could be felt on his back and shoulders. "Perhaps, though I wonder if they were caught off guard there as well."

"What do you mean?"

"I have no real reason to think this, but it may have been an experiment of sorts. The spirit they summoned may have been more than they bargained for."

"Perhaps, but the question still remains… Why?"

"I wish I knew, Your Grace."

Zhabyn looked over at him and smiled. It seemed to Nikandr that there was respect in his eyes, and gratitude. "Well, I'm sure your father's men will keep us safe. I only wanted to thank you for what you did. It was bold thought and actions that saw my son safely home. I fear he would not be here today"—he waved one hand, indicating where Nikandr and Borund had slid along the snow—"able to take baths, were it not for you."

Nikandr bowed his head, remembering how angry Borund had seemed about the scene by the harbor and the attack by the Maharraht. He realized, then, that Borund had perhaps felt inadequate himself. He had always taken to bullying his way through problems; perhaps he had felt upstaged by Nikandr.

"Atiana." Zhabyn finally turned to face Nikandr. "My daughter."

"Your Grace?"

"When my wife first told me of the arrangement she had made with your mother, I was disappointed."

With the warmth long since having left and the cold beginning to invade, Nikandr began to shiver. "As you say, Your Grace."

Zhabyn forced a smile and slapped Nikandr on the shoulder. "I was wrong, young Prince, and I'm not afraid to admit it. Anyone who protects my son like this will surely do so for his wife."

Nikandr smiled.

"Is it not so?"

"Of course I would, Your Grace. Of course." He said the words, hoping he might someday think more of her than simply a woman he needed to protect.

Zhabyn seemed to notice, for his smile faded and he stared at Nikandr with a serious glint in his eye. "That is good." He slapped him on the shoulder one more time.

Then he did something most strange. He glanced over at the other men, who were still rolling around in the snow, and Nikandr swore it was Borund he was spying. He leaned in toward Nikandr and said, "I can understand your reluctance, you know."

"Your Grace?"

Zhabyn smiled, the most genuine smile Nikandr could ever remember him wearing. "Don't tell my son, but I was horrified when my mother told me of my marriage to Radia."

"Surely you're only being kind."

"*Nyet*, I am not. I nearly refused, though I knew in the end it would be done whether I wanted it or not."

Nikandr blinked, at a complete loss for words.

"But know this... Radia has been more than I could have dreamed for. She is a good woman, a good mother to her children, and she is a beacon to our family."

"Of course, Your Grace," Nikandr said simply. He had to bite his tongue. Radia had long been known to be the most subservient of the Matri. No doubt Zhabyn's high estimation of her stemmed from her willingness to bend to his will following their marriage.

Behind them, the other men were heading inside. Steam from the bath billowed outward as they opened the door and filed in.

"Come," Zhabyn said as he guided Nikandr toward the door, "you're shivering. Time to get warm."

The day continued with Nikandr meeting and greeting each and every member of the Vostroma contingent except Atiana, which included, unfortunately, Mileva and Ishkyna, who seemed too polite and much too pleasant. He kept eyeing them, wondering what they were up to, until it occurred to him that that might be exactly what they were after. He tried to ignore them after that, but it was impossible—one or the other or both kept inserting themselves into his conversations.

It felt as though the rest of his life would be spent answering questions about his plans for Atiana, his plans for family and livelihood. It was endless and painful beyond description, not in the mere voicing of it, but in light of the fact that he doubted he would live to see those years. The wasting was growing within him. He knew this. And despite whatever small hopes he might harbor of finding a cure, he understood deep down that he might very well die before he saw his first child born.

Eventually—thank the ancestors—it was time to prepare for dinner. He changed into the shirt and kaftan made for him for this night. He kept his own boots, however. There was to be a dance, and he would not engage in battle with Atiana wearing unbroken boots. After downing a healthy portion of the elixir—and an herbed biscuit to mask the odor—he left for the grand ballroom.

When he arrived, he was taken aback. He knew the celebration had been cut back in favor of the wedding itself, but this? The ballroom could hold nearly five hundred, and ten years ago it would have, but the room before him had tables for a third of that, perhaps less. They were widely spaced over the floor, making the room look anemic, and though it was clear that Victania had tried to cover for this by decorating each table with towering arrangements of fresh flowers, it still seemed like something that would cause insult to a man like Zhabyn Vostroma.

Victania entered the ballroom a moment later. A smile came to Nikandr's lips, decorations forgotten, as she wove through the tables toward him. She wore a dress of bronze, sewn with pearls patterned into a school of tiny fish. Hair the color of dark walnut was pulled up into an impeccable bun, revealing her delicate neck and the iridescent quality of her chalcedony soulstone. She looked grossly thin despite months on a special diet of fatty fish and goat and fibrous foods like celery and radishes and asparagus, but there was a gleam in her eye, a flush in her cheeks, that hadn't been present even that morning.

"Nischka, Nischka, Nischka," She took both of his hands and swooped in to kiss him once on each cheek. "Let me have a look at you."

"There's nothing to see, sister."

"Ah, but there is!" She took him in from head to toe, an approving smile on her face. "You're actually presentable once you've been thrown in a bath and given fine clothes."

"I am little more than an oaf in costume. You, however, are stunning."

She favored him with the smile the two of them reserved for one another. "So good of you to notice." She turned toward the room, smile faltering. "I hope it's all right."

He squeezed her hand. "It is more than I could have hoped for. Truly."

"If you would hope for anything, Nischka"—she glanced toward the ballroom's entrance—"hope for another bride. It's almost too late…"

He nearly laughed, but Victania was staring to one side, her nostrils flaring momentarily. She seemed confused, and then an expression of disbelief came over her face. She looked him over as if she'd just seen something she had completely missed moments ago. She had probably done the same thing while looking into her mirror, coming to grips with the fact that she had the wasting. He knew he couldn't hide the disease forever, but he couldn't let it be known now, not with the wedding so close at hand.

Before she could say anything he squeezed her hands and said, "I'd better find my seat."

As she stared into his eyes, her expression softened. She knew as well as he did how important this wedding was for their family. "Well, dear brother, if you'll excuse me, I have a function to attend to before—how did you put it this morning?—it *dashes against the rocks*?" And then she was off, headed toward the great fireplace, snapping her fingers at two servants setting the silverware.

Nikandr breathed a sigh of relief as the ballroom continued to fill. On the dais at the head of the room, Nikandr's father stood next to Zhabyn, both of them sipping kefir, looking as stiff as Nikandr could ever remember. They had never been comfortable with one another, and despite whatever words Zhabyn had spoken to Nikandr in private, the looming marriage seemed to be pushing them further apart.

On a golden perch behind the head table was a large rook. The bird was preening itself, which meant Mother had not yet assumed the bird's form, but she would when the time came.

Nikandr wondered when Atiana and her two henchmen would arrive, but then, as if he'd summoned them by the mere thought, she swept into the ballroom wearing a stunning white gown. Her hair was powdered and piled on top of her head, and she looked as if she were balancing it, like it would topple down if she were to tilt her head in the smallest degree. Her skin was powdered as well, with a small amount of rouge applied to her cheeks. She wore rubies at her ears and wrists, and her soulstone hung from a beautiful gold chain at the nape of her neck. Atiana turned and sent a small but insistent wave into the hallway, and Mileva and Ishkyna strode in, each of them a near perfect simulacrum of their sister.

Victania greeted them, though she was anything but warm. There was still a bit of protectiveness to her that Nikandr was secretly appreciative of. It was better than Ranos's constant haranguing about making children.

"Now how could you resist a woman like that?" Ranos stepped by Nikandr's side, and put his hand on his shoulder. Nikandr looked at Ranos, who had a huge, childish grin on his face.

"Tell me, brother. Which one is Atiana?"

Ranos considered them, the bridge of his nose pinching. "You have me there, but I tell you truly, any one of them would do."

As the last of the guests were arriving, Ranos and Nikandr wove their way to the head table. The contingent from Vostroma was respectable, but they were dwarfed by the Khalakovos, who had traveled from all seven islands and beyond to see Nikandr's new bride. Only Mother was notably absent, but she was much too infirm to attend a function such as this for more than a few minutes. Better she stay in her cold basin deep beneath the Spire; as old as she was and as long as she'd been controlling the aether, that was where she was most comfortable.

Everyone was seated—from highest ranking to lowest—and then food was rushed in by dozens of servants wearing simple black kaftans and dresses. It was interesting to note just how many people dove into the meal with a recklessness that spoke of ravenous hunger, particularly among the socialites and lower-ranked royalty. How many had forgone one or two meals to save a handful of rachma? Most had probably not eaten this well in years, even though they were of royal blood. One woman even took bread and slipped it into her knit purse, a woman Nikandr knew to be married to a wealthy merchant. At least, he was wealthy at one time… With the blight and the increasingly bold attentions of the Maharraht, their families' fortunes may well have reversed. It had taken quite some time for the blight's effects to trickle their way upward, but it was clearly being felt by everyone now.

Nikandr's appetite was not strong, but with so many people watching he forced himself to eat. It probably wasn't a good idea, considering the dance that would immediately follow dinner, but Atiana was eating healthily, and something in him wouldn't let her beat him, even at something as simple as that.

When dinner finally ended, the center of the room was cleared. As was custom, Nikandr walked out to the empty floor and held his hand out as the crowd gathered round. The rook on its perch seemed to be watching intently now—Mother had joined the festivities, however briefly.

A lute and a harp and a skin drum took up a dancing song as Atiana stood and made her way toward him, pulling pins from her hair as she came. The crowd whooped as her long hair fell about her shoulders, giving her a wild and most unladylike look. Her words from the eyrie rushed back to him. *I look forward to it*, she'd said. As simple as that. But the words had dripped with meaning.

She arrived at the center of the floor, but rather than take Nikandr's hand and wait meekly for the dance to begin, she pulled him into a tight embrace, the typical pose dancers took for this particular song.

The crowd laughed. Nikandr felt his cheeks flushing, partly from the embarrassment of Atiana taking the lead, but more so from the sheer surprise of this woman—who had always been the meekest of the three—taking charge of the situation. He found himself not only impressed, but *attracted* to her. She was turning out to be vastly different than the girl from his memories.

"Are you so eager to dance?" Nikandr said as the dance began.

The scent of jasmine and facial powder laced the air as she leaned into him, chest to chest, and whispered, "Not to dance, Nikandr Iaroslov, but to teach you a lesson."

"And what lesson is that?"

"That a Vostroma is no woman to be ignored."

"Were you ignored?"

"Avoided. Snubbed. Choose the word you wish."

He found a smile coming to his lips, but he suppressed it. "And a dance will even the ledger?"

"*Nyet.*" As they stalked in the opposite direction, she leveled upon him a steely gaze. "It merely begins to tip the scales, Khalakovo."

As the drum sounded a heavy beat, she spun on one heel and stood straight as a sword, her hair flaring before falling about her shoulders. All was silence. The preliminaries were over, and now the real dance would begin. The story the song painted was one of a young man and woman—two people that had wandered through life, searching for love but never finding it. It detailed a defining moment in their lives, one in which each of them saw through to the heart of the other for the first time, and their love began to blossom. What followed between the two lovers was grand, and the music played it so, slowly at first but with a steadily quickening rhythm.

Atiana spun in a circle and took one step forward. She kicked her outer leg in a high arc, over Nikandr's head as he dropped to a crouch. He balanced on the balls of his feet as she stared down at him.

And there came that wicked little smile. The one she used when she wanted him to know that she'd tricked him. No one else would even notice, but Nikandr knew it all too well. The smile he'd suppressed earlier returned, and this time there was nothing he could do to stop it. Atiana had come to dance, and he had not been tested in a very long time indeed..

As the lute and harp strummed a heavy chord, the crowd collectively clapped. In time, Atiana spun and brought one leg low over the ballroom floor, her dress flourishing as it did so. Nikandr jumped into the air, clearing her sweeping leg, and kicked both legs out, touching his toes with the tips of his fingers.

A collective gasp filled the room. Nikandr had jumped very high, partially to impress, but also to let Atiana know that he had accepted her challenge.

The second chord came, the crowd clapped, and Atiana repeated the low sweep of her leg. She was very good, Nikandr realized, her motions fluid. No doubt she had practiced only to drive her superiority home in front of as many people as she could manage. Nikandr jumped again, and the crowd murmured.

The progression continued, Atiana spinning, Nikandr leaping, as the pace of the music increased. It was a time where the two lovers were exploring their emotions after being lonely for so long, a celebration of their newfound love. The clapping came faster, the music more lively. The crowd became more animated, some people yelling "Hup!" as Nikandr leapt and kicked his legs straight out.

Typically the woman, even if she were more fit or a better dancer, would end the dance when she saw her partner begin to flag. Atiana would do no such thing.

Nikandr was no stranger to this dance, and certainly not to dancing in general, so he was able to continue for quite some time, but the demands on the male partner were great. His stomach began to tie in a knot and the muscles in his legs tired as the crowd clapped in a frenzy and the music marched on.

Still, Nikandr thought, her efforts would be taking their toll. Part of him hoped she would slip or be unable to sweep her leg, or that she would simply stop, her breath coming too quickly, but another part hoped that the challenge would not be so easy.

Nikandr's breath came in ragged gasps as he dropped to the balls of his feet, ready to launch himself into the air once more. His thighs began to burn as if they'd been replaced with bright, molten lava.

He launched himself once more. And again, knowing he had only a few more in him.

And Atiana knew it. He caught that same little smile as she spun around once more.

She would fail, he told himself.

She would stumble.

She would fall.

Nikandr pushed himself harder than he ever had. He sounded like a wounded animal as hard as he was breathing, and he barely cleared her leg as he leapt into the air. He was no longer able to touch his toes, and he couldn't extend his legs completely. It was an embarrassment to the form.

And then.

He could neither leap high enough, nor fast enough. He raised himself up, but Atiana's leg caught his ankles, sending him sprawling to the floor.

The crowd went mad, clapping and yelling and laughing, some sending piercing whistles about the room.

CHAPTER 11

Nikandr's knee flared with pain where it had struck the marble tile. He sat, nursing it as the crowd continued to roar.

Atiana stood over him, extending a hand while staring down at him. Laughing, Nikandr grabbed her hand and allowed her to help him to his feet.

The Vostromas clustered on the dais were all of them laughing or smiling. The rook was beating its wings against the air, twisting its head, a clear sign of displeasure.

As he stepped back and snapped his heels, a curious smile touched the corners of Atiana's mouth. "It seems Vostroma has won this round," Nikandr said.

The words were met with a raucous round of applause, particularly from the Vostromas. "Next year, Nischka!" a voice in the crowd shouted, referring to their anniversary dance, where couples would reprise this dance. Often the partner who had won would defer to the other, but Atiana would not yield—not in a year, not in ten—and Nikandr found a part of him that bore respect for that.

He spent most of the night dancing with the other women of Vostroma, but after a time, he and Atiana, as per custom, were allowed to leave the ball to speak with one another in something resembling privacy. They stood outside in the central hall with Atiana's Aunt Katerina standing a good distance away, ready to act as chaperone. Whether it was the awkwardness of finding themselves together after what had happened with their dance or the fact that they were suddenly being watched not by a crowd but by a single person, Nikandr didn't know, but neither he nor Atiana appeared ready to say anything to the other. It was intensely awkward, but he was pleased to see Atiana mirroring his own feelings.

"Would you care for a walk outside?" Nikandr asked.

"A walk, *nyet*. But a ride would do nicely."

74

And Nikandr, despite himself, smiled.

With Atiana riding to his left, Nikandr urged his pony along the road leading down toward Volgorod. Katerina hadn't been pleased at all that they had wanted to ride, but it was the prerogative of the wedding couple, and so she could do little but put on a sour face and go along with them. With the recent attack, a full desyatni of streltsi were sent as well, five on the road ahead, and five behind. They stayed far enough away, and the two of them were used to such things, so it didn't bother them overly much to have an escort. Atiana's aunt, on the other hand, was a different story. As old as they were—Nikandr twenty-four and Atiana twenty—it felt strange to have a chaperone, but Katerina seemed to be taking her duty very seriously.

The city of Volgorod far below them was almost entirely hidden in the darkness, but there were a few taller buildings near its center that had lights in their windows, giving some sense of its size and shape. Somewhere amid them, Nikandr thought, was Rehada's home. He managed to prevent himself from glancing over at Atiana, but felt conspicuous in doing so. A part of him wished he could ride to the city and spend the night with Rehada, but another found himself glad to be alone with Atiana. He had decided shortly after realizing the wasting had taken him that he would share it with his bride. He had not found it in himself to tell another soul, even Victania, but Atiana was different. She deserved to know, deserved the option of backing out of the marriage if she so chose. All she'd need to do was tell her father, and in all likelihood he would have the contracts declared dead.

"Come," he said, pulling the reins of his pony over and heading northward over the tall grasses of the highlands. He needed to remove the sight of Volgorod, if only to get the feeling that Rehada was watching him out of his mind.

Atiana followed, and soon they had gone far enough that the city was hidden. Only the lights of Radiskoye could be seen, and he decided that that was the right of it, no matter how much he might wish for something else.

"I've always loved Radiskoye," Atiana said.

"You have?"

"Don't be so surprised. Galostina is too spare. Radiskoye is grand and stately."

"Galostina is proud."

In the moonlight, he could see her shrug. "Proud, perhaps, but she was built with only one thing in mind." She pulled her pony to a stop and slipped down off the saddle to the snow-covered ground in one smooth motion. She began walking, leaving her pony to nibble on the exposed grass. "Was my father hard on you today?"

Behind them, Katerina pulled her pony to a stop. Nikandr couldn't see her expression, but her stiff posture told him all he needed to know.

Nikandr dropped down to the ground and walked alongside her. "Your father? *Nyet*. He was kind, if a bit severe."

She laughed. "My father is nothing if not severe."

"There is something I would share with you," he said.

She stopped, forcing him to do the same.

Nikandr stepped to one side, so Katerina couldn't see, and pulled the stone from inside his shirt. He was surprised how difficult it was to share, particularly after how openly he once wore it. With the proximity to his mother—or perhaps the mausoleum—it glowed, but it was much dimmer than it should have been, and the cracks that ran through it could be seen clearly.

"So dim," she said.

"The hezhan," he told her. "When it attacked, the stone cracked."

"Does your mother know why it is so?"

"She does not."

"Will you have another?"

"*Nyet*," Nikandr answered simply. He didn't know what this gem had in store for him, and so he would honor it as he always had. "If you will, I would touch stones."

She paused. In the darkness he had trouble reading her face, though when she pulled from her coat her own necklace, there seemed to be no hesitation in the movement. Her stone was bright in the darkness, and uniform in its intensity.

He held his out, wondering what she would think when she discovered his other secret.

She lifted her stone, and the two of them touched. Nikandr felt a brightening within his chest, a new connection that had not previously been there.

Atiana pulled away and grabbed her gut. By the light of the moon he could see the look of shock on her face. "The wasting?"

He slipped the stone back inside his shirt, though he could feel her still, however faintly.

"How long have you known?"

"Months."

"Before the wedding was announced?"

"Shortly after."

"And you said nothing?"

"I was not sure at first—"

"But you became sure, and you held your tongue."

"I'm saying it now."

"When there's little enough to do about it."

"Atiana?"

Nikandr and Atiana both turned. Katerina was on her pony, sitting with that same prim posture. "Are you well?"

"I must go," Atiana said with a clear note of finality.

"Atiana, please."

He held his hand up to forestall her, but she slapped it away and walked past him. Soon, she was on her pony and riding back toward the road. Katerina sent him a chilling stare before pulling her reins over and calling after Atiana.

The desyatnik of the streltsi approached on his black mare. "My Lord Prince?"

"Accompany them back to the palotza," Nikandr said.

"My Lord, my orders—"

"Come back for me if you will, but make sure they arrive safely. All of you."

"My Lord—"

"Go!"

"Of course, My Lord."

They left, and in little time he was alone with the moon, the silver landscape of snow and stone, and the sighing of the wind. He tied his pony to the snow-covered branch of a spruce, preferring to walk among the trees to clear his mind. He wandered in what he thought was an aimless path, but soon he stopped, his fear over what Atiana might do replaced instantly by dread.

He had arrived at the very place where he had spotted the Maharraht only two days before.

He slipped off his pony and moved to the edge of the cliff, stopping when he arrived at the position from which the Maharraht had leapt. He stared at the tree line far below and the shore beyond it as a brisk wind blew upward along the cliff, lifting his hair and blowing it about. They had been trying ever since the encounter on the *Gorovna* to determine what the Maharraht had been hoping to do—Father had sent a qiram to search for answers; two dozen streltsi had combed the area, hoping to find any small clues; Mother had searched as well—but those efforts had so far provided only the most tenuous of rationales for the presence of the Maharraht.

Somewhere behind him there came the sound of approaching footsteps, crunching softly over the snow. He thought at first it was the streltsi, but they hadn't been gone long enough to have made it up to the palotza and back again, and so he wondered if it was the Maharraht.

Making as little sound as he could, he stepped into the cover of the trees nearby and crouched down. As the crunching came closer, he pulled the flintlock from its holster at his side and slowly pulled the striker until it locked into position with a heavy click.

Movement came further down the tree line. Nikandr trained the weapon on the dark form that stepped out from the trees, but then lowered it when he realized that it was not a man, but a boy.

He felt something deep within his chest, eerily similar to what he had felt when Nasim had been staring at his soulstone as they stood on the eyrie. He turned, pressing his hand against his chest to quell the dull-but-growing sensation while squinting ahead as Nasim moved to the edge of the cliff and stood where Nikandr had only moments ago. He stared downward, his arms hanging loose at his sides, showing none of the pain and discomfort he'd had on the eyrie.

Somewhere far below, a fox began to yelp. Another growled, but then began yelping as well. More and more joined in, and soon, the forest was filled with their calls.

A chill ran down Nikandr's spine. He swallowed involuntarily; his throat felt as though it were closing up, his chest as if it were being pressed from all sides, as if he'd been thrust into the deepest part of the ocean. His breath came in short gasps—inhaling brought excruciating pain.

The horizon began to tilt, and he wondered in fascination whether he was about to die.

Then, of a sudden, the pain was gone, absent, replaced by a feeling of comfort and peace the likes of which he'd never felt.

And the wind rushes around him, carrying him aloft over the city that lies below. He allows it to carry him down toward a tall tower that shines by the light of the moon, a pillar of white standing tall against the varied landscape of the proud stone buildings around it.

He lands on the tower, and the wind subsides. He breathes deeply of the chill night air. He tilts his head back and studies the constellations as if he'd never seen stars before. He has come far in these past few months. He feels ready, at long last, to take the next step, to begin the healing of this place that has for too long been a little more than an open wound upon the world.

And it all came down to acceptance. He feels as though he is part of this island, as if it is a part of him. He feels as if he *belongs*. It is freeing beyond comprehension—not the *notion* that he is integral to this place, but the *understanding*—and it is in such opposition to the feelings that had been running through him only weeks ago that he giggles from the excitement.

"Why do you laugh?"

He turns. A woman steps up from the stairs built into the roof. Her long golden hair sways as she takes the last of the steps and stares at him with a humorless expression. It has been years since they saw one another—or has it been decades?—but her appearance has not changed. She is still the woman she was when the three of them ripped the island asunder over three hundred years before.

"I laugh because I am ready, Sariya. I am finally ready."

She stares up at the constellation he'd been considering. It is Iteh with his harp, holder of the northern skies. "Muqallad has returned."

A chill runs through him. His resolve, his satisfaction, both so complete a moment ago, begin to crumble.

She waits, speechless for a time. "Not so ready as you thought, then."

He smiles. "As ready as I'll ever be."

"You're fooling yourself. We need him, and you know it."

"He will not bend. You know this."

"He has returned…"

"To convince me to walk the path he's chosen."

She shrugs. "We will only know by speaking to him."

He walks to the edge of the roof. The grit of the stone is alive beneath his sandals. The city below sprawls outward, nearly lifeless except for those few souls they'd managed to save when they'd torn the veil between worlds.

He has searched for a way to heal the damage they'd caused without Muqallad. After he'd left, after he and Sariya had banished him from the city, he'd hoped that the two of them would be enough. But he'd known all along, deep down, that three would be needed to heal what three had done.

"He will not listen."

Sariya stands beside him. He can feel the warmth of her shoulder standing next to his. "We can but try."

He nods, knowing she is right. "We can but try."

As suddenly as the vision came, it faded, and the discomfort returned. Nikandr stared at Nasim, but the light of the moon upon the white snow became so bright he had to squint against the sting in his eyes.

Nasim took one tentative step toward his position, and then he began to pace confidently forward.

A burning sensation built within Nikandr's gut and expanded to fill his chest, his arms, his legs. He felt as if he would burst, so powerful had it become, and he found himself tightening his arms around his waist and gritting his jaw to hold off the pain.

"Nasim, don't," he cried, lowering his weapon.

The pain rose to new heights.

Nasim stopped at the edge of his spruce and crouched down, looking within.

While Nikandr aimed his pistol.

And pulled the trigger.

CHAPTER 12

The pan flashed. Nikandr's arm bucked, and he dropped the pistol into the snow. He hadn't been able to hold his aim. The shot had gone wide.

The pain became too much. He pitched forward onto the ground.

He heard the crunch of footsteps as Nasim approached. He kneeled down and stared into Nikandr's eyes, while Nikandr could do little but hold his stomach and wait. He couldn't prevent Nasim from doing whatever it was he wished. Not anymore. The pain was too great. "Stop, Nasim, please." Each inhalation felt like a searing iron.

The boy stared while Nikandr fought to draw breath. "Your stone was so bright," he said.

Even through the haze of pain Nikandr was surprised. Ashan had said that he rarely spoke, and when he did, his words were practically meaningless. He might have been lying, but Nikandr didn't think so. For some reason, this place had brought out in him a moment of clarity.

"My—stone?"

"Blinding. Brighter than the sun."

"On the—eyrie?" Nikandr shook his head, groaning through clenched teeth. "Not blinding. It was—hidden."

Nasim had somehow sensed Nikandr's stone, even broken as it was, so in a way he didn't doubt Nasim's words, but they sounded like the ravings of a madman. It occurred to Nikandr that perhaps he'd seen it *because* it was broken. But that made no sense. And how could it have been blinding?

Nasim shook his head. "There was a hezhan."

The pain began to ebb, and Nikandr let it as the snow began to melt against his cheek and hair. It was cold, but he was burning so badly he was glad for it.

"The havahezhan? The one that attacked my ship?"

He nodded, but that made no sense either. Nasim hadn't even been on the island then.

"Lord Khalakovo!"

It was the desyatnik. The streltsi had returned.

Nasim jerked his head toward the sound, and the pain in Nikandr's chest became white hot.

He opened his eyes, face buried in the snow, realizing he'd been knocked unconscious from the pain. He rolled onto his back, feeling an ache in his chest, but none of the feelings that had overwhelmed him moments ago.

Somewhere nearby, men were tracking slowly through the snow.

"Lord Khalakovo?"

They were close.

"Here," he called weakly. "Over here!" he cried again, louder this time.

"To me!" the desyatnik called. "The Prince has fallen!"

They helped him to his feet and onto his pony, which they'd found and brought with them. His chest still hurt, but that was more from his muscles tensing like harp strings.

The desyatnik pulled his pony alongside Nikandr's. He remained close, clearly worried Nikandr was going to tip over.

"You will not accompany me," Nikandr told him. "Take your men and comb the countryside west of here. Send two along the road and the rest through the woods. Look for an Aramahn boy, eleven years old. If he's found, bring him to the palotza. He is to come to no harm if it can be avoided."

"My Lord Prince, if you were attacked—"

"I'm no longer in danger. He is on the run."

The desyatnik nodded and ordered his men to spread out and sweep westward as Nikandr kicked his pony into action and headed for Radiskoye.

"It was just the boy?" Father asked.

Nikandr nodded. "Just him."

The two of them were seated at the head of the long table in his audience room. Isaak stood by the fireplace, tending to the fire that acted as the room's only source of light. Between Isaak and Father was a stand with Mother's favorite rook, Yrfa. The bird was quiet; after a quick briefing from Nikandr, Mother had left to speak with Ranos in Volgorod and then to scan the grounds to the west to search for Nasim.

At a knock, Isaak opened the door and Jahalan entered. In the heavy shadows, with his sunken eyes and hollow cheeks, he looked as lean as death. "I was told there was trouble."

Nikandr retold the tale he'd just told Father for Jahalan's sake, everything from the point at which he'd left Atiana until the ride back.

"How could he have done this?" Father asked Jahalan.

Jahalan looked just as confused as Father. "You said a pain in your chest?"

"*Da*," Nikandr replied.

"And the feelings before the pain—euphoria, you said—had you experienced such a thing before?"

Nikandr shook his head. "*Nyet.*"

Jahalan spread his hands, making it clear his thoughts on the subject were tenuous. "There are some among our people who feel euphoria when they become one with a place or a time."

Father shook his head. "Explain."

"The Aramahn hope to arrive at unity with the world around us, and most times, sometimes our entire lives, we fail to do so even once, but there are rare occasions, after long contemplation, after opening ourselves to the world, that we feel as though we have come to understand a thing for what it is, and in turn we believe that we are understood as well. Perhaps Nasim was feeling this as he looked down from that cliff. Perhaps Nikandr was somehow party to it."

"And the pain?" Father asked.

Jahalan turned to Nikandr. "You said the boy looked discomforted on the eyrie."

"To put it mildly," Nikandr replied.

"I cannot explain how a connection between you might have been made, but assuming it was, it would make sense that you would feel both Nasim's euphoria *and* his pain, not just one or the other."

"I was feeling his thoughts?"

"Not exactly. They may have been your thoughts, just triggered by Nasim. He acted as tuning fork, but what you saw, you saw from your own perspective, your own experiences."

These words rang true, Nikandr thought. The experience hadn't felt foreign, only out of place and unexpected.

"The boy mentioned a hezhan," Father interrupted, looking at Nikandr. "He said nothing else?"

"*Nyet.*" Nikandr shook his head. "He heard the streltsi and ran. He must have been referring to the havahezhan."

Father looked to Jahalan.

Jahalan pulled himself from contemplation and nodded. "I suppose it must be, but how could he have known? It was days before his arrival on the island."

"Simple," Father said. "He is Maharraht. They told him."

"Nasim?" Jahalan considered the words. "I suppose he might be, but I doubt very much he would be in the company of Ashan if he were."

"It is the only explanation." Father said. "He traveled to the very spot from which the havahezhan was summoned, the place the Maharraht had gathered. It must be so."

"As you say, but it doesn't answer the more important question. How could he have done such a thing to your son?"

As they considered the question, Nikandr remembered the dream from the cliff. "There was a city," he said, almost breathlessly. He stared at Jahalan, knowing he'd seen a vision of a place, a city that in all likelihood no man from the Grand Duchy had ever stepped foot within. "I was speaking to a woman, Sariya, and she mentioned another, a man name Muqallad. Have you heard of them?"

Jahalan shook his head. "I have not. You say it was a dream?"

"A dream, but very real. It felt like something Nasim had seen." The words felt false. The one from the dream was a man grown... How could the memories have been Nasim's?

"You may have seen one of your past lives," Jahalan said.

Father snorted.

Jahalan looked hurt, but he held Nikandr's eye.

Nearby, the rook flapped its wings and clicked its beak several times. It launched itself forward and landed on the back of the chair opposite Nikandr. "The boy is nowhere to be found."

Father bristled. "Then we must—"

"Still your words, husband. I bring news. Ranos is sending a full sotni to cover the road to Iramanshah. With the fifty men we've sent in addition to the ten from Nikandr, it will be enough. If the boy can be found, he will be."

"And Ashan?" Father asked.

"The *Braga* is in flight already. We will ask the mahtar for permission to speak with Ashan. If they agree, he will be brought to Volgorod, to the Oprichni's house."

Father's gaze turned steely as he studied the rook. He glanced at Jahalan, shaking his head. "We should play no games of diplomacy with Iramanshah. The dukes will be arriving tomorrow."

"I know who arrives on the morrow, husband, but there is little enough to present the mahtar with, and nothing of Ashan."

"He is the boy's keeper!" Father said.

"And what will that mean to them?"

Father fumed, but he knew Mother was right. It was forbidden to take the Aramahn by force unless laws had been broken. Even then, the Palotza was to present their evidence to the mahtar to let them decide if taking an Aramahn was warranted.

"What if they don't agree?"

The rook stretched its neck back and released a series of harsh caws.

"Then it will be dealt with." It pecked at the table and then winged back to its perch. "I have much to do before the sun rises."

The bird shivered, the orange glow of the fire playing against its slick black coat, and then it was still.

Father asked to speak with Jahalan alone, and this time Nikandr didn't mind.

"Nischka?" Father said as he reached the door.

Nikandr turned.

"Tell no one of this."

"Of course, Father."

And then he left.

He was bone tired, but he couldn't go to sleep just yet. He had to deal with Atiana before she told anyone about what happened on their ride. He was worried that she'd already told her sisters, but there was a chance she would have kept quiet about it, at least these last few hours, and that she was cool enough that she would listen to reason.

He took a small lamp and walked to the far side of the palotza, to the bath house. It was empty and cold and dark. Beyond the massive tub in the center of the room he opened the door to a small closet, reached beyond the stacks of towels on the lowest shelf, pressing a certain space along the wood. He heard a click and the shelves swung inward. He stepped into the frigidly cold passage and closed the door behind him.

The passageway was lined with bricks, but as he traveled lower, he was walking through the body of the mountain itself. He knew these passages well, though even he—who'd scoured them whenever he'd had a chance as a child—didn't know all of them. He knew enough, however, to make it to a similar closet in the wing where the Vostromas and their retinue were staying. He reached it after several brisk minutes of walking; then he left and padded down the tall hallway toward Atiana's room.

After reaching it, he knocked on her door softly.

He heard nothing inside.

He tried again, louder.

Further down the hall, a door swung open, and Nikandr's heart leapt out of his chest. A woman leaned out into the hall—Mileva or Ishkyna, he couldn't tell which. Her hair was pulled up into a sleeping bonnet, and she wore a thick nightdress, but her feet were bare. A curious look came over her when she recognized him, like a cat catching a mouse it hadn't known was there. Then the look was gone, and she padded toward him over the cold tile floor.

"My dear Nikandr," she said, her words soft, "have you become so smitten with Atiana that you feel you must steal into her room in the middle of the night? Is she such a treasure?"

Ishkyna.

"She is a jewel beyond measure," Nikandr replied, just as softly.

One of Ishkyna's delicate eyebrows rose. "A jewel you wish to polish before it's been given to you properly?"

"A jewel I would look upon, nothing more."

She stared at his shoulder, perhaps at the dust he'd collected on his way there through the hidden passages. He waited for her to speak, refusing to rise to the bait.

"This is highly irregular. What would Aunt Katerina think?"

"She would frown, but you, I think, will not."

"And how can you be so sure?"

"There is little harm in a talk between a man and a woman two days before their marriage."

She took a step forward. She was close enough to touch now. "That depends on what happens after the words are done, Nischka." She took another half-step forward. "Words can lead to many things, can they not?"

He could smell the alcohol on her breath, the powder in her hair. The tight line of her lips arced in a meaningful smile as her eyes closed once. Her nipples stood out, her breasts rising in the cold air of the hall. She was beautiful, as Atiana was, and he found his throat tightening at the thought of where, indeed, words could lead. He had always thought of these three sisters as girls, children, but this was no girl standing before him. Ishkyna was a woman grown.

"I only wish for a word, Ishkyna."

She glanced at Atiana's door, then her head tilted toward her room, and finally her gaze returned to Nikandr, daring him to take this one step further. When it was clear he would not, she took a half step back and said, "Pity," and then she turned the handle of Atiana's room. It swung open soundlessly as Ishkyna swept back to her room and closed her door behind her.

CHAPTER 13

Atiana heard the click of a door opening. She was so tired she thought she was in her own bed within Palotza Galostina, and she fell immediately back to sleep. But then she heard a single word being spoken, soft but clear—"Pity"—and soon thereafter came the faint sound of a door closing.

She sat up, saw the silhouette of a man, his back to her, the light from the lamp he held wavering over the walls and ceiling.

"Who's there?"

The floorboards creaked as Nikandr turned. "May we speak?" he asked softly.

She shivered though she was not cold. When they had touched stones, standing outside the palotza walls, she had *felt* the disease gnawing away at him, slowly but surely. She had touched stones with others and felt similar things, but it had been so strong with Nikandr. It had felt for a moment as if *she* had had the wasting, and it had shaken her.

"You shouldn't be here."

"Atiana, I merely wish to explain."

"There's little enough to explain. You lied."

He nodded. "I did, to everyone else, but I *chose* to share it with you." He sat on the edge of her bed, his face growing worried. "The Khalakovos need this marriage, as does your family."

She felt a lump forming in her throat. She understood what he'd done, even shortly after touching stones. What *he* failed to understand is how she might react to it. To him, this marriage was a burden, and he probably felt she shared his opinion.

"It would be foolish," he continued, "to jeopardize that by telling your father of something that cannot be changed. No one has to know. In another week, Council will be over, and they'll all be gone. I'll reveal everything once it's safe."

"Safe from what? Why hide it in the first place?"

He stared at the lamp he still held in one hand. "I thought I could cure it. I thought, somehow, I'd be able to find a way. There are those…"

"What, that live with the disease? They all succumb eventually, Nikandr."

"I know." He stared at her, his eyes brimming with emotion.

"You must have known all this. Victania…" She stopped, because she realized what Nikandr had been hoping to do. He had hoped to cure himself, true, but he was *desperate* to save Victania.

It was touching, his connection to his sister, but also selfish. There were two families to consider in his decision.

But that wasn't what hurt the worst. Atiana had come to Khalakovo, despite the constant words of her sisters, with hope—hope that Nikandr would accept her; hope that they could come to love one another; hope that she would one day bear his children, and that they would grow to be strong. She didn't want a marriage like Mileva, who shared with her husband a cold tolerance for one another. She didn't want to live like Ishkyna, who moved among beds as rapidly as she could, as if that could somehow fill the life her cruel husband drained from her. She didn't even want a marriage like Mother and Father, where one took knee for the other. She wanted respect. She wanted love. She wanted passion.

Perhaps that had been a foolish list of demands with which to land on Khalakovo's shores. Perhaps she should be happy that she knew him well, and that he would most likely come to tolerate her. But she was who she was, and she could see clearly now that she would take second seat to Nikandr's other women: his mother, his sister, even the Aramahn whore he was rumored to be in love with.

"Tell me, Nikandr, would you do for me as you do for Victania?"

The answer was plain in his eyes.

"Then perhaps there is no need for marriage. Perhaps our fathers will allow the documents to live without the compact of blood."

"You know they won't."

"*Nyet*. Perhaps you're right." How foolish she'd been, to think that he would welcome her. "Go," she said. "I'll not reveal your precious secret." Her resolve finally broke, and tears gathered at the corners of her eyes.

He stared at her with a confused look on his face.

Rather than let him stare at her, she lay down, facing away from him. "Go!"

After a moment, the shadows being thrown around the room waved wildly, and he left without another word.

Then, alone once more, she allowed herself to cry.

Atiana stood before a tall mirror and took a deep breath while her hand-maid pulled mercilessly at her corset strings. Mileva stood next to her in the same state of dress while Ishkyna sat on the bed, cross-legged, wearing only her shift.

Her future sister, Victania, stood nearby, watching with a critical eye. It was early in the morning, and the Grand Duke was not set to arrive until after noon, and still Victania's powdered wig and white makeup were impeccable. One would think that the wasting would make her appear weak, but in fact it was just the opposite; though she was frail physically, she had the air of a woman who had taken the disease by the throat, refusing to grant it an inch. It was something Atiana might admire if Victania didn't treat her as if she were a symptom of the wasting.

Victania stepped between Atiana and the mirror, looking more closely at her hair. She reached out, checking the length at her ears, and it was all Atiana could do not to pull away.

Victania's mouth pursed. "You won't be infected," she said as she continued to draw Atiana's hair along the side of her cheeks.

"I wasn't thinking that I would."

Victania's sharp eyes focused on hers. "*Nyet?*"

Atiana remained silent, a surge of jealousy rising up within her. She could never hope to compete with Victania for Nikandr's love.

Victania moved behind her and checked the back. "I'll send for the barber," she said, dropping Atiana's hair as if it had insulted her.

The door to the room opened, and Yvanna Khalakovo, Ranos's wife, stepped inside, dressed as impeccably as her sister.

"Khazabyirsk has arrived," she said to Victania, "and they're flying the wounded flag."

Victania looked sternly between the girls and Yvanna. "They won't be ready in time."

Yvanna nodded. "The Duke will understand, of course."

"*Da,* but I doubt that Mother will." Victania stiffened her jaw and released a pent-up breath. "Be ready, girls, by the time we return." And with that she and Yvanna were gone.

Ishkyna rolled her eyes. "Be ready, *girls.*"

"Mind your manners," Atiana said.

Ishkyna stared at her impassively. "As if the Dame of Khalakovo would deign to listen at doors."

Mileva smiled. "You would think *she's* getting married."

"She probably wishes she were," Ishkyna said as she fell back on the bed. "She loves no one more than her precious Nischka."

"Shkyna!" Atiana said, though the thoughts echoed her own. "In a day she'll be my sister."

As her corset strings were cinched even tighter, Atiana tried to smooth the goose bumps on her arms. The wind was howling outside, which only served to remind her of how long she would have to wait as the flotilla of royalty arrived. The royal eyrie had been cleared for the event, but it would still take hours for all seven ships to land and for the royalty to disembark.

The handmaids, finished with the corsets, helped Atiana and Mileva to step into their cream-colored dresses. They were padded and bulky and would no doubt ruin their figures, but Atiana didn't care as long as they provided even one dram of warmth.

Ishkyna pulled her dress onto the bed and began smoothing away the wrinkles. "What do you think he'll be like?"

Mileva smiled, glancing at Atiana from the corner of her eye. "He'll be soft."

"Soft?" Ishkyna laughed. "Have you so little faith in your sister?"

Atiana felt her face warm.

Ishkyna's eyes went mischievous. "*Nyet*. He'll be hard as oak, ready to welcome our dear sister to his family properly."

Atiana frowned, little pleased with Ishkyna's tone, even less pleased by the look in her eyes, the one that said she knew something her sisters didn't. "You'd do well to worry about your own husband."

"Oh! You see how she is, Mileva? She's already gazing at us over the shoulders of Khalakovos."

"I am not."

"Well, you soon will be, Tiana. In no time at all Victania will have you wrapped around her wretched little pinky and you'll be singing for her just like all the Khalakovo women."

Atiana stood straighter, to the consternation of her handmaid, who had nearly finished lacing the back of her dress. "I am Vostroman, and I will always be so."

"I wouldn't be so sure if I were you. Once Nikandr has ridden you like the surf, you'll open up to the ways Khalakovo."

"Shkyna, that's the second time you've spoken of my husband—"

"*Future* husband."

"You never did so with Mileva's."

"Viktor is twenty years her senior. He's hardly worth the effort."

"Nevertheless, if you speak of Nikandr again, it will be civilly or I'll toss you over a cliff myself."

"So territorial… You'd think she would wait to see what lies below before—"

Atiana turned—batting away her handmaid's attempts at keeping her in place—and stormed over to the bed. She pointed her finger at Ishkyna's face, her blood boiling at the smug look that greeted her. "I gave you warning."

"And as it's the day before your wedding, I let it pass unnoticed."

Atiana didn't know what happened. She had fought with her sisters before—countless times—but never had she been so angry as to raise her fist with the intention of striking. Yet before she realized it she had slapped Ishkyna across the face.

Ishkyna's head snapped to the side. She held one hand tightly to her cheek. She took breath for long, tense moments, and then lowered her hand. When she turned back, Atiana could see a red mark already beginning to swell along her cheek. Her face was calm, which made Atiana shiver—a calm Ishkyna was nothing if not trouble.

Mileva took Atiana around the shoulders. "Enough." She guided Atiana back toward the handmaids. "We haven't traveled together in some time. It's merely a symptom of being cooped up with one another again. Do you remember how viciously we used to fight?"

"The only reason we fought," Atiana said, "was because the two of you are so insufferable."

Mileva laughed, looking to Ishkyna, who merely glowered.

"Come, Shkyna," Mileva said. "It was the very reaction you were trying to provoke."

"A slap across my face as the dukes are set to arrive? *Da.* Exactly what I was hoping for."

Mileva turned away, giving Ishkyna time to cool. "Have you looked into his woman, this Rehada?"

"In case you haven't noticed, I've had more than a little to attend to."

Mileva scoffed. "It's not something you should ignore, Tiana. A week before our wedding, I had Viktor's women quaking in their boots at the mere mention of my name. I allow him to see one, if only to keep his interests at a distance, but she's clean. You know nothing about Nikandr's."

"Other than she's a Motherless whore," Ishkyna said.

The words were meant to rile, but they were exactly what Atiana had been struggling with ever since hearing the rumor. She had been ready—after an appropriate delay—to accept a courtesan of Landed blood. But an Aramahn? Why? What could he see in her?

She'd decided on the voyage to Khalakovo that she would learn more, but there simply hadn't been time.

"If you wish," Mileva said, "I'll look into it myself. There's little else to occupy my time."

Atiana shook her head. "I'll deal with her in time."

"Well," Ishkyna said, "there's a bright side to everything, is there not?

Perhaps our dear Atiana won't have to worry about Nikandr's wandering attention for long."

Atiana jerked her head to look at Ishkyna in the mirror. "What is that supposed to mean?"

Ishkyna held Atiana's gaze, her jaw set, her eyes smoldering. And then Atiana remembered. Last night. Someone had spoken to Nikandr—*pity*, she'd said—and then a door had softly closed. It had been Ishkyna.

As sure as winter was cold, Atiana knew she'd returned after leaving. She'd overheard their conversation.

She knew about Nikandr's affliction.

The door swung open, startling Atiana. Victania flicked her fingers at Atiana as if summoning a servant girl, and then she left. After one last meaningful glance at Ishkyna, Atiana followed.

Yvanna was there as well, and she fell into step with Atiana as Victania led the way down the tall hallways of Palotza Radiskoye. Their collective footsteps echoed like a handful of stones dropped down a deep, dark well. They left the palotza proper and made their way along an impressive marble colonnade. The entablature protected them somewhat from the drizzle but did nothing to shelter them from the harsh winds. On the right, Khalakovo's massive black spire towered over Radiskoye. It looked ominous, standing there against the roiling gray clouds.

They entered at the base and descended a long, spiraling set of stairs. Atiana's anger with Ishkyna was slowly being replaced by fear of the meeting that lay before her, and the deeper they went, the more her stomach began to turn. She wasn't ready for this. She didn't know how she would measure up to the woman Mother spoke of with such reverence.

The stairs landed within a circular room with two sets of intricately carved doors. Two pairs of streltsi guarded them, berdische axes and curved shashkas at the ready. An old servant woman, standing by the doors straight ahead of them, bowed as Victania and Yvanna turned to Atiana.

"She will be weak," Victania said, "for she has only just removed herself from the aether."

Atiana wanted to bite her tongue, but Victania's mothering tone and the row with Ishkyna had frayed her nerves. "I am well aware of what the aether does to a woman."

"Oh?" Victania pursed her lips as her gaze traveled Atiana's length. "Tell me, then, how long does my mother require a warm fire before her joints begin to ache?"

She swallowed the first response that came to her mind. "I do not know, My Lady."

"What sort of tea does she favor upon awakening?"

Atiana lowered her gaze. "Forgive my outburst, dear Victania. I have only just completed the voyage here, and I fear the length has made me testy."

Victania's eyes did not soften. "Difficult voyage or not, see to it that you curb your tongue. The Matra will not stand for it."

"Of course not."

Victania turned to Yvanna. "You can prepare her?"

Yvanna nodded.

"Good." She turned on her heel and headed into the room with the servant woman, leaving Atiana alone with Yvanna in the cold, dark antechamber.

"Forgive her," Yvanna said as she blew warmth into her cupped hands. "She's very preoccupied with your wedding. She doesn't say it, but she wishes the best for you both."

Atiana smiled, not wanting to offend. "She *does* hide it well."

"Make no mistake, if she didn't care for you, she would tell you so."

Atiana had her doubts. Victania knew as well as everyone else that this marriage was crucial for both families. Atiana's father needed ships to bring goods to Yrstanla, and as light as their coffers were, the only sensible way to get them was by marriage. And Khalakovo had been one of the worst struck by the blight. Nearly two-thirds of their cabbage and potato crops, if reports were to be believed, had been devastated in the last several years. Now more than ever it needed its precious wood and spices and gemstones to be sold in the Motherland. They would need much to weather the coming storm.

A shiver traveled down Atiana's frame as one of the great doors suddenly opened. Victania motioned them into the room known as the drowning chamber. At the far end of the long, low room, Saphia Mishkeva Khalakovo sat in a wooden chair a goodly distance from the fireplace. An amber-colored stone of chalcedony rested in the circlet upon her brow. Victania stood next to her, a comforting hand upon the Matra's shoulder.

Every one of the nine families had a room like this, and Khalakovo's looked eerily similar to Vostroma's: dark-as-night stone, Aramahn tracework running along the support columns, a basin sitting in the center of the room, all of it laid out almost exactly the same as Galostina's chamber. The only difference seemed to be the iron lantern holders spaced about the room and the marble busts of the Matri from Khalakovo's past.

Atiana strode forward as confidently as she could manage. When she stood before Saphia's chair, she kneeled, waiting to be kissed, hearing only the Matra's labored breathing.

"Stand, child," Victania said. "She cannot kiss you."

Atiana complied, realizing just how much Khalakovo's Matra had sacrificed for her station. Sunset had already fallen on her fiftieth year, but she looked much, much older. The bones of her hands and wrists stuck out as if she'd been starving herself for months. Her eyes were recessed deeply into their sockets, and her cheeks were little more than hollows. Her white hair was damp and stringy from her time in the cold water that allowed her to touch the aether. She was leaning a bit to one side, and Atiana realized that Victania was standing there, not in any statement of solidarity, but to ensure that her mother didn't tip over.

Despite all this, there was a regal quality in the way she held her head, the way her steely gaze evaluated Atiana. It gave proof to the supreme effort of will that *any* Matra needed, much less Saphia, the woman who had tamed the aether the longest in memory.

She looked not so different from Victania, both in form and bearing. The difference was that where Victania *demanded* respect, Saphia knew it would be given to her.

A golden perch stood behind the Matra's chair, and a tall rook rested upon it. Rumor had it that so strong was Saphia's connection to the aether that she could assume a rook for some time after leaving it, but the rook seemed inattentive, uninhabited.

"Touch stones." Victania's expression and words were filled with impatience.

Atiana hurriedly pulled at the chain around her neck to retrieve her soulstone. She touched this to Saphia's circlet, and both stones brightened briefly. She couldn't help but think of when she'd touched stones with Nikandr, but unlike then, Atiana could feel a strong connection with Saphia, stronger than the one with her own mother hundreds of leagues away.

"Your voyage has delivered you healthy and whole." Saphia's voice was a horrible croak.

"It has, Matra, thank you."

Saphia nodded, a satisfied expression on her face. "It will be good to have another woman in Radiskoye. Too often it teems with men."

"As you say, Your Grace."

"Do you know why I've brought you here?"

"I assumed it was to meet in the flesh."

"There is that," Saphia allowed. "Can you think of nothing else?"

"Well, there is the pending marriage…"

Saphia barked out a short laugh, an act that brought on a coughing fit. Victania supported her mother until she had regained herself. "*Da*, there is that as well."

"I'm afraid there's nothing else I can think of, Matra."

Saphia's gaze shifted to Yvanna momentarily. "The last several months have made us aware of a small yet growing problem. One of my good daughters is losing the ability to touch the aether."

Yvanna, staring at the floor and holding one hand tightly in the other, looked embarrassed. Victania, however, was staring at Atiana, daring her to make mention of it.

"Like the other Matri, I have found the currents more and more difficult to tame, but I never thought the ability could be lost outright."

"And now you think it can?" Atiana asked.

"A year ago, Yvanna could have stayed under for hours. Now, she cannot stand it for more than a handful of minutes."

Disturbing news, indeed. The aether was what connected the islands. It was what allowed them to ride the winds with their ships, but it also acted as their primary path of communication. Collectively, the Matri touched the aether to commune with one another, to trade information and to make important decisions. Each of the nine families had one who performed the duty primarily, but all had at least two others trained in harnessing the currents in case the Matra took ill or—ancestors protect them—died.

"Why does that concern me?" Atiana asked.

"Because, dear child, I chose you in part because of your strength in the dark."

Atiana felt her face pale, and she prayed that in the dimness of the room no one had noticed.

"I have little ability," she finally said.

"You do. You *and* your sisters. You just haven't been allowed to use it."

It was true that she hadn't lain in those cold basins for years—beyond Mother, it was Aunt Katerina and Borund's wife who held those duties, and Atiana was only too glad to cede it to them. To be rubbed in animal fat and submerged in water colder than the bones of the world itself was not something she would willingly do, and here was the mother of the man she was about to be married to telling her she would need to do just that.

"We were told we were too heavy-handed."

"That may be so, but consider this: at least you have the ability. Control can be learned. Raw ability cannot."

"Forgive me, Matra"—she tried to keep the desperation from her tone— "but my mother told me I would not need to."

"She should not have."

"You assured her I would not be needed in this capacity." She could hear her voice rising in volume.

"I told her that I expected you to be trained."

"But—"

"Are you a member of this family or are you not?"

"The wedding has not—"

"Your father has signed documents. You are Khalakovan now whether you like it or not, and your family's needs take precedence over your own. Or do they teach you different in the halls of Galostina?"

"I will fail, Matra."

"You will try, and that is the end of it."

Atiana bit her tongue. She was sure that Mother had inquired about the need to take the dark, knowing her innate fear of it, and she was just as sure Saphia had chosen her words carefully so Mother would come away with the answer she'd been seeking while Saphia would be able to claim later that there had been an unfortunate misunderstanding.

Misunderstanding or not, it didn't change the fact that she was now bound to the Khalakovos. There was no backing away from this request. Not yet, anyway. Perhaps in time, once she had her feet under her.

"So I was chosen for marriage simply for my ability."

Saphia smiled, an expression that looked truly evil on such a skeletal face. "Not only for that, child. You have other redeeming qualities."

"Such as hips ready to bear children?"

Saphia laughed again, a thoroughly unpleasant sound. "And a father with shipping contracts to Yrstanla. Do you find any of these reasons distasteful?"

"The women of Vostroma are not accustomed to being treated like prized cattle."

"But you are in a *prized* position, Atiana Radieva. There are dozens of women who would gladly take your place."

She knew it was so. There were always duties expected of a young bride, some distasteful, some less so. "Of course, Matra. I'll gladly help the family in any way I can."

The silence in the room lengthened, broken only by the whuffle and snap of the fire. Saphia nodded, though even that small motion seemed taxing for her. "Good and good. You can tell your mother when next you speak with her."

Victania closed the conversation shortly after, and Yvanna led Atiana away.

On the way out, she was amazed at how different the basin seemed. Before it had merely been an implement she would never need to use—not so different from needle and thread or a butter churn—but now it looked so much different, terrifying.

It was with a heavy heart that she left the room and took to the long flight of stairs. Moments later, the doors to the drowning chamber boomed shut behind her.

CHAPTER 14

The wind was bitter, and for the first time in years, Rehada truly felt it. She was trudging through the knee-deep snow behind Bersuq, Soroush's older brother, along a game trail in the forest below Radiskoye. Despite working hard to climb the trail, despite the three robes she wore, her feet and hands were numb, and her teeth were chattering. Soroush had told her to release her spirit the night before, and so she had, but it felt strange to be without it. Everything felt different, as if she were walking in someone else's body.

Bersuq, who had pulled ahead of her, turned and barked, "Keep up."

She had never felt a feeling of kinship toward Bersuq, even in the days of Ahya's early childhood, but she didn't begrudge him that. He was not unkind. He was simply hard.

She pushed herself as hard as she was able, and eventually the slope leveled off. Radiskoye could not be seen, but its presence could be felt. With the landing of the dukes commencing today, a dozen ships were patrolling the sky over the palotza and the mountain that housed it, Verodnaya.

The trail they followed was bordered by a ridge on their left and the forest to their right. The ridge was rocky and clear of trees, probably from some landslide years ago. Distant but still visible beyond the tree line was the outer wall of the palotza.

Rehada was startled when ahead of her, Soroush stood from a deep crevice. She calmed her nerves as she approached.

"Have you found it?" Bersuq asked.

"It has been difficult, but I think it will be best here."

"Be sure," Bersuq said as he scanned the sky above them. "The location is dangerous."

Soroush nodded. "I am sure."

For the next hour, she, Bersuq, and Soroush trudged into the nearby woods and brought firewood, throwing it into the crevice. The pile climbed higher and higher until it stood above ground nearly as high as Rehada.

They were nearly done when Soroush darted for cover of the spruce, waving Bersuq and Rehada to follow. No sooner had they hidden themselves than a Landed brigantine sailed overhead, its pair of landward masts barely clearing the tops of the trees. Rehada thought they had been spotted, but the two men watching from the lower masts were scanning the ground further east, toward Radiskoye.

The ship sailed on, turning westward toward the eyrie, picking up altitude and cresting the ridge above them. Finally it was gone.

Rehada felt her heart pounding. It reminded her of her first days on Khalakovo, her first few times with Landed men. Her first lies. This, acting in secret against the interests of the Landed, was no different; it felt just as shaming.

"Is it wise to taunt Radiskoye?" Rehada asked.

"It is past time."

"All for a stone?"

"Not just a stone." Soroush returned to the pile of deadwood and used flint and steel to spark the base of it to life. Soon the pile was burning high, the heat rising. "It is a facet, one of five."

"To what end?"

Soroush stared into the fire, as if it would pain him to look upon her. "When we have them all, we will be able to tear the rift asunder. We will give to Adhiya what it wants, a taste of life."

Praise be, Rehada thought. Before speaking with him at Malekh's hanging, she had felt defeated. Her anger had overflowed, but it had felt directionless. Even after speaking with him, she worried that the tide had turned against them to the point that they would never realize their goal, never avenge the deaths of her people at the hands of the Landed. But now, with Soroush so self-assured, and with them so close to achieving what they had long worked for, she was enlivened.

Soroush turned and faced her. "The ancients never used stones to create a bond, did you know this?"

She shook her head.

"They bonded, and the stone was formed. It was a manifestation of their experience, not a tool to be used to control."

"I do not control."

He shook his head. "You don't think of it in that manner, but you do. The hezhan does not come willingly—or not completely so. In the early days of this world, the bond was a way to share, to learn. What is it now?"

She found herself becoming angry, but Soroush did not mean for his words to be taken as such. He was young, but he was learned; he was wise, as wise as any arqesh. She thought on what he said, and it frightened her.

To use no stone to create a bond… She had never done so, and the thought of attempting it was already making her palms sweat. "How will they know I have come?"

"Go with an open heart. Do not bring fear. Do not bring anger. Bring curiosity. Bring life. Bring a yearning for the things that have always eluded you."

There was a part of her that wanted to ask him what would happen if a hezhan did not come, but she knew the answer to that. More importantly, she knew the question could not be entertained once she stepped into the fire, and so she set it aside and steeled herself while pulling the clothes from her frame. Naked, the wind tugged at her hair, and the sound it made through the trees behind her, a howling, seemed to laugh at what she was about to do. She had had doubts before—when her master had shown her the way of qiram. She had been afraid, but she had been raised by a strong mother. She had been given over to a wise teacher. She had traveled far and she had come to know the ways of flame. She would do this, no matter what the wind might say.

She stepped forward, feeling the heat from the fire against her stomach and thighs. The wood crackled and spit, sending steam and smoke into the sky. She put one foot forward to the edge of the snow-covered earth. A spike of fear rose up inside her with the knowledge that she wore no stone, but the stories of the ancients all spoke of qiram who were able to summon hezhan without the aid of such things. She would trust to them. Trust to her teachings. Trust to Soroush, who had never led her astray.

One more step forward, and she fell among the flames. The branches gave way, cracking loudly, as sparks swirled into the air. The heat soared, higher than she had ever felt, even during her times of penance. It seared her legs, her arms, the skin over her stomach and back. Her eyes were closed, but she forced them open, knowing she must face this squarely or lose herself to the pain.

Her breathing was labored, her lungs barely able to take breath. She managed to remain standing, but it felt like her skin was blistering, blackening, cracking. She felt no hezhan; she surely would have had she been wearing a stone. She tried to reach out, to call to one, but the things she felt were very different from the normal ritual. They were much more open now, without bounds, and it was frightening.

She was barely able to turn—so painful was the movement—and look up toward Soroush. To her surprise, his face was locked in an expression of pride.

"Soroush!" she cried as the pain became too great.

"Silence!"

She grit her teeth. Tried harder.

But it was no use.

She fell to her knees. The heat was no longer satisfied with burning her skin. It licked at her insides. She dropped to one hand, unable to prevent herself from curling up against the searing heat that was building inside her. If she were but to open her mouth, she could breathe flame; she could light the forest afire with but one brief sigh.

She reared back and spread her arms wide to the sky.

And released her building fury in a drawn-out cry.

She felt, while doing so, another presence. Something clean and white among the madness around her. She could feel him both in the flames of the material world and on the far side, in the shifting currents of Adhiya. He felt ancient, as old as the stars.

Suddenly the flames above her blackened with smoke. A sound like a rockslide filled her ears. She was thrust downward, hard, into the ashes. The sky above her clouded over, obscuring her vision. She heard a hollow thump, felt the heat above her plummet. She coughed against the glowing white embers swirling in the air, and when they finally settled, she was able to see what lay before her: a form as tall as a tree, as wide as a wagon. Stout and flaming.

A suurahezhan. It had crossed from the world beyond—to what purpose she did not know. Unlike the suurahezhan she used the tourmaline gems to bond with, she had no control over this creature, none whatsoever.

The hezhan stood, unmoving, perhaps taking in its new surroundings, but then it lumbered around and focused its attention up toward the palotza. It hesitated, and then began to stalk up the hill along the fault line.

Soroush spoke, but she could not understand him. Words made no sense.

"Quickly!" he shouted. "Search among the ashes."

She did as he asked, not knowing what she was looking for. A moment later she felt something small and hard among the brittle embers and powdery ash. She picked it up.

A tourmaline—deep red, almost black, and beautiful beyond description.

"Daughter of Shineshka"—Soroush, so hasty a moment ago, paused and bowed his head—"rejoice, for never have you done so well."

Rehada paid him little mind, nor did she wish to examine the stone. She had felt something deeper in the woods, and she could see among the shadows a boy poking his head out from behind a tree.

Nasim? Had that been him when she was at her most vulnerable? Had he *helped* her?

Soroush held his hand out but stopped short of touching her. She would still be much too hot. "Come."

She looked at him, suddenly angry over being disturbed.

"Come," he said, more forcefully this time.

She stepped up from the crevice, but when she looked toward the trees again, the boy was gone.

CHAPTER 15

The rest of Atiana's day proved to be just as tense as the morning—from luncheon, where they met the delegation from Khazabyirsk, all the way through to the greeting ceremony on the palotza's eyrie.

Father came for her as the sun was peeking through tall, white clouds. Though he waved away any attempts at complimenting him, he looked grand in his tooled leather boots, his sheepskin cherkesska and ermine kolpak. Katerina came minutes later, and together they led Atiana and Mileva and Ishkyna from the palotza to the eyrie by way of a cobbled path. The eyrie was one of the oldest among all the islands, and it was one of the most breathtaking. It stood one thousand feet above the seashore. Each of its four perches were made of sculpted stone; the curved supports beneath them were filled with the intricate traceries of the Landless artisans. Two of the perches were occupied by Khalakovo's royal yachts, but the other two remained clear, waiting for the incoming ships.

Three dozen royalty, including the contingent from Khazabyirsk, stood on the landing in their best finery, waiting for the first ship to dock. It was good to see that Khalakovo was taking their recent threat of the Maharraht seriously. By all accounts they hadn't been seen again on the island, but still there were more streltsi than usual for the landing of council: both patrolling the curtain wall and standing at attention.

Nikandr, dressed in a fine gold kaftan and polished leather boots, stood behind his father. Zhabyn and Katerina bowed to Iaros, who, after waiting for a healthy pause, stepped aside, allowing Nikandr to take Atiana's gloved hand in his.

He stepped in and kissed both cheeks with an iciness that surprised her.

She was still angry with him, yet she found herself wishing he would take her hand, to warm one small part of her on this cold spring day. She tried to forget Mileva's words, but as she stood there, her hand aching from neglect, she couldn't help but think of Rehada, his lover. Did he hold *her* hand? What had he told her about the wedding? Had they gossiped about her while lying in each other's arms? Had she laughed when Nikandr told her what a poor wife Atiana would be?

Her hands, of their own volition, clasped themselves before her in a pose that was much like her sisters'. Mileva seemed to notice, but she returned her gaze to the retinue of Duke Rhavanki, who were just now stepping down the gangplank of his impressive yacht.

As ships came and left, Atiana had a growing awareness of being watched. Ishkyna, standing between her father and Mileva, was watching her. No one else might have noticed it, but Atiana knew Ishkyna better than anyone—even Mileva—and there was jealousy in her eyes. *Ishkyna* was jealous of *her*. It was an occurrence so rare that Atiana wondered if she were imagining it, but as the last of the ships approached, the feeling intensified, and she knew she must be right.

A willful Ishkyna was never a good thing, Atiana thought to herself, especially when you were the object of her attentions. She decided she would have to watch her sister carefully these next few days.

The Grand Duke's ship was the last to arrive. The thing was absolutely massive for a yacht. It could practically double as a cargo ship; given the dire straits the islands had been in of late, perhaps that was the plan. Or it may have been the Grand Duke's pride that had forced him into such an extravagant decision.

The Grand Duke himself, Stasa Olegov Bolgravya, a man who had seen seventy winters, stood at the bow wearing a heavy fur coat and a tall black hat. He had not come to the last council. He had made his excuses and had sent his first son, Konstantin, in his place. No one had thought much of it—it happened from time to time with all the dukes—but now everyone saw why he had refused to come.

The Stasa that stared at them all from the gunwales of his ship was not the same man. He had always been a large man, barrel-chested and meaty about the arms and legs. His face had been plump, his cheeks red. He had possessed steely eyes. He was quick to anger, and he rarely laughed, but when he did, his eyes held that same keen edge, as if he were granting you some favor by allowing the display of his mirth.

This Stasa was crooked. He listed to one side, as if the position pained him but was the *least* painful position he could find. His cheeks were drawn, and they sagged about his chin like an old bloodhound. His lips drooped at the edges, giving him a permanent frown. And his eyes... They were sunken eyes, defeated eyes, as if they were tired from the mere viewing of the world.

Why he had come when the wasting had nearly taken him already, Atiana couldn't guess. Perhaps he knew his death was near and wished to meet his fellow dukes one last time. Perhaps there were agreements he wished to negotiate, a final show of power before the fates finally took him.

It was disheartening to see him like this. Among the squabbles of the dukes, Stasa had always ruled with something akin to fairness. It felt like the wasting, or the blight itself, had taken him, and with him gone it would only be a matter of time before the rest succumbed as well.

Atiana's attention was caught by a motion from Nikandr. He was touching his neck with a curious look on his face, but when he noticed her watching he dropped his hand immediately. It must be his soulstone, though why it had attracted his attention now she had no idea.

Stasa's son, Grigory, stepped onto the forecastle deck and made his way to stand by his father's side. Though he was fourth in line for the scepter of Bolgravya, he had learned the lessons of a prince well. As he swept his gaze over the crowd, he kept his face stern, as if it were *his* iron fist that ruled the islands, not his father's.

A moment later a broad-winged rook flew over the eyrie, cawing loudly. "A suurahezhan approaches! Prepare! Pre—" It never completed those last words, for it dropped from the sky as if it had been shot. It struck the ground heavily and lay there, twitching. Then it went still.

The crack of a musket was heard. A soldier shouted orders, and then two more muskets rang out. The soldiers who had fired immediately sprinted along the wall, looking over their shoulders at something that had clearly shaken their resolve.

Then, over the curtain wall, flowing like flames over a burning log, came a form twice as tall as Atiana. It looked vaguely manlike, but its chest was compact, its arms long and fluid, its head little more than a featureless mound. Its form shifted—growing here, shrinking there. It burned orange with wisps of yellow and white, and though it was still twenty paces away she could feel the heat of it against her skin. The sound was like a heavy wind as it blew through winterdead trees.

The eyrie devolved into bedlam.

Shouts and screams filled the air. Several of the royalty pulled their pistols and fired. Many retreated along the stone pathway toward the palotza. Others edged toward the cliff and the perches, while a select few pulled shashkas from the sheaths at their belts. Nikandr, pistol in hand, stepped in front of Atiana and edged her backward while keeping his eyes fixed forward.

The wind shifted, bringing with it an acrid and choking scent. Atiana's eyes began to tear as more musket shots rang out, some from the curtain wall and a few from Bolgravya's ship. It was impossible to tell if the hezhan was affected as it plodded through the garden, singeing the squat evergreen bushes as it went. Where the musket balls struck the hezhan's skin—if skin was what the gaseous surface could be called—it darkened as embers did when struck with water, but then it quickly returned to its previous brightness, all evidence of the wound gone.

Two jalaqiram, Aramahn water masters, rushed forward, calling in their lyrical language. The one closest to the fiery beast spread his arms wide, and the azurite gem on his brow glowed brighter. A pool of water built around his feet, but before he could use it, the suurahezhan charged forward and brought him to the ground with both casket-sized hands, snuffing the life from him in an instant.

A handful of streltsi rushed out from the palotza carrying dousing rods, circles of pure iron with long, leather-wrapped handles affixed to them. They were typically used against enemy qiram, but they were effective against hezhan as well. As the musket fire continued the streltsi surrounded the spirit, attempting to fence it in using the rods. For a moment, it seemed to be working. The suurahezhan paused, its form shrinking as its color turned deep red. Then, like a cornered dog, it shot between two of the soldiers. A deep moan escaped the creature as the iron struck its arms and sides. Where the metal touched the hezhan turned deep red, almost black, but the price had apparently been worth it. It was free of its containment.

It charged forward as more shots hit home, passing mere yards away from Atiana. Nikandr was sure to place himself between her and the creature, but she still felt the heat of it on her face as it passed. Once it was clear it was headed for the ship, Nikandr pushed Atiana with a firm hand toward the palotza.

"Go," he said, alternating glances between her and the hezhan.

She backed up, but found it impossible to turn away from the unfolding carnage. The five streltsi on Bolgravya's ship were reloading their muskets. The suurahezhan waded forward, the heat of its body burning right through the rigging. In seconds the soldiers were dead, and the fire was raging higher through the yacht's sails.

The Grand Duke's wind master, standing near the center of the ship, moved her arms forward, palms facing the suurahezhan. A cyclone built around the spirit, pulling air away, but before it could have any discernible effect, the suurahezhan reared back and blasted a gout of flame toward her. She was buffeted backward and over the edge of the ship's railing, gone in the blink of an eye. With one last gust the winds dissipated.

The Grand Duke had backed up from the gunwales, but now with the hezhan so close he retreated to the ship's starward mainmast. The hezhan followed, its footsteps thumping hollowly against the windwood deck.

Many men tried to use their tall axes to protect him, but the creature was of one mind—it no longer appeared to care if it came into contact with iron. Dozens of strikes hit home, darkening the creature's skin, but it plodded onward.

Grigory ran forward, drawing his shashka from its scabbard, but several streltsi grabbed him, preventing him from reaching his father. Few of Stasa's retinue had been on deck, preferring to leave the decks clear for the crew, but now many were climbing up and heading for the ship's side. With the gangway still in its away position, the crew and passengers were leaping to the safety of the perch.

The suurahezhan, standing over Stasa, crouched and stared into Stasa's eyes. With one huge wail, and a heat that Atiana had never felt before, the creature reared up, facing the sky and throwing its arms wide. Stasa's soulstone was aflame—much brighter than a soulstone ought to be. Moments later, the mainmast was ablaze, and the entire center of the ship was engulfed in a column of crackling orange fire. Stasa was lost in it, though there was a brief moment where Atiana thought she could hear his cries, high and desperate, mingling with the wail of the suurahezhan. They were eerily similar in those brief moments, but then both were cut short.

The suurahezhan's form seemed to be drawn into the flame. And then it was gone altogether, leaving behind a raging fire that had burned away a healthy portion of the mainmast and eaten a wagon-sized hole through the decking.

The boom of a cannon shook Atiana's entire body. They had been aiming at the hezhan, but the creature was now gone and the shot clipped the weakened mainmast. The mast cracked and began to lean toward the windward side.

Then the ship began to descend. People were continuing to leap to the safety of the perch, but the acceleration was already increasing. Atiana saw Grigory's sister launch herself from the gunwales, but she didn't leap far enough. She fell screaming a moment later.

Grigory was still fighting against the men who were holding him back. Tears streamed down his anguished face. Nikandr stood near the edge of the quay, swinging a rope. He tossed it to the deck and shouted at the soldiers to take hold. They pleaded with Grigory to come, but he ignored them. Over a dozen men anchored the rope behind Nikandr and took up the call, their voices becoming more and more insistent as the pace of the ship's descent increased.

Atiana thought surely Grigory had decided to spend his last moments with his father, but just as the ship's main deck was dropping from view, he seemed to sense for the first time what was happening around him. He looked toward the perch, and then stood and grabbed the rope. The men on the eyrie bore down to hold Grigory and the soldiers. As they began heaving in time to pull them to safety, the ship's tall, flaming sails slipped from view. Then it was gone, leaving only black smoke curling high into the cloud-stippled sky.

CHAPTER 16

Even while pulling Grigory to safety, Nikandr watched in wide-eyed horror as the yacht slipped from view. A great cacophony of snapping wood and rigging followed. Grigory was finally pulled up to solid ground. He immediately stepped to the edge of the perch, screaming in rage and confusion. Nikandr tried to hold him back, but Grigory shoved him away.

Father and Ranos arrived and ordered the streltsi to escort everyone inside. "For your cousin, if not for yourself," Iaros said to Grigory when he appeared reluctant to leave.

Grigory looked at young Ivan, who stood nearby shaking with fear, though he was clearly ashamed of it.

"Stop your trembling," Grigory said, "and get yourself inside."

Ivan looked afraid to take a single step.

"Go!"

Ivan shivered, looking smaller than a boy his age ought to, and then complied.

To Nikandr's surprise, Grigory pulled himself taller and faced Father like an equal. "I will not hide indoors like some shivering child, not while there is any chance of survivors. My men and I will accompany the effort to save them."

This was of course a *demand* that a rescue effort be waged, for no mention of one had been made so far. Grigory had always been a bold young man—he was Stasa's son after all—but he had never seemed so much like his father as he did just then.

Father did not balk at Grigory's tone. He merely nodded and turned to the sotnik of the streltsi. "Take the ships. Have the *Broghan* scour the area around Radiskoye. The *Tura* should search the rest of the island. And have men accompany Grigory to the harbor. Send two waterborne ships to the cliffs and have them search for survivors."

"Father," Nikandr interrupted, "let me take the *Broghan* down to the sea.

Help from Volgorod will arrive too late."

"*Nyet*. The winds at the base of the cliffs are too dangerous."

Grigory stepped forward and pointed a finger at Father's chest. "No effort will be spared, Khalakovo."

Father turned calmly. "Take yourself away, Bolgravya, before I have you dragged and thrown in with the women."

Grigory glanced at the nearby ships, knowing that any delay could mean the lives of his family below, and then he turned crisply and strode away.

"We cannot risk it," Father said once he was out of earshot.

Nikandr lowered his voice. "But if there's any chance that some survive, we should take it."

"Nikandr is right," Ranos said. "And despite Grigory's brashness, think on what is going through everyone's minds. It's bad enough this happened in front of the entire Grand Duchy. If we're to save any face, we need to show our best effort."

"I cannot risk more lives," Father said.

"Nikandr has done it before, Father. With Jahalan and Udra, he'll be safe."

Father hesitated, his gaze wandering to the smoke trailing up from the base of the cliff. He stepped forward and took Nikandr by the shoulders, and then pulled him into a tight embrace. "Go." He kissed Nikandr on the forehead. "Save what can be saved, and come home safe."

And with that Nikandr was off. Grigory and the three Bolgravyan windmen who had leapt to safety joined him. Jahalan and Udra were already waiting near the ship. They assembled a crew from the available men and pushed off as soon as they were able.

Once the mooring ropes were released, a half-dozen men used poles to push the ship into the wind. Nikandr took the helm himself and ordered the sails set along all four mainmasts.

Flying this close to an island always held its risks. A windship, unlike a waterborne craft, had three keels, each of them a shaft of obsidian running through the center of the ship. One ran lengthwise; one ran from the starward mainmast, through the ship and down the seaward mainmast; and the final one ran from the landward mainmast to the windward. The ends of each shaft were attuned to the aether such that it would align in a particular manner, each end pulling along ley lines drawn by the complex arrangement of islands and sea. This close to a cliff face, the currents were little more than whorls of aether, shifting and swirling with no discernible pattern. This was the reason eyrie landings were so difficult and the most seasoned pilots were called upon to perform them.

If it were only the aether that they had to contend with, Nikandr would not worry so much; it was the added danger of the wind, which was at best unpredictable, at worst deadly. There was little to do about it now, however. They could not abandon any survivors to the seas, no matter what the risk might be.

Udra willed the *Broghan* to descend. Jahalan summoned the winds to push them away from the cliff face, but already they were being blown back toward it. Nikandr used the three levers on the bridge to control the ship's alignment. Jahalan could only do so much; he used his bonded wind spirit, a havahezhan, to manipulate the winds, but fine control was impossible, so it was up to Nikandr to harness them properly and guide the ship away from the looming rock.

Finally they approached the sea. Spikes of rock jutted up from the water like the ragged teeth of a leviathan lying in wait just below the surface. Stasa's ship lay in ruins between two of them, the massive hull shorn near its center. The masts were crooked and broken like the trunks of once-proud trees following a terrible cold snap. White, frothy water rose and fell with the surf. Bitterly cold spray flew off the crest of every wave and was thrown against the ship, against the exposed skin of the crew.

Men crowded the gunwales and scanned the water for any sign of survivors. For minutes on end, Nikandr struggled with the rudders, fighting the tendency of the wind to send them toward the rock. Jahalan was doing his best, but even one as strong and skilled as he could not coax the havahezhan bound to him indefinitely, especially when there were so many other wind spirits gathered in places like this, ready to foil the wishes of the Aramahn masters.

"There!" Grigory shouted from the gunwales. "Near the rock! Two of them!"

Grigory pointed toward two men who were clinging to the rocks, too weary to pull themselves higher.

"Ready—" Nikandr lost his breath when the wind threw the cold ocean spray into his face. "Ready the ropes!"

Four of the crew shimmied along the landward mainmast, carrying ropes that were fed to them from the deck. Nikandr ordered men to the windward mainmast so the ship's delicate balance would be maintained. There was no need to speak with Jahalan and Udra. Jahalan knew his part—to keep the winds as steady as he could—and Udra stood ready to right the ship as the new weight was taken on board.

The wind buffeted the ship, first away from the rocks, then toward, then fiercely downward. All the while Nikandr guided the ship steadily closer to the stranded men. The crewmen on the mast heaved the ropes toward the rocks, but they had to be reeled in, because the survivors were either too weak to leave the safety of the rocks or too scared to brave the waters.

The cliff and the tall, jutting rocks prevented them from moving directly above the men, but Nikandr brought the ship as close as he dared.

The sound of the wind fades. The numbing cold and the tug of the wind soon follow until all of his senses have been robbed from him.

Until there is nothing.

Nothing save for a keen yearning. A summons.

It tugs at his soul. It clambers for life. It is a need so great that it threatens to overwhelm him. It is the call of the spirits beyond the veil. One has reached through and taken hold of his soul, but there are many, many more, ready to scratch and claw in any way they can for the life that lies within him.

The world slipped into view.

Grigory shouted from the gunwales. "What are you doing? Bring her in closer!"

Nikandr realized the *Broghan* was slipping away from the rocks, but he didn't care. Jahalan was clearly concerned over Nikandr's actions, but he continued to command the winds as he always had—with a steady hand.

He rails against the hezhan that hungers for him as others approach. Several men have already succumbed. Surely more will follow if they attempt to save the men on the rocks. Soon, if he allows it, the entire ship will be lost to the hunger of the spirits.

One of the two crewmen on the mast slipped free and fell to the white-capped waters below. Another man standing on deck near the head was screaming, scratching at his face, leaving dark runnels of blood. Nikandr understood what was assailing them. He also knew they had to flee, now, before they were all consumed.

"Rise, Udra, rise! Jahalan, hold steady!"

The ship rose immediately as the winds shoved the ship toward the rocks. Jahalan was ready—he commanded his havahezhan to thwart the elements yet again.

Grigory's eyes went wide. "Are you mad?" He stalked over from the gunwales, his eyes in a craze. "You cannot leave! They are just there!"

"We cannot stay," Nikandr replied, unable to articulate what had just happened.

"Your own man has fallen in the waters!"

When Nikandr did not reply, Grigory pulled the ornamental kindjal from its sheath at his belt and stalked toward Nikandr.

"Take her back!" he shouted, but before he could come within striking range, three streltsi swarmed in and seized his arms.

Grigory's countrymen broke away from the gunwales, ready to help their Lord Prince, but the crew of the *Broghan* took them by force, preventing them from interfering.

"I am a son of Bolgravya! You will release me!" When they did not, Grigory turned to Nikandr. "Turn back, coward! There are lives to be saved!"

Despite Grigory's pleas, Nikandr knew he could not, and though his face burned with shame from the screams of the men below the ship, he would not throw away a ship—along with the lives of a score of men—when the spirits themselves had somehow risen against them.

CHAPTER 17

"My Lord Prince?" Isaak, the palotza's seneschal, was standing in front of Nikandr with a look on his face that made Nikandr wonder just how long he had been standing there.

Nikandr had always been a sure-footed man, but he'd had a terrible case of vertigo ever since his return to solid ground. It was another symptom of the wasting, one often associated with the latter stages of the disease, but Nikandr hoped that it had somehow been brought on by his strange experience and that it was merely lingering because of his condition.

He couldn't get the scene from the *Broghan* out of his mind.

The crewman who had been attacked by the spirits, an old gull with a wide jaw and heavy growth of beard, was standing nearby. He was pressing a bloody kerchief against his self-inflicted wounds. He looked at Nikandr with something akin to solidarity—he understood Nikandr's confusion—yet at the same time he looked embarrassed, as if he felt weak for admitting that he had succumbed to this unexpected attack.

It mirrored Nikandr's own feelings precisely.

"I'll be fine, Isaak," Nikandr said. "I'm only a bit shaken. Where did you say I could find my father?"

"I said *His Highness* would find *you*. He asks that you retire to the Great Hall to assist Ranos in *staving off the wolves*, as he put it."

"Where has he gone?"

"Have you heard a word I've said?" Isaak asked.

The sounds of screaming came to Nikandr again. Closing his eyes only made matters worse.

Isaak stepped forward, lowering his voice. "Are you quite well, My Lord Prince?"

Nikandr waved him away. "It's nothing."

"There is trouble afoot, My Lord. Your father, the Duke, is with the Matra, and he'll return as soon as he is able. If you're well, as you say, then best you get to the Great Hall now, before things turn sour." He turned and walked briskly away, and when he reached the end of the hallway, he turned. "The Great Hall, My Lord, the Great Hall."

Flanked by the old seaman, Nikandr made his way there. The doors stood open, and Nikandr entered as an argument played out at the head of the hall. Some noticed his entrance, but they remained silent as Nikandr and the crewman made their way to the dais. The screams of the men on the rocks, the silence as his man slipped free of the mast and fell to the sea, the clawing feeling he'd experienced as if his very soul had been held in the balance, all of it still swirled within his mind as if it were still happening.

He paused, nearly retching at the discontinuity. He took deep breaths as Ranos shouted over the noise of the crowd. "I have told you thrice, Vostroma. We have secured Radiskoye, Nikandr and Grigory are attempting to find any survivors, and our Aramahn are searching for signs of foul play."

"*Foul play*?" Zhabyn barked. "Can there be any doubt?"

"Spirits have crossed randomly before, Duke."

"And if you believe that's the case here, then you're less prepared to follow in your father's footsteps than I thought." Zhabyn stabbed a finger toward the eyrie. "What happened out there was murder. No more, no less."

Nikandr reached the dais. When Ranos took note of him, he tipped his head, indicating Nikandr should join him. "We don't know that yet. Your blood is boiling, I know. Mine is as well. But we can discuss this further once more is known."

Voices rumbled about the room, clearly perturbed that Ranos was questioning the obvious.

"Discuss?"

This came from Duke Leonid of Dhalingrad, a heavyset man with a crooked shoulder and a long white beard that shook as he spoke.

"You wish to *discuss* when the Grand Duke himself has been murdered on your very doorstep? This is a time for action, not wandering about asking polite questions while you hide your cock with your hand."

"Spirits cross when they will, Dhalingrad," Ranos replied.

"Not only when they will," Duke Leonid said. "They can be summoned, as you very well know. It happened to your brother. This might have been planned days before Council"—Leonid opened his arms wide—"from within these very walls."

Ranos's face turned hard, mirroring Nikandr's own feelings. "If you have something to say, Dhalingrad, you'd better come out from hiding and say it."

"Dhalingrad hides behind nothing!"

Then, striding through the open doors at the rear of the hall, came

Grigory, his face a study in anger and indignation. When he reached the open area before the dais, he spit upon the floor and pointed his finger at Nikandr. "You have much to account for, Khalakovo."

Before Nikandr could speak, Ranos strode toward him. "Watch your step, Bolgravya."

"I will not, not when my father burned before my eyes, not when my blood has been offered to the sea."

"I told you what happened, Griga," Nikandr said.

Grigory's look hardened at the use of his familiar name. "Do you expect me to believe that hezhan were *attacking* you?"

"I do."

"When your own Motherless slaves say they felt nothing?"

"I felt the hezhan as I feel my own thoughts. They were clamoring for us. Our man felt the same."

Nikandr motioned for the crewman at the head of the crowd to speak, but before he could summon the courage, Grigory scoffed. "He will spout any story you've fed him."

"I saved lives, including yours! They took one of my own men."

"Then you should be doubly ashamed for abandoning him!"

Voices were raised, people taking sides, others looking for answers. Nikandr saw Borund, standing near his father. They had grown up together, had attended many Councils with one another. Borund had spent a summer on Khalakovo, and Nikandr had done the same on Vostroma. He was Nikandr's closest friend among the aristocracy, a man Nikandr considered a brother. Ever since Borund's arrival their relationship had been strained, different. Nikandr had written it off to his own reticence to marry Atiana, but the look on Borund's face… He was staring at Nikandr as if he were looking upon a coward, as if he were ashamed that he had ever considered Nikandr a friend. It was a strange reality to be faced with, and it made Nikandr realize just how dangerous a position they were in. Tensions had been high. Distrust and the urge to look after one's own family had been rising above the long-fought-for solidarity among the Duchies. If Borund were looking at Nikandr in this manner, what must the other dukes be thinking, especially those from the south, who typically aligned with one another?

An echoing boom resounded through the room—once, twice, thrice. Everyone turned toward Zhabyn, who was slamming the heel of his boot against the wooden floor. Once quiet had been restored, he nodded to Nikandr. "Tell us what you know."

Nikandr complied, at least so far as he was able. Grigory interrupted several times, but each time he did Zhabyn stomped his foot, cowing the young man back into silence. When Nikandr was done, Zhabyn turned to the crewman and asked the same of him. And finally, it was Grigory's turn. He relayed the events at the base of the cliff, painting Nikandr as a man more craven than anyone the islands had ever seen. It would seem, by the time Grigory was done, that Nikandr was responsible for everything from the presence of the suurahezhan to the very blight that threatened their way of life. Perhaps that was Zhabyn's plan, to allow Grigory to paint himself into a corner with his own words, relieving the pressure that was building on Nikandr and the Khalakovo family. Then again, given Zhabyn's disapproving look toward Nikandr when Grigory finally fell silent, perhaps it wasn't.

"This is strange business," Zhabyn said to Ranos, essentially waiting for an official reply.

"Khalakovo was hurt as much as anyone by what happened here today."

"As anyone?" Duke Leonid said. "I think not."

The silence in the room yawned like a sleeping beast preparing to wake.

"Don't mince words, Dhalingrad," Ranos said quietly.

Before Leonid could continue, Duke Yegor of Nodhvyansk stepped out of the crowd, his arms wide. Yegor was young—Ranos's age—and still impressionable, but his family had always been a friend of Vostroma. "He's saying what we're all thinking, that the one man who stands to gain the most from Bolgravya's death is the man hosting this Council."

Ranos moved to the edge of the dais, perhaps ready to challenge Yegor for such an insult, but before he could, Father's voice called out from behind him.

"You're saying I would kill my oldest friend?"

Nikandr turned to find his father standing in the doorway that led to the hall's antechamber. Before him, sitting in a padded chair fitted with wheels, was Mother.

The entire assemblage went deadly silent and took to one knee. Father pushed Saphia Mishkeva Khalakovo forward, the wooden wheels thumping over the floorboards, until he reached the edge of the dais. When he stopped, everyone rose to their feet.

"You're saying," Father continued, "that I would risk my youngest son and his new wife? You're saying I would risk the lives of my *own* wife, my elder son, even *yours* to a rogue spirit such as that? I would sooner have fired a musket into Stasa's chest than release a creature like that into my family's midst."

Yegor opened his mouth to speak, but there came from the wheelchair a voice so rarely used it croaked with every utterance. "I have conferred with the other Matri," Mother said. The effort, as small as it was, proved taxing; she breathed rapidly several times before continuing. "The crossing of the suurahezhan appears to be spontaneous."

As she recovered herself, Grigory opened his mouth to speak, but Father stomped his foot down hard, forcing him to silence.

"An investigation will be conducted, and as we are on … Khalakovan ground, my son Nikandr … will undertake it."

The room began to murmur.

"We will share with you our findings … but until such time as it is complete … you will remain welcome guests … of Radiskoye."

Zhabyn Vostroma bowed his head. "Forgive me, Matra, but have *all* the Matri agreed to this?"

Nikandr saw his mother smile, and it was wicked. "They have, Vostroma."

Grigory pulled Ivan from the crowd and placed the young man before him. "Forty of our countrymen are dead!" Grigory's face went beet red. "Someone must pay!"

"And they will," Iaros said. "Khalakovo will find those responsible."

"Then start with your son! He left two of my men to die on the rocks below like a baseless thief!"

Father glanced at Nikandr, but it was Mother who spoke. "My son has answered your questions. There was a tear in the aether … made, perhaps, when the suurahezhan returned to the world beyond."

"I felt nothing," Grigory said.

Saphia laughed, and her face pulled back into a rictus of a smile. "Tell me, Grigory, when was the last time you spent time in your Matra's chamber?"

Grigory's face went red. "I don't have to touch the aether to know a lie when I hear it."

"Speak to your Matra. Discuss with her what happened. Until then, speak no more of my son."

Grigory opened his mouth to reply, but Father spoke over him.

"And Khalakovo will find who is responsible, good Prince. Have no fear of that."

The entire room went silent. Grigory stared at Father for a long time, clearly enraged at being treated like a pup.

"It had better be soon." And with that Grigory marched from the room. Even with all his confidence it was strange watching him leave. Bolgravya had always had the largest retinue at Council. It felt like a herd of men should be leaving with him, but besides Grigory there was only the one sorry remainder of their strength: young cousin Ivan.

Nikandr expected the tension in the room to drop, but strangely, it intensified.

Duke Heodor of Lhudansk, a squat man with a piercing gaze, cleared his throat. "If there's no one who will say it, then I will. We need to consider who will fill the seat of Grand Duke."

Father gave no outward sign of emotion at Heodor's words. He, as the eldest reigning duke, should fill the imperial seat, but with Stasa's blood staining their house, the vote would be in question.

Duke Andreyo of Rhavanki shook his fist angrily. "The Grand Duke is dead not an hour, and you're calling for his replacement?"

"There is no sense ignoring what needs to be done," Heodor said.

Yegor pointed to the dais. "You might as well stand behind Khalakovo now, Lhudansk."

"*Nyet*, Heodor is right," Zhabyn said. "The Grand Duke is dead." He turned to Iaros, looking up at him on the dais as if he were a son who had disappointed him. "But the cause is in doubt. A vote cannot be held until the matter is settled."

Several of the dukes nodded, and Father nodded along with them. Nikandr knew his father well enough to know he would gladly take the mantle of Grand Duke, but he was also wise enough to realize that others would not be pushed. A week would pass, perhaps more, and they would find out what happened in the eyrie. Then, a vote would be held and honored.

"We will wait," Iaros said. "There is much to be done in any case, not the least of which is my son's wedding day."

There were a few somber nods among the crowd, but most eyes turned to Zhabyn, whose rigid stance had not changed. "It would be best, I think, if the wedding were postponed as well."

Iaros eyed Zhabyn for long, uncomfortable moments, but it was Saphia that Nikandr watched closely. This was a grave insult indeed. Saphia had been the one to finally convince Zhabyn's wife, Radia, that the marriage would be in the best interests of both families. It would benefit them at a time when their strength was dearly depleted.

The decision, strictly speaking, wasn't Zhabyn's to make. The Matri had arranged it, and by tradition, only *they* could undo it. But Radia had never been a willful woman; if Zhabyn declared the marriage to be dead, she would follow, and then there was little Khalakovo could do except hold the offered ships and trade agreements as bait.

When Saphia spoke again, she spoke slowly and deliberately. "Plans have been made, Vostroma. Documents have been signed."

Zhabyn didn't flinch. "Winds change, Matra. Should we ignore them when they do?"

Saphia seemed to lift herself up higher in the chair—an act that would take a supreme amount of will in her weakened state. During the pause that followed, the entire room seemed to lean forward. Finally, Saphia nodded once, politely, though there was no graciousness in the dour expression on her face. "A small delay will hurt little."

And with that she reached up and patted Father's hand, which rested on her shoulder. Father then turned her chair around and strode from the room, Ranos and Nikandr behind them.

CHAPTER 18

It had been three days since the attack on the eyrie. Nikandr was out beyond the palotza walls, hiking down the trail the suurahezhan had taken, his fourth time doing so. He came to the spruce a thousand yards from the palotza's walls where the husk of the burned streltsi had been found. The scent of cardamom still laced the air, one of the telltale signs of a suurahezhan.

Little had remained of the man who had bravely charged forward to stop the threat of the suurahezhan from reaching those he had vowed to protect—a bit of cloth, charred flesh, but by and large it had been little more than a blackened skeleton.

The body had been taken away for interment two days ago, but Nikandr still whispered a prayer of thanks to the soldier, and for a life of honor and peace in the world beyond for the service he'd given. The poor soul had been on his stomach when he'd died, his arms stretched outward as if he'd been trying to claw his way across the frozen ground while burning to death.

Nikandr took a long swig of elixir.

The wasting had been troubling him all morning, and now he was getting the shakes. These symptoms normally passed after he'd taken a few mouthfuls, but today the effects were lingering. After tucking the flask back into his coat he continued downslope. A light, fluffy snow began drifting down from the bright but sunless sky. He had found three more clusters of streltsi, all of them similarly burned. Again he whispered prayers before continuing.

Finally he came to the site of the crossing, an unremarkable clearing that lay at the base of a century-old landslide. Three streltsi, armed with tall muskets and berdische axes, stood guard by five stout ponies. When they saw Nikandr coming, they slapped their heels together and bowed their heads. Nikandr bowed back and continued on toward Udra.

She was kneeling at the edge of a massive black stain that marred the surface of the clearing. Her eyes were closed, and every so often she would set her palms to the snow-covered ground before her and bow. Running across Udra's path was a natural fault that still contained the charred remains of a large fire. The fault ran upward toward the palotza—a fact that seemed significant, though how, Nikandr couldn't guess.

It was strange how bent the suurahezhan had been on Stasa—strikingly similar to how the havahezhan had attacked Nikandr on the *Gorovna*. He knew it had something to do with the wasting—there could be no other explanation—but he didn't know just what the connection meant. Did the wasting attract the hezhan in some way? Did it anger them? Or was it perhaps that they were looking for a way back to Adhiya, the spirit world? Those with the wasting might provide some channel that allowed them to return to their natural place.

But if that was true—that there was some connection with the wasting—why had it chosen Stasa over Victania or Nikandr or one of the other nobles who had taken ill? Stasa was clearly in the final stages of the disease. Did that have some effect? Or perhaps his age had something to do with it; Stasa had lived a full life, and it was known that the hezhan thirsted for the experience of the real world.

The other dukes, of course, would have none of this talk. They believed it to be no more, no less, than assassination. The Maharraht were bent on their destruction. What better way to reach their goals than to throw the Grand Duchy into chaos during Council? Attempts had certainly been made before, and though the ancestors had been kind in that no duke had yet fallen to those attacks, others had—princes, boyars, posadni, polkovni, magistrates.

As the wind picked up, blowing the light snow into his face, he couldn't shake the feeling that Nasim had been involved. He was a curious child, with powers that in all likelihood even his guardian didn't understand. And the other night he had seemed innocent, albeit out of touch with reality. How could someone so unpredictable be such a crucial part of the Maharraht's plans? Yet in this lay another problem: the Aramahn were able to commune with spirits across the void of the aether. A century ago it wasn't all that uncommon to find those with the ability to guide them across the black and into the material world, but those days were long gone—as far as he knew, no Aramahn had been able to summon a spirit of any size for decades. The reduction in their abilities was felt to be part and parcel of the blight, the increase in storm activity, and the scarcity of fish and game. Had the Maharraht somehow uncovered some lost bit of knowledge? Had they now perfected it?

If so, it would seem that Mother would have sensed it. Father had questioned her mercilessly on this subject, and she claimed that she had sensed no summoning. Could she have been mistaken? Could her attention have been focused elsewhere? Mother was resolute, and the other Matri had apparently—grudgingly in some cases—agreed. Not that the Matri were always perfect. They weren't. There had been times when they had been fooled by particularly gifted qiram, but those times had been in those now-ancient days when the Landed women were first learning to touch the aether. They were so much more aware now that Nikandr doubted they could be fooled in any significant way.

Udra finally opened her eyes. She touched a finger to the soot and rubbed it between her fingers. She drew in a long, slow breath. Satisfied, she set her palms against the burnt earth and closed her eyes, the heavy wrinkles along her eyes and mouth deepening.

He stalked over the grass and stopped just short of Udra. "For the love of the ancients, have you found nothing new?"

She opened her eyes, still keeping her palms to the burnt earth. Then she stood deliberately and regarded Nikandr. "Is this not important?"

"It is."

"Then leave me to my work."

"I would know what you've found."

She stared at Nikandr as if she'd just sucked on a lime. He suspected it was because she had so far been unable to learn the nature of the crossing.

"The hezhan crossed, but no Aramahn drew it."

"Then it crossed through a crease."

"*Neh.*" She turned and regarded the burn. "There are indications that it was drawn."

"But you said no Aramahn was present."

She nodded. "That is what I said."

"I don't understand."

"Neither do I, and I never will if you don't leave me to my work."

"Nischka!"

Nikandr spun, ready to bite the head off the strelet who had spoken to him so, but he was surprised to find Ranos on his roan pony, beckoning him. A black rook on Ranos's shoulder, thrown off balance by his movement, flapped several times before settling.

The day of the attack, a rook had been sent to Iramanshah to treat with the mahtar. They claimed that Ashan and Nasim had both gone missing. Nasim had left the night before the attack, and Ashan had gone searching for him. Neither had been seen since. Mother asked for permission to search Iramanshah and the lands around it themselves, and the mahtar had eventually agreed. Ranos had gone himself and was just now returning.

Sparing a frown for Udra, Nikandr mounted his pony and rode to meet Ranos. Together, they headed through the trees back toward the palotza road.

"What news?" Nikandr asked. Just then a wave of nausea struck him so fiercely he was forced to lean forward in his saddle to keep himself from vomiting over himself and his pony. He breathed deeply, pushing himself into a normal riding position.

Ranos was clearly lost in thought, for he answered as if nothing had happened. "They allowed me to search the rooms Ashan was given for his stay. There was nothing useful. A few blankets. A small telescope. Everything else he took with him when he left to find Nasim. And what's worse, the mahtar refused our petition. If Ashan and Nasim are found, they claimed the right to take them into custody themselves until we present more evidence of their involvement."

The nausea began to pass, and Ranos's words began to sink in. It was not the best of news. A covenant had been drafted long ago, outlining the terms under which the Aramahn would lend their services to the Grand Duchy. Much of it related to the number of Aramahn that would be granted to each Duchy every month, their duties and compensation, which largely consisted of passage from island to island and a measure of the stones they used to bond with hezhan. It also detailed the strictures of how the Aramahn would be treated, especially with respect to those suspected of committing crimes under Grand Duchy law. Except in cases of a select few crimes, the Aramahn were to be given the option of trial by their own people, and they were to be allowed the right to decide punishment. The murder of the Grand Duke certainly qualified as serious, but there still needed to be some evidence tying the accused to the crime itself, and at this point they had practically no evidence whatsoever.

"Nasim is involved, Ranya. I'm sure of it."

"That may be so, but they will claim, rightly, that the Maharraht were behind the attack, and without something concrete, they will have rights to withhold their qiram from service to Khalakovo."

They came to the road where a dozen streltsi waited on ponies, ready to accompany Ranos toward Radiskoye. Every third man held a dousing rod instead of a musket. Six went on ahead, while the others fell to the rear.

"So what do we do?" Nikandr asked.

Ranos paused, the hooves of their ponies muffled by the thick blanket of snow over the road. "We find them before Iramanshah does."

Five sotni had been sent to search for them, but even with five hundred men, it was doubtful they would be found. Three days had already passed and they'd found nothing. It would help their chances greatly if Mother could spend her time searching, but she could not. It was too important to monitor the land directly around the palotza for immediate threats. If she went too far afield, she risked missing another attack entirely, and that was something Khalakovo could not afford. So it would be left to the soldiers, and even if they numbered in the thousands, it would still be difficult to locate someone who wished to remain hidden. The mountainous island positively brimmed with small, hidden valleys that would be difficult to navigate before the summer thaw. And besides, it was entirely possible that they'd left the island; by now they could be on Duzol, Grakhosk, Yfa, even Kravozhny.

Ranos cringed as the rook on his shoulder cawed raucously and flapped its wings.

"They have been found," the rook said.

"The Maharraht?" Ranos asked.

"The boy and his guardian, south of the lake."

Nikandr reflexively looked northward—as did Ranos—to the high ridge above them.

The rook craned its neck as the feathers along its head and neck crested. "Send men to Jahalan and have him search the lake immediately. A larger ship will follow." It cawed several more times as Mother left its body, surely to spread the word.

Ranos was looking at the men, probably deciding which he would send.

"I'll take them," Nikandr said before Ranos could order them to go alone. His heart was beating madly.

Ranos snapped his head toward Nikandr. "You cannot go, Nischka."

"I must."

"Leave this to the streltsi."

Nikandr bowed his head to the men. "I will, but I can help." He pulled his reins over, waiting for Ranos to give the word.

Ranos stared at him, clearly conflicted. He glanced up at the ridge, toward the lake, and then nodded to the four nearest men with muskets at the ready to follow him. "Be careful, Nischka."

"I will, brother."

The wind was bitterly cold near the peak, but there had been no time to find proper clothing. The skiff bucked with the currents, though Jahalan was doing his best to control them. The clouds had parted, and the snow had dropped to light flurries. They soared over the westward side of the mountain and saw the crystal reflection of the sun off the dark, deep lake nestled into a plateau about a third of the way down the shallow slope. They had made the circuit of the lake once, but so far they'd seen nothing.

Nikandr's stomach had been strangely silent since he'd left the palotza, but it was beginning to grumble once more. He didn't take his elixir out for fear that the streltsi would expect the traditional passing of the flask.

A forest of spruce and windwood and fir crowded most of the shoreline, but there was a wide meadow to the north, an area that led to a sheer cliff.

"Check near the meadow again," Nikandr said.

Jahalan began adjusting the wind, pulling at the ropes tied to the skiff's billowing sail.

They had just crossed the center of the lake when Nikandr felt something in his gut—a deepening of the wasting combined with an awareness that broadened well beyond the mundane senses. The wind was loud in his ears, but as time passed, he felt the currents about him, felt snowflakes drifting downward, felt the drifts shifting ever so slightly over the flat landscape of the frozen lake. He felt the wind as it funneled through the branches of the trees, over hills, into the dens of winter wolves.

It was similar to what he had felt with Nasim, but it was not so all encompassing as before. He guessed it was what a qiram must feel, as if his mind were now opened to the element of wind. It was unlike anything he'd experienced before. It was freeing, humbling, terrifying—all in the same breath.

"East, Jahalan," he said in a deep, steady tone. "Head east."

Jahalan glanced down at him from his struggle with the sail, but then complied. They followed the line of the cliff, which shallowed until eventually low and high ground met at a steeply falling slope. Folds of the mountain met there, and in spring a healthy stream would flow as the snow melted, but for now it created a natural pathway for anyone to trek downward from the heights of Verodnaya.

"There!" one of the streltsi shouted.

"Lower your voice," Nikandr said, scanning the ground where the strelet had pointed.

And there they were—a half-dozen men in heavy winter robes making their way down the streambed. Nasim walked between the men. He moved easily, as if he'd been born among the mountains. Ashan was behind him. It was easy to tell, for he wore no turban where the others did. His brown curly hair was blown by the strong wind.

"Ready muskets… Jahalan, move in directly behind them and drop us down slowly."

The streltsi trained their weapons over the edge of the skiff and pulled the hammers to full cock. Nikandr did the same with his own musket. He stared down the barrel, but found it difficult to concentrate. He had hoped his sense of the wind would weaken, for it made it nearly impossible to focus, but it was intensifying. Branches swayed. Snowflakes fell onto individual pine needles. Wind flowed through the folds of cloth in the Maharraht's robes. He even felt Jahalan's havahezhan manipulating the wind to control the direction of the skiff.

His mind was no longer wholly his own, and he wondered how he could sense such things. Even his mother could not see the bond to a qiram's hezhan or the hezhan itself; she was limited to sensing the magic the qiram employed as it was drawn through the aether.

The skiff was now less than a hundred yards away. The men were itching to fire, but Nikandr withheld the order. Muskets were inaccurate, and he wanted to get as close as he could.

The Maharraht at the rear of the line—the very same one Nikandr had winged with his shot from the *Gorovna*—turned and scanned the sky above.

"Fire," Nikandr said softly.

The Maharraht shouted in Mahndi.

Four muskets barked, the light from their pans flashing.

One of the Maharraht dropped. Ashan grabbed Nasim and ran for the nearby trees. Two Maharraht turned to face the skiff. They raised their hands, their eyes closed in a look of concentration. Wind began to howl around the ship, overwhelming Jahalan's attempts to prevent it.

Nikandr sighted along his musket, aiming at the closest of the Maharraht wind masters, but at the last moment he adjusted, aiming it at Ashan.

He squeezed the trigger. The musket bucked just before the skiff was thrown roughly downward, and he lost sight of his target in the confusion.

Jahalan struggled against the sudden attack. Their descent was arrested, but the skiff still struck the ground hard. Nikandr held tight to the gunwale and lost his musket in the harsh landing. One of the streltsi screamed. Another was thrown backward. He hit his head on the thwart behind him and lay at the bottom of the skiff, unmoving, blood streaming from a cut beneath his blond hair.

The snow flew upward around them, turning the world white. The sound of it was like a roaring waterfall. Jahalan, who was within arm's reach, lifted his hands and a great gust of wind shook the skiff and swirled the snow upward. He was trying to stave off the attack, but it wasn't working.

More snow piled up around them. Nikandr recovered his musket and tried to reload it, but the wind was so strong there was no way he could prime the pan—the wind blew the powder away before he could close the frizzen. One of the two streltsi still conscious had managed to reload his weapon, but he had nowhere to aim. They could see only snow. Impossibly thick snow. It was already up to the gunwales, and climbing higher.

Jahalan screamed in rage or pain or frustration.

"Come!" Nikandr shouted. "This way!"

Jahalan allowed himself to be led out of the skiff. The snow was up to their chests, and though it looked to be powdery and easy to navigate, it was not. They sunk deeper with each step, and it seemed to be compacting as the seconds wore on. Before they had gone further than a dozen paces movement became nearly impossible. Nikandr tried using his musket to lever himself forward, but this got him nowhere.

The others were no better off. The snow continued to pile, reaching their necks, then their mouths. Finally it was up to their ears and they were fighting just to climb their way out of the rapidly deepening drift.

Nikandr struggled his way higher, but the snow, already tight against his body, became tighter with the movement. The snow piled above his head, sending his fear to new heights. The bright light of the sky dimmed. Then, as the snow continued to pile higher, it darkened, until all around him was blackness and the only thing he could hear was the desperate sound of his own breathing.

CHAPTER 19

As the howling of the wind began to deaden, Nikandr felt his bond to the wind intensify—the gusts around him, the whorl of the snow from hundreds of yards in every direction, the touch that the two Maharraht and Jahalan had with their hezhan—and it was then that he recognized a bond to one other.

Himself.

A hezhan.

Bound to *him*.

Impossible. He was not Aramahn, to bond with a spirit. He had no stone of alabaster; he had performed no ritual.

Why then? Why had a hezhan bound itself to him?

His breathing had begun to weaken. His body was deathly cold. His heart beat softly.

He fought against the elements, fought for life, and though his body did not answer the call, the wind did.

It blew from the west, swooping in and scouring the landscape behind them. It gouged at the snow where it was thin, biting at rock and soil when the snow had been scraped away. It ate at the drift where Nikandr and the others were buried, ablating it like the rare, summer sun against the winter pack. Large chunks cracked and were blown away, and soon, he was free down to the shoulders.

A hail of stone and ice struck him from behind. He willed the wind to stop, and just like that, it was gone. One last gust, and then silence reigned once more.

He was chilled to the bone. He ached like he had never ached before. He was also still encased in the snow, his arms barely able to move. More alarming than these sensations, however, was the fact that he could no longer sense the hezhan. It was gone, and rather than provide any sort of comfort, it felt as if a limb had gone missing, as if the hezhan had always been a part of him, and now that he'd been awakened to it, a deep yearning was all that remained.

Footsteps crunched across the snow. Nasim was walking toward him, alone. Ashan was nowhere to be seen. Nikandr's shot must have struck true, though he hoped that it had only wounded him.

Nasim dropped to his knees and stared into Nikandr's eyes.

He was crying.

The sun, casting dark shadows over much of his face, made the tears falling down his cheeks glint like stars.

"Why do you cry?" Nikandr asked.

He didn't answer—Nikandr wasn't even sure the boy had understood the question—but he began digging Nikandr out of the snow with his bare hands.

Finally, Nikandr was able to crawl out of his prison. Jahalan was out as well, and he moved to help the streltsi, but Nikandr kneeled before Nasim, who looked miserable. He was hugging himself, refusing to look Nikandr in the eye.

"Nasim, they're gone. All is well."

Nasim began shaking his head slowly, but then with more speed, until it seemed he was possessed. Nikandr pulled him into an embrace, holding his head so he wouldn't shake it so. "Nasim, it's all right."

"There are so many," Nasim said. "So many."

"So many what?" Nikandr asked.

Nasim gazed over the snow-swept landscape, his eyes watering, a look of inexpressible fear on his face. "I can't stop it." His expression turned to one of discomfort, and then outright pain. He gripped himself tighter, and then he groaned and doubled over in pain.

"Nasim?" Nikandr caught him as he fell. He turned him around, but Nasim was unconscious.

The caw of a rook caught Nikandr's attention. He looked up and saw one of the palotza's birds winging over the landscape. Beyond, cresting the high ridge behind the lake, was a windship.

Jahalan crunched over the snow, looking down at Nasim with an unreadable expression. "There is something altogether disconcerting about that boy, son of Iaros."

Nikandr looked down. Nasim's face, even while sleeping, was troubled. "Of that, Jahalan, there can be no doubt."

The gaoler opened the door, stepping back and bowing as Nikandr entered the room. Ashan lay on a lush bed set against the far wall.

They had found him beyond the tree line in a gully, unconscious and bleeding from a leg wound. The Maharraht were nowhere to be found, not that they had searched overly long for them. The search would resume in the morning. The important thing was that they had Nasim and Ashan.

"Leave us," Nikandr said, holding his hand out for the gaoler's iron ring of keys.

The gaoler handed them over and left, closing the door behind him.

Nikandr moved a chair over to Ashan's bedside. It creaked when he sat down, and Ashan woke with a jerk.

He stared at Nikandr, a look of fear and confusion on his face, but as he took in his surroundings, his expression calmed. "A rather elegant room for a prisoner, is it not?"

The chair groaned as Nikandr relaxed against the chair back. "There have been a number of occasions when aristocracy were… accommodated in these rooms."

"As prisoners."

"As *very* welcome guests."

Gritting his teeth, Ashan pulled himself up in the bed, resting against the headboard. "It would not do to give them a hovel in which to stay, now would it?"

"It most certainly would not. Now why don't you tell me how you came to be with the Maharraht on the far side of the mountain."

Ashan nodded with a small smile, as if he were about to tell an old friend a long and complicated tale. "Nasim," he began. "He acted strangely after meeting you on the eyrie. He seemed out of sorts. Troubled. He even mumbled your name several times. Names are difficult for him to relate to, and so he hardly ever repeats them, even mine.

"It lasted until that night when we reached Iramanshah. He went to sleep next to me, and when I woke, he was missing. He has done so before, though I usually found him nearby. This time he was simply gone. I spent the following days tracking him through the forests around Verodnaya, coming close but never quite finding him. It was only hours ago—" He glanced around the room. "It was only hours wasn't it?"

Nikandr nodded. "Why didn't you seek help from Iramanshah?"

"I thought he would be close. And by the time I found his trail, it seemed foolish to leave it and return for help. I did eventually find him, but unfortunately Soroush had found him first, so I allowed myself to be taken rather than let Nasim go alone."

"As simple as that?"

Ashan nodded—not innocently, but as a matter of fact—and Nikandr found himself *wanting* to believe him even though there was another, altogether real possibility.

"You are wondering, perhaps, whether I'm in league with Soroush."

"Of course I am."

"It is a difficult position to be in."

"Me or you?"

Ashan smiled, showing his crooked, yellow teeth. "Both. I wonder, son of Iaros, if you might humor me with a question or two. It may help you in your decision on whether or not to believe me."

Nikandr waved his hand, bidding Ashan to continue.

"I wonder if you know what happened when you and Nasim met on the eyrie. A bond was created, was it not?"

Seeing no reason to deny it, Nikandr nodded.

"Will you share with me your suspicions as to how it was formed?"

Nikandr paused. There were two possibilities, and one he was not ready to discuss with Ashan. He had discussed his cracked soulstone with several, Jahalan and Udra included, but so far they had come to no real conclusions, so he pulled it out from beneath his shirt and showed it to Ashan, hoping if nothing else Ashan might be able to find the answer to this riddle. He told Ashan of the attack, of the havahezhan and the way it had honed in on him. "The moment my soulstone cracked, it was gone."

"May I see it?"

Nikandr slipped the chain over his neck and handed it over.

"In the past"—Ashan examined the stone closely, running his thumb over its surface—"Nasim has become interested in certain people, certain places, though it has never been for long. I wonder if his connection to you is stronger, more permanent."

He looked up, his eyes piercing, as he handed the soulstone back. "Nasim was raised by the Maharraht, primarily by a man named Soroush. You saw him on the mountain, the one with the scarred ear. He and his followers had great difficulty communicating with Nasim. They tried for years, and may have gained some small insights into his nature, but not his mind. They could no more relate to him than they could a dog or a horse. But they understood that in Nasim lay a treasure the likes of which this world has not seen in centuries."

"What do you mean?"

"I believe that Nasim walks between worlds. He touches Adhiya and Erahm, both, but because he was raised with no knowledge of this, he cannot tell the two apart. It is beyond confusing for him. It tears at his soul. He doesn't understand the nature of this world, though he wants more than anything to do so. When the two of you met on the eyrie, he found something in you—perhaps your stone, perhaps your very soul—but it grounded him. It gave him a way to tell the two worlds apart, and in turn gave him some small amount of solace."

"Nasim came to the site of the havahezhan's crossing two nights before the attack." Nikandr told him of how they had met after Atiana returned to the palotza, of the pain and euphoria he had felt. "Jahalan said something similar. He said that I was sharing what Nasim was feeling."

Ashan nodded. "Jahalan has long been a wise man."

"When I first saw him on the eyrie," Nikandr continued, remembering the city with the tall towers, "I saw a vision of a city, an empty, abandoned place. And then on the cliff it happened again. I was walking among the streets with a man named Muqallad. We came to a tower, where a woman waited for us."

Ashan blinked and his head jerked back. "What name did you say?"

"Muqallad, and I was sure, in that moment just before I came to my senses, that they had somehow betrayed me."

Nikandr waited for him to reply, but Ashan only stared.

"Do you know them?"

Ashan shook his head. "Muqallad is a name that holds great weight among the Aramahn." He turned to Nikandr soberly. "He lived on an island named Ghayavand, an island lost, taken by the winds of Adhiya."

"Taken how?"

"The arqesh became too bold. They pushed too hard, played with arts that were better left alone for the end of days." Ashan frowned. "But it cannot be him."

"Nasim couldn't have met him?"

"Muqallad died three hundred years ago, along with the island itself."

Nikandr moved on, hoping to keep Ashan in a talkative mood. "How could you have heard of Nasim if he were so important to the Maharraht?"

"They were careful, but something so powerful and mysterious as Nasim cannot be hidden forever. Word of him came to me, and I thought it something worth investigating."

"So you simply made your way to their doorstep and begged permission to see him?"

Ashan's smile was pleasant, but grating all the same. "Nothing so simple as that. It was a delicate negotiation, to be sure, but eventually they allowed me near him."

"Why?"

"If you're wondering if I agreed to aid them in their cause"—Ashan shifted in the bed, wincing from the pain—"I did not."

"Then why would they have allowed you near him?"

"My refusal to aid them does not mean that they could not benefit from my presence."

"Then you were helping them."

"I was helping Nasim."

"Who is a tool of the Maharraht."

Ashan's face grew cross for the first time. "He is a child who is lost. A child who needed my help. I answered that call, and I would do so again."

"No matter what might happen to the Grand Duchy."

Ashan stopped, his eyes serious. "I care for the lives of the Grand Duchy, son of Iaros. Have no fear of that."

"As you care for the lives of the Maharraht?"

"As I care for all in this world."

"If that were so, you wouldn't have forged a weapon for them to use against us."

"*Nyet*? You would rather I had left Nasim where I'd found him? Let them find what they may?"

Nikandr's nostrils flared. "This sits not well with me."

"That is because I am no tool of Khalakovo."

"It is because you seem to be a tool of the Maharraht, willingly or not."

Ashan shook his head calmly. "Both mean little, son of Iaros." He placed both hands over his heart. "What matters is what lies within, what we give to the next life, not that which comes and goes in the blink of an eye."

Nikandr's gut began to churn, the feelings of nausea from earlier returning. "Did Nasim summon the hezhan?" he asked, more hastily than he'd meant to.

"Nasim is no qiram. He has no ability to bond with spirits."

"Did he summon the hezhan?"

"It would have been impossible. Nasim can affect the ability of qiram to lure and bond with a hezhan—he may even make crossings more likely by his mere presence—but he cannot summon them himself."

"How can you be so sure?"

"How do I know the sun will rise tomorrow? I simply know."

Ashan's voice was calm, which was all the more infuriating. But there was no doubting that he seemed sincere.

"Where was Soroush taking him?"

"They did not consult with me, son of Iaros."

"Do not jest, *son of Ahrumea*. They are murderers."

"They do not kill indiscriminately."

Nikandr laughed. "Tell that to those who lie in their graves from their discriminating tastes."

"No matter what you may think, they treasure life. They believe the world has been set off course. They are merely trying to correct it."

"If I didn't know better, I'd say you wished you could join them."

Ashan appeared saddened by these words. "I neither hope for their success nor wish for their defeat."

The feelings of nausea in Nikandr's stomach advanced. He swallowed several times without meaning to.

Ashan seemed to notice, for his expression turned to one of confusion, of concern.

Nikandr stood, knocking his chair back in his haste. "Did Nasim summon the hezhan?"

"I told you he could not have."

"We could hang you, Ashan—you and Nasim both."

Ashan seemed unfazed. "Of that I have no doubt."

His stomach was growing worse. "You would do well to consider your answers more carefully the next time we meet."

He left, locking the door with the gaoler's keys, and rushed up the hall. Then he bent over and vomited, the contents of his stomach pattering against the stone. He heaved again and again—more and more sour liquid coming up. He knew Ashan could hear him, and the knowledge burned, but what was worse was the fear that was starting to well up inside him. The symptoms were growing stronger. Soon, everyone would know; it would be plain as day. And then, the long march toward death would be all that lay before him.

He stood, clearing his mouth of spittle.

Nasim's door lay just ahead. He moved to it, listening for any signs of movement within. For no reason apparent to him, he was afraid.

Softly, he placed the key into the lock and turned it. It opened with a soft click. He found Nasim kneeling in the center of the room, holding his gut and rocking back and forth, a look of profound misery on his face.

Nikandr stepped inside. "Nasim?"

The boy didn't respond.

"Nasim, can you hear me?"

Nothing.

Nikandr crouched down, hoping the boy would acknowledge him in some way. But Nasim only rocked, his breath coming in short gasps through flared nostrils.

"Nasim, please, speak to me."

Father was going to demand answers, and soon. The life of the Grand Duke had been taken. The lives of everyone on the island—the gathered aristocracy included—were threatened, and they would all be looking toward these two to provide answers.

But Nasim appeared unready to grant this request, so Nikandr eventually left.

CHAPTER 20

Rehada often took walks around Volgorod. She told herself it was to steep herself in the ebbs and flows of the city, and that was true, but she knew deep in her heart that it was also because she was lonely. She catered to the richest of the Landed, pleasing them in the ways of the flesh, but none of them other than Nikandr had ever given her pause. She was shunned in Iramanshah for her refusal to cross the fires, to forgive those who had taken the life of her daughter, Ahya. Soroush, Ahya's father, had told her many times to do so. What was one more lie in the stack you've created, he used to ask. There were many things she would do to make her life among the Landed appear innocent, but forgiving the murderous souls who'd taken Ahya from her wasn't one of them. She would never forgive them. Never.

So she lived half a life—always on the periphery of Royalty, of the Aramahn, of the people of Volgorod. She traveled not only through the city, but all around the island and the others in the archipelago. She attended festivals, celebrations, even funerals, where the Landed would bury their dead in the ground instead of setting them onto skiffs and letting the wind take them where it would.

She approached the line where peasants stood in line for their dole. Today it was four blocks long, people waiting with barrows or straps to take home the grain they would be allotted. There were many of them—more than normal, it seemed—and they looked haggard, gray, as if they were slowly but surely becoming part of the stone of the city around them.

"Rehada," a woman called, beckoning Rehada closer.

Her name was Gierten, and she was a woman Rehada had met several times at the summer festival in Izhny. She was holding the reins of a sickly donkey saddled with two baskets—one empty, the other with a nest of faded brown blankets.

She approached, trying to appear pleasant. Gierten had been heavy with child the last time she'd seen her nearly a year ago. Rehada had no real desire to see the child, nor talk to Gierten, but impressions must be maintained.

"How old now?" Rehada asked as she approached the basket.

"Praise to the ancients, she nears her ninth month, and she is healthy as can be."

Rehada pulled the blanket back to reveal the red face of a babe. Gierten was thin, with a wiry strength to her, but this baby was round in the cheeks with strong color to her skin. She looked nothing at all like Ahya, but still it drove a knife through Rehada's chest merely to look upon this child, this *Landed* child, while hers was gone, ripped from her when she had only begun to blossom.

"She is hale, indeed," Rehada said to prevent herself from crying. She looked along the line, to those that seemed like it was a struggle just to remain standing. "I wonder, then, why you've come here."

"We need grain as much as the next family."

"Last year your husband's nets were full."

Gierten shook her head. "The fish have all gone. Even two months ago we could find enough to live on if not sell at market, but now we can't even do that." She smiled as she reached down and pulled the blanket over to protect her child from the breeze. "And my Evina needs all the food she can get."

It was then that Rehada noticed something from the corner of her eye. Beyond the line, nestled between several tall stone buildings, was a patch of snow-covered ground with three white fir trees standing over it. On the far side, near the mouth of an alley that led up toward the Boyar's mansion, stood a man. He was in the shade of the trees—with the clouds in the sky and his dark clothes it was difficult at first to pick him out. It was Soroush, still wearing his double robes, his ragged turban, daring anyone to notice him and call attention to it.

She pulled her eyes back to Gierten, for she couldn't let on what she'd seen, but as they continued to talk—Gierten regaling her with all manner of meaningless stories about the baby's first months of life—Rehada caught several more glimpses of Soroush. Clearly he had been following her, or had been waiting, knowing somehow she would walk this way.

She bid Gierten *dasvidaniya* and began heading along the line, hoping to cut across and speak with Soroush, but when she looked for him again, he wasn't there. She rushed across the street to the trees, looking up along the alley, but she did not find him.

She shivered, and not from the wind tugging at her robes. For some reason she felt more alone than she ever had since coming to Khalakovo.

Rehada woke to a soft knock at the rear of her home. She stood, wiped the crust of dried tears from her cheeks, and pulled her robe over her naked form. Another knock came—more insistent—as she took a small lamp from the mantel and limped along the creaking hallway to the rear of the house.

A third knock came as she opened it.

Standing there was Soroush, lit in golden relief by the light of her lamp. She had known he would eventually come, but she still felt watched from the scene in the city earlier that day.

She bowed her head, stepping aside to allow him entrance. It was not lost on her the parallel this made to Nikandr's visit only three days before, the only difference being that Nikandr had used the front door while one of her own was forced to use the rear. She was ashamed, though she had to admit she wasn't sure whether it stemmed from the fact that Nikandr had become so familiar with her or that Soroush, even after all they'd been through, still was.

Doing her best to disguise the pain she felt in her feet and shins as she walked, she led him into her sitting room and offered him vodka. He turned his nose up at that, clearly expecting araq or the sour citrus wines from the south of Yrstanla.

"It has fallen out of favor."

"Even in Iramanshah?" His voice was deep and smooth, like the voice of a mountain. It was something she'd been so long without she'd forgotten how reassuring it could be.

"In case you've forgotten, the picture I'm painting is not of a woman in Iramanshah."

He smiled. "You could still have a bottle hidden beneath the floorboards."

She returned his smile and poured him a drink of the vodka anyway. "Perhaps I no longer prefer it."

He accepted the glass, firelight flickering off of the golden earrings in what remained of his left ear. "Then I would know you had finally turned."

He sat within the mound of pillows, his face haggard, his eyes heavy, as if he hadn't slept in weeks. As she sat across from him, she tried to hide the pain in her feet and ankles.

Soroush glanced down, then toward the fire, and finally he met her eye. "I would have guessed you would give that up long before the araq."

She took a sip from her vodka, hoping he would take the hint and leave the subject alone. The fire crackled as the sting of the liquor crept down her throat to lie heavy, deep within her gut. She couldn't bring herself to move closer to him, though she admitted there was still a part of her that wanted to. Despite his scars—or perhaps because of them—he was a deeply attractive man. But to think of Soroush she had no choice but to think of the pain that had been laid at their feet by the bloody hands of the Landed.

"Do you have a place in the city?"

"That isn't something you should know."

She knew the reasons for this, but it still hurt to be treated like a risk that he was forced to weigh. "Then why have you come?"

"It has been too long, Rehada. It is time for us to sit. To take drink with one another."

She shook her head. "I am no girl just taking to the winds, Soroush. You have come for a reason."

His dark eyes shone in the firelight. "Tell me first what you've heard."

"Of the hezhan?"

He nodded.

"It crossed the wall of the palotza and murdered the Grand Duke. Dozens died with many more wounded. Bolgravya's grand ship was lost."

Soroush stared at his drink with a look of regret on his face. He took a healthy swallow and closed his eyes, perhaps wishing the dead a better life on their return to Erahm. "Your Prince?"

"Safe as far as I know."

"That is good. We may have need of him before this is done."

"In what way?"

"Who can tell?"

Rehada shook her head. "Fine, keep your secrets."

"Bersuq has been having trouble with the third stone."

She laughed. "I've given you your stone."

"You have." He shook his head, ignoring her jibe. "We thought we had mastered the way to sense the weakest points in the rift. You saw the effects yourself."

"I did, but I may have had help."

"What do you mean?"

"I don't think I would have succeeded in summoning the hezhan were it not for a presence I felt at the end. I was lost utterly, and the presence cleared my mind, allowed me to focus against the pain. When I woke there was a form in the woods. It must have been Nasim."

His head tilted incrementally. "Why didn't you tell us?"

"It was not until hours later that I was thinking clearly. Memories were streaming from my mind, and it was all I could do to sort them from reality. I thought on it for a long while afterward, and I think it was him. I think he was watching the whole time."

He downed the last of his vodka in one gulp. His face soured as he stared at the glass, then he set it aside and gazed into the fire. He looked like the Soroush of old, then. Peaceful. Contemplative. He had been a man on a path toward greatness before Ahya had been killed.

"Did you know he is in the palotza, taken by your Prince?"

She was surprised at how strongly her heart beat at even this small bit of news of Nikandr, but the alcohol was already helping to mask her emotions.

When she remained silent, he continued. "Don't worry. Nasim will keep well enough in the palotza. What's important are the stones. Bersuq has tried several times to summon the vanahezhan. But the way has proven blocked."

"We have time."

"*Neh*. There is no time left."

"You have always preached patience."

"I have, but where has patience gotten us these last dozen years?"

"We have done much," Rehada said, insulted.

"What have we done? Stolen a handful of ships, destroyed a few more, and all the while the Landed have pushed us from two more islands in the north and further cemented their hold on one of the others *despite* the blight."

"They cannot hold forever."

"And neither can we. You have been gone a long time, Rehada, and I've hidden much of the truth from you, so you have no idea how thin our ranks have become, but believe me when I tell you that the situation is dire. We have so little food that some are taking to the winds simply to feed themselves, and who can blame them? More of our qiram have been scarred by the Aramahn, leaving our ability to attack the Landed tenuous at best. We are in much more danger of driving ourselves off the edge of our islands than the Landed will ever be."

"We will recover, as we always have."

He waved his hand as if she were a girl offering him dates. "There comes a time when one must act and trust to the will of the world."

"The will of the world may be against the Maharraht." Rehada surprised herself by voicing those words, but Soroush's response was even more surprising.

He shrugged and avoided her gaze, not with any sense of discomfort, but with contemplation. "If it is so, then it is so. I am willing to give myself to the will of indaraqiram, but I will have its answer now, before there are none of us left to hear its words."

Rehada considered this thought, finishing her drink while doing so. They were strong words. Had they come from any other man, she might have found herself repulsed, for such had been her upbringing, but Soroush's ways had always been an intoxicant for her. She had found herself attracted to him from the first day they'd met.

"What can I do?" she asked.

Soroush stood and held his hand out to her. "We'll have those words soon. For now I would simply hold you, as we once did."

She paused and found herself thinking of Nikandr, and what *he* would think of this. It wasn't fear of discovery, she realized—her life would be forfeit were Nikandr or any of the Landed to discover the truth—it was fear of how it might hurt him. She had never wanted to fall in love with Nikandr. Their first meeting had been a random one, and she had taken it for a blessing of the fates. In their four years together, she had always felt in control until these last few months—the point at which, she realized with growing horror, Atiana had come into the picture.

"There is *fear* in your eyes," Soroush said, still holding out his hand.

She took a deep breath. "Not fear, my love." She stepped forward and fell into his embrace. "Uncertainty."

She warmed herself and in so doing warmed him.

"Treat me not like a man from the Hill bearing coin." He pulled the circlet roughly from her brow. A chill fell over her as if she had plunged into the waters of the sea.

She hid her eyes from him. It was an insult, what he'd just done, but the look on his face made her feel like *she* was the one at fault. "I am sorry. I did not mean—"

He pulled her chin up until she was gazing into his deep brown eyes. He leaned down and kissed her. His beard tickled her neck, but his lips were warm, and she could feel him rising as she held him longer and their breath fell into time.

Without another word, they pulled their clothes from their bodies. She saw upon his shoulder a fresh wound—stitched—a puncture from a gunshot, perhaps. When she moved to examine it, he grabbed her hand and stared down into her eyes fiercely, as if acknowledging the wound were an insult. He had always been this way—proud, too proud at times—and she knew better than to challenge him.

She pulled him down among the pillows, kissing him to make him forget. As the night deepened, as their bodies became one, for the first time in a long while she no longer thought of the Prince of Khalakovo holding her.

She woke with Soroush watching her. They were in her bedroom, and he was propped up on one elbow, watching her as the faint light of dawn shone through the small window on the far side of the room.

He was holding in one hand a stone of red jasper. When she had propped herself like he was, he slid it toward her. "Take this to the woman you were speaking with today."

Rehada picked it up and examined it. It seemed unremarkable. "Why?"

"It will accelerate the wasting. Bersuq believes that when someone of stone dies, he will be able to summon his vanahezhan."

"Gierten doesn't have the wasting."

He shook his head, slowly but seriously. "*Neh*, but the babe does."

"How can you know?"

"I know."

Rehada felt the blood drain from her face. The babe. Gierten's nine-month-old daughter.

"The Matra will take notice."

He nodded, a sober gesture. "We hope that it is so."

"But why?"

"Because it is nearly time."

She pressed him for more, but that was all he would say on the subject. He pulled himself from the bed and began to dress. He stopped as he picked up his turban cloth. "Do you find this distasteful?"

The babe has done nothing to us, she thought. The words were on her tongue, ready to speak, when Soroush cut her off.

"The fates play strange games, do they not?" He began wrapping the cloth around his head. "The babe had two cards played against her. She is of earth, and she was born to the Landed. That is enough." He finished with his robes and stared down at her while cinching them around his waist.

She returned his gaze, emotions warring within her. She had resolved herself that doing what she did on this island might lead to deaths, even those of children. She might even be called to take up the knife herself. But to inflict something upon a babe when her Ahya had suffered the very same fate. It didn't seem right.

But Soroush's smoldering expression of anger reminded her of how strong she needed to be. He was an undying flame, a ceaseless wind. If he could do all that he did, even after losing his ability to commune with hezhan, then she could give up one child.

"What must be done?"

"Place the jasper near the babe. The stone will do the rest."

She stared at the jasper, an unremarkable stone the color of salmon flesh. Such a dangerous game they were playing. It felt like they were stepping in the paths of the fates, and it rested uneasy in Rehada's gut. But perhaps that was what needed to be done, as the fates had so far seemed unwilling to aid their cause.

"It will be done," she said shortly.

He nodded once, and then was gone.

Rehada approached the house, her heart thumping madly.

Gierten was sitting on the front porch in a chair, her hands working quickly to repair the fishing net that lay across her lap. A basket was nearby, the same one that had been hanging from the donkey two days before.

Gierten looked up, her thin face staring at Rehada with a mixture of confusion and charity. "Rehada, welcome. What brings you?"

Rehada shook her head. "I was on my way to Izhny, and I thought I'd stop by to offer you a present for your daughter."

Gierten waited, her hands pausing in their work, as Rehada stepped onto the porch.

Rehada could see the babe from the corner of her eye, but she couldn't find it in herself to look at her just yet. Instead she held out a string with a piece of coral in the shape of a windwood tree. She had made it for Ahya, and though parting with it was like chopping off a finger, she would give Gierten's babe something to guide her in her next life. "We give them to our children for luck. I have no need for it anymore, so I hope you'll accept it for Evina."

Gierten didn't move, and she looked like a woman who was about to make excuses for a gift that made no sense to her, but Rehada talked over her before she could protest.

"You would be doing me a favor. It brings only bad memories. It would please me to know that it was doing some good in the world instead of dredging up the past."

Gierten paused for a moment, and then she smiled. She accepted the gift, nodding once. "It would be an honor. Thank you."

Before she lost heart, Rehada kneeled before the babe, palming the stone of jasper in one hand. "Do you mind if I held her?"

She plunged her hands into the basket and picked Evina up without waiting for permission, leaving the stone among the folds of the padding blanket at the bottom as she did so.

She held the baby, staring into her eyes, fighting off the tears that were threatening to surface. She knew she should be rocking the babe, should be bouncing her on her hip and telling Gierten what a wonderful child she had, but she could not. She could not go so far as that when she had just condemned this child to die with the simple act she'd just performed.

She laid the baby back down as quickly as she'd picked her up, to the confused looks of Gierten. Then she made her excuses and left, unable to stare Gierten in the eye any longer.

It had been so simple. Soroush dealt with death often; perhaps it came easily to him. But it was shocking just how much this simple act shook Rehada. By the time she had reached the path leading back to the road between Izhny and Volgorod, she was running, her tears flowing freely.

CHAPTER 21

Atiana stood before the tall windows in Radiskoye's solarium, staring at the maelstrom raging outside. Cold rain fell down along the thick glass in heavy sheets. Lightning flashed. In the ghostly image that quickly faded she could see the blinding brilliance of a dhoshahezhan. They often slipped into the world for split seconds during lightning strikes, but it seemed to her that there were many more than one would normally see. The unseasonable storm had settled over the islands two nights ago and hadn't budged since. It had brought life on the island, especially the palotza, to a standstill. Father and several of the other dukes thought it strange timing after the suurahezhan, but Khalakovo's Matra claimed it was benign, a coincidence.

"As likely a coincidence as Stasa's death," Father had said. But their own wind master, Kaeed, doubted Saphia was lying. Father's reply had been to send Kaeed away and to recount all the ways he'd been wrong over the years.

Each of the families had been given their own wing of the palotza, but the solarium had become a council chamber of sorts for those dukes that stood behind Zhabyn and Grigory in this slowly building crisis. Borund and Grigory were sitting on a curving couch, listening to Duke Leonid boast about his son's exploits over the southern seas.

She returned her attention to the skies, drawn to the lightning and the ghostly images, losing herself as the chill from the windows settled over her skin.

"You'll catch your death." Borund came to a halt next to her. In one hand he held a snifter filled with a healthy amount of rosemary vodka, which he handed to her before wrapping an arm around her shoulders. He was warm, and it felt good to be held.

She took a sip, feeling the pleasant burn trail down her throat. "Then you'll just have to protect me," she said, handing the snifter back.

"Don't I always?" Borund replied.

Atiana smiled and tipped her head until it rested on his shoulder. "Soon you won't have to."

Borund went silent and deathly still.

"He *will* be my husband, Borund."

"Things are not so clear as they were a week ago."

"How surprising you've sided with Father."

"This Council smells foul, Tiana. I know you sense it too."

Atiana pulled away and faced him. He wore a brown kaftan, and his beard had grown longer, giving him the look of a scowling bear.

"Why are men so distrustful?"

"Because there's always trouble about, especially when you're not looking for it."

Atiana reached up and smoothed the cloth of his kaftan. "Don't think it isn't appreciated, but really, I think there's little enough to worry about."

"There you're wrong, sister. Trouble has come, and it's already started to simmer. Father has ordered two more ships sent to Khalakovo."

Atiana's brow creased. "What of Leonid and Bolgravya?"

"Them as well."

"Why?"

"To prevent Khalakovo from dictating terms."

"They've done nothing of the sort."

"Tiana, just because a dog has never bitten you is no reason to believe it won't someday do so. It's why you put them on a leash and whip them when they misbehave."

"This is madness. Everything will be resolved shortly."

"If that is so, then the ships will be sent home. No harm done."

"Perhaps no harm, but certainly insult. Saphia will learn of it."

Borund shrugged. "The offense to Khalakovo is a risk we're willing to take."

"We are *guests* here."

Borund snorted and downed the rest of the vodka in one gulp. "Guests… Have you not been here these last five days? We have heard nothing from the Khalakovos since Stasa's death. Nothing. Ranos has come twice, and he did little more than prattle about inquiries. Nikandr came once to ask me to hunt with him. To hunt! As if we were still boys hoping to while away our time far from the foolishness of Council. And Iaros, that coward, has hidden himself away ever since that farce of a speech by the Matra. Nothing will come of their inquiries. They will attempt to blow this over as if it had never happened, and then—mark my words—they will attempt to install Iaros as Grand Duke, and they'll expect us to smile as he takes his seat."

Borund's face had filled with color as he talked until he was positively red. She had had no idea he was so angry over the matter. He had, for the last several years, become progressively more absent from Galostina as he shouldered more of the shipping contracts to Yrstanla. Their time together had become by necessity more brief and perfunctory. Here, with the death of the Grand Duke so fresh in everyone's minds and tempers starting to rise, she realized how similar to their father he had become.

As she worked this through in her mind, another realization struck her full in the face: she had become protective of *Nikandr*, even against Borund. She had come to Khalakovo dutifully, ready to fulfill the needs of her family. She hadn't expected to feel more for Nikandr than that. Yet the way he had tried to best her at the dance those many nights ago—he had been obstinate about it, true, but she also felt like he had been doing it to win her over, like he had truly wanted to show everyone in the room that he would win her affection. Perhaps she was fooling herself, but she felt in her heart she was right.

Aunt Katerina waved Atiana over. "Come, niece. I grow tired of winning."

Katerina and Ishkyna were sitting at a large ebony table pitting their skills at trump against those of Mileva and Grigory's young cousin, Ivan. Katerina wore a fine black dress and her dark hair was tucked under a beaded cap. Her traditional raiment contrasted sharply with Atiana and her sisters, who wore embroidered dresses of emerald green, their hair high and powdered with lazy ringlets falling near their ears. Ivan, a boy of only fifteen, looked like a peasant among queens, but he didn't seem to mind—or notice for that matter—for he could be caught staring doe-eyed at Mileva as often as he did his cards.

Atiana's stomach was turning too much for her to sit still for any amount of time, but before she could decline, the doors of the solarium opened, and in strode Father, bootsteps echoing, looking as cross as he ever had.

Without saying another word, Borund moved to meet him. Katerina stood as well, her dress sighing as it slid over the parquet floor. "What news?" she asked.

Father glanced at Atiana and then pulled Borund and Katerina away to speak with Grigory and Leonid.

A shiver traveled along Atiana's frame. Father had been treating her as if she'd already married Nikandr, as if Ishkyna's prediction of shifting allegiances had already come true. She moved casually to the card table and took the vacant chair, doing her best to feign indifference.

"Don't mind him," Ishkyna said while dealing the cards with practiced ease. "He only fears you'll let something slip should you ever be allowed to meet Nikandr again."

Atiana sorted her hand, unwilling to admit that Father had gotten to her over the last few days. "I bid three."

Ivan, having paid much more attention to the three sisters than he did his own hand, quickly ordered his cards. "Four," he said, more of a question than a statement.

Ishkyna glanced at Ivan and rolled her eyes. She leaned in toward the table. "It's just us, Tiana. You don't have to hide the fact that you're enamored of him. I bid six."

"Ah, but she does, Shkyna," Mileva said. "What would good Bolgravya think if she were to show any outward sign of affection toward Khalakovo? Seven."

Ivan's face went bright red. Had he been older—or had hotter blood run through his veins—he would have stood from the table and left, but he was clearly enamored of the sisters, Mileva in particular.

Atiana set down her cards, allowing Mileva to capture the blind. "Show some respect." She squeezed Ivan's wrist tenderly. "He has lost much this week."

"Ivan knows how much respect I have for him and his family. It was a warning for *you*, sister." Mileva finished selecting her final hand and they began playing, the sisters moving quickly, practically without thought, Ivan choosing his cards carefully, often looking to Mileva for approval as if she could somehow see his cards before he played them.

"And why would I need a warning, Leva?"

"Because," Ishkyna answered for her, "it's clear to everyone you're chafing at the bit to gallop for Khalakovo when you *should* be headed home."

Atiana slapped her highest trump onto the table and swept in the trick. "I had a notion that this *was* my home now."

Mileva took the next. "The longer we stay, sister, the likelier it will be that your wedding bed will forever stay cold."

Atiana wanted to scoff, but there was a ring of truth to those words. She had thought the matter would be settled within a day, but then came rumor that the Khalakovos had found a Landless qiram and were questioning him deep beneath the palotza. They neither confirmed nor denied the rumor, but Leonid had men asking about Volgorod for news, and they said that some of the Landless had come to the palotza, treating with Iaros to have their kinsman back.

"Perhaps if you spoke with young Khalakovo, away from prying ears."

Atiana did not look at Ivan. She knew that this was as much for his ears as it was for hers. "And just how would I do that?" she asked, providing the requisite nibble on the bait.

Mileva shrugged. "There are hidden hallways in Radiskoye, are there not, as there are in Galostina? I would even wager that Zvayodensk has a tunnel or two hidden away from curious eyes."

Ivan blushed again, playing a pitiful, off-suited card.

"Perhaps," Ishkyna said, playing a high trump, "but who will be left to tread them?"

As Mileva played her final card, winning the trick and the hand, Ivan's face changed. Instead of a deep red, his face went white. After staring at the table for a time, meeting no one's eyes, he stood, bowed, and without a single word strode away.

"Really, Shkyna," Atiana said. "The boy has just lost a dozen in his family, and dozens more countrymen."

"And we lost two cousins and a ship only a month ago. That is life among the islands. The sooner Ivan learns that, the better off he'll be."

Atiana raked in the cards and tumbled them into the deck, unable to deny the truth in her sister's words. When she was young she had been heartbroken at the frequent deaths in the family, but she had soon learned to put such things in perspective. She realized, too, that Ishkyna had played Ivan well. He was angry now, and would probably tell others what the sisters had brewing. It would no doubt come back to Father, and then *he* would expect that she would have already gone to question Nikandr.

But she didn't care if she was being manipulated by her sisters or if her father would have expectations. She wanted to see Nikandr. So late that night she demanded a simple dress of one of their servants. She donned it and left her bedroom to the sounds of whispering from her sisters. She held a small, unlit lamp in one hand even though there were whale oil lamps set on ornate marble tables along the hallway. The passageway to her left led to Radiskoye proper—the most obvious way to reach Nikandr, and also the most watched. She turned instead to her right and padded down the hall until she reached another, smaller hallway where Father and the other dukes were housed. She came to a small linen closet and opened it. After stepping inside, she felt among the shelves of sheets and pillow cases for the catch Mileva had assured her was there. She found it at the back of the bottommost shelf. It clicked and the entire rear of the closet creaked backward at her touch.

After lighting her small lamp, she entered the secret passage. Stairs immediately took her downward. She guessed it to be two stories, perhaps more. It was difficult to tell with no landmarks to guide her. She reached the bottom, and by the flickering light of her lamp she could see a narrow stone tunnel running to the right. She followed it, holding her arms tight to her side, partly because of the cramped space and partly because of the horrible draft. Her lamp was equipped with a glass shield, but it still guttered and threatened to go out if Atiana moved too quickly.

She tried to retain her sense of direction, but the tunnel took several turns, and none of them at right angles to one another, and so soon she had no idea where she was going. She finally reached a fork in the passage, and was forced to stop. Mileva hadn't mentioned such a thing, and so she had no idea which one she should take. What if there were more? What if she got lost in these tunnels and never found her way out again? Who knew how extensive they were? Radiskoye was among the largest of the palotzas; she might find herself caught in a place from which no amount of screaming would rescue her.

She took the right-hand fork, vowing that she would head back if she came across any more. But after another, she told herself that she could find her way back as long as she consistently chose one direction to follow. It happened a third time, and still Atiana went on, taking several flights of stairs upward.

Thankfully this tunnel came to an end.

She searched for a latch and eventually found it. On the other side was the rear of a similar closet within the bath house. One large pool was set into the floor here, and another smaller one, for children, lay beyond it. She had been here a few times and knew that it lay two levels below the floor where the Khalakovos slept. She was nearly there.

She padded to the bath house door and opened it slowly. The hallway was empty, so she left the bathhouse and walked to the main stairwell serving this wing of the palotza. She took it two levels up.

And stopped.

For sitting on a bench was a large black rook. It watched her closely with intelligent eyes, and by the time she had taken two steps forward, she knew that Saphia had assumed the bird, and that she had been found sneaking about like a thief in the night.

CHAPTER 22

"How may I serve, Matra?" Atiana asked.

The rook emitted several clicking sounds before speaking. "Have the hallways of Radiskoye so caught your interest"—it clicked again—"that you must skulk among them while the sky lays dark?"

"*Nyet*, Matra."

"Another reason, then…"

"I only thought…"

The rook cawed. "Go on."

"I wished to speak with your son, to apologize to him."

"*Apologize?*"

"For my actions the other night. For besting him at our dance." It wasn't a lie, exactly, but it was the only thing she could think of.

The rook cawed again, and to Atiana it sounded like a laugh. "There's little enough for you to apologize for. You held your own, child, which is more than I can say for Nikandr."

"He did very well, Matra. I practiced that one dance for weeks before coming here."

"To show him you were better."

Atiana pulled herself taller. "To show him I would not stand in his shadow, but at his side."

The rook was motionless for a time, staring. "As it should be."

Atiana suppressed a small smile. "As you say, Matra."

"You asked how you may serve…"

For the first time Atiana realized there was more to this meeting than had at first met the eye. "Of course, Matra."

Footsteps echoed from down the hallway, and out of the gloom stepped Isaak, the palotza's seneschal, holding a large, unlit lantern and wearing thick winter night clothes.

"You can accompany Isaak to the drowning chamber."

Isaak bowed his head and held out a night coat as the rook flapped up to his shoulder.

With no small amount of trepidation, Atiana accepted it and pulled it over her chilled frame. She walked the cavernous halls of Radiskoye with Isaak, their footsteps echoing off into the immensity of the palotza. The old chancellor said nothing the entire way, the Matra sitting on his shoulder.

When Atiana had last spoken to the Matra, they had discussed her abilities in the dark and the need for someone to take up the slack where Yvanna could not. Surely she didn't mean for Atiana to begin now. It must be something the Matra wanted kept secret, something that needed to be told directly.

Her dread increased the lower they went, and by the time they crossed the colonnade near the base of the towering black spire, her heart was pounding in her chest, and it was all she could do not to turn and run.

Finally, after reaching the antechamber at the bottom of the interminable stairwell, Isaak knocked thrice upon the imposing iron doors and led Atiana into the drowning chamber.

If the stairwell was chilly, the chamber was positively frigid. It began seeping through Atiana's clothes the moment she stepped in. As bitter as the memories were, she remembered her training—while her whole being wanted to tighten, she needed instead to relax.

Saphia sat in the stout chair near the fire—though not *too* near. A servant woman—an aging, gray matron—fussed around the Matra, fixing the blanket just so while the rook alighted from Isaak's shoulder and flew to the golden perch standing behind the Matra.

This was another subtle indicator of Saphia's prowess with the aether. No other Matra could assume the form of an animal while outside of the drowning basin. Saphia, if reports were to be believed, could do so for hours after leaving it, and it made Atiana wonder what other powers she might have that no one knew about.

Suddenly the rook began cawing and beating its wings furiously, an indicator that Saphia had returned to herself.

Atiana kneeled and bowed her head. "How may I serve, Matra?"

The Matra sipped from a thick, earthenware mug and worked her mouth before speaking. "Rise, child. What I need is trifling, though you may not think it so easy to give."

Atiana stood, her head still bowed. "What I have is yours."

A smile spread across Saphia's skeletal face as she raised the mug to her lips and sipped noisily. "We shall see soon enough." Her hands shook, as did her head when not in direct contact with the mug, but her eyes were bright and spry. "Victania is unavailable, and Yvanna's inability has grown worse since our last talk. I need rest, child. I have not slept properly in weeks, and it is taking its toll. Take the dark. Watch over our island for a time, and that will be enough."

"Forgive me, Matra, but my father has said the marriage is in doubt."

"You're near enough to a Khalakovo, child."

"But Father—"

"You think the men will halt a wedding their Matri have arranged? Not likely. Not while your mother and I live. They may scratch and they may claw, but you will be married. Be sure of that. Besides, your inclusion in this family has nothing to do with it. A Matra can choose who she will. Is it not so?"

"It is so, but shouldn't Victania—"

"I told you she is unavailable." Atiana thought Saphia would tell her to simply suck in her gut and prepare herself, but she did not. She stared at Atiana while the fire lit one side of her face in a ruddy glow. "You are afraid."

It was not a question.

"I will do it, Matra, if it will give you rest."

Saphia continued to stare, the hollows of her eyes like black pits. "I lied to you the other day," she said, "or at least I didn't share with you the whole truth. The Matri always discuss those that will be allowed to take the dark. It was decided years ago that you and your sisters were too much of a risk to be allowed to ride the currents."

Atiana tried not to let her surprise show. "And what, may I ask, changed your minds?"

"I should think the answer was obvious."

And of course, it was. The dark, for whatever reason, was becoming progressively harder to control. Though the aether flowed over the seas, over the entire world, in chaotic currents, the islands grounded it, creating natural channels through which the aether could flow. It was still too wild to be used without further refinement, however. The spires allowed the Matri, collectively, to guide the flow of aether between the archipelagos. Without them, ships would be lost among the winds, their keels useless among the fickle currents.

But just like everything else on the islands, the aether had become unpredictable. The Matri had had to work harder to control the currents, which was the main reason that those weaker in the craft were practically useless, and masters like Saphia were taxed more heavily each time they took the dark. Most believed the blight to be a drought that would one day pass, but Atiana wasn't so sure. What if it *never* passed? Or passed so many years from now that it made little difference? What would become of the

Duchies of Anuskaya? Would they be forced to live only among their own archipelagos, forgoing the dangerous flights to the farther islands? How many would die from starvation as conditions worsened and they were cut off from trade?

"If it's a simple matter of ability," Atiana said, "then Ishkyna or Mileva would do better. They seemed to enjoy it."

"Ishkyna is an unbroken filly, always trying to prove herself, always pulling at her reins. And Mileva is too cunning for her own good."

"Which leaves me."

"Which is no small matter. Take the dark, child. The Matri will guide you, as they have in the past. There is little to fear now that the winds are calm."

"Mother says there is *always* something to fear in the dark."

Saphia began to laugh, splashing tea over the shawl on her lap. The servant came quickly with a napkin and dabbed the wet spots, making sure to send a wicked glance in Atiana's direction while doing so.

"This is another reason I think you're ready. You recognize the need for balance—hold the reins too tightly, and the aether will fight you; loosen them overly much, and it will trample you roughshod."

Atiana stood there, cold and perfectly unwilling to become colder, but also out of reasons not to. "Very well," she finally said.

Atiana knew she was no fledgling needing protection from the cold, but the abilities of the drowning basin to steal warmth was something even the stoutest of women could not prepare for, and so when she stripped she was—despite the nearby fire—already shivering, and as the servant woman spread the rendered goat's fat over her arms and breasts and stomach, it grew worse.

"Control yourself," Saphia snapped, "or you'll fail before you've dipped one toe into the basin. The storms have been strong of late, but if you keep to the spires, they will guide you."

Atiana nodded.

"And remember what you see, Atiana Radieva. It is important."

And with those words came some amount of control. Nerves calmed. Muscles relaxed. Blood flowed more freely, and finally she was able to control the shivering to a degree.

She stepped to the edge of the basin—now empty—as the servant woman pulled a lever on the wall. Water from the mountain's internal streams flowed through a channel and began filling the basin. The water rose slowly. It was all Atiana could do to control her breathing. She managed to only by telling herself that once she entered the dark her body would become a faint memory.

Until she woke...

But she would deal with that when the time came.

The basin full, Atiana stepped inside. The cold clawed at her feet and ankles and calves. She knew it was foolish to enter the basin in slow increments, so she laid back until it was up to her neck. She grew rigid from it, her muscles rigoring painfully. Her left foot began to cramp. She flexed her toes against the pain as the breathing tube was pressed into her mouth. She drew in desperate lungfuls of air through the tube as her body screamed at her to rise from the basin, to extricate herself from the water's iron grip.

But she could not allow such thoughts to control her. She was Vostroman.

She would not bend.

She slowed her breathing, relaxed muscles so tense they were nearing the breaking point. Her skin became numb, and at the same time—as it had so many years ago—the aether began to suffuse her frame, providing a subtle warmth that was not unlike those first sips of mulled vodka after hours in the howling winter wind.

Her body lost its tension, lending her a confidence that had been lacking, but she knew this was the time she had to be most careful, for before she knew it—

Her eyes, clenched tightly, lose the telltale signs of light. Her stomach sinks. She hears nothing save the low susurrus of the aether and the currents of the dark. She sees one bright light among the endless sea of midnight blue surrounding her. It is Saphia, the Matra, still strong, still caressing the dark as if she could submerge herself at any time she chose. There is a weariness in her, a fatigue that cannot come from mere sleeplessness. It is a wonder she can function at all, much less enter the dark and guide the flow of its currents.

Atiana leaves the Matra, not wishing to tax her unnecessarily—indeed, not wishing to touch the physical world so soon after leaving it. Such a thing can be dangerous, especially for one such as her.

She expands her sphere of awareness and senses the servant woman, though only vaguely, as one knows that someone is near upon waking. She sees the rook on its perch clearly, and if she so chose she could assume its form, but she has not done so in years and there are risks with even a small thing such as this. She senses the roots of the spire, which run deep beneath the obelisk, and then the spire itself, towering above Radiskoye like a stern and overprotective parent. The aether licks at the spire as if it were curious over its existence, but like a ship too bold for its own good, it is caught in the maelstrom and pulled down into the depths of the mountain.

She sees the people spread throughout the palotza, all of them small, meaningless, like flies buzzing over fruit. She senses the dogs in their kennels, the ponies in their stalls, the rats running through the walls of the palotza, even the bitterly cold trees and grasses that blanket the island. The city of Volgorod and the Landless village of Iramanshah enter her consciousness like dim candles in a misty bog filled with countless, twinkling wisps. The island itself, now that her mind has expanded, has an ebb and flow. It has life, little different from the body floating in the drowning basin deep beneath the spire.

When her awareness expands to the sea, she recalls the warnings of her mother. A realization grows. She is granting too much to the aether, but the will to heed those warnings begins to wane, while the desire to lose herself in the vibrant currents grows.

The ocean teems with life. Fish and coral and mollusks and the great white goedrun that make long sea voyages so difficult. And the air. Though the sun has yet to rise, and the winds are high, there are thousands of gulls swooping along the southern cliffs, diving for fish. Grouse are sleeping in their nests. Owls continue to hunt.

She knows that she is becoming lost, that she is coming ever closer to the point where she will no longer be able to return to her body, but she has lost the will to care. The life and death surrounding her is too beautiful for her to willingly turn her eyes away.

And then a note—the pluck of a single harp string—calls to her. She senses, among the chaos, the minds of the other Matri. She feels them supporting her, willing her return. They are too distant to offer much beyond this, but the realization that they are there is enough. She draws herself inward, focusing more closely on the spire.

Returning to the lessons drummed into her so many years ago, she attunes herself with the spire. Her soul reverberates against its power. It drives her. She feels the whorls and eddies around the island. They are strong, but it is not so difficult to amplify them, to focus it southwest toward the spire on Duzol, and the two beyond that on Grakhosk and Yfa, and eastward to the other islands in Khalakovo. Soon, like a spider on her web, she is in tune with all seven spires, strengthening them, guiding the currents of aether among them. It is something that Saphia does without thinking, but for Atiana, it takes minutes, hours.

Some time later—she knows not how long—a whorl appears.

So lost is she in her task that she doesn't recognize the source, but soon she comes to realize it is not so far from where she lies, nearly frozen, deep beneath the palotza.

She propels herself southwest of Volgorod, along the coast, beyond the

156 · BRADLEY P. BEAULIEU

eyrie and toward the shifting currents. She hovers outside a home sitting near the shoreline, hidden in a strip of forest. It is nearly black among the thin currents of the aether, and inside there is a woman, bright blue, nearly white. She kneels before a cradle, staring down at the babe lying within it. Though Atiana can hear no sounds, it is clear the tiny girl is crying—her mouth wide open, her eyes puffy, no doubt from the sheer intensity and duration of her fit. The babe's imprint in the aether, like her mother's, like all creatures of this plane, is blue, but there is a tinge of yellow, lending her a greenish tint.

Curious, Atiana floats closer, sensing a hunger from the child, a hatred. She has no idea how this could be, or why, but she does know one thing.

As surely as the wind blows, this child is dying.

CHAPTER 23

Though the child is dying, Atiana is powerless to prevent it.

The woman picks up the child and holds her against her bared breast, but the child will have nothing to do with it. The mother holds the babe tight and rocks her, shushes at her ear, but it helps not at all.

Mother, she calls. *Mother, please hear me.*

There is no response. She tries to reach Saphia, but she is asleep and will remain so for hours, perhaps even a day or more.

Currents swirl around the darkening babe. She is tainted blue still, and a tinge of green remains, but she is fading to midnight, the color of the stout brick walls or the thick pine beams running along the ceiling.

Pressure builds around Atiana. She feels tight, crowded. She is new to the currents of the dark. She knows this. But she knows that this should not be. The aether, though it stands between the worlds, is not bounded in such ways. Adhiya's presence can be seen, but it cannot be *felt*. The same is true of Erahm. What then, could be pressing in on her so?

The pressure becomes worse. She feels constricted, choked, feels as though the breath is being pressed from her slowly but surely.

And then, as the light from the babe fades altogether, the feeling is gone.

She is unable to focus on these feelings, for she is too caught up with the emotions that are clear on the face of the mother.

Though she may not realize it yet, she holds a dead child. It is all Atiana can do not to call out. She might try to touch the woman, to give her some indication of what has happened, but before she can the woman realizes. She shakes the babe—not violently, but enough to wake a sleeping child. She begins to cry, and she shakes her daughter harder. She holds her up, listening for signs of life.

Then she leans her head back and unleashes her pain to the fates. She hugs the babe to her chest, tenderly yet fiercely, her whole body wracking from the realization.

Atiana feels ashamed that she cannot share in the woman's grief. She watches for a long time, wishing she could have helped in some small way, but in the end she can no longer stomach the limitations of the aether, and she pulls away.

When Atiana woke, it was not like waking after a full night's sleep, nor was it like stirring from a lazy daydream—it was more like those dreams she had had as a child where she was standing at the edge of the tall black cliffs near Vostroma's palotza, staring down at the churning sea, her stomach bubbling with a mixture of excitement and fear. She was convinced in those dreams she could fly, though it would still take her long minutes to summon the courage to leap into the air like the wide-winged gulls flying far below her. Her stomach would lift as she plummeted, and she would wake with a gut-churning jolt to find herself sitting stock upright, breathing deeply in the cold air of the bedroom she shared with her sisters.

So it was now as she sat upright in the drowning chamber, frigid water splashing around her. She fully expected to find herself in the darkness of Galostina, but of course she did not. She was somewhere else entirely.

The light of the nearby fire was low, yet she was forced to clench her eyes in order to bear it. It took Atiana long moments—her eyes tearing and blinking involuntarily—until she realized Victania was sitting on a chair close to the fireplace. She was watching Atiana, silent, her face devoid of emotion.

And then the past came rushing back. The Matra's summons. Her request. Atiana's eventual capitulation.

Already her time in the dark was fading, a dream that only moment ago had been reality. As she had been taught, she began reliving the moments backwards, so that one link in the chain would reveal the next, and the next. It worked to a degree, but she was unable to remember everything. There was something crucial missing. Something terribly disturbing.

Her eyes began to acclimate.

"Do you require help?" Victania asked, her voice echoing against the harsh stone walls.

It was insulting, what Victania had just done. She knew as well as any that those who had just surfaced from the dark required help. Her question was an attempt to make Atiana feel small.

Atiana shook her head while struggling to gain her feet. The water dripped noisily from her arms and hair and breasts as she steadied herself on the basin's stone walls. Her legs could hardly support her weight and her arms were little better. She stepped out onto the granite floor, and her knee buckled. She fell to the floor, her head crashing hard against the stone.

Victania was at her side in a moment, helping her to her feet. As Atiana steadied herself, Victania held out a hand towel, a brief look of regret on her face. When Atiana did not accept it, she motioned with it toward Atiana's head. "You're bleeding."

Atiana took it, wincing as she pressed it against the lump that was already forming. Victania, using a large white cloth, scrubbed the goat's fat economically from Atiana's naked frame. Then she helped Atiana into a thick woolen robe.

It was warm—almost too warm after the bottomless cold of the water. Atiana's skin began to prickle, but she let it, for it was a welcome tether to reality.

Victania motioned to the Matra's padded chair, then made her way to the hearth, where a kettle hung from an iron hook. Using a thick woolen mitt, she poured steaming tea into the lone cup that waited on a wooden table. She raised one eyebrow when she realized Atiana hadn't moved to take the offered seat. "She gave her permission if that's what you're worried about."

It felt presumptuous to even consider taking Saphia's chair, but she didn't have it in her to do battle in her weakened state, so she sat and accepted the tea that Victania offered her.

Victania resumed her seat. She sat rigidly upright, as if it pained her to lean back in the chair. Atiana wondered if there were *any* position that would offer her comfort. She looked haunted from the wasting. Saphia might seem frail, but there was a silent strength to her, while Victania looked as if she were being eaten from the inside, as if her inner structure was now hollow and the next thing to go would be her thin and crumbling shell. One small bout with a cold, Atiana thought, and she would not be long for this world. She would have felt sorry if Victania didn't lord herself over Atiana at every opportunity.

"You were gone quite a long time," Victania said.

Atiana sipped from the sweet tea. The warmth of the liquid trailed down into her gut. It was too much, too soon, and her stomach rebelled. "How long?" She asked, setting the cup down.

"You've been under for well over a day."

Atiana shook her head. It didn't seem possible. "More than a *day*?"

"*Da.* A passable length of time." Was there a bit of envy in her voice? "What did you find?"

Atiana opened her mouth to speak, but she found that she could remember nothing. Her memories had already been muddled the moment she woke, but the shock of finding Victania here, the pressure of being questioned after her awakening, had caused her to forget.

"I don't remember," she admitted.

Victania took her in, from her bare feet to her head, a prim look of disgust on her face. "Think."

She tried. She recalled the last few moments in the aether, as well as a strong feeling of discomfort, of grief, but the more she tried to pin the memories down, the more focused she became on the simple act of wakening.

"My mother, the Matra, asked you here to take the dark. Did they teach you so little—"

"Stop," Atiana said. That one word, *mother*, had brought about the glimmer of memories.

"—the first thing you do—"

"Silence!"

Atiana glanced around the room, struggling to hold on to the faint memory of a mother holding her child. "There was a babe"—her words were practically a whisper—"in Volgorod."

Victania watched carefully, but held her tongue.

Atiana shivered. Her eyes watered. She had not known the woman, but the aether made things seem more personal and emotional than they would have been under the light of the sun. She had felt, not that she *was* the woman, but that she had as much at stake in that child as the mother did. It was personal, and stepping out from under the aether's spell had done nothing to lessen the feelings.

She told Victania the story, slowly, for the words came in fits and starts, and she feared if she spoke too quickly, it would all come out in one tearful gout. When she was done, she was finally able to meet Victania's eyes. There was no shock in Victania's expression, no sense that anything Atiana had said was new information.

"You know of this…" Atiana said softly.

"It has been happening for months."

"To babes?"

"*Nyet.* To the old, to the sick. It was only a matter of time before the young were affected too. Children will be next. And then…"

Victania didn't have to finish. They both knew what was at stake. The blight had started by affecting the health of their crops, their game. Why wouldn't it move on to the very people that inhabited the islands?

"Does my mother know this?"

"Of course."

"Then why hasn't she told me?"

"Because this news cannot be spread. The people look to us for protection.

There are already weekly disturbances in Volgorod, and scattered incidents in Tuyal and Erotsk and Izhny. How long do you think it would be before there are riots in the streets? How long before they march on Radiskoye to demand that we shelter them?"

Not long at all, Atiana thought, but it still hurt to be marked as an untrustworthy by her own mother. Then again, she had never shown the least bit of interest in taking the dark, nor in matters of politics—why *would* Mother trust her with the information?

Why would *Saphia*?

It was a clear sign of just how desperate things had become when the Matra of Khalakovo had been forced into depending on Atiana for the protection of her Duchy.

"There must be something we can do," Atiana said.

Victania shook her head. "There is nothing, nothing save coming here to lend us your strength, to continue to give the Matra her needed rest during these troubled times."

CHAPTER 24

Nikandr trudged up the stairs, fighting off another yawn, as crisp footsteps rose in volume behind him. "You didn't think you'd be allowed to lay your head down, did you?"

Nikandr turned and found Ranos on the stairs below him. He looked to his left, to his room near the end of the long hall, dearly wishing he could just ignore his brother and get some sleep. The last few days felt jumbled, like all the minutes of all the hours spent in the donjon with Ashan and Nasim were piled on top of one another, none of them distinguishable from the others. It didn't help that he and Jahalan had made no real progress. Ashan claimed that Nasim couldn't have been involved in the summoning of the suurahezhan, though he also admitted that he hadn't been there when it happened. Nikandr's focus had been to find ways to reach Nasim, to find out what might have happened that day, and though Ashan was forthcoming about the tricks he used to reach Nasim, none of them had so far worked. Nasim was more cipher than boy.

"What might I do for the Boyar of Uyadensk?" Nikandr asked, bowing his head in mock sincerity.

"Put on your uniform, Nischka, and come with me."

Nikandr took his brother in again. He was wearing his suit of office: the uniform of the Boyar. He ran to his room and retrieved his own, pulling it on as quickly as he could manage. "What's happening?" he asked as he fell into step alongside Ranos.

"The Aramahn… They have come once again to petition for the boy's release."

"Why would that require my presence?"

"You'll see soon enough."

They made their way to the first level of the palotza and traveled a long hallway to a chamber where Father held audience for matters of state. Dozens of Aramahn were waiting outside. Nikandr assumed they would shortly be allowed inside to speak with Father, but he was mistaken. When he opened the Duke's entrance, he found the room packed wall-to-wall with robed Aramahn. There were some he recognized, but most he did not. This was not strange in itself given their transient nature, but the sheer number of them was. He had never seen so many of them in one place. Even in Iramanshah, large gatherings were rare, many of them preferring to meditate or to converse in small groups. They were an isolated lot, and this solidarity was troubling.

At the head of the room was a raised table with a dozen chairs facing the audience. Father's secretary was calling the room to order. The array of men were seated: Father first, Pavol Andreyov, Polkovnik of the Streltsi, Veliky Pytorov, Admiral of the Staaya, Ranos and the four posadni of Uyadensk, and finally Nikandr.

"Who comes?" Father asked.

At the front of the crowd stood the seven mahtar of Iramanshah, all of them aged and venerable, their time among the winds behind them. Fahroz stood at the center, the honored position, and when the sounds of the gavel died away, she stepped forward. Her eyes mirrored the fiery layers of her robes, which were colored a deep orange. "My name is Fahroz Bashar al Lilliah."

"State your cause."

"We have come to petition for the release of Ashan Kida al Ahrumea and Nasim an Ashan."

"Both are being held in the investigation of the death of Grand Duke Stasa Olegov Bolgravya."

"As we well know, Duke Khalakovo. What we do not know is what gave the Duchy cause to suspect them and what has been discovered since."

"As I'm sure you understand," Father said in a rote manner, "with an investigation such as this is, our findings cannot at this time be shared."

"*Cannot* or *will* not?"

A murmur ran through the crowd, and Father stiffened, striking the gavel several times until order was resumed.

"*Will* not."

"Under the terms of the Covenant—"

"I know well the dictates of the Covenant, but it clearly allows us to defend ourselves against threats to the Grand Duchy."

"You speak, of course, of the threat the suurahezhan represents, that it could very well have been summoned and sent by one of our own."

Father remained silent.

"I will assume your silence, My Lord Duke, to mean assent. What I believe you fail to understand is that we are just as concerned. We are not so naïve as to think that the Aramahn are incorruptible. Far from it. We have only to look to the Maharraht to find examples. And so I hope you will share what you know so that we can assist, so that we can root out the infection in our midst before it spreads."

Father was quiet for a time. Fahroz was speaking as if she believed the assumption that the Aramahn had been involved—in this lay her only hope to sway Father—but everyone in the room knew this was a sham. She was not lying, but she was trying to coax Father into sharing the information in any way she could or, failing that, make the entire Duchy look foolish for refusing.

"Your request is noted but denied."

"We urge you to reconsider."

"Noted," Father said.

Fahroz nodded, as if she'd expected this answer. "We have been generous up to this point—"

Father knocked the gavel thrice. "*Generous*?"

Fahroz bowed her head respectfully, but this only seemed to raise Father's hackles.

"Consider it generous that I haven't tossed the lot of you from these halls for coming here daily. Consider it generous that Ashan hasn't been summarily hung based on the evidence we already have. Consider it generous that we grant you gems for communion." Father stood, his face turning red. "But do not enter these halls and tell me that *you* have been generous with *me*."

Fahroz bowed her head again. "Generous, indeed, and so we will grant you time to reconsider. But take care, Duke. If too many suns rise without clear evidence against Ashan or Nasim, we will ask that all Aramahn refuse your *generous* gifts of gems, your *generous* offer of travel aboard your windships, your *generous* acceptance of our presence on these islands."

Father leaned down and slammed the gavel fiercely against the block as the din of the crowd rose to new heights. "Do not presume to threaten."

"That was no threat."

And with that Fahroz turned and strode from the room, the crowd parting for her as she passed. As one, the Aramahn began leaving through the far door. It was more than rude to leave without a request from the officer in residence—a final exclamation on the seriousness of Fahroz's words.

Father marched past Ranos and Nikandr to reach a door at the rear of the platform. He stepped inside and left the door open behind him. The other officers of state all stood and followed him. Ranos and Nikandr did as well, but the moment Nikandr stepped inside the room, Father was there, holding him back.

"Your presence is not required here, Nikandr." What he was saying, of course, was that Nikandr's place was in the bowels of the palotza, speaking with Ashan and Nasim. "You have two more days." And with that he closed the door.

Nikandr felt a chill course down his frame.

The sun had long since set over Radiskoye. Darkness lay heavy over the northern courtyard, but the moon gave enough light that Nikandr could see the outlines of the buildings, the shape of the wall that circled the palotza. It was cold, and he had nothing to do but wait, but he couldn't find it in himself to return indoors. He paced along the stone walkway, looking every few moments toward the arch that led to the palotza's main entrance.

He heard the clop of hooves well before the crunch of wheels on gravel. An enclosed coach with a single horse approached. The driver pulled up when he reached him, taking down the bulls-eye lantern and moving to the door. He opened it and Nikandr stepped forward to help the lone occupant of the coach to navigate the steps.

She wore a heavy cloak, and the cowl was pulled up over her head, hiding her face well. The driver had been given only the location of her home and a note. He might know her—enough in the palotza did—but he was a trustworthy man. He nodded to Nikandr and returned to the driver's bench, pulling the neck of his cherkesska higher against the cold, as Nikandr led the woman inside.

"Don't you think it's time," Rehada said as the door closed shut, "that you share the reason for your summons?" She pulled her arm away as if she were insulted that he'd had the presumption to take it.

"I need your help."

She pulled the cowl back, allowing it to fall around her shoulders. She stared at him with a curious expression. Disappointment?

"Nasim?" she asked.

Nikandr nodded. "Things have become serious. Fahroz has threatened to withhold the services of the Aramahn. It will start in a matter of days, a week at the most. Father has given me two days to reach Nasim. Somehow."

"And you want *me* to help?"

He nodded.

"I know nothing of him."

"You know enough. And you are observant. Another viewpoint would be of great service to me. And there is the matter of your alignment."

Rehada considered his words. "He may indeed be aligned with fire. If you wish, I will commune with my hezhan and see what comes of it."

Rehada acted strangely on the way to Nasim's room. She was quiet, unreadable, as if she were guarding against emotion. As they approached, there was a clear note of expectation in her stance, in the way she looked at the door, as if this were something she was very much looking forward to.

Nasim sat on a circular carpet that lay at the foot of the large bed. His legs were pulled up to his chest, and he was rocking back and forth slowly. If he noticed them, he gave no sign. His movement spoke of discomfort, and his face revealed the depth of it. His brow was furrowed, his lips pinched. His jaw worked. And his eyes… They were fixed upon a point on the far wall, well below a painting of a bleak, wooded landscape caught in the throes of winter. He seemed on the verge of crying, but there was a resoluteness to him that was immediately apparent. He seemed, in fact, noble.

Nikandr had no idea that such pain could project from a child—this or any other. It was humbling, and he found himself wishing he could lift the misery from him.

Rehada kneeled on the carpet. "Nasim?"

He neither moved nor noted her presence. Nikandr doubted he was truly here in any case. More likely he was seeing things from the other side, from Adhiya, the land of hezhan, and he wondered what it would be like to truly *see* such a thing. He had had one inexplicable meeting with a hezhan, but that was probably as close as he was ever going to get to the world that lay beyond.

Rehada reached out and touched his arm. "Nasim."

Nikandr sat in a chair at the round table in the corner. "He has not spoken since he arrived, but Ashan said he has done so in the past, sometimes for hours on end."

"This may take some time," she said.

He nodded, knowing that would be the case.

Rehada closed her eyes.

Nikandr was entranced as he watched. Rehada was nervous at first, tentative, but then her breath deepened. Her shoulders slumped. Her mouth fell slack. Their breathing fell into sync so completely that they seemed of one breath, of one mind.

But then differences began to appear. Rehada's brow furrowed. Her throat swallowed several times. Nasim began shaking his head, and the motion grew in frequency and intensity.

A moan escaped Rehada. Her eyes were still closed, but they were clamped shut, as if she feared to open them. He knew she was communing with Nasim, but he had no idea what she might be seeing.

"Rehada?" he asked.

She didn't respond.

Nasim was shaking his head more fiercely.

"Rehada?" he repeated as he kneeled next to Nasim and held him, trying to quell his violent motions. Nikandr felt heat and knew immediately it was coming from Rehada.

"Rehada, wake up!"

Smoke began to issue from inside her robes.

"Rehada, wake up now!"

It trailed out from her neck and along her face. Nikandr hauled Nasim away, hoping to break their bond.

It seemed to have no effect.

Then Rehada's clothes began to burn.

By the ancients, what was happening?

He laid Nasim down in the corner and grabbed the sheets from the bed and threw them over her, hoping to smother the flames.

But the flames grew, and Rehada began to scream.

CHAPTER 25

Nikandr swatted at the flames, hoping Rehada would wake on her own. He was nearly to the point of striking her to jar her from her trance when her eyes shot open.

Her face turned purple. Her eyes were wide as they searched the room. A sound uttered from her throat, more like a rusted hinge than an inhalation. Then, finally, she took in a deep, rasping breath. She began coughing immediately after, pulling herself into a ball like a child afraid of the night.

He continued to beat at the flames until finally all of them had been smothered. "Can you hear me?"

She nodded weakly.

"What happened?"

She didn't answer. Her eyes were wild, afraid. Her breathing was still coming in long, wheezing draws.

"What happened?" he repeated. He hoped that by keeping her talking, it would prevent her from slipping back.

"I found him," she said. "But my hezhan rebelled."

"Rebelled?"

She nodded, cringing as she touched her neck. "I fear it was some effect brought on by Nasim's presence."

Nikandr's expression became concerned. "What does it mean?"

"It means that I will need to try again."

His heart sank. "There cannot be a next time, Rehada. I can't allow you in again."

She stared into his eyes with a look that made it clear how disgraced she was. "It would be impossible to bring him to me."

"I'm afraid so."

He helped her to sit up. She looked down at the remains of her clothing, nearly all of which had been burned to cinders. Nikandr sent the gaoler to find clothes, and as he and Rehada waited, his sense that he'd made a

168

terrible mistake by bringing Rehada here grew by the moment. Finally the gaoler returned with acceptable—if overly large—clothes for Rehada. She put them on and Nikandr led her back the way they had come.

When they reached the large hallway, Nikandr froze when he realized they were being watched. One of the triplets—Ishkyna, he thought—was standing far down the hall, hair disheveled, the smile on her face fading as she looked between Nikandr and Rehada.

One of the palotza's guardsman was standing near her. His hand had been at the small of her back, but the moment he saw Nikandr, he dropped it and straightened.

Ishkyna glared at Rehada with an expression that even from a distance could only be interpreted as severe disapproval, and then she took the guardsman's hand and alighted the stairs, giving Nikandr one last look that dared him to make mention of it.

Of anyone—even Atiana—Ishkyna was the last person he would have chosen to see him like this. Not only was she indiscreet. She was devious. Hopefully he could speak to her before she ran her mouth.

"Was that her?" Rehada asked.

"*Nyet.* Her sister, Ishkyna."

Rehada pulled her lips into a compressed line. "Is Atiana as pretty?"

Nikandr shook his head, laughing softly. "Prettier."

Rehada smiled. "Then you have done well."

With that she turned and walked away, toward the door through which she had entered. Nikandr saw her into the waiting coach and nodded to the driver. He snapped the reins, and in moments the coach was gone.

His stomach was beginning to turn as he returned to the cells. He took out his flask to take some of the elixir but was surprised to find that there was only one swallow left. He had refilled it only yesterday. Had he drank so much already?

He finished it off and walked to Ashan's cell and found him sitting cross-legged on the ornate carpet in the center of the large room. His hands rested on his knees. He watched calmly as Nikandr closed the door and collapsed into a nearby chair.

Ashan seemed concerned—making it clear he had heard the commotion—but Nikandr wasn't ready to speak of it. He needed a moment to let his stomach settle.

"Do you know Rehada Ulan al Shineshka?" he finally asked.

"I do. She is an accomplished suuraqiram, and a woman her mother can be proud of."

"She is a woman I care for deeply. At my request, she came, hoping to commune with Nasim. She woke from her trance not long ago, her clothes burning. She was unharmed, but it occurred while she was trying to reach Nasim. He seemed to become agitated just before it happened."

In their talks with one another, Ashan had always seemed like a carefree man. He could be serious, but more often than not he was quick to smile and light of heart. But now for the first time, as he considered Nikandr's words, he seemed deeply troubled. "There is something I wish to share with you, son of Iaros, something that may be difficult for you to believe." He took a deep breath before continuing. "Nasim is gifted, as you know, and I have long been trying to understand how it might have come to be. When we are born, there is some part of us that is taken from our previous lives. A kernel only. A seed. It allows us, fates willing, to expand our awareness as the world grows older. Some retain more of their past, some less.

"I no longer have any doubts that the first possibility is the one that applies to Nasim. We spoke of Ghayavand… It is a dead island, I told you, which is true. What I did not reveal are the reasons behind it. Over three centuries ago there was a troika of powerful arqesh, each as close to vashaqiram as any in our history. It was the end of the last age of enlightenment, and they believed the time was right to merge the two worlds."

It was one of several possible ways the Aramahn believed the world would end. Indaraqiram, the point at which Adhiya and Erahm become one, when all souls meld, both here and beyond. The Grand Duchy gave no credence to such beliefs, citing the failings of the most powerful of the qiram as proof. They believed, rightly, that one's ancestors watched over a person, that by building one's legacy, by paying homage to those that came before, that they would protect their progeny from beyond the grave. One day they would become more powerful than the fates, making them masters of their own destiny.

"They were unsuccessful," Nikandr said.

Ashan granted that with a tilt of his head. "*Da*, but not completely so. There are many who believe that those three qiram lived on beyond the devastation they caused. The life they lived—halfway between Erahm and Adhiya—twisted their souls. Eventually they went mad from it. They fought with one another for supremacy, none ever quite able to swing the balance fully in their favor. Many feared that when one finally did win out that it would mark the beginning of the end of the world—the path of destruction instead of the path of enlightenment."

Nikandr remembered the rush of the wind as he flew down to the tower, the feelings of oneness with the city around him, the island, the sea and the world.

Nikandr swallowed. "You're suggesting that Nasim was one of the three."

Ashan nodded. "I believe this to be true. There are many signs.

Nasim's ability to walk between worlds, the way the aether shifts around him…"

"The way the hezhan cross when he is near?"

"*Nyet*. Do not make the mistake of discounting Soroush. He has discovered many secrets from Nasim, not the least of which is the ways in which the aether has shifted. There are rifts that have been forming for years. They may be the cause of the blight, of the wasting."

"All this from one boy?"

"Not from one boy, but from his *absence* on Ghayavand. If I am right, his death would have caused a severe imbalance around the island, not only from his absence but from the renewed battle between the other two."

"Preposterous," Nikandr said, leaning back in his chair. "Nasim is no more than twelve. The blight has been building for decades."

"When we pass, we are not reborn immediately. We live a life there before returning. No one knows how long. The arqesh who was Nasim could have easily spent that time in Adhiya before returning. Since his rebirth he has been struggling to understand the world, but it is no longer with the perspective of a man who had the time to absorb the ways of flesh and bone. He was raised struggling, always, to tell the difference between the material and the spiritual. It is what causes him such pain, his inability to reconcile the two while living within the shell of a boy." Ashan stared at Nikandr meaningfully. "Until he met you…"

"Our link?"

"Just so. He has taken great strides. You have provided a grounding for him, allowing him to relate to the world around him in ways he never has before. The nature of this connection still eludes me, but it certainly exists."

Nikandr grabbed his gut as a wave of nausea washed over him. He was tired and at the moment unable to hide the effects of the wasting. Surprisingly, he found that he didn't really wish to in front of Ashan. The man had a calming influence, a way of making one want to confess.

"I didn't tell you everything the other day." Nikandr pulled his soulstone out from beneath his shirt. Though only days ago he had worn it openly, he had come to feel exposed when it was not tucked away. "I have the wasting."

Ashan eyed the stone. He seemed to be looking at it anew, revising his assessment.

"Stasa Bolgravya," Nikandr continued, "had been struck as well. In him the disease was very advanced, whereas in my case it is early. Still, it is a connection that may have been overlooked. That day we found you near the lake, I *felt* a havahezhan, and unlike the ship where I had been attacked,

I could control it, as a qiram must do. I've thought on it much, and it may be that Nasim was the one in control, not I, but I have no doubt that I would have felt nothing were I not near him. It is as if Nasim is at the heart of a storm, and all those that come near are drawn toward it."

"Can there be any doubt as to Nasim's nature?"

Nikandr didn't know what to think, but he had to admit the possibility was real. "What if it is so? What would you propose we do?"

"Give me time. Let me speak with the two of you together."

"You don't understand." Nikandr tucked the stone back into his shirt. "The halls of Radiskoye grow tense. The dukes ask thrice each day over the progress we've made."

"What do you tell them?"

"We tell them to wait, that we will soon find resolution."

"And do they believe you?"

Nikandr shook his head. "At first they were content to let us conduct the investigation as we saw fit, but they are now requesting that they be allowed to ask the questions."

If there was any concern in Ashan's heart at these words, he did not show it. "Will you allow it?"

"I think my father may already have agreed were it not for your brethren. They have come, in numbers greater every day. I have just come from their latest appeal for your freedom."

Ashan smiled—a genuine gesture, it seemed to Nikandr. "Shall I prepare for my departure?"

Nikandr chuckled sadly.

Ashan pulled his knees up to his chest and hugged them, not unlike what Nasim did when the worst of his pains were upon him. "Allow me to speak with them."

"Father will not allow it."

"Fahroz will give you a week, perhaps, but no more."

"*Da*, and then they will call the qiram away from our fishing ships. Then trade ships. Then the military. It would seem to put pressure on me to get an answer from you."

"I know you not well at all, son of Iaros, but I know you better than that. I would tell you what I know of Nasim—I think you know this—but the answers still lay hidden. I need more time."

"Haven't you been listening? We don't *have* time."

"Last month, Nasim began to scream when he saw a woman's red scarf. He was inconsolable. The month before that he laughed hysterically at a dead turtle we found lying on the beaches of Samodansk. He does these things, and there is little to connect them. I must consider carefully before I speak."

"I thought I made our situation clear."

"A situation every bit as clear as mine, My Lord Prince."

"Were the Duke of Vostroma to be given the boy, believe me, he would find evidence, one way or another—the dukes that rally beneath his flag will allow nothing less. They will make the boy talk or they will hang him as a traitor to the Grand Duchy and fabricate the rest. Either way, your young charge will be dead, and you will never be able to say that you were powerless to prevent it."

"You know in your heart that Nasim is innocent."

"Innocent or not, Nasim was involved. Silence now leads to the gibbet. We have waited so long to give the dukes news that they believe Khalakovo was in league with you. They believe we arranged for the murder of Stasa."

"Preposterous."

"Not at all. Our history is rife with murder. It gives everyone pause that an arqesh would be involved, but you are a man, like they are. No matter how peaceful you prove yourself to be, they will always think you capable of it. The only way to help Nasim now is to give me answers so I might convince the other dukes that this was merely—"

Nikandr stopped, for there was a feeling within his chest, a discomfort that felt like heartburn. He swallowed, unable to speak.

Ashan stared, clearly confused.

The feeling of discomfort intensified, and suddenly Nikandr knew unerringly the direction from which it came. Ashan glanced toward Nasim's room and stood as Nikandr backed away toward the door. Ashan looked like he wanted to accompany him, but Nikandr stepped outside and ordered the guardsman to lock it. Then he rushed up the hall to Nasim's room.

Nasim was sitting on the floor, cross-legged. The carpet had been rolled up and sat against the bed. The floor was made of hard granite tile. Nasim was working a piece of the tile—pulling it upward, thinning it, shaping it like clay, until it was as thin as a cord. It pulled away from the floor when he gave it a sharp jerk. Then he placed it among dozens of others, all of them forming an impossibly complex sculpture made from the stuff of the floor itself. It was similar to the skills of the vanaqiram, the Aramahn stone masters—they altered the form of stone to recreate it in ways both practical and beautiful. These cords, however, when Nasim released them, did not remain still. They moved, flowing like strands of kelp in a calm sea.

Nasim, apparently oblivious to Nikandr's presence, sat up straighter and smiled as if he were an artisan completely lost in his work. He motioned one hand toward the center of the creation. And then, Nikandr felt a clutch at his heart as the center of it flared to life.

Nikandr fell to his knees, grabbing his chest as pain blossomed from within.

CHAPTER 26

Khamal stands on a stony beach, watching the waves roll in. The day is cloudy, an omen not altogether unexpected. His relationship with Muqallad has always been this way. Why should this day be any different?

The stones crunch as he squats, and while he runs his hand along the rocky shore, feeling the weight of it, the water mingles among the stones with gentle sighs.

Out to sea, the water begins to swirl. It froths and boils, and Khamal can feel it as he touches the stone. A form can be seen moving up from the depths, and soon the surface of the water breaks, and Muqallad begins to rise.

His hair is black and curly. His beard is braided with golden rings woven into the strands, making him look like a king from beneath the sea. His eyes are dark, and he is bare-chested. He stares at the island, failing to see Khamal from the shroud Khamal had placed over it long ago—when Muqallad had left.

Khamal finds a single rock among the countless others, a rock of reddish hue, with striations of black and silver. He stands and holds it out at arm's length.

And Muqallad turns. He stares straight at Khamal, though surely he cannot yet see through the shroud.

He has learned much. Perhaps too much.

But what is there to do now?

Khamal allows the stone to drop. And the shroud falls away.

Together they walk toward the city. As they fall into step, neither he nor Muqallad leads the other. They talk, of their travels, of knowledge gained, of loves found and regrets discovered. It is as if the past five decades had never occurred, so easy is it to speak to him.

As it was of old.

But as they reach the edge of Alayazhar, they both go silent. Among the streets, though they cannot be seen, are the akhoz, the wanderers, the lost. The forgotten. It had been Muqallad's idea long ago to shroud the city in illusion, painting it as whole and pristine when in reality it was a broken and tragic thing. Khamal allows the veil to fall away, only for a moment. There are three of them, all children once, standing nearby. They are naked. Their lips are black. Where their eyes once were is now smooth skin. They raise their noses to the sky, somehow still able to smell them despite all their attempts to mask their scent. As Muqallad and Khamal continue, the akhoz scrabble after, their noses to the sky, their lips pulled back in rictus grins.

Khamal allows the illusion to fall back into place. He has never been able to look upon them for long.

They approach a tower, a pinnacle of ivory that stands near the harbor. The air between them grows even more tense. Both of them know who awaits here. Both of them remember what happened.

When they come to the black iron gates surrounding the tower, the wooden door at the tower's base opens. There stands Sariya, she of the golden hair, she of the blue eyes and graceful face. She is a child of autumn, a child of the dying day. A child of indecision. Khamal should have thought of this when they agreed, together, to banish Muqallad from the island.

Muqallad opens the gate and holds it for Khamal. As Khamal steps through, Sariya studies him, and the skin beneath her brow pinches. It is a momentary thing—there one moment and gone the next—but Khamal knows instantly that he has been betrayed.

"My Lord Prince!" the guard stood at Nikandr's side.

Realizing where he was and what had happened, Nikandr waved him away and stood. Thankfully the pain was already beginning to subside.

"My Lord?" He was staring at Nikandr's chest.

Nikandr looked down. Something was glowing beneath his shirt. He pulled out his stone, and found it to be glowing just as brightly as the light from within Nasim's living sculpture.

"Leave us," Nikandr said to the guard. "And speak of this to no one."

"Of course, My Lord."

When the guard had stepped into the hall and closed the door, Nikandr met Nasim's eyes. There was an awareness Nikandr hadn't seen in him before, an awareness that spoke of a clear grounding in reality.

"That was you, wasn't it? You were Khamal."

Nasim's face became tortured, and Nikandr felt fortunate that he couldn't remember the things that seemed to haunt the boy so. "I was many people."

"Do you remember them all?"

Nasim shook his head. "Not all." He smiled, a fleeting thing. "Not yet."

"Does Ashan know these things?"

"He may. He is wise. Wiser than I have ever been, I fear." Nasim pulled his knees up to his chest, the position now eerily familiar. "Will you kill him?"

Nikandr was confused at first, but quickly came to understand that he meant Ashan. "I would not wish it."

"But it is not in your hands."

He debated lying to Nasim, if only to calm him. This sudden clarity in the boy was an opportunity he did not want to waste. But the Aramahn valued honesty above almost everything—excepting perhaps the sanctity of life—and the boy seemed to know much more than Nikandr would have guessed only minutes ago.

The light within the living sculpture, which had been sparkling white, shifted so that red was mixed in, and the fronds seemed to quiver rather than wave.

"It could be. I need only discover what happened when the suurahezhan crossed to this world. Can you tell me about that day?"

Nasim blinked several times. He looked lost in thought, perhaps recalling the events in his mind.

"Please," Nikandr urged. "Tell me what happened. Was it you that summoned the suurahezhan?"

He was shaking his head, but he wasn't sure if it was because of some growing discomfort or if it was in answer to his question. "She was there."

"Who was there?"

Nasim's face transformed from a boy deep in thought to the expression he'd worn so often since coming to the palotza, a blank expression that told Nikandr that this moment of lucidity had passed.

"Nasim?"

Nearby, the delicate structure of stone crashed to the ground. As the cords struck the floor, they shattered into hundreds of pieces. His soulstone dimmed until it was just as it had been before its sudden resurgence.

"Nasim?" Nikandr prompted. "Nasim, can you hear me?"

He tried for long minutes, but Nasim had gone back to whatever place so occupied his mind, and Nikandr, for the life of him, couldn't figure out what any of this meant.

He touched his chest—the pain still fading—and felt his flask. A numbness spread through him, the kind one feels when struck with something so certain that it didn't seem possible.

The elixir...

He had used it each time he'd felt a connection with Nasim. The eyrie.

The cliff. The frozen lake. Here in the donjon of Radiskoye.

It had to be the reason, though why that could be he had no idea.

Nikandr rode next to Borund on a well-worn trail along the southern border of Khalakovo's largest forest. The ground tapered slowly down to the sea. The day was bright if not warm, and it was good to feel fresh wind upon his face again.

The storm that had been raging over the island abated during the night. Nikandr suspected that it had had something to do with Nasim, but Mother said that she had felt no connection from him to a hezhan. With a storm the size of the one that had gripped the island for the past week, it would take a very ancient spirit indeed to sustain it, and though Mother said that she didn't believe the boy capable of such a thing, Nikandr guessed that she was starting to form doubts. The boy had done what he had done without Mother even sensing it. The fact that she hadn't known was cause for great concern, and Nikandr could tell even if she wouldn't admit it that she was worried.

"I was pleased to hear that you'd decided to join me," Nikandr said as they crested a grass-covered knoll.

They had both been awkwardly silent since leaving the palotza. For Nikandr's part, he was angry with Borund but trying not to let it show. Father had told him early that morning that Mother had sensed ships coming from the south, ships meant to bolster the position of Vostroma and his allies.

Borund, no doubt, was angry for his own reasons.

"It was time to talk, *da*?"

They approached a meadow, which was blooming with snapdragons and brightbonnets. Both Borund and Nikandr pulled their ponies to a stop. Berza, Nikandr's mottled brown setter, had pulled up short and was standing stiff—crouching a bit, begging to be set free. Borund maneuvered his flintlock off of his lap, but Nikandr raised a finger, telling him to wait and see.

Nikandr couched the stock up against his shoulder, sighted to the center of the meadow, and pulled the flintlock back. As soon as the striker clicked into place, Berza bolted into the meadow. She leapt gracefully over a small thicket of heather, scaring two red grouse into flight. Nikandr led the lead male and pulled the trigger. A moment later, sparks shattered against the pan. The musket kicked and the crisp air exploded.

Black bits of tail feather splashed against the blue sky, but the bird continued with its mate beyond the forest—insulted, perhaps, but otherwise unharmed.

Borund started laughing—a chest-heaving affair—but then recovered himself at Nikandr's look.

"It's been a while since I've been to the fields," Nikandr said.

"No doubt! Even with that nifty trick you taught my dog, you managed to miss."

When they were young, Khalakovo's master of hounds had gifted Borund with a puppy. He loved it and begged his father to let him take it home, but Zhabyn refused, and so Borund had had to settle for visiting with her during his rare visits to Khalakovo. The dog—no thanks to Borund—had grown up to be an excellent hunter, and she'd sired a progeny that all seemed to have the same excellent traits as their matriarch, but that didn't stop Borund from claiming all of them as "his dogs."

"Laugh while you can," Nikandr said, as he spurred his pony into action, "you'll have your chance soon enough." They galloped away, Berza jumping ahead through the meadow. Nikandr took a deep breath before speaking. "But we have more to speak of than grouse."

Borund rested his musket easily in the crook of his arm. "I was beginning to wonder if you had the nerve to speak of it."

"Atiana, I would like to extend my apology to you as well as your father, which I will when I see him again. I have acted the child. Had I acted as I should, Zhabyn might not have delayed the marriage."

"Such a change of heart… You could hardly stand the thought of marrying her a week past."

"I have had time to think on it, Bora. You, of anyone, should know how difficult it can be to accept the one chosen for you."

Borund's face reddened, and Nikandr realized at once he had made a mistake. Borund had married Nataliya Dhalingrad, daughter of Duke Leonid, and it had not been Borund who had been unreceptive, but his new bride. Borund had confessed years ago how cold she had been in their wedding bed, and how it had continued until Borund had beat her in a fit of anger. She now accepted his affections, but little more than that.

Nikandr continued, "Father is furious that he would be so taken to task in front of the entire Grand Duchy. He doesn't deserve mistrust, especially when it was his wife who suggested the arrangement."

The color in Borund's face slowly faded as he reined his pony around a heather bush. "Father is merely being cautious."

"Caution is all well and good, but his fears are unfounded."

"Are they? Then answer me this, Nischka. Do you or do you not have the wasting?"

Nikandr felt his face go hot. Borund wasn't even watching him, so sure was he of the answer. Nikandr wanted to deny it, but there was no point.

Atiana must have told him.

"I do, but that doesn't mean our families cannot profit from this wedding."

"It is not the disease I care about, but that you felt it necessary to hide the fact from us. Was Khalakovo so desperate for these contracts?"

Nikandr did not want to admit that that was true, even though both of them knew it was so. Vostroma needed it as well. Khalakovo had the deepest supply of windwood and alabaster among the islands—crucial to the flow of trade among the Duchies and to Yrstanla—but Vostroma had the shipping lanes. They needed one another, but they had been at odds for so many years that it had been difficult to overcome. If Nikandr wasn't careful, he'd reopen those wounds.

"I am in the early stages, Borund. I had hoped to find a way..."

"To what? Cure it? When no one has so far been able to?"

Nikandr shrugged, feeling foolish.

"Set aside for the moment the wedding and your lies. There is the seat of a Grand Duchy to fill. Until that is resolved, there is little sense pursuing a union that would only get in the way."

"I wonder what it would be getting in the way of. You were hardly viewing your sister's marriage as a nuisance when Ranos showed you the ships that came with it."

"Those wrecks with wings?"

"You know which ships I mean."

"Ah, the ones you were so gracious in showing after making an ass of me in front of the entire eyrie."

"It wasn't—"

Borund pulled his pony to a stop and regarded Nikandr squarely. "Bolgravya is dead, Nikandr. There is treachery afoot, and my father is hardly unwise for waiting until we hear more of the affair. What I should be hearing instead of a shrill plea for the hand of Vostroma's daughter is news on what you've found after your *extensive* enquiries."

"We have been working diligently, Borund."

"To what end? Why haven't we heard more about the Motherless qiram and his boy that were spirited into the bowels of Radiskoye?"

Nikandr was not to give out any information of Ashan and Nasim, but this conversation had gone in the completely wrong direction. Borund was his oldest friend—at one time his best friend. If anyone in Vostroma's camp would see sense, it was him.

"We found them three days after the attack. The qiram is strong, but neither Mother nor Jahalan were able to detect a guided crossing. Your own mother corroborates that, does she not?"

Borund allowed himself a nod.

"And the boy is just a boy, a boy that has no talent with hezhan."

As Borund stared, a cold wind passed over the meadow, making the grasses look like waves lapping against the taller heather. Even the tops of the pine trees swayed with a similar rhythm. Berza was sniffing along a rivulet—chasing a meadow mouse, perhaps.

"If this is so why have you not yet freed them?"

"Because of the seriousness. We have to be sure."

Borund's face steeled and his eyes thinned. "Then give the boy to us. Let Ellayah question him."

"I told you, he is not the one. There is little talent within him, certainly none for an elder spirit."

"Then there is nothing for him to fear. It will take little time—days, a week at the most—and if all is as you say, the boy will be returned, none the worse for the wear."

Nikandr sat up in his saddle. "You are my friend, Borund, but be careful of your tongue. You are on Khalakovan ground, and our court rules here. Not your father's. Not Leonid's, nor his henchmen. Not even Stasa, ancients preserve him, could tell Khalakovo what to do. So, *nyet*, we will not give you the boy."

"I understand your father, Nikandr, better than you think. He was always one to ignore the tides around him, to ignore the signs brought to him on the wind. You, I thought, were different. I can see, though, that you have fallen too close to the tree. I was embarrassed for Iaros when I first heard of your offer to come hunting. Had my father not bid me to accept, I would have refused, and I would have spat upon Khalakovo's table for sending his son when duke should have sat with duke."

"The meeting was my idea," Nikandr said.

Berza, a dozen yards away, had resumed her half-crouch. She was pointing her muzzle toward the open field, but her ears were swiveling toward Nikandr.

"Then he has lost control of his own house. And if you believe—"

Borund raised his musket to his shoulder and pulled the striker to full-cock. Berza sprinted away over the meadow.

"—that I would raise friendship above my own family's interests—"

Three grouse, fifty paces away, fluttered into the air.

"Borund! Don't!" Nikandr pulled his reins over and kicked his pony into action.

Sparks flew from the hammer.

The gun cracked.

A brief flash of red against Berza's brown coat.

A yelp.

And then she was lost among the tall grasses.

"—then you are sadly mistaken."

Nikandr, his breath loud in his ears, pulled his pony up short, unable to comprehend what had just happened. He studied the grass for any sign of Berza, but there was none. The shot had been all too accurate.

"Think, Nikandr." Borund urged his pony into a walk. He held the gun up, waited for Nikandr to meet his gaze, then threw it onto the ground between them. It landed with a dull thump. "One Landless boy against the entire Duchy seems like an ill exchange to me."

And then his pony trotted away as Nikandr dropped from his saddle and sprinted across the meadow.

CHAPTER 27

Nikandr, carrying Berza, took the path just inside Radiskoye's western wall to the eyrie. The streltsi on guard, clearly confused, said nothing.

Berza was heavy in his arms, a limp weight. She hadn't deserved this. She had been a faithful friend to Nikandr her entire life. She had been loving and devoted, and well mannered save for her penchant for finding rats in the stable and eating them at the foot of Radiskoye's grand entrance. Nikandr had never been able to rid her of that one love. Perhaps it had come from her inability to down the grouse she'd been trained to chase.

He followed a trail to a quiet place along the cliffs—a place he used to come as a child to study the water far below. In the manner of his people he set Berza down and whispered words to her departing soul. For some reason he felt shamed more than betrayed. He should have sensed Borund's mood. He should have charged Borund's pony, fouled the shot.

He was preparing to drop her over the edge when he heard the crunch of footsteps coming his way. When he turned he hoped to see Victania—he needed a friend just now—but instead he found Atiana coming his way, and as soon as he had he turned away. She was just about the last person he wished to speak with now.

She either didn't sense his mood or purposely ignored it. She squatted down next to him, her dress folding over his right knee as she stared at the body of Berza. "Oh, Nischka… I had hoped they were lies." She rubbed his back, a gesture that was wholly infuriating.

"What did he say?" Nikandr asked.

"He joined us late for midday meal, boasting at how well the hunt had gone, how true his one and only shot had been. Father asked what he had felled. Borund looked at him and smiled and…"

"Don't hide it from me."

"Nischka—"

"Tell me!"

Atiana shifted away, the stone crunching beneath her boots. "He barked like a dog. And then he set to eating his elk."

Nikandr rubbed Berza's coat tenderly, realizing he was powerless to avenge her death. There could be no repercussions. Not now. Not over a dog.

He wanted to ask Atiana to leave. He didn't want the sister of the man who had done this to see his last farewell. But she had become more than that. She had come here when it was unwise to do so. If she wished to help him, then he would accept it gratefully, no matter what their future might be.

He picked Berza up, holding her in his arms while looking to the horizon. He heard Atiana whispering next to him, and when she was done, he tossed Berza from the edge of the cliff. He watched her fall, saw her splash into the white ocean waves, his eyes watering as the image of her running over the field and falling to a small spray of red played over and over within his mind.

He didn't know how long he had been watching, but suddenly Atiana was pulling him away from the edge. She brushed dirt from the shoulder of his coat, and then looked up at him with a hardened expression.

He shrugged her away. "Did you tell him?"

"Tell him what?"

"Of the wasting?"

"*Nyet.*" Her confused expression was so masterful Nikandr wasn't sure if she was telling the truth or not. "I would not have, Nikandr. I told you so that night."

"Then how would he know?"

She shook her head. "I do not know. Perhaps he guessed."

"We have barely seen one another, Atiana, and I have been careful."

Her face grew cross. "I am telling you the truth."

"*Da*, something the Vostromas are very good at."

"We aren't the ones hiding a disease that should have been revealed months ago. We aren't the ones secreting away Aramahn that should be handed over."

"You side with your father, then?"

"Why should I not? His demands are reasonable."

Nikandr paused, breathing heavily, weighing his words. He was angry now that he had shared his last few moments with Berza. He should have sent her away—he should send her away now to rot with the rest of her family and their traitorous allies—but he realized she was the one small link he still had to the Vostroma family. And more than that, she was not his enemy.

"Ashan is innocent, Atiana. The boy—I am not so sure, but if he was involved, it was as a tool. He would not do something so violent."

"How can you be sure?"

He pulled out his soulstone and showed it to her. She cringed, though whether this was from concern of his well-being or embarrassment that she might still marry a man with a broken past, he wasn't sure. "When I first met him, he noticed my stone even though he couldn't see it. We are connected, he and I. I know not how, but I do know this—that boy is no murderer." He motioned toward the nearby cliff. "He is as innocent as Berza."

She stared at the stone a moment longer, then met his gaze. "I believe you."

"You do?"

"Strange things are happening. The blight. The wasting. When I took the dark for your mother, I saw a young girl die in her mother's arms, taken by a hezhan. Who would have thought to see such things in our lifetime? If you say there is a link between you and the boy, if you say he is innocent, then I believe you."

He was so shocked he found himself unable to speak for a moment. "Thank you, Atiana."

Her eyes went far away. It was a look he knew well. It meant she was scheming. Calculating.

"What is it?" he asked.

"If it's proof my father needs, there is one way you could provide it."

"How?"

"The Matra could assume him."

Nikandr sat across from Father in his drawing room, waiting for Mother to join them. A black rook, which had been sitting idly on the nearby perch, suddenly launched into a fit of flapping wings and cawing. The display ceased as soon as it had begun, but now there was a look of intelligence in the eyes that hadn't been present moments ago.

"Good day, Mother," Nikandr said.

The rook arched its head back and cawed once. "Quickly, Nischka. I have little time."

"I wish to discuss Nasim." Father opened his mouth to speak, but Nikandr talked over him. "There is little enough to report, which is why I needed to speak to you both."

"Go on," Father said.

"I want Mother to assume Nasim's form."

The moment Atiana had said it, Nikandr knew they had to try it. He was surprised he hadn't thought of it sooner. He was surprised his mother hadn't, until he realized that she probably had. It was a dangerous thing to do, made no less dangerous by Nasim's unpredictable nature. And there were other considerations as well. It was a practice that had been used long ago by the earliest of the Matri against the Aramahn—sometimes to gain information, sometimes to control them for short periods. It was a practice that had been forbidden as part of the Covenant between the fledgling Grand Duchy and the Aramahn. Were they to resume the practice and be discovered, there would be serious repercussions from Iramanshah.

The rook flapped its wings several times.

"Impossible," Father said as he reached up and stroked the black feathers of the bird's breast. "Has Ranos not told you the steps Fahroz has taken?"

"All the more reason to do something now, before it's too late."

Aramahn were already refusing to work on Khalakovan ships. Some were still arriving, but word had already spread among the archipelago, and fewer ships bearing goods and food were arriving because of it. As hard as Volgorod had been hit by the blight, they could sustain no more than a few months without the Aramahn.

"That isn't all," Father said. "Zhabyn, as I feared, has delivered an ultimatum. Either we give him the boy by tomorrow morning or he and the traitor dukes leave to join the incoming fleet. He has threatened a blockade, allowing no ships to pass in or out until we give him up."

"The same choice left to us by Fahroz."

Father allowed himself a smile. He looked haggard, but then he turned casually toward Nikandr, a steely look in his eyes. "Barring a confession or conclusive evidence, we have two clear choices. We can give the boy to Fahroz or we can give him to Zhabyn, though the latter seems no choice at all. He will simply torture the boy to find the information he needs, and I have no doubt it will be skewed to his side of the conflict. Which leaves the Aramahn… It grates that they have demanded the boy, but they are in the right here. We have nothing to offer them for evidence, so if we assume the boy's mind and word ever reached them that we had, we would be left with nothing."

"It isn't whether or not he had something to do with the crossing. It's in what capacity. Who used him, and why? Can they do so again? And if so, when?"

"It's too dangerous."

"No one will know. We'll find an excuse to keep Jahalan and Udra away, and we can move Ashan to another cell. Even if Nasim understands what's happening to him, he'll most likely never tell a soul, and even if he does, it would be easy to deny."

Father stared into Nikandr's eyes, clearly doubting the soundness of this decision, but then the rook croaked and pecked at the crossbar it was standing on. "We will do it."

Father looked shocked. "You are sure?"

The rook cawed. "You are right to worry over the threats we face from the dukes and the Aramahn, both, but I fear we have not been paying enough attention to what this boy might have done. What he might have leveraged here on Khalakovo to summon such a beast. If there is some small risk of giving offense, then I say the risk is worth it."

Father considered this for a time, but then nodded. "It will be done. Tonight."

CHAPTER 28

Rehada, flying high over the island under a bright and cloudless sky, adjusted her hold on the sail lines, maneuvering the skiff to a more westerly course. Unlike the larger Landed ships, the skiff had only a single keel running fore to aft that kept the craft aligned with the ley lines of the island below her. It was a simple craft, not so different from the ships used in the early days of exploration, granted life by the nature of the windwood hull and the dhoshaqiram shipwright who had cured and shaped it.

There was much to do today, but Rehada's thoughts kept slipping back to her time with Nasim deep in the roots of Radiskoye. The heat. The pain. So intense. She had never been at the mercy of the elements in that manner. Always, even when she was young, even while she was learning, she had been in control. Even when she offered herself up to the flame in penance for her thoughts, she was in control. There, sitting with Nasim, she had been at his mercy.

And there was no doubt that he had been the one pulling the strings. The only question was whether or not he had understood what he was doing, whether it was malicious or not. She didn't think so, mainly because of what had come before.

Over the years—especially when she was new to the ways of bonding—she had hoped through her bonding that she could understand more about the world beyond and so learn more about *this* life. She had hoped to learn what she could expect when she passed and how she might better prepare herself for her next life—all in hopes of one day reaching vashaqiram.

But she, like nearly all Aramahn who tried such things, had been disappointed. She had been unable to feel anything more than a vague sense of *otherness* that emanated from the hezhan she bonded with. Her time there would often evoke memories, especially ones she had long forgotten, and some she could not remember at all—memories from prior lives, or perhaps those she had yet to live—but never had she felt like she was experiencing Adhiya.

But there in Radiskoye, while allowing the suurahezhan to occupy her consciousness, she had felt another soul. Nasim. She bid the hezhan to approach him, and when it did, she felt something so unexpected that she nearly cried. He was so miserable in the real world. But there... There, he was in rapture. He was filled with joy, with wonder, with love beyond understanding. She had often wished she could see the world beyond, to touch it and taste it. Feeling some small amount of what Nasim felt, she knew these to be foolish urges. Who needed eyes when such heights of emotion were possible? Who needed to taste, to hear, to feel, when the mind could soar high along the firmament?

She craved to bask in his light, but she knew she had to speak with him, not for Nikandr's benefit, but her own.

Nasim, she called.

His attention shifted. It felt as if a bright star had focused its rays upon her, and though it burned, she did not care.

Nasim, it was you that day, wasn't it? You were there when I summoned the suurahezhan.

There was no response, but she could sense that he was listening. How many others had done what she was doing now? What had Ashan spoken to him about? And what had he learned?

We hope that you will join our cause. We wish to rid these islands of the taint from the Landed. She paused, but when she heard no response, she continued. *We wish you to open the rift, the same rift used to allow the suurahezhan to cross.*

She repeated these thoughts many times, but Nasim only continued to watch, to wait.

Did you know that men died that day?

A flare.

Dozens, Nasim.

She felt, at last, an emotional response.

Dozens of Landed died from one hezhan. Imagine what you could do were the rift to open wide.

And then her world was pulled out from underneath her. Her awareness had been fixated, pinpointed, but now it expanded so rapidly she felt lost. She felt the island, the currents that ran through it. It was a reflection of the material world as seen from Adhiya, and it was beautiful beyond description, the currents of life, shifting, slipping, mixing, reforming into innumerable combinations.

But it was not complete. A wound ran through it, so deeply that she knew it immediately for what it was. The rift that Soroush had discovered forming on Uyadensk, the place she had called home for the last seven years. The rift moved like the slow tide of magma on the active southern volcanoes. It drew life from everything around it. It was a corruption, a tear between the worlds, and it was affecting Adhiya as much as it was Erahm.

Yeh, Rehada said, *this is what we wish you to—*

Pain coursed through her like a river during springtime melt. She felt the misery of the island, the pain that the rift was wreaking on its slow trek across the landscape. It poisoned everything it touched, and though she realized the rift would one day close, she also knew another would replace it, and another, until the rifts became so large, so voracious, that they would consume everything.

She pleaded for Nasim to release her, but she realized with a growing horror that Nasim had gone. He had left her to the devices of Adhiya, leaving the rift and the suurahezhan that now fed upon her to do with her what they would.

She railed, fighting the spirit with all the strength that remained. She thought surely it would take her, would draw her through the veil to Adhiya to begin her life beyond, but finally, after one last panicked surge, she felt it release her.

She had woken with Nikandr beating the flames from her clothes, staring at her with wild eyes. The stench of burned wool filled the air. The dying madness was at odds with Nasim, who sat emotionless on the floor nearby.

She had left Radiskoye with feelings of inadequacy and smallness in the face of what she had seen. She'd had terrible dreams, visions of Ahya being burned alive, of Gierten's baby girl being swallowed by the earth, and when morning had finally arrived, she had known she would come to remove the stone she had placed beneath Evina. It was a small thing, she knew—Soroush would merely take another if not this one—but it was all she could think to do.

She pulled several of the small opals attached to the inside of the hull off, placing them in a bag affixed to the mast. As the skiff descended, she maneuvered it toward the water, landing it in a clearing between the trees. She headed off toward Gierten's home. She could hear the sound of the surf to the south. The wind was pleasant, and it brought with it not only the loamy smell of the forest but also memories of the times she had spent with Ahya in places like this, running through the trees and laughing.

She reached the home a short while later. It was squat, with a thatched roof and a gravel path that led from the shoreline to the front of the home. She stepped onto the porch and squinted into the dim interior. With the sun directly overhead it was difficult to see into the room that had only a small window set high in the wall, but she could still see a hearth, a small table, and a rocking chair. "*Privyet*?" she called.

When no one answered, she walked around to the rear and found Gierten kneeling on a piece of wood, tending to a sickly patch of garden twice the size of their modest home.

Beyond the garden was a well-tended graveyard bordered with a low stone wall. Inside were a dozen cairns, each of them marked with a tall piece of obsidian shaped like Radiskoye's spire. They held no words of remembrance, but they had a small, uncut chalcedony stone near the top.

Gierten wore a skirt and a man's shirt, the sleeves of which were rolled up beyond the elbows, revealing grossly thin arms. She was using a wood-handled trowel to pull the weeds among the potatoes and onions. Every so often she gathered enough of the weeds that she would toss them behind her onto a large pile.

Gierten was alone; Evina's basket was nowhere to be seen.

The cairns… One of them was small, and the earth beneath it was dark, fresh. By the fates, she had come too late.

Rehada began backing away, hoping Gierten wouldn't notice. She moved one step. Two.

And then a voice spoke from behind Rehada. "What's this?"

She turned and found a man, perhaps forty, staring at her. His name was Ruslan, and he was Gierten's husband. She had seen him at the midsummer festivals in Izhny. He wore simple peasant clothes, and a string of small blue mackerel hung over his shoulder.

Gierten turned and wiped her brow with the back of a grimy hand, regarding Rehada with a wholly uncharitable look. Her cheeks were sunken. Her eyes had dark bags beneath them. "What are you doing here?" Her voice was listless and gray.

"I merely came to see how Evina has been faring." She tried to make it sound as if she didn't already know that Evina was dead, but she knew it sounded unconvincing.

"*She* brought the necklace?" Ruslan said to his wife, though he stared hard at Rehada.

Gierten nodded.

Rehada willed herself not to look at it, but she could see a fisherman's knife within a sheath at his belt. "I've made a mistake. Please, I'll leave. I won't trouble you again."

She made for the path, but he stepped in her way. Her heart was pumping madly, and she was just touching the aether to summon her bonded spirit when Gierten grabbed the circlet from around her brow. Instantly her connection was broken, leaving her stomach lurching from the loss of contact.

She felt instantly cold, and her skin prickled along her legs and arms.

Ruslan pointed to the circlet. "It's forbidden to use them against us."

"I would not have. I swear to you."

"You were. It was glowing."

"I should leave." She backed away, ready to run. The circlet and the gem could be replaced. "I'm sorry to have caused any trouble."

She stopped when she heard footsteps coming from behind. A balding man with damp white hair hanging down in loose curls stood by the corner of the house. "You had something to do with my granddaughter, didn't you, you filthy Motherless wretch?"

"*Nyet*, I—"

Rehada turned to run, but Ruslan grabbed her around the neck.

She tried to scream, but the only thing that came out was a muffled caw, like a diseased and dying gull. She kicked, but the older man stepped in and punched her in the gut. The air rushed from her lungs as pain blossomed in her stomach and ribs. She fought for air, to no avail. Nothing was coming, and the man's hold prevented her from breathing. They dragged her toward the house. She kicked viciously, catching the old man off guard. Her heel connected hard with the left side of his face. He shouted and doubled over, holding his ear.

Ruslan threw her to the ground and pulled the thin boning knife from its sheath. He grabbed for her hair. She recoiled, kicking at his legs, but the other man had recovered, and he moved around behind her and grabbed her shoulders.

"Let her go," Gierten said, still holding the circlet tightly in both hands.

"Get yourself down to the shore," Ruslan said. "I'll get you when we're done."

"She's been kind… She wouldn't have harmed Evina…"

Before she could say anything else, Ruslan stalked forward and slapped her across the face. "Get yourself down to the shore!"

Gierten held her cheek, a frightened look on her face. She glanced at Rehada, saying nothing, and then she turned and walked down the gravel path.

"Please don't leave—"

The old man struck Rehada, hammering her ear so hard it began to ring.

"That's for the kick. Now stop fighting or it won't go well at all."

Rehada didn't listen. She kicked and thrashed, spun around on the ground, trying to loosen their grip on her. She screamed.

Ruslan managed to lay himself over her legs and climb up until he was straddling her waist. His father pinned her arms over her head.

"Please don't do this. You don't know who I am."

"Don't I?" He reached down with the knife. "You're Landless. You're nothing."

"She is Maharraht—"

Gierten's husband looked up just in time to see Soroush rushing forward with a khanjar gripped tightly in one hand.

"—and she is worth more than you and all your ancestors."

CHAPTER 29

Soroush drove the khanjar deep into the fisherman's gut while fending off a hurried counterattack. Ruslan's eyes went impossibly wide. His face reddened. The knife fell from his grip and thumped softly against the earth. He grabbed at Soroush's wrist, trying to pull the khanjar free, but Soroush was strong, and the man was already beginning to weaken.

The older man had been too shocked to move, but then he dove for his son's knife. He never reached it. He was pulled backward and off of Rehada by Bersuq.

Rehada scrabbled away and reached her feet.

Bersuq was nearly fifty, but still he grabbed the other man around the waist and flipped him to the ground as if he were felling a lamb. He drew his own khanjar—a curving blade with runes worked along its length—and brought it down hard into the old man's chest.

A ragged inhalation of breath accompanied the man's panicked attempts at removing the blade, but mere moments later he fell back, lifeless. Rehada, breathing heavily, her fingers tingling, studied his face as she approached. As Bersuq pulled the knife free and stood, she reached his side, seeing details in the man she hadn't noticed before—the deep lines in his tanned face; the spots along his brow from his days on the sea; his rough, gnarled hands; the scars that ran through the light white stubble covering his chin and neck.

His soul, even now, was crossing over to Adhiya, to join the hezhan until such a time as the fates decided he should return. She wondered if he would be reborn as Aramahn or Landed. There were those among her people, especially the Maharraht, that believed Landed returned as Landed, Aramahn as Aramahn. It was foolishness—an attempt to further divide the peoples of the world—and as it always did when she saw the loss of life, it reminded her of her daughter's passing, of the day *she* would pass, of how much had changed for her people over the last few generations.

As always, death was making her question the choices she had made, her decision to join the Maharraht and their thirst to reclaim a thing that was said to be owned by no one: the land itself. If anything, the *land* owned *you*. She questioned whether or not she could continue with such willful hatred.

But then she remembered her daughter's blackened skin in the smoking wreckage of the house—her clawed hands and curled-up form. She had been told of the streltsi, how they had chased a pair of Maharraht to a simple home on the outskirts of a village not unlike Izhny. The Maharraht had taken refuge and had refused to leave. The couple that lived there—a couple Rehada knew well—had been watching Ahya while Rehada took breath on the tallest mountain on Nazakhov. Hoping to protect both Ahya and the Maharraht, they had shut the doors to Bolgravya's soldiers and refused to open them. Rather than force their way in, the soldiers had secured the doors and set the structure ablaze. The windows were too small to crawl from. They had no chance to escape.

Rehada had returned hours later from a time of extreme peace. She had felt, before being told what had happened, like she had made great strides toward an understanding of this island. It was exhilarating. So many of her experiences had combined on that mountaintop, and she felt as though the road had been paved for even more in coming travels. But then she had found the blackened ruins of a home where her daughter had been trapped by the soldiers.

Rehada's stomach turned while the memories of that day played within her mind. She knew she had lost lifetimes of progress on her way toward vashaqiram with the decision she had made—along with Soroush—to join the Maharraht. But the ways of the Landed could not continue. She was glad she could do this, that her brothers and sisters might be spared; she was glad to sacrifice so that the entirety of her people would not have to suffer the same.

Soroush released a short, piercing whistle. Bersuq scanned the ground over Rehada's shoulder.

Rehada turned and found Gierten standing near the corner of the cottage, training a musket on Soroush. Soroush darted to one side while Bersuq sprinted toward her, releasing a melodic war cry as he went.

She changed her mind, aiming for Bersuq. She squeezed the trigger, but nothing happened. She looked incredulously at the musket, as if it had betrayed her, and then she threw it at Bersuq, who dodged easily and grabbed her by the hair. In one quick motion, he was behind her, his arm locked around her throat. Bersuq tightened his hold. Gierten's face went bright red. Mere moments later, her eyes closed and she went limp. Bersuq lowered her to the ground, where she remained, unconscious, the musket lying just next to her.

As Bersuq began dragging Gierten toward the trees, Soroush rounded on Rehada. "A pretty hole you've dug for us," he said in Mahndi. "What were you doing?"

Rehada stared down at the men, shaking her head. More and more to atone for, she thought to herself. "We should leave."

"Answer my question."

"I hoped to secure the stone," she lied, "to leave no evidence behind."

"You should have left it to us."

"I have been careful to construct a life here, Soroush, a life free of suspicion. I would not wish it to unravel in a matter of days."

"Your life here is nearly at an end, Rehada."

"Think well on this, Soroush. All of this could still fall around our ears. I still have Nikandr's trust. Would you throw that away for nothing?"

He paused, breathing heavily, glancing eastward toward Radiskoye. "That will not matter after tonight."

"Why?"

"We are taking Nasim back."

She paused. Things were moving so quickly. She did not trust Nasim, but she wasn't yet sure she wanted him in Soroush's hands. "You are sure?"

"I am sure."

Bersuq had returned after dragging the men's bodies into the forest. He motioned to Soroush. "Toward the westward shore."

Soroush glanced in that direction, and then faced Rehada squarely. "Return to Volgorod. Wait for word."

They left, trudging through the forest undergrowth carrying two shovels and a pick. When the two of them could no longer be seen, Rehada stepped inside Gierten's simple home. A wooden table and chairs occupied one corner, a potbelly stove another. The hearth was made from rounded stone and aged mortar. The mantel held several pieces of carved bone, a hobby of Ruslan's, perhaps. A hand-woven rug covered the floor nearby, and a rocking chair sat by the window near the front door.

An entire home, wiped away in an instant. What had they done to deserve it?

They'd done nothing. They had had the misfortune, as Soroush had put it, of being born Landed. When would all of this end, she wondered. And what would come of the rift? If Soroush had his way, Nasim would be back in his hands soon. Would he wipe away the life on Khalakovo as he'd done in this simple fisherman's home? Would they return enlightened? Or would it continue the cycle of discontent that seemed to have gripped the world?

She took a deep breath, readying to leave, when she noticed movement among the trees. A woman dressed in Landed riding clothes was moving stealthily through the forest. She moved with a certain grace, but she was no woodsman, and her raiment was fine. Fine enough for royalty.

It struck her all of a sudden. This woman was strikingly similar to the pale, blonde-haired beauty she'd seen in the halls of Radiskoye. And for good reason. This was no other than Atiana Vostroma. What would she be doing here, and what would have possessed her to follow two Maharraht?

Rehada nearly let her go, nearly let her walk into the jaws of the wolf that would meet her on the nearby shore, but too much blood had been spilled this day, and she realized with a numb sense of horror that she was jealous of this woman. She had taken something of Rehada's, no matter how tenuous her hold had been, and she didn't like it. Those were the exact emotions she had been trying all her life to root out.

So she followed this foolish Vostroman woman to see what she was about.

CHAPTER 30

The coach taking Atiana and her sisters to Volgorod jumped as it struck an excessively large hole in the road. Ishkyna pounded the roof, her expression making it clear she would gladly have replaced the roof with the driver's head.

"I don't see why you couldn't go by yourself," Ishkyna said as she settled herself back into her seat.

"You can walk back to the palotza if you'd rather."

Ishkyna rolled her eyes. "You're as sensitive as an open wound these days, Tiana. I was only wondering why you couldn't just ask Father for permission."

Atiana nearly unleashed her bottled up anger on Ishkyna for telling Borund of Nikandr's disease, but Ishkyna would only deny it. Atiana would bide her time. She would even the scales.

Borund had kept it quiet until after his hunt with Nikandr, then he'd told everyone who would listen, acting as if it were the greatest insult imaginable. Many supported his position—largely, she suspected, because Father was the one everyone assumed would take over the mantle of Grand Duke. The wasting was often hidden by royalty—some for reasons of vanity, others because they perceived it as weak. Stasa himself had hidden just how bad the disease had become.

Grigory had been only too pleased to hear this news. He spoke longer and louder than even Borund, telling everyone how craven Nikandr was. He stopped short of demanding a duel, however—even Borund would think twice over that. Nikandr was known by everyone to be an expert shot.

Atiana didn't like hearing their words. Though she and Nikandr hadn't been formally married, she felt as if she were honor-bound to defend him. There was also the feeling that it had been something she and Nikandr alone had shared. As far as he knew, he hadn't told anyone else, and even though she'd stumbled upon it accidentally, it felt like something special, something cherished. It was a foolish thought, she knew, but still she harbored no small amount of resentment toward Ishkyna for letting it out.

The coach crossed a stone bridge, the sound from the ponies' hooves going from a soft thumping to a rhythmic clatter and back again. Atiana turned her back to Mileva, who sat in the seat next to her, and Mileva began pulling at the cords of her dress.

"I've seen twenty winters." Atiana slipped out of the dress, pulled off her dainty shoes and began pulling on her riding trousers. "I have no inclination to ask Father for something that is mine by right."

Ishkyna laughed. "Which is exactly why you told him we'd be visiting Lady Kirelenko the entire day."

Mileva tapped Ishkyna's knee. "Come. There's nothing wrong with a bit of a diversion, and what Father doesn't know won't hurt him." She turned to Atiana, who was just now pulling on a gun belt, complete with an ornate flintlock pistol. "It *is* only for a look around, isn't it? We won't be hearing news about a Motherless woman floating face-down in the bay, will we?"

Atiana felt her face flush. "Would you blame me if you did?"

Yesterday Ishkyna had seen Nikandr speaking with the Landless woman inside the palotza, and then saw them embrace. It had been no perfunctory gesture, Ishkyna had said. It had been filled with desire—on the woman's part if not Nikandr's, she was quick to amend.

Rehada and Nikandr had apparently been quite close over the past few years. They had tried to keep their relations a secret, but there was no such thing among the aristocracy. In truth, Atiana didn't really blame him for it. The fact that he retained a lover was no surprise at all, but to be faced with her presence in Radiskoye, to be presented with her *name* and a description of her dark beauty, was another thing entirely.

Mileva stared at Atiana with the expression she used when they were alone—as if *she* were the only sister allowed to pass moral judgment.

"Enough," Atiana said. "If I have a mind to be alone in a city I've seen precious little of since I arrived, that's my prerogative."

"Well, we'll be sure to keep your little secret," Ishkyna said.

"Don't you always?" Atiana asked.

"Always."

After Atiana pulled on her fitted cherkesska, she was dropped off at the central square near Volgorod's state buildings. Ishkyna and Mileva continued in the carriage toward Lady Kirelenko's while Atiana continued on foot. When the carriage was finally out of sight, she headed to an inn near the edge of the old city that kept ponies. She bought one for the day and headed west. The buildings, many of them four stories or higher, were made of stone. That changed to curving streets and smaller brick homes that looked exactly like one another, and finally the land began to open up into farmland as it rose steadily toward the high ridge running the entire length of the island.

Atiana followed the southwesterly road and took to the grasses once she came close to the eyrie. The fewer people that saw her, the better. She saw nothing of the eyrie itself, for the bulk of it was facing toward the sea. It took her another hour of riding, but finally she came to a small set of wagon tracks that veered off the main road that led toward the small fishing village of Izhny. The wooded trail led her to the sea. An empty pier jutted out into the water of the cove. The wind was brisk, but not unpleasantly cold. The trail continued through the thickening trees and, far ahead, led to a simple, earth-covered home.

She pulled her pony to a stop as she came closer, her heart immediately beginning to race. Through the trees she saw two Maharraht heading into the woods to the west of the home. They were old, perhaps as old as Father. Both wore loose trousers tucked into leather boots. They had a tight inner robe wrapped by a wide belt of cloth, and an outer robe that trailed nearly down to their ankles. Instead of the traditional cap many of the men on the island wore, they wore turbans, with the trailing ends hanging down over their shoulders and along the front of their chests. One of them was carrying two shovels, the other a pick.

Her pony pulled at the reins. Atiana immediately loosened them and smoothed the hair along his neck—she could not afford to be heard, now of all times.

She scanned the landscape behind her. She set her gaze through the alder and ivory-skinned birch, toward Volgorod. She should let these men go. A woman had no business following men like this.

And yet this seemed too important to ignore. They had come to the very home she had seen in the aether. What connection did they have with the baby, to the hezhan that had taken her life?

She had to know.

She grasped the soulstone at her throat and closed her eyes.

Saphia.

She waited for a moment, but the only response she heard was the sound of the surf and the rustle of the wind through the trees.

Matra, I need you.

She knew the Matra might be far afield, spying on one of the other islands, or she might be deep in communion with the other Matri. Either way, it didn't make much difference right now.

She pulled the pistol from its holster at her waist. When the men were lost from view, she tied her pony deeper into the woods and padded after them.

They were not moving quickly, and it took her little time to catch up. They walked until they reached the edge of the wood, at which point they trekked into the jumbled landscape of tall, rounded boulders that split the forest from the water. The air smelled of sea and earth, both. The tide was low, so the rocks would be slippery, but the men navigated them with ease.

Atiana kept pace until they stopped between several large boulders. The nearby surf broke white and frothy against the rocks before crashing apart into rivulets, frothing to a stop near her feet.

The older Maharraht crouched and with his eyes closed ran his hands over the rocks. There was a golden setting at the center of his brow, worked into his turban, and within the setting was a gem of jasper. A vanaqiram, then, a master of earth. Atiana had seen few in her life. Very rare were earth spirits, and rarer were those who could control them. She studied the gem closely. It was difficult to tell, as the jasper was striated and blood red in color. It seemed lifeless, and so she could only assume that he was unbonded.

The other man had a horrible scar where the lower half of his left ear should have been. The crest of his ear was festooned with a half-dozen golden earrings. This close, she realized who he must be. Everyone on the islands knew of him. He could be no other than Soroush Wahad al Gatha, the leader of the Maharraht.

The very thought made what little courage she had left drain from her. But what could she do now? To leave would be to alert them to her presence.

The older one, apparently satisfied, stood, and the two of them spoke in Mahndi to one another. Atiana knew little of the language, but it sounded harsher than the way Father's servants spoke it. After a short discussion, they set to work digging in the rocky soil using the shovels they'd brought. The going was slow at first, but once they hit the sandy-clay soil, they went much faster. Soon they had formed what Atiana could only describe as a grave.

After tossing the shovels aside, the two hugged, then kissed, and then the one with the graying beard laid down in the pit. Atiana's eyes widened as Soroush began pushing the mounded soil back into the hole. In little time, the moist earth had been piled upon the buried man. Soroush moved himself a few paces away, and there he crouched, closed his eyes, and began humming an ancient and arrhythmic melody.

Atiana grasped her soulstone. *Matra, please, hear me.*

But she sensed that the Matra would not.

She gripped the pistol, gaining some small comfort from it. She debated on whether to fire upon Soroush while he was alone. She could reload and take the other as he crawled from his grave—*if* he crawled from his grave. She pulled the striker to full-cock, pouring a bit of powder into the pan for good measure. She was a decent shot, but she had never fired *at* someone.

These men were ruthless, she told herself. They would kill her without a thought if they found her. She was merely protecting the interests of her family.

Which family? she asked. *Khalakovo or Vostroma?* Lately, she had felt as if she were of neither, but here, as she readied her aim, she felt as though she belonged to both.

She trained the pistol on the Maharraht. *Fire now,* she told herself, *fire.* But her arm was shaking so badly she was sure she would miss. Using two hands only seemed to make matters worse.

And then the earth shivered. A great crack rent the sound of the pounding surf. Atiana felt it in her feet and in her bones. Another crack pierced the air, and this time she felt the rock move. She leapt away, hoping she could make it far enough that she wouldn't be spotted, but she lay there awestruck as the rock she had been standing on unfolded into a tall, stone beast. Much of it was a mottled gray color, but its front—the portions of the hezhan that had moments ago been folded within itself—was black as night and glittering, as if it had swallowed the midnight sky, stars and all. It stood on two massive legs, and it had four oddly segmented arms attached to a chest the size of a wine tun.

She raised her pistol, aimed at the thing's face. She squeezed the trigger. The pan flashed as the gun pounded her wrist and forearm. A cloud of scree exploded from its head. For a moment everything stood still. But then the dust and rock cleared and it was obvious that her ill-advised shot had done nothing.

She thought the beast would step forward and place one foot upon her chest and press the life from her, but instead it turned and began digging at the earth where its master lay buried. Soroush helped, though while he was doing so he would every so often glance her way.

Atiana backed away, preparing to run, but before she had taken three steps the other raider stood from his grave, covered in wet earth, staring straight at her. His eyes were hard, as if he were furious that he'd been discovered even though Atiana had seen little. The vanahezhan raised its arm—

Atiana's eyes went wide, and she scrabbled away as quickly as she could.

—and the earth flew upward in great gouts, plowing ever closer to Atiana. The sound of it was like a landslide.

She leapt, but the spraying rocks tore into her left leg. She screamed while rolling away. When she found her feet, she had trouble standing, so sharp was the pain in her knee.

The hezhan raised its palm once more, and Atiana readied herself to dodge, but before she could the water among the rocks in front of her began to hiss. Steam rose up and filled the air, and in a flash everything around her was as hot as a steam bath and the air was thick with fog.

The ground shook with the footsteps of the vanahezhan. It resolved out of the fog, mere paces away. Atiana tried to run toward the relative safety of the larger rocks, but the pain in her leg allowed her little more than a shambling gait. The beast followed, knocking aside a massive boulder with a swat of two of its trunk-thick arms. She retreated further, but the beast was catching up. Soon, she had no more rock to hide behind. There was only open land between her and the forest. The sound of the surf suddenly intensified, but Atiana could spare no time to look.

The vanahezhan picked up a huge boulder and prepared to launch it at Atiana. The rock itself began to hiss, and the front of it began to glow dully red. It cracked in half as the beast attempted to throw it. It crashed into the beach halfway to Atiana.

Footsteps crunched over the stone behind her. Atiana turned and saw a woman—an Aramahn woman—running toward her from out of the mist. "Come quickly," the woman said as she grabbed Atiana by the wrist and led her toward the water. She was beautiful. She had long black hair cut straight across the brow. A glowing tourmaline gem rested in the center of a circlet upon her brow.

Atiana couldn't believe her eyes. She had only a few descriptions of the woman, but she had no doubts. For reasons known only to the ancients, Nikandr's Aramahn whore had come to save her.

CHAPTER 31

"Into the water," Rehada said, her voice tight.

Atiana could do little but obey. The vanahezhan was already pounding its way toward them. Steam rose from the hissing rocks, covering their retreat. They had gone a dozen paces into the surf when Rehada said, "Swim." She yanked Atiana's arm, pulling her off balance. "Do not allow your feet to touch the seabed."

Through gritted teeth Atiana sucked in a lungful of breath as the icy water enveloped her. She swam backward as the vanahezhan reached the edge of the water and stopped. It swayed its head back and forth like a bloodhound. Then it raised its four arms up high and brought them down together against the beach. A great plume of water and rock and mud rose up into the sky.

The fog around them was thick, and soon they lost sight of the hezhan entirely.

"It will not find us as long as we don't touch the rock," Rehada said.

"Grand. Then all we need do is swim to Duzol and we'll be safe."

"It will leave soon enough."

"How do you know?"

"They know they have been discovered. When they do not find us, they will hide."

"How can you be so sure they won't find us?"

"I can't." Rehada leaned into the water and began to swim in a direction parallel to the shoreline.

Atiana was forced to decide whether she would follow, but there was little choice, and she soon began swimming after Rehada. The water was numbing, drawing away her energy, but she was still high with fear, and so they were able to go quite a long distance. The fog finally dissipated. As they swam beyond it, it rose up behind them white and thick while the way ahead was clear and bright under a cloudless sky. They headed for land after seeing no one on the shore, and by the time they dragged themselves out of the heavy surf, Atiana's arms and legs were leaden. She kissed her soulstone, not particularly willing to show weakness in front of Rehada but even less willing to ignore her ancestors, who had clearly been watching over her this day.

"Come," Rehada said, "this is no time to rest." And then she was off toward the trees.

Atiana gritted her teeth against the pain throbbing up her left leg and limped after her. They moved as quickly as they could, Atiana often looking behind them to see if anyone was following.

"That was Soroush, wasn't it?"

Rehada ignored her.

Atiana grabbed Rehada's arm and turned her around. "What was the leader of the Maharraht doing here?"

The Landless woman jerked her arm free and stared down at Atiana. Atiana hadn't realized how tall she was until just then.

She resumed walking, forcing Atiana to keep pace. "You were foolish to follow them."

Atiana's mind swam with questions. "How did you come to be there on the shore?"

"I followed you."

"From Volgorod?"

"From the eyrie. I was taking breath in the hills above it."

Taking breath was the Aramahn term for meditation. It was possible that she had met newcomers on the eyrie—the Aramahn often did so to acclimate those who had arrived—but something in her story smelled foul.

"I was nowhere near the eyrie."

"You were near enough."

"I saw no one."

"Nevertheless, I saw you."

"Then tell me why you followed me."

They had nearly reached the house. Rehada stopped and faced Atiana after taking a good long look behind for signs of pursuit.

"You know who I am." She stated it flatly, barely a question at all.

Atiana nodded.

"I was curious."

"Curious…"

Rehada swallowed. This tall, beautiful woman was somehow cowed. "I should not be speaking of this."

Atiana remained silent, a demand that Rehada continue.

"Your husband has spoken of you, and… I know my place in the world.

I know it is not with Nikandr. He will be with you. But I was curious to see the one who would take him away from me."

It felt strange hearing these words from a woman who had bedded the man who would be her husband. If anyone had asked her the day before how she would have reacted, she would have said she'd have the woman's eyes put out. But here, standing before her, there was a strange sense of camaraderie that she would never in a thousand years have predicted. She could not be angry with a woman who was jealous of her. But neither could she speak to her of Nikandr—it made her stomach feel queasy just thinking about it.

"We should go."

Rehada agreed. In little time they had reached the wagon trail that led from the house to the short pier. Atiana made to go after her pony, but Rehada stopped her.

"Leave it. We cannot remain on the ground, not when they could still find us, perhaps with reinforcements."

"Then how—" Atiana stopped, for she had just realized how Rehada had spotted her, and how she hadn't known. She had been on a skiff, the smaller windships the Landless use to fly between islands and ferry themselves from Volgorod to Iramanshah.

Once they had reached a thick copse of trees near the beach, Atiana saw it: a craft shaped like an overturned turtle with a single mast in its center. They entered, and once Rehada had placed several opals into the small brass fittings worked into the hull, the vessel lifted into the sky.

"Where will we go?" Atiana asked.

Rehada wore leather gloves. She used them—already looking completely at home—to hold the two ropes tied to the lower corners of the simple, triangular sail that billowed ahead of them. "I will take you to Iraman-shah. A healer will look at your leg, and you can arrange transportation to Volgorod."

As long as it was alone, Atiana thought.

Her earlier acceptance of Rehada was starting to wear thin; she wanted, at the moment, to be anywhere Rehada was not.

She tried to study the landscape for signs of pursuit, but the winds were playing with the ship, making her stomach turn, and so she kept her eyes on the horizon until the skiff had settled into the wind. The currents were easterly here, and they grew stronger the higher they rose into the sky, but the sail and the ship's keel were guiding the ship northward.

The house was soon lost from view, but Atiana could see the beach where she and Rehada had fought with the vanahezhan.

"Why wouldn't they follow in a skiff of their own?"

Rehada stared down at Atiana coldly. "I would think that was obvious."

Atiana stared back, shivering. The wind was strong, especially this high up, and her clothes were still wet. She realized they were growing warm, and then she realized why.

"*Nyet!*" she shouted, refusing to allow this woman to warm her. She would freeze to death first.

Rehada, the tourmaline gem upon her brow still glowing, shrugged and returned her attention to the sails.

Immediately, the temperature plummeted.

"If they didn't want to attract attention from the Matra," Atiana said after a time, shivering once more, "they wouldn't have summoned a vanahezhan on her doorstep."

"That was different."

"Why?"

"The place where it was summoned marked, I believe, a location where a vanahezhan had left this world."

"You mean entered it."

"*Nyet.* Left. The spirits are tied to this world as surely as we are tied to theirs. They hunger when they've been too long without it, and when they finally get a chance to experience it, it lingers with them, and they remain near the place where they exited our world and returned to theirs."

"But how could a vanahezhan have entered our world?"

Rehada stared toward the horizon. "I do not know."

The wind began to whistle louder in Atiana's ears. She knew why the raiders had come. She knew how the vanahezhan had created a crease in the aether.

Rehada was pulled forward, nearly against the mast, but she regained her footing as the skiff tumbled through the air.

"Do the spirits hunger for us?" Atiana asked.

Rehada frowned. "Hunger?"

"For life, for our souls."

"They thirst for a *taste* of this life, not for any particular part of it."

"Perhaps they've changed."

"Why would they?"

"The blight… It's changed everything. Why not the spirits as well?"

"*Nyet,*" Rehada said flatly. "Hezhan do not do this. There is an imbalance, but it will heal."

"That house back there"—Atiana motioned outside the skiff, back the way they had come—"I saw a babe two nights ago, taken by a vanahezhan."

"*You* have taken the dark?" She said it as if she didn't believe Atiana could do so in a hundred years.

"I did," Atiana said, pulling herself upright.

Rehada's eyes thinned. "Then you were mistaken."

"I was not. I was there in that woman's home when the vanahezhan drew the life from the wailing babe she held in her arms."

"Was the babe sick?"

"I don't know."

Rehada pulled a strand of hair from her mouth. "Perhaps the hezhan was simply curious. Perhaps the babe was near death and was close to crossing the aether to reach their world. Perhaps that's what drew it to the babe and not some ridiculous explanation such as yours."

Atiana wanted to bark back a reply, but what Rehada was saying made sense. Perhaps the babe *had* been sick. Perhaps, in those moments before its death, it had attracted the notice of the hezhan and had given it the crease it needed to enter this world.

But it seemed strange after what had happened on the eyrie. Physical manifestations of spirits were once common among the qiram, but now they were so rare that even the wisest among the Landless knew little of them. And here, on Khalakovo, there had now been three in the span of a fortnight.

The shore was distant, and the place where she'd turned off the road to Izhny was barely visible, but she thought she could see—though she could not say for certain—two men standing among the trunks of the birch and alder.

Perhaps they were watching them leave.

When Atiana turned back, she found Rehada looking as well. One moment, there was a look of profound worry on her face, but then it was gone.

A violent shiver ran through Atiana, not only from the cold.

After the incessant cold of the skiff, the frigid air within the village was unwelcome. Atiana had been pacing the length of a small room deep within Iramanshah for nearly an hour. After Rehada had landed the skiff, a mahtar named Fahroz had taken Rehada away while Atiana had been led into the heart of the mountain.

The only light present in the room was a glowing blue gemstone. She could see through the doorway to the far side of the stone corridor, but beyond a scant few paces, all was darkness.

An Aramahn man stood outside her room, not to force her to stay, but to prevent her from becoming lost in the darkness should she try to leave. She wouldn't have in any case—she needed their help. Radiskoye needed to know what she'd seen.

But who will you inform? she asked herself. *Your family or Nikandr's?* She struggled with that question for a long time. In the end, instead of answering it, she stalked out into the hallway and faced the Aramahn.

"I would speak with Fahroz," she said.

He turned to her, his brown eyes placid. "And Fahroz dearly wishes to speak with you."

"Then take me to her."

"I cannot."

She tried to walk past him, but he motioned to the room behind her. "Please, she begs your patience."

"I am a daughter of Vostroma!"

"Then I would have credited you," said a voice behind her, "with more composure."

Atiana turned to find Fahroz—a mature but vibrant woman—walking toward her with a glowing stone, a siraj, in her hand. She wore a black shawl with intricate tracery running through it. Unlike many of those who rose to the rank of mahtar, she wore no stone. Instead, a gold chain with a medallion hanging from it was strung across her brow.

"Where is Rehada?" Atiana asked, seeing two Aramahn women she'd never met before standing behind Fahroz.

"She has left."

Atiana paused, feeling small and alone. That such feelings were caused by Nikandr's lover made her doubly angry over it. "Why?"

"That, I'm afraid, will remain between me and her. There are more pressing matters, are there not?"

Atiana pulled herself higher. "I need to return to Radiskoye. They are in danger, which I'm sure you're well aware of by now."

"Radiskoye has little reason to expect favors from Iramanshah."

"They must be warned."

"Is that so?"

Atiana stared into Fahroz's eyes, knowing that she had been the one to take up the cause of the Aramahn. From the accounts, she had stood face-to-face with Iaros Khalakovo—no simple feat—and demanded the return of the mysterious boy and the arqesh.

In the end, it was Atiana who flinched first.

Fahroz turned and began walking away. "Are you coming?"

The two women parted, allowing Atiana to follow. They made several turns, passing rooms both large and small, but rarely did Atiana see another light. Iramanshah, like all of the villages, had dwindled in population if not in grandeur. She had been to the one on Vostroma only once, and it had seemed like a sad reflection of what it once was, but also somehow proper, as if the fading of the Aramahn were a necessary part of the rise of the Grand Duchy. She had been young, then. Now, she was not so naïve as to think that the Grand Duchy could live without the Aramahn—they needed one another, as surely as wildflowers needed bees.

Fahroz took them down a long, curving set of stairs. It felt strangely familiar, though for a long time she couldn't place why.

It struck her as they neared the bottom. "Where are we going?"

"You said you needed to warn Radiskoye."

"I do."

They reached the landing and took the single tunnel that led out from it. The tunnel, which was carved as the rest of the corridors had been, became rough, natural. Soon after, they reached the first of a set of wide, rough steps that seemed to be hewn by hand instead of guided by the skills of a vanaqiram. Shortly after, the tunnel opened up into a massive cavern. Atiana could see the rough stone wall on her left and the stairs ahead of her, but the space to her right was fathomless and black. The roof of the cavern, which had provided some small amount of grounding, faded from view the further they went.

Atiana drew in breath as a twinkling came from the darkness below. They reached the shore of a large black lake, where water lapped ever so gently against the rough stones and gritty sand.

"You would find," Fahroz said as she guided Atiana toward a stone pier, "the water as cold as your drowning basins."

Atiana stopped, forcing Fahroz to do the same. "You wish me to take the dark? Here?"

"I believe you can, with our help."

The lake felt foreboding—somehow ancient and raw, whereas the basin within the drowning chamber felt tamed in comparison.

"Did you not say it was important for Radiskoye to know as soon as possible?"

"I did, but—"

"Then take the dark. Warn them if you would."

Fahroz led her out to the end of the pier. Lamps on decorative stone posts lit as they approached. The light was meager—beyond a certain distance the cavern swallowed it whole—but it was enough to shed light on the lake bed some two stories below the surface of the crystal-clear water.

Atiana shivered just looking at it. "Why would you offer this?"

The smile of Fahroz's face made her seem patronizing, but Atiana doubted she meant it in such a way—she, like so many of her race, was unnaturally calm, and it could lead to a misinterpretation of their moods if one wasn't careful. "I will admit that my goals are not wholly altruistic. Over the years, there have been some who have learned to touch the aether, as you have."

Atiana glanced at the two women, who waited patiently on the shore, then she looked at Fahroz under an entirely new light. She wore no stone. This was common among the Aramahn—perhaps only one in twenty became qiram—but it *was* rare among the mahtar. Most who rose to that status had mastered two or three disciplines. Why, then, if Fahroz could bond with no spirits, had she been allowed to take that rank?

"You?" Atiana asked.

Fahroz nodded, her arms clasped before her. "I ask only to observe."

"Toward what end?"

"Would you not agree, Atiana Radieva, that the islands have become a dangerous place to live? We would do well to understand it, to learn from it."

"I go only to warn Radiskoye."

"But you have seen more. The babe…"

"That was by mere chance."

"Then perhaps luck will be with you again. Allow me to observe. Share with me what you find when you return."

This was a strange position to be in. She was a visitor on these islands, after all. It felt as though she would be betraying the trust of the Matra were she to take the dark unbidden.

Perhaps sensing her hesitation, Fahroz walked forward until she stood at the pier's very edge. She beckoned Atiana closer, and when Atiana was at her side, she motioned toward the vastness of the lake. "Did you know that there is a lake like this in every Aramahn village?"

"*Every* village?"

"Every one that is still populated. Some have been drained by earthquakes. They were repaired if possible, but if it was not, if they ran dry, the village was eventually abandoned."

Atiana struggled to understand why Fahroz was telling her this. "Not merely for lack of water…"

A sad smile touched Fahroz's lips. "*Nyet*, not merely for lack of water. They connect us, these lakes. There was a time when we could speak to one another much as the Matri do now." She stopped speaking and the silence lengthened between them, and Atiana realized that she was crying. "It is one of a dozen things—a hundred—that we do not understand since the islands were taken." She said the words not with anger, but as simple fact, as if the War of Seven Seas had been no different than an earthquake draining one of their lakes and a village with it. "The babe you saw, if you care for it at all, if you care for the others—Aramahn or Anuskayan—then you will do this."

"It may not work."

"A choice I leave to the fates…"

Atiana had never felt close to the Aramahn—they had never been allowed to be a part of her or her sisters' lives—but this woman, this leader of people, struck her deeply. She wished, somehow, that she could know as much as Fahroz did, that she could face the world with as much poise.

In the end, Atiana bowed her head. "I will share as I can."

Fahroz nodded and led her back along the pier. "You may find taking the dark here in the village vastly different from the spire. It is the mountains, after all"—she motioned to the roof of the cavern—"that once acted as the spires do now. In those early days of exploration, they guided us from place to place, even if we weren't yet sure where we were headed. They are our lifeblood, and we are theirs. You will be experiencing this place as many of the ancients did—or nearly so."

The lake looked like it would chill her to the bone just as quickly as the drowning basin had.

"I will require a balm."

Rehada motioned to the two women. "We have some at the ready."

Fahroz disrobed. As soon as she was done, one of the women began rubbing a salve over her. Atiana disrobed as well, feeling more self-conscious than she had in years. Her skin was white as snow; it was expected of the gentry, but next to the darker skinned Aramahn she felt sickly and small. After the second woman rubbed salve over Atiana's back, Atiana did the same over her front. It was similar to what the Matri used, except it smelled strongly of sage. Soon it was over, and she was left a woman naked in a place she hardly knew, ready to submerge herself in water that would take her life as soon as cradle her.

There were steps along the left and right sides of the pier she hadn't noticed. Fahroz took the steps to the right, wading out into the water without hesitation.

Atiana followed, and although the water seized her ankles and calves and thighs, she waded forward, intent on controlling herself better than she had those days ago in Radiskoye's drowning chamber. She leaned back. The woman caught and supported her. She felt like a fish out of water wriggling its way back toward the sea. "Is there nothing that could support me?"

"This is how it is done."

A sliver of fear crept inside her, but she took deep breaths to calm herself. When she felt as ready as she would ever be, she allowed herself to sink beneath the water. She forgot that she was deep within Iramanshah, a veritable prisoner for the time being; she forgot about the Maharraht and the events of the day; she forgot about her embarrassment, her nervousness, her feelings of vulnerability; she forgot about Rehada, though this was the most difficult of all.

And soon…

She sees herself floating in the water. She feels the cavern, its immensity, though in only moments the size of it seems natural—one small part of the mountain that contains it. She feels the streams that feed the lake, and in turn the streams that the lake feeds. She feels the bowels of Iramanshah, the winding tunnels, the rounded rooms, the traceries carved by the careful craftsmanship of men and women long since dead.

She expands her awareness. Unlike the last time, she is confident, though this in itself is cause for concern. She cannot take the aether for granted. She cannot…

The peaks of the mountains, the ridges that connect them, the forests and prairies and the brackish northern swamps enter her awareness. It allows her to suffuse herself among the bowels of the island. She dives deeper, so deep she can feel the heat of the world itself, still cooling from when the fires of the creation gave birth to the world and the stars. She feels the age of the land, and for a moment she feels as though she could tell its entire history, from inception to destruction at the hands of the long-dormant volcano. She knows this is dangerous. If she remains this way she will become part of the island, her body abandoned as her soul merges with the larger life that surrounds her, yet it is the only way she knows to find what she searches for.

She waits for the aether to call to her. Eventually she feels something, a disturbance, though it is nothing like the babe. This is more like the presence of the Matri. She slips back toward Iramanshah, and she drifts down into the cavern where her body still floats. She finds the old Aramahn woman floating in the darkness. Fahroz. She is in the aether, but it is like dipping her toe in the water. She wants to go deeper, but like a child hoping to fly with the mere flapping of her arms she is unable to. There lies within her a yearning and a deep sense of anxiety. She fears over what has come to pass, what *will* come to pass. She feels powerless to prevent the coming storm.

Atiana does not blame her.

She realizes, however, that the disturbance does not reside in Fahroz, but the lake in which she is submerged. There are similarities to what happened with the babe. The walls of the aether feel close, so different from the times where she is at peace with the shifting currents. Instead of free breath in an open field, it is dark water pressing against her, deep earth. She thinks at first it must be her that is causing it, but as she continues to float, leaving her mind aware and awake, she begins to doubt this conclusion.

But then, as soon as it had come, it is gone. She searches for long moments, but is unable to sense it again.

Knowing that time is moving quickly in the material world, she moves on toward Radiskoye. Saphia rests in the drowning chamber deep beneath the spire. Victania watches over her. And now Atiana understands why she was unable to speak with the Matra. Her attention is focused not on the islands, not even on Volgorod, but on an Aramahn boy who rests in a chamber among the lower levels of the great palotza. The boy seems unremarkable. He is colored blue, a gem of sapphire against the black velvet backdrop of the palotza's interior.

It becomes clear that the Matri is not simply watching him. She is surrounding him. She hopes to assume him, as she would a rook, but she moves slowly so as not to disturb, to give him no warning when she finally knows his mind well enough to supplant it.

It is bold, what Saphia is doing, an affront of the worst kind, to supplant that which is most precious to the Aramahn: their soul. Such is the desperation of the Khalakovos.

A voice speaks within her mind. *What are you doing, child?*

She recognizes it immediately, but it has been so long since they'd spoken to one another that it feels strange, foreign.

It has not been so long, daughter, the voice says.

Mother, she replies.

In her first foray into the dark, she did not attempt to speak with her mother—it takes much concentration, and at the time it would have been too dangerous—but she is stronger now, more confident, and she finds herself able to strengthen the bond to her mother with no ill effects.

Her view of Nasim is another matter entirely. Try as she might, the vision begins to fade, and she realizes it is not a failure on her part. Her mother is pulling her consciousness away.

I asked you a question...

I am trying to speak with Saphia. To warn her.

They've had their warnings, child.

I mean to warn them of the Maharraht.

It matters not.

She can no longer sense Saphia or Nasim at all, but her mother's presence is clear. She can feel three other Matri as well: Dhalingrad, Nodhvyansk, and Bolgravya.

Where are you? her mother asks. She moves closer—with an ease and an efficiency that is impressive—and then on toward Iramanshah.

Atiana blocks her way, barring her mother from moving forward. Fahroz placed herself in Atiana's trust; even though this is her mother, she does not feel right breaking that trust so quickly. Were her mother nearer she would have succeeded in bulling her way past Atiana, but as distant as she is, such things are difficult, and Atiana holds her ground.

Mother's presence retreats.

Do you test me?

The Maharraht are on the move, Mother. There are those, our family among them, who stand in harm's way.

You are not in Radiskoye.

It is a statement, not a question, and in that one moment, Atiana feels her mother's guard slip. She also feels thoughts that weigh heavily on her mind. She is worried because Atiana is not where she should be, because decisions have been made and are now being set into motion.

A feeling of dread grows within Atiana like a gathering storm. *You are attacking the palotza?*

A pause. *It is nothing they've not been asking for since the moment Stasa died.*

You would risk war over a boy?

Risk it? Khalakovo has demanded it, Atiana.

You cannot.

She does not wait for her mother's response. She moves quickly toward Radiskoye.

Stop, child!

She rushes among the halls until she senses a rook. Without thinking, she pours herself into the bird. She feels its weak resistance. Worse, she feels her control over the aether slipping. Her arms lengthen. Feathers sprout. Her legs bend and contort, and her talons grip iron. She manages only a rough caw before she is drawn roughly away.

In the precious moments that follow, she is too confused to fight, and by then she is too far away. It does not prevent her from trying, though. Like a woman drowning beneath the waves, she flails for the surface, ready to gasp for breath.

But it is no use. The Matri have worked in concert for years. If their intent was to prevent one lone woman from assuming a rook, then it would be so.

She kicks one last time and feels her control betray her. She feels the island, the sea, the air above, the stars beyond. She feels herself breathe, her skin prickle, her bones ache…

CHAPTER 32

Atiana felt a beating upon her chest. Lips pressed to hers and air filled her lungs. She coughed. The beating ceased.

She was dying. She knew this in her heart.

She tried several times to open her eyes, but they wouldn't respond. Neither would her voice comply when she willed it to speak. A simple word would do, any word, so that she could ground herself more fully in this reality.

And yet, despite the vague sense that she should be struggling for her own survival, it felt so peaceful that she no longer cared what the outcome might be. She would let death take her. She would welcome it with open arms.

She fell into herself, hoping it would be so if only to make the pain go away.

Then silence…

Followed by a single note, fading in and out of her consciousness.

Then a string of syllables, more song than voice.

Someone was speaking—who, she couldn't guess.

They were speaking another language.

Mahndi.

She was still among them. She hadn't died.

Her eyes finally fluttered open.

She licked her lips once … twice … still unable to speak.

"What…" The word came out in a croak. "What happened?"

The voices stopped. A face moved into her field of vision.

Fahroz.

"You nearly crossed to the other side, Atiana Radieva." Her voice carried with it a completely unexpected note of concern.

Atiana's bones ached. It felt as if someone were driving a spike through her hips as the Aramahn women levered her up. They forced upon her several sips from a steaming earthenware mug. She felt the mulled wine drift down her throat, down her chest, and it was the most wonderful feeling she could ever remember experiencing, except that its warmth suddenly made her fingers and toes feel deathly cold.

She began to shiver uncontrollably. "It is … painful."

"That is to be expected," Fahroz said, wrapping a new, dry blanket around her shoulders. "Come. We will take you to a place where you can rest."

She was allowed to pull on her clothes, but immediately after they left the great cavern and reentered the rounded hallways of Iramanshah. She could remember little of her time in the dark, but one thing was clear.

"I f-found no rift," she said, her teeth chattering.

"We can discuss that once you've rested."

Atiana nodded, but more and more of her voyage was coming back to her. Her time in Radiskoye, her search while feeling the island.

Atiana sucked in a deep breath.

Fahroz tightened her grip on Atiana's shoulders. "What is it?"

She could not answer, for she had remembered her battle with her mother and the other Matri. The ships allied with Father were ready to attack. Tonight. She had to get back to Radiskoye before it was too late. But she couldn't tell Fahroz. There was no telling if they would allow her to leave, not with an attack imminent.

"The time in these tunnels weighs heavily on me." She hoped Fahroz couldn't hear the lie in her voice. "I can barely breathe from the weight of it. Please, I wish to be in clean air. Take me outside."

"You shouldn't go—"

"You will lead me from this mountain!"

They walked in silence for several paces, but finally Fahroz nodded. "Ushai will escort you. When you feel well enough, come inside and warm yourself."

Fahroz and one of the women stopped. There was a bit of silence as, perhaps, they watched Atiana continue on with Ushai, and then she heard their footsteps receding.

The village was a labyrinth of maddening proportions. Every time Atiana thought she recognized a hallway, a room, a stair, she turned out to be wrong. When they finally reached the main gates and stepped outside into the valley that housed the entrance to the village, she released a breath of air she hadn't realized had been pent up.

The sun was setting in the west, spreading golden light across the top of the valley's ridge. In the stone-lined court that lay at the foot of the entrance's stairs, a fountain bubbled. Several women stood in the water, chatting and washing clothes while their children played stones near its base. As was true for most Aramahn villages, several buildings were positioned near the entrance: a granary, a mill, several large animal pens, and the place Atiana needed the most, the stables.

"Might I walk for a time? Alone?" Atiana asked.

Ushai was not much older than Atiana. She stared at Atiana severely. Finally, she nodded and moved to the fountain and began scolding one of the children in Mahndi.

Atiana strolled around the fountain, holding the blanket tight around her frame. She was still chilled to the bone, and what she was about to do brought her no comfort in that regard. The ride to Radiskoye was going to be long and miserable.

And dangerous.

She had no choice, though. There was no way to warn them other than to ride there. So ride she would, setting sun be damned.

She bided her time, acting as if her walk was aimless. Finally Ushai began talking with the other women, and Atiana knew it was time. She made her way toward the stables, and when she reached it, she stayed a while—becoming, she hoped, part of the background.

When she thought it was safe, she ducked inside.

She had chosen her pony well. It attacked the inclining slope not with impressive pace but with a steadfastness that would hopefully get her to the palotza in time. She felt her stomach flutter as she glanced at the western sky. Little light remained, and that would be gone in less than an hour.

Now that she was out of the valley, and pursuit was hopefully far behind, she pulled the pony to a stop. She gripped her soulstone and tried desperately to reach Saphia. She felt nothing in return.

Her pony shivered her mane and stomped her forehooves.

"Be good"—Atiana patted the pony's neck soothingly—"and take me home."

And then she kicked her into a full gallop.

She rode like she had never ridden before. She rode until the night had robbed the western sky of all but an indigo swath. She was forced to slow to a trot, the stars giving barely enough light to keep her on the trail. She urged the pony into a faster pace as the moon rose in the cloudless sky. Her stomach churned as she came closer. She was sure she would arrive too late.

She crested the ridge running the full length of the island. She would be only an hour or more away now. She reached the spur in the road that led to the eyrie, then Volgorod itself, and still she rode, her pony's breath coming hard and heavy.

By the time she reached the road leading up to Radiskoye, she saw it. She slowed her frantic pace, tears coming to her eyes.

By her ancestors, she was too late.

A fire rose in Radiskoye, tainting the clouds high above a tender shade of yellow.

CHAPTER 33

Nikandr returned to the cells deep beneath Radiskoye. He had taken a healthy amount of elixir before he'd come. He felt lightheaded because of it, as if he'd downed a mouthful of vodka.

He found Nasim staring at him as he entered. He had no doubt that it was due to the elixir, but he still felt watched and somehow vulnerable. He had never come to Nasim with ill intent. He'd only wanted to discover his nature—to find how, and to what degree, he'd been involved with the summoning of the suurahezhan. This time was different, and he found his heart beating at what he and Mother were about to do.

"Are you here, Nasim?"

Nasim stared at Nikandr as he moved into the room and took a chair at the table.

Nikandr pulled the necklace over his head and set it on the table, the heavy chain coming to rest with a sound like jingling coins. "Can you sense it?" He pushed the stone toward Nasim. "Do you remember what you did to me? Do you remember allowing the hezhan inside me?" Nikandr had thought on this much. The hezhan near the lake. His shared bond with Nasim must have allowed it. But perhaps it hadn't merely been the bond. Perhaps Nasim had compelled it.

Nasim, as if in a daze, drew his eyes closed and opened them again. He swallowed and stared at the dead stone as if he were about to cry.

"Tell me about it, Nasim. Why did you do it?"

"The gap narrows." Nasim's voice was hoarse, and it came out so suddenly that it startled Nikandr.

"What gap, Nasim?"

"The gap within me. Within you."

"I don't understand."

The look on Nasim's face was one of profound misery, and when he turned and looked at Nikandr it was as if he were pleading with Nikandr to make it stop. "It hurts."

Nikandr kneeled. "I know." He pulled Nasim into an embrace. "I know, Nasim." He rocked him, hoping to ease the life of a boy whose world was a living agony.

"It will soon close if we are not careful."

"What will close? The gap?"

Nikandr felt Nasim nod. And then the boy stiffened, and a keening moan escaped him. Nasim always suffered in silence, so this took Nikandr by surprise. Nasim's eyes were opened wide and he stared up with a look of wild fear. "They are coming."

The hair on Nikandr's arms stood on end. His breath sounded loud in his ears. "Who is coming?"

Nasim arched back and screamed. He tilted his head up toward the ceiling and threw his arms wide. His entire body shook, and Nikandr knew Mother had just assumed him.

He stood and grasped his blackened soulstone. "Mother, *nyet*! Please, let him go!"

Nasim fell to the floor, shaking, eyes clenched shut and neck muscles taut. The skin along his face and neck was blue.

Nikandr dashed from the room. Had he been able to reach the drowning chamber in time, he would have gone there, but he went instead to the only other place he thought could provide help.

The strelet at Ashan's door opened it for Nikandr as he approached. Ashan was already near the door, a look of worry on his face.

"Bring him," Nikandr said to the strelet.

The three of them raced down the hall. The moment they entered Nasim's room, Nikandr lost his footing. He felt Ashan fall on top of him as piercing cracks rent the air like a series of musket shots going off in tight sequence. The floor shook. It felt as if the walls were about to buckle.

Nikandr stared in horror, wondering how this could be.

A great wedge of stone crashed into the corner bookcase, sending splintered wood and books about the room. The ground shook for a moment more, and then, blessedly, all was still except for a fine sifting of dust that was pattering to the floor near the corner.

Nikandr made it to his feet, surveying the damage. On the far side of the room, a gap wider than his fist ran from floor to ceiling. He and Ashan moved to Nasim, who was unconscious.

Nikandr heard footsteps coming from down the hall.

"Lord Khalakovo!" It was the strelet's voice.

There was a pause, then a scuffle.

"Halt!"

Gunfire erupted. Two men cried out. There was silence for a moment, and then Nikandr heard a man draw in several wet, halting breaths. One final shot filled the air, and then the footsteps of many men approached.

"Who comes?" Nikandr said, getting to his feet. He hadn't so much as a knife to defend himself, so he stood there, waiting, but all he heard were the sounds of men reloading their guns.

Then a man stepped into the open doorway, and for a moment Nikandr couldn't believe his eyes.

It was Borund.

And he was aiming a pistol at Nikandr's chest.

CHAPTER 34

Borund wore a thick cherkesska, the type one would wear on a long journey, and his cheeks were flushed as if he'd been in the elements.

Nikandr stared at the pistol, realizing he had come for Nasim. "Never did I think to see this day."

"Then you're as blind as your father." He pointed to Nasim with his pistol. "You should have given him to us the day you found him."

"You would have done the same in our place."

Borund paused. "You are right. We all have our pride. But I think, all things being equal, we would not have placed the life of two Motherless so high that it would cloud our vision."

"There is more to him than meets the eye," Nikandr said.

"We will be the judge of that—not you, not your father, and certainly not that Motherless qiram. Now come." Borund waved his pistol, indicating that Nikandr should step into the hall. "I would rather this trigger go unpulled."

Nikandr complied. A dozen Vostroman streltsi stood at the ready in heavy winter coats. In the other direction were two dead guardsmen.

Three of Borund's men moved into the room—one of them hoisting Nasim over his shoulders, the other two pointing their pistols at Ashan.

Ashan looked completely helpless. He held his hands before him in a gesture of peace. "Please don't hurt him."

Their only response was to shove him into the hall. They all left en masse, seven soldiers to the fore, then Nikandr, Ashan and Nasim, and finally Borund and the remaining men. The gaoler had also been shot. He lay behind his desk, a sea of blood pooled beneath him.

As they took to the stairwell leading up, it was clear Borund's mission had not gone unnoticed. A smattering of gunfire could be heard above, and by the time they reached the ground floor, the clash of swords rang through the halls of Radiskoye.

Nearly two dozen Vostroman streltsi had set up a host of tables and statues as barricades, but the Khalakovan soldiers had broken through, and there was now a violent skirmish being waged not twenty paces down the hall. The polkovnik of the royal guard was among them, and when he saw Nikandr he shouted for his men to push, and the fighting intensified.

Borund pressed his pistol into Nikandr's back. "Come, quickly, and you'll live to see another day."

Nikandr allowed himself to be taken. They moved southward, toward the eyrie, and Nikandr wondered how much damage had been done in order to capture one small boy. How many men had been killed?

They moved through a set of tall glass doors and into the garden. The eyrie lay just beyond, and a great fire was raging through the rigging of the *Tura*. As he watched, flames washed over the deck of the *Gorovna*, which was moored to the perch.

Nikandr swallowed, his hands balling into fists at his side as the flames began climbing the starward mainmast. Gravlos had worked day and night to repair the ship, completing it well before his estimates in hopes of appeasing Zhabyn Vostroma. But now it was another victim in this cowardly attack.

Nikandr turned, but Borund had guessed his intentions and had his pistol raised and aimed at Nikandr's chest.

"Don't be foolish, Nischka. It's only a ship."

Gunfire cracked over the eyrie, coming from the walls. One of the streltsi on the *Gorovna* screamed and fell. Two of his countrymen carried him. A dozen more returned fire and retreated toward Vostroma's ship.

I am lost, Nikandr realized.

He would be taken as a hostage, a bargaining chip to force Khalakovo to do as the southern alliance commanded.

He could not allow it, but he could see no way out of it other than simply leaping from the eyrie or getting shot in the back.

Shortly after Radiskoye came into view, Atiana's pony collapsed. She was thrown to the ground, dirt and stone biting the palms of her hands as she rolled away. She whispered a prayer of thanks to the ancients for giving the animal such strength as she jogged up the hill.

Her will was strong and her need was great, but the pitch of the road soon slowed her. A smatter of gunfire came from the palotza, echoing moments later against the cliffs of Verodnaya. By the light of the flames she could see Khalakovan men firing into the palotza grounds—aiming, no doubt, at her countrymen. Atiana bent over, grasping her knees as her lungs burned. After only a moment, she spit to clear her mouth and pushed on, worried now not just over Nikandr, but her family as well.

When she came within a hundred paces of the wall, where the ground finally leveled off, a cannon blast lit the night. She felt it in her chest, and she saw outlined in the white flash the streltsi manning the weapon.

The gates were closed, and Atiana saw no one manning them. Most likely they were on the far side of the barbican, training their muskets toward the courtyard. She approached and was just about to call out when another cannon lit the wall. The blast had also lit the low clouds, giving off enough light to reveal the forms of men—a dozen or more of them—crawling up the wall.

She stood stock still, afraid to move, afraid to give her position away. As the flash from the cannon fire faded and her night vision returned, the glow from the fire gave her enough light to detect the dark forms of the men climbing upward. They were already halfway to the top.

It was the Maharraht, she realized. In moments they would gain the battlements.

"On the wall!" she screamed, hoping she wasn't making a huge mistake. "On the wall, attackers!"

She didn't know if they could hear her, but the Maharraht certainly did. Several of them looked her way, and she could see the dull glow of the jasper gems upon their brows. Two slid down the wall, reaching the ground in less than a breath. They sprinted toward Atiana as she continued to yell. "To the wall! To the wall!"

Atiana made for the barbican as quickly as her leaden legs would allow.

One of the Maharraht was just below the crenelations along the curtain wall. As he reached up, the report of a flintlock broke the crisp night air. He struck the earth with a hollow thump. Another Maharraht flung his arm. A spray of rock flew from his hand toward the strelet who had fired. Like the spray of grapeshot it cracked along the top of the wall. The strelet screamed, grabbing his face with both hands, losing his musket. Three more streltsi arrived and were treated to a similar attack.

Atiana reached the huge doors and began pounding them with her fists. "Open! It is Atiana Vostroma! Open the gates!" She heard footsteps approaching from behind. "Please, hear me!" Her fists felt like mangled pieces of meat.

She turned around just before the men reached her, but her face was stung by dirt and stones as the wind picked up and swirled around her. It howled, and the only thing she could do was ward her face with her forearms and press backward into the door.

Suddenly she lost her balance, falling backward as the door opened behind her. She was grabbed by the elbow and pulled inward. The sound of the wind dropped. There was light, but her eyes stung so horribly from dust and dirt she couldn't see.

The door slammed shut and several men secured it with three massive wooden beams. Atiana blinked, her eyes watering, but she could see by the lantern light a tall Aramahn man walking down the stairs. She recognized him as Jahalan, one of Khalakovo's wind masters. Behind him came Ranos, who was bleeding from several cuts along his forehead. He looked fierce as his eyes met hers.

Atiana cringed as another cannon blast shook the room and trails of dust filtered down from the stone ceiling.

"The Maharraht," Atiana began, unsure of what to say amidst all this madness.

"We know." Ranos came to her side and took her arm in a painfully tight grip. "Come," he said while leading her toward the inner gate, "the Duke would speak with you."

Nikandr ducked as a canon blast struck the Vostroman yacht *Olganya*. For the first time, Nikandr noticed Zhabyn standing on the foredeck, watching the scene play out before him. His eyes met Nikandr's momentarily as the streltsi led Nikandr toward the ship. His eyes were smug, but there was a tautness to his frame. He had not expected things to go so badly.

Several of the streltsi boarded the ship, but as Ashan was being led toward the gangplank, a horrendous rumble filled the eyrie. One moment the stone of the westernmost turret was bulging outward and the next its entire face, including the cannon emplacement, was tumbling to the ground. Nikandr felt it in his feet, in his chest and shoulders. Several streltsi were caught in the fall. Their bodies were dashed like pebbles upon the surf. A cloud of dust exploded into the air, turning ochre and orange from the nearby fire.

Nikandr was shoved onto the ship by the streltsi. Ashan and Nasim were right behind him.

"Prepare to cast off!" Zhabyn yelled.

Before the last of the stones had settled into place, a massive form lumbered out of the cloud. The backs of its arms and legs were smooth, mottled stone. The front of it was dark as night and glittering. Its eyes twinkled, and to Nikandr it seemed to have singular purpose as it stalked forward.

Retreating from the palotza, the remaining Vostroman soldiers moved in formation, firing at the hezhan as they went. Many fell as they were shot by Khalakovan muskets, forcing them into an all-out retreat for the *Olganya*.

Behind the vanahezhan were several men dressed in the loose clothing and ragged turbans of the Maharraht. They reached the edge of the garden that bordered the eyrie. One of them was shouting and pointing toward the *Olganya*, and Nikandr knew he was pointing at Nasim. Ashan placed his body between the boy and the violence.

Several of the men on the *Olganya*—and even among the Khalakovan streltsi—began firing at the Maharraht instead of the hezhan. They had found a common enemy.

The hands of the Maharraht were gripped into tight fists as they walked, and the expressions on their faces were ones of concentration and even pain. Tufts of fabric lifted and tore free of their frames, but otherwise they seemed unaffected. Then a shot struck the closest—an aging man with a long white beard—and a bit of his cheek split from his face as if he were made of stone. Of all the Maharraht, he was the only one who had a glowing gem of jasper fitted within his turban. He was the closest to the vanahezhan, and it soon became clear that he was the one controlling the beast.

"Cast off!" Zhabyn shouted while Borund ordered their men to return to the ship.

The streltsi tried, but the hezhan lowered itself and placed fists the size of beer casks on the ground. The stone at its feet flaked like dried mud in the rare heat of summer. The effect spread, faster than the men could run, and soon it had swept beneath them. The loose stone shifted beneath the soldiers' feet, and many of them slipped and fell. One slid with the sound of scraping gravel as he approached the gangplank. He slid off the edge of the perch and plummeted soundlessly downward.

Shots continued to fly.

"The one with the white beard!" Nikandr shouted.

Few heard at first, but then more and more concentrated their fire on him. The old warrior cringed, no longer able to move forward. Seeing their success, the remaining streltsi lined up near the palotza's walls shouted "*Kozyol!*" and fired at the wounded man. The Maharraht pulled his arms tight around himself in a vain attempt at protection as several musket shots bit deep. He fell to the ground, twitching as many more shots struck home, and then his gem went dim.

The vanahezhan reared back, shaking its head to and fro. It dropped to its knees and struck its head twice against the stone. Huge, echoing booms shook the courtyard. And then it stood and stalked toward the ship.

The blast of a cannon shook the deck of the ship. The shot tore into the creature's chest. The center was pulverized, and the remains of its torso cracked into several large pieces. It crumbled into a heap, and the men, both Khalakovan and Vostroman, raised their fists in a rousing and unified cheer.

The respite had given the remaining Maharraht time to rush forward as the *Olganya* pulled away from the perch. Zhabyn's dhoshaqiram sat at her post near the center of the ship, palms laid against the deck, giving lift to the windwood from which the ship had been made. The havaqiram stood just behind her, calling the winds to pull the ship back. He spared one hand to raise a wind near the perch, sending dust and stone to flying around the Maharraht.

Soroush, the one with the golden earrings running through the scarred remains of his ear, ran toward the ship, which had nearly cleared the perch.

"Halt!"

Nikandr turned in time to see Ashan shoving Nasim toward the windward gunwale, away from the Maharraht. Ashan then lunged forward and grabbed the circlet from the brow of the havaqiram.

The wind swirled. The sails snapped. The rigging swung wildly as Ashan took two loping steps toward the gunwale.

Soroush shouted a command in Mahndi. The Maharraht stalked forward, pushing aside the streltsi who stood in their way. Ashan picked Nasim up and then tipped backward over the gunwale. He was gone, lost from view, taken by the howling wind.

A moment later the wind pulled sharply at the skiff lashed to the edge of the *Olganya*'s deck. It rocked against its restraints, slamming the deck louder and louder, until finally the moorings were ripped free. Then it was gone, just like Ashan and Nasim.

The streltsi had been in complete disarray with the Maharraht among them, but they had regrouped. A dozen stood near the stairs leading belowdecks. The front six kneeled, the back six stood. The sotnik shouted, "Fire!" and the guns cracked in unison. Four of the Maharraht were struck as they tried to leap free of the ship. The other two reached the perch and ran along its length. Soroush hopped onto the back of the other, who crawled down along the perch's stone supports like an insect. He moved quickly downward toward the surf before Zhabyn's streltsi could reload. Several fired once they had, but with the winds and the distance to their targets, their shots would be ineffective.

For several moments the only sounds were from the burning ships. Then Father's voice called out from the eyrie. "Zhabyn!"

Zhabyn, for the first time, seemed unsure what to do. He measured the carnage around him. Perhaps in that one moment he had come to regret what he'd done, but then the look was gone and he strode across the deck toward the gunwale.

As Zhabyn stared downward, Borund moved closer to Nikandr, pistol in hand. What Zhabyn saw, Nikandr couldn't guess. He said nothing—only stared—but he was stiff, as if what he saw below had come as a complete surprise.

The *Olganya* had slipped toward the *Tura*, which was almost completely engulfed by fire. The bowsprit of the *Olganya* was momentarily caught in the rigging of the starward mizzenmast.

With most of the streltsi reloading, Nikandr ran for the bow.

Borund shouted behind him, "Nikandr, stop!"

He didn't. He couldn't.

A pistol fired.

Nikandr felt his shoulder flare in pain as he leapt for the rigging.

Ranos held Atiana's arm in a tight grip as they made their way through the halls of Radiskoye. When they reached the long hallway that led to the eyrie, they found the Duke of Khalakovo standing behind a dozen streltsi, speaking with a man dressed in the uniform of a sotnik. The soldiers were filing outside, taking aim and firing on her father's ship, the *Olganya*.

Before Ranos and Atiana could reach him, a rumbling shook the foundations of the palotza. It increased in intensity, and Atiana saw from the corner of her eye the crumbling of one of the palotza's turrets. It happened at an impossibly slow pace, as if everything were caught in honey.

Then the leaded glass within the row of tall windows crashed inward. Atiana raised her arms, turning away as the sound intensified. A deafening roar filled the air, and she screamed as bits of glass tore into her arms and shoulders.

The roar subsided, followed by the sound of impossibly heavy stones clacking hollowly against one another. Other sounds entered her consciousness: the coughing and moaning of wounded men, a shrill cry for help, the sporadic crack of musket fire.

Ranos dragged Atiana to her feet. Bits of glass tore into the palm of her hand as she steadied herself, but she did not cry out. She refused to let Ranos hear such a thing.

"Up!" shouted the sotnik. "From the wall! Defend yourselves!"

A vanahezhan—the same one that Atiana had seen on the rocky shoreline—had stalked out of the great cloud of dust surrounding the fallen turret and was bearing down on the *Olganya*. A half-dozen Maharraht followed. Fear welled up within her as she recognized the two from the seashore. Their attention appeared fixated on the eyrie's perches, however.

The rate of musket fire increased, both from the *Olganya* as well as from the Khalakovan soldiers, but the hezhan kept stalking forward, its huge arms held up before it as if it could feel the bite of the shots tearing into it.

Ranos pulled a pistol from a holster at his belt. Watching the garden closely, he pulled her before Iaros, who was wiping vainly at the dust on his fine golden coat. He looked up and stared at Ranos for a time before turning his head slowly toward Atiana. His face was smeared with dirt and bits of broken glass littered his graying hair and long white beard. He blinked, and Atiana thought surely he had struck his head, for there was a fresh wound on his forehead. Blood dribbled down his cheek and into his beard—a river of red against a snow-swept field.

Whatever disorientation he felt seemed to vanish the longer he stared at Atiana. "What, child, are you doing here?"

Atiana held her tongue. This was not a question to be answered lightly, not with the Duke *measuring* her so.

How it was that emotions had boiled over in a single day she couldn't say, but she was not entirely surprised. Grigory had been beating the drums of war ever since Stasa's death. Leonid had been of a similar mind, and although Father had nominally stepped within their circle, Atiana thought he would have been able to control them. None of this, however, gave her any clue as to why she had been abandoned.

"I came from Iramanshah, to warn you."

"The Matra was attacked"—he glanced outside, toward the eyrie—"by the boy your father has stolen from these walls. Did you lead them here?"

Atiana was stunned. He meant the Maharraht. "*Nyet,* I came to warn you."

Iaros looked to his son.

Ranos shrugged. "We heard her just before they gained the wall."

Atiana could see the muscles in Iaros's jaw working.

"Please, I came—"

"*Da,* to warn me. But"—Iaros turned, pointing toward the eyrie where the fighting had made its way onto the deck of the *Olganya*—"your father has committed murder within these walls."

The blast from a cannon rose above all else, but Atiana could not tear her gaze from the eyes of Duke Khalakovo.

He, as well, seemed so intent on her that he barely noticed the world around them. "Your father has stolen away men who were not his. And yet he leaves his daughter here."

Atiana had always been able to keep a straight face when being questioned. She was as competent in this as Ishkyna and even better than Mileva. But this was different. Truth was on her side, but Iaros wouldn't believe a word of it.

Her throat had gone dry. "It—" She cleared her throat. "It must have been a mistake."

"My son is on that ship."

Atiana swallowed again. "I am sorry."

Iaros's expression hardened. He snatched Atiana's arm and collected the pistol from Ranos and then marched her down the hall. Her heart was already beating heavily, but now she felt it pound within her chest. She felt blood course through her ears. Her fingers and toes began to tingle.

Pulling Atiana behind him, Iaros pushed open the heavy doors leading to the garden. The fighting had subsided. The *Olganya* had begun to pull away from its perch, while the two ships next to it were fully ablaze. The Maharraht had gained the ship, but as Iaros stalked forward, his grip like an iron shackle, an angry shout spoken in Mahndi came from the *Olganya's* deck. A moment later two bodies fell downward beyond the far edge of the ship. They were followed moments later by a skiff.

A flurry of new shots rang out, and Atiana cringed. Two men—Soroush and the other from the beach—leapt from the ship to the perch, the tails of their turbans fluttering behind them like pennants. They landed, at which point one of them crawled onto the back of the other. The two slipped over the side of the perch and were lost from view.

After several more musket shots from Father's men, all was silence save for the sounds of the wounded and the roar of the nearby fire.

Duke Khalakovo summoned a lungful of breath and shouted. "Zhabyn!"

Several moments of silence followed. Iaros's grip on Atiana's arm tightened, and she feared that if her Father did not show himself Duke Khalakovo would simply shoot her like a mongrel dog.

Finally Father came to the edge of the ship and looked down. The ship was beginning to list.

Iaros's breath came in great heaves through his nostrils. She couldn't look at him. All she could do was stare at Father, who looked down on her with a steely expression.

Iaros raised his pistol and pointed it at Atiana's temple.

She could *feel* the barrel, could feel it in her bones, in every part of her being. Part of her wanted to cringe, to curl up into a ball and pray to her ancestors that the trigger would not be pulled. But she would not—she would stand tall and accept her fate. She was Vostroman, after all.

The seconds passed, and the ship continued to drift. The bowsprit had caught itself in the rear rigging of the ship next to it.

Her brother's voice bellowed from the deck of the *Olganya*, "Nikandr, stop!"

And Nikandr's form leapt from the deck of the ship.

CHAPTER 35

Nikandr's shoulder flared in pain as he leapt. He grabbed the gaff rigging and slid downward. His hands slipped, but he caught the rope in the crook of his arm. It burned his skin until he slammed into the rigging block, barely catching himself.

He looked up as the heat from the fire below him intensified. Borund stood at the gunwale of the *Olganya*. A moment later, his father appeared next to him. They were in dire trouble. Without a havaqiram they would be at the mercy of the winds. It was possible to control a ship without a havaqiram, using the keels to control the heading of the ship against the prevailing winds, but the larger the ship, the more difficult it became. The *Olganya* was no Aramahn skiff, and would not respond well to such maneuvers.

Nikandr slipped over the side of the ship and made it to the nearby perch. The heat from both ships was strong—so strong that he was beginning to feel lightheaded. He held his sleeve to his mouth. He wished he could run toward solid ground, but the fire was licking the perch closer to the fore of the two ships. There was no way he would make it past them.

He felt something small strike his head. Then again.

He used his finger to probe his hair, worrying that embers from the fire were striking him, but the palm of his hand came away wet. More water fell, primarily on the *Gorovna*. The water cooled the air just enough for Nikandr to run the length of the perch. By the time he made it clear of the heat he was exhausted, and he couldn't seem to clear the smoke from his lungs.

Two jalaqiram standing within the stone garden had their arms spread to the sky. Azurite gems glowed brightly in the dim light as they commanded the rain to fall against the ships. Rain hissed and steamed as it struck the *Gorovna's* deck.

Nikandr saw Father standing nearby. With the blood along the side of

232

his face, the dirt and glass in his hair and beard, the haggard look upon his face, it looked like he alone had defended Radiskoye against the traitor dukes. He stared at Nikandr with a strange mix of emotion on his face, so much so that Nikandr felt uncomfortable.

Ranos broke away from several soldiers and gave Nikandr a long hug, breaking the spell. "I didn't know if I would see you again."

"Nor I you."

Movement caught Nikandr's eye. Near the broken doors leading into the palotza, he saw a woman being watched by a strelet. He didn't recognize her at first—she wore a dirty riding outfit, and her hair was tied back behind her head in a long tail—but it was Atiana. She stared at him with a soft expression, a worried expression. Stranger than the show of emotion, however, was her mere presence. He had thought her gone with the rest of her family. What was she doing here? And what had happened on the eyrie when Zhabyn had been called to the edge of the ship?

Three sotnik and a polupolkovnik came and spoke with Father, and as they did Jahalan and Udra arrived. The skiff that Nikandr had seen returned to him in a moment. "Father, forgive me, but I beg your permission to take the *Gorovna*."

Father turned and regarded Nikandr anew.

"The skiff that was ripped from the *Olganya*... Ashan escaped with it—he and Nasim, both. I can still find them, but I must leave now."

Father looked to the east. The night still reigned, but there was a band of indigo along the horizon. "The sun is already starting to rise. The blockade will find you before you could find such a small ship."

"That's why I need to hurry."

"Ashan could be headed anywhere."

"*Nyet*. He is headed toward Ghayavand."

When Nikandr had last discussed it with Ashan, he had seemed mystified by the possibility that Nasim might be one of the three arqesh who had destroyed the island. Whether or not that was true was no longer the point. Ashan believed it, and he would take Nasim there to discover the truth.

He also understood that Ashan would need him. The bond that was shared between him and Nasim was unmistakable. It was the key to a very large and complex problem—he'd admitted as much when they'd spoken of Ghayavand. Nikandr didn't care, though. He sensed a need to discover the nature of their connection as well, and if it meant traveling to a distant island to do so, then he would answer the call.

Nikandr explained as well as he could, as quickly as he could, to his father. "I'll bring them back for you, Father," he concluded. "Please."

"You won't find them."

"If I fail, I'll return. I'll bypass the blockade. It hasn't truly begun in any case."

"They have two dozen ships, Nischka, with more on the way."

Outside, the two jalaqiram had put out the fire on the *Gorovna* and were trying to stem the tide on the *Tura*, but it was too little, too late. The ship was damaged beyond repair. By now the fire would have compromised the ability of the windwood to maintain its buoyancy. Soon the ship would sink and snap its mooring lines, as heavy as any waterborne craft.

"Father," Ranos said, "they wanted the arqesh and the boy. Surely with the two of them gone they'll stop this madness."

Father pulled a grimy hand down over his mouth and along the length of his beard while looking at Atiana further down the hall. "There is his daughter to consider now."

"He'll have her back. Surely you won't—"

"He won't be satisfied with just her. He needed the marriage for the ships we were to provide. Nothing has changed. He needed them then and he needs them now. He had hoped, clearly, to use Nikandr as a wagering chip, but with that unavailable he will demand his daughter *and* the ships and offer nothing in return."

Nikandr watched as Jahalan and Udra and a half-dozen other Aramahn gathered in the garden. They spoke amongst themselves, looking occasionally to the bodies of the dead Maharraht and the section of the palotza wall that now lay in ruins.

"Father, forgive me, but you said it yourself. Mother is ill, and I saw with my own eyes what happened to Nasim when she was attacked. He may be the only way to revive her."

Father considered his words, but just then two young men were carried in on canvas being used as makeshift stretchers. They were alive, but unconscious. They looked bloodied and broken. Father watched them go by. His jaw worked and he seemed to become smaller. But then he stood tall and took a deep breath.

"Go to your mother, Nischka. Keep her company in her time of need."

"Father—"

"Go!"

Nikandr remained, the blood settling in his veins as Father paced toward the room where several dozen people were being administered to by the palotza's small and suddenly overwhelmed cadre of healers. Atiana, escorted by her assigned strelet, went as well, perhaps to comfort her wounded countrymen.

Outside, Udra had stepped onto the *Gorovna*. She reached the starward mainmast and looked along its length, her arms spread, her head to the sky. It looked as if she were mourning the ship—and perhaps she was considering how intimately she'd been involved in the curing of the ship's wood. Dhoshaqiram looked upon the ships they'd built as children, and although the *Gorovna* wasn't dead, it had been sorely wounded.

Jahalan was speaking with the other Aramahn, and a dozen other men—streltsi and servants—were still clearing away and organizing the bodies of the dead.

Nikandr coughed, a ragged sound. He tried taking in a deep breath, but that only made things worse. Ever since the fire it had felt as if he had been buried alive, the air slowly being squeezed from his chest. He felt completely powerless. He had been so close to reaching Nasim, and now it felt like it had all slipped through his fingers.

Before he knew it, he was walking toward the doors that would lead him to the eyrie.

"Nikandr."

He turned and saw Atiana standing near the infirmary. He nodded to the strelet, and Atiana stepped forward, her eyes darting toward the eyrie as she came. She stopped just before him, and Nikandr found himself confused. A part of him was enraged at what her father had done, but another part, the part that remembered how she had looked at him upon seeing him safe, saw a woman he wanted to take into his arms, especially considering what he was about to do.

Atiana spoke softly, "You will find him, won't you?"

He nodded, seeing no sense in denying it.

"There is something in that boy..."

"There is, and he may just be the ruin of us all."

Father's voice echoing into the hallway caught Nikandr's attention. Time was slipping away. If he didn't leave now, he would never be able to.

"I must go," he told Atiana.

"Wait." She gripped his wrist. Her skin was warm. With her other hand she pulled out her stone from within the depths of her white riding shirt. "Touch stones."

He pulled his own necklace out, and Atiana gasped.

He looked down and understood what had surprised her.

His stone... by the ancients, what had happened?

It lay dead as a piece of granite.

PART II

CHAPTER 36

The day was warm and humid in the lowland swamps of Uyadensk, one of the first true days of summer. White-barked trees crowded the waterways, their roots exposed and arthritic, their canopy shielding out the sun. Clouds of biting insects swarmed everywhere, breaking only when dragonflies swooped through them to feed. All manner of sounds could be heard, from the croaking of frogs to the screech-screech of insects to the melodic call of the sparrows that plagued the upper reaches of the canopy.

Rehada had entered the swamp with the first light of dawn. It was nearly midday already, and there was some ways to go yet. She had traveled the swamp many times, but the last had been some years ago, and she was beginning to doubt her memory. She should have come across the island by now.

Well used to the balance of the thin raft, she drew her pole up from the putrid water and allowed it to slip through her hands until striking bottom. She used it to propel the raft through a narrow artery that seemed familiar.

In the distance, the boom of cannon fire played across the swamp. It had been four days since the attack on the palotza. The traitor dukes had been making these not-so-subtle reminders of their presence ever since their retreat from Radiskoye and the commencement of the blockade. It had taken several days for word to trickle down to Volgorod. The fight had been vicious—duke attacking duke as well as Maharraht. Rehada knew that Soroush had been after Nasim and Nasim alone, but some claimed that the traitor dukes had hired the Maharraht as mercenaries. Others believed they had come to finish what they'd started with the Grand Duke.

Some rumors, spread by Radiskoye, said that all the Maharraht had been killed, the all out attack an indication, the palotza claimed, of their growing desperation. Others spoke of another hezhan that had been summoned. The people of Volgorod, already tired and hungry, were becoming fearful over what this might mean. With the blockade now in full effect, preventing aid from coming in from Yrstanla or the outlying Duchies, unrest was threatening to spill over into all-out revolt.

Rehada had feared that Soroush's body would be counted among the dead. Later she heard that some of the Maharraht had escaped, and she knew in her heart that he had not died, but her relief soon gave way to fears over what Soroush would do to her in retribution. She had stolen Atiana away from him, and there had been no time to explain. She could only hope that he would listen to reason when she saw him again. And see him she must. Allowing him to come to her was not an option; she must seek him out.

He hadn't shared where he and the Maharraht had hidden themselves, but when he had come to her after Malekh's hanging, she had smelled the rot of vegetation and noticed on his boots the remains of a bright green algae that only grew in the lowland swamps.

Relief washed through her when, shortly after midday, she came to a broad bank of land. It was the tip of a long island, one of the largest in the swamp and the only one that had enough stone to form natural caves.

She pulled the raft up onto the bank and headed inland, warding the tall grasses away from her body as she went, careful to avoid the webs of the bright yellow spiders. She was obvious in her approach; she would be watched, and she would not wish the guards to kill her before they knew who she was.

As she was heading toward a rise, where the first of the caves would be, a Maharraht dropped down from a massive cypress. He was young, no more than fourteen, as were most that joined the Maharraht these days.

He didn't appear threatening. He merely pointed toward the caves and said, "He hoped you would come."

He led her to a camp that was set up beneath a group of ancient willows. A dozen Maharraht were gathered around a small fire, one of them cooking flatbread over a baking stone. Several were eating, others conversing. They looked thin, these men, emaciated, but their eyes were sharp, and none of them looked defeated.

They all stopped what they were doing as she approached. Their expressions were not unkind, but neither were they charitable. She nodded to them, and most bowed their heads in return.

Her young guide took her to the edge of a hillock. Beyond a stand of grasses, set into a face of exposed rock, was a hole that led into the earth. He motioned to it, then turned and left.

Rehada got onto hands and knees and crawled into the hole. Once she was inside, the temperature dropped. For a while the way ahead was pitch dark, but then her eyes adjusted and she saw faint light up ahead. She heard words being spoken, too soft to distinguish, and they stopped as she came near.

She reached a small, natural cavern lit by a glowing pink stone, a siraj, set onto a ledge. Her fears had eased when the boy had told her she was expected, but when she saw Soroush lying there in the cavern, wounded, all of them returned in a rush. He lay on a blanket padded by folded grasses. One thigh was wrapped in bandages dark with dried blood. His head was propped up by a rolled blanket. He was watching her, but the effort of contorting his neck seemed to cause him pain, and he rolled his head back until he was staring at the roof of the cavern.

Bersuq sat cross-legged nearby, as did another—an old, barrel-chested man with as much gray hair poking out from under his cap as there was black. His name was Muwas. Rehada had met him when she was twelve. He had been leaner then, but she recalled his stocky frame and the odd way he waddled when he walked.

They remained seated, staring at her as she approached.

"Leave us," Soroush said.

Muwas stood and bowed his head to Rehada before stepping past her. Bersuq, however, gave Rehada a severe expression, weighing her.

"Go," Soroush repeated.

Bersuq, silent as the earth, stepped past her, leaving the air scented with his heavy musk.

Rehada kneeled and placed a long, tender kiss on his forehead. "What happened?"

"I took a musket shot to the leg and passed out as Bersuq was taking me to safety. I nearly died in the waters below the palotza before Muwas found me and pulled me to the boat."

"And Nasim?"

Soroush shook his head. "We nearly had him, but he escaped with Ashan. Your Prince left in a ship shortly after to chase him down."

"He is not my Prince."

"As you say."

"Will you have them followed?"

He considered for a time, his chest rising and falling. "I don't think it will be necessary. Ashan goes to Ghayavand, and if the fates are kind, he will return here with Nasim."

"What makes you think he won't run?"

"Because Ashan cares too much. If he can unlock Nasim's secrets, he will return to close the rift. And if that happens, those secrets will be unlocked for us as well."

"And if we *don't* find him?"

"Then the fates have chosen our course. Now tell me"—he turned his head with obvious discomfort—"for I cannot think of an answer that will appease Bersuq. Why did you take the woman?"

"She is Princess Atiana Vostroma. Nikandr's bride."

Soroush smiled, and then laughed. "And you *saved* her?"

"I didn't know if she had been followed. She saw little enough that the Landed didn't already know. It seemed unwise to beg the entire Duchy of Vostroma—not to mention Khalakovo—to come hunting after us."

He stared into her eyes, considering her words, but then he relaxed into the roll beneath his neck. "There have been times when I've thought the fates were set against us, but then something like this happens, and it renews my faith."

"What do you mean?"

"Open the satchel there."

He motioned to the other side of the fire, where Bersuq had been sitting. She upended the soft leather satchel, and three stones poured out onto the woolen blanket: jasper, alabaster, and tourmaline. The jasper must have come from the beach when the vanahezhan had been summoned, and the tourmaline, of course, she had liberated herself. She stared at the stone of alabaster, stopping just short of touching it. She knew from Soroush that this had been liberated when the havahezhan had been summoned. It had been the one to attack Nikandr.

Soroush was watching her carefully. "I have been blessed, I think, to be with Nasim for as long as I have. He did not mean to, but he taught me many things. It is because of him that I can sense the rifts, the places where the hezhan can cross. It is because of him that I know of the stones. And I've also been able to sense, starting with young Khalakovo on his ship, those souls that are brightest, that will attract the hezhan. We have known that the Landed are aligned with the hezhan, as we are. What we *didn't* know was how hungry the hezhan would be for them. Nikandr. Stasa Bolgravya. The babe taken by the wasting. And now Atiana Vostroma."

Rehada's head jerked back. "Atiana?"

"She is of water. Azurite. It is she that will bring the fourth stone to us."

"But how?"

"By drowning her, Rehada. There is one place on the island where the veil is so thin that her death is all it will take."

Rehada felt the blood drain from her face. The look in his eyes as he stared at the stone above him was one of satisfaction, of something akin to smugness. He believed that the fates had shined on them, but also that this was her reward for taking Atiana without his leave.

"Where must I bring her?"

"To the lake in Iramanshah."

CHAPTER 37

As the door to her cell opened, Atiana remained seated at the lone table. She was expecting her noon meal. She hadn't been spoken to by anyone from the Khalakovo family since she'd been placed here—only guardsmen bearing food and clearing her chamber pots and providing water and the occasional clean dress to wear—so she expected nothing but more of the same. A strelet *did* enter—the serious one she saw most often—but he merely bowed his head and stepped to one side, allowing Yvanna Khalakovo to stride in with a silver tray.

As the strelet closed the door, Yvanna set the tray down and sat across from Atiana. The lids of her eyes were heavy. She seemed unable to focus, but then she seemed to remember who and where she was, and she motioned to the tray, almost angrily. "You *must* be hungry."

The tray held a plate covered by a polished silver dome, ornate utensils, and a carafe of white wine sitting next to an empty wine glass. The scent of roasted goat and onion and garlic was heavy in the air. Atiana was not merely hungry—she was ravenous—but she refused to show it in front of Yvanna, so she stood instead and moved to her bed.

"What is it you want?" Atiana asked.

Yvanna took a deep breath, seeming to gain a bit of vitality as she did so. "I need to speak to you of the dark."

"What of it?"

"You know of the boy, Nasim? The one who—"

"Of course I know of him."

"Of course—of course you do. Did you ever see him?"

She meant in the aether, but Atiana had not seen him long before Mother and the other Matri had pulled her away, so she shook her head, confused over why Yvanna would ask.

"I need the truth."

"I saw him, but only for a few moments, just before Saphia tried to

243

assume him."

If Yvanna was concerned by Atiana's knowledge of the forbidden practice, she didn't show it. "He is… He is powerful, Atiana. More powerful than any of us could have guessed." She paused, and when she spoke again, her voice was soft, as if she feared being overheard. "Mother *did* try to assume him. He stood against her and won. She's been unconscious since."

"Her need must have been great to take such a risk."

"The Matra wanted some sense of what he was about, whether he had anything to do with the summoning of the suurahezhan."

"How is she now?"

"She has not woken since the night of the betrayal."

"Is that what they're calling it?"

One eyebrow on Yvanna's elegant face rose. "What would *you* call it?"

So deep was her shame over what her father had done that Atiana could not respond.

Yvanna's anger drained away, and she suddenly became reluctant to meet Atiana's eyes. "She grows weaker every day. My difficulties with the dark continue, and I would ask…" Yvanna licked her lips. "I would ask for you to take the dark, to see if you might help."

Atiana tilted her head. "Victania is trained in the dark, is she not?"

Yvanna *did* meet Atiana's eyes then. There was no anger, only resignation. "She is no longer able to." She smoothed the tablecloth absently. "Perhaps from the wasting. Perhaps from the storms over Khalakovo. No matter what she does, she wakes within minutes of slipping under."

"Is it the same for you?"

"*Nyet.* I can no longer enter. Victania has the potential to be as strong as Saphia, but she tries too hard. The aether has come to mistrust her, or she mistrusts it, and she overcompensates."

"And you wish *me* to help?"

"She was to be your mother."

"She is head of the family that is holding me hostage."

"You are a member of a sisterhood. You cannot turn your back on it now."

"A rather convenient perspective, don't you think? The Grand Duchy has been split, and here I stand with one leg on either side. What I do here might tip the conflict in your favor."

"You are thinking like the men."

"I sit here because of the men."

"It is a baseless conflict."

"Yvanna, come. When has reason ever stood in the way of politics?"

"My mother *needs* you."

Atiana paused, remembering the way Saphia had spoken to her. She had not been kind, but neither had she been harsh. She had been matter-of-fact, and that was something to be valued among the halls of the Duchies.

"If you need it," Atiana said at last, "I will try."

Yvanna stood, a grateful smile on her face. "Then come."

They were heading for the door when the strelet unlocked it. Victania strode in, her face a picture of rage. As she stared at Atiana and Yvanna, she seemed to gather strength, like an approaching storm cloud before it unleashes its fury. "You would come to *her* for help?"

"We need her, Victania."

"We need many things, Yvanna, but a forgotten Vostroman whelp isn't one of them."

"Would you abandon your mother to her fate?"

"Leave us, Yvanna."

Yvanna stood, pulling herself to her full height, which was still a half-head shorter than Victania.

Victania stabbed her finger toward the door. "I said leave us!"

Yvanna glanced at Atiana, a brief look of apology on her face, and then she strode from the room.

"I would help your mother if I could," Atiana said.

"You are deranged," Victania said as she stepped forward, "if you think I would let you near my mother. It is because of *your* family that she is ill."

Atiana met her, refusing to be cowed. "It is because of her presumption. Nasim is no rook to be assumed as she will."

Victania's hand lashed out and struck Atiana across one cheek. Her cheek flared white with pain as her head snapped to one side.

"Do not think to judge my mother," Victania said.

Atiana's chest heaved as she fought down her anger. She nearly raised her fist, but thought better of it—it was the very thing Victania was hoping for. Instead, she sat at the table, ignoring Victania as she began eating the food from her tray. She refused to meet Victania's gaze, so she couldn't judge her reaction, but she could sense the tightness in Victania's stance, could hear the rapid pace of her breathing.

She thought it a small victory, but when Victania strode from the room, her footsteps echoed down the hallway in sharp, satisfied strokes, making Atiana feel small and defeated.

Two days passed. The routine of the previous days resumed: meals and water brought only by the guardsmen. She nearly asked them to speak to Yvanna, but decided against it, wagering that Victania had left strict orders to be informed of any such overture.

Late on the third night, Atiana heard the door to her cell being opened. She woke, groggy, to find Yvanna standing at the door.

"The Matra?" Atiana asked.

Yvanna nodded. "She is gravely ill. Please, if you care for her at all, you will come."

"What of Victania?"

"She hasn't slept properly in weeks, but she sleeps now. We won't be disturbed."

"Then I will come." She dressed and together they moved quickly and quietly down the hall. The strelet and the gaoler were gone, and Atiana asked no questions. "What can I do?" she asked as they took the stairs up.

"Be quiet," Yvanna whispered.

Yvanna stopped at a landing and pressed something behind a marble statue of a rearing horse. The wall behind it swung inward, and soon they were taking one of the tunnels that threaded its way through the interior of Radiskoye. They continued and took a steep set of stairs downward, and then another set upward before Yvanna spoke again.

"Her breathing is shallow. There are times when she moans and we think she's ready to wake, but she does not. Each time, she returns to her slumber, weaker than before. I fear she will live only a day or two more if this continues."

"And you believe the solution to this lies in the aether?"

"It must be so. I have tried to take the dark, but each time it becomes more painful, and I see little or nothing. Victania managed to take the dark for nearly an hour, but she was unable to find her."

"What do you mean, *unable to find her*?"

"That is all she said."

They reached a fork, where Yvanna turned left. The draft in the tunnel became markedly stronger, chilling Atiana's skin. The tunnel here was cut directly from the rock, the smooth whorls in the stone indicative of an Aramahn mason's hand.

"Has there been news from my father?" Atiana asked.

"Little. With no Matra, negotiations have been slow, but the Lord Duke has spoken with your father."

"Has he asked of me?"

"I don't know—My Lord Father has not deigned to share it with me—but do not worry. As long as the blockade continues and we aren't attacked, I imagine your release becomes more and more a likelihood."

Atiana had resigned herself to living here on Khalakovo as Nikandr's bride, but these last few days had been an entirely different matter. She felt abandoned. Forgotten. Betrayed. Not by Father, but by Ishkyna and Mileva.

She had thought long and hard on how such a thing could have happened, and the only answer was that they had told Father that all was well, that Atiana would be safely away with the rest of the family.

Yvanna stopped suddenly.

"What is it?"

"Be quiet!" Yvanna whispered.

Far ahead, a dim light shone in the tunnel. Yvanna waited, perhaps wondering—as Atiana was—who was coming to meet them.

Atiana took a step back, preparing to flee.

"Stay where you are," Yvanna said. "It's only Olgana."

The pace at which the light was approaching quickened, and a voice filtered up to them. "Lady Yvanna, please come quickly!"

Yvanna rushed down the hallway, perhaps feeling the same sense of dread that was building within Atiana. Olgana's face became visible as they approached. She looked like she feared for her life... Or someone else's...

"What is it, Olgana?"

She swallowed hard, her chest heaving like an overworked bellows. "It's the Matra, Yvanna. I think she's dead."

CHAPTER 38

"Dead?" Yvanna asked.

"Please, hurry!"

They rushed down the tunnel, practically running. They took the slope as fast as they could handle, and several times on their harrowing run Atiana nearly tripped. When they came at last to the end, the tunnel opened up into a long hallway—impossibly tall and intricately decorated by Aramahn hands. They stepped out from behind a statue of a stout man wearing a thick coat and cloak, but they did not pause to close it. They continued down a hall with several shorter spurs diverting from it. Among each of these were glowing stones set into ornate marble plaques. They had come to Radiskoye's mausoleum, where the soulstones of those dead but not forgotten were mounted.

They hurried to the end, where two large doors lay open. They were into the stairwell that lay deep beneath the spire and into the drowning chamber moments later. Far across the room lay a bed, and in it—illuminated dimly by the fire in the hearth—was the Matra.

They reached her side, all of them breathing heavily. Olgana moved to the other side of the bed and stroked the Matra's hair as Yvanna put two fingers to the pulse point of her neck. Yvanna closed her eyes and waited. Long moments passed, certainly long enough for Yvanna to discover the truth of the matter. A tear slipped down her cheek, and she opened her eyes. She sniffed several times, composing herself before speaking. "The Matra is dead."

Olgana opened the Matra's robe and pulled from its recesses her soulstone. Yvanna gasped. The chalcedony stone was dark. Saphia's had always been brilliant, brighter than any Atiana had seen, including her own mother, who had been treading the aether nearly as long as Saphia had. But there had been the briefest of flashes when Olgana had touched the setting.

Yvanna seemed not to notice, however. "It cannot be…"

"The stone," Atiana said breathlessly. "Did you not see it?"

"See what?"

"When first you touched it, it glowed, however briefly." Atiana stepped closer, opening her mind to the aether, as she supposed Saphia did while she was outside of the drowning basin. She passed her hands over the gem, feeling nothing at first, but when her fingers brushed its surface, she felt the cool touch against her skin, like a ripple in an underground lake.

"I see nothing," Yvanna stated flatly.

"It is there." Atiana still had the stone, and she was trying desperately to keep her mind open for any small sign, but the harder she tried, the more numb and clumsy her senses seemed to become. "And there will be more to see in the aether."

Olgana looked to Yvanna, who looked nervously down at Saphia. She seemed ready to send Atiana back to her cell, perhaps afraid of what it might mean if Atiana were caught, *Yvanna* having freed her.

But then she looked up to Atiana, perhaps realizing how vulnerable all of them were. She needed Atiana, and she knew it. After taking a deep breath, she nodded to Olgana in response.

Atiana moved to the drowning basin and undressed as Olgana prepared the jar of goat fat. Atiana was rubbed down hastily but efficiently, and then Olgana moved to the lever that allowed the chill mountain water into the sluice.

Water crept up the sides of the drowning basin while Atiana took deep, measured breaths. She had nearly resigned herself to the fact that she wouldn't be taking the dark, and now that she found herself here, about to do just that, she felt unprepared, unbalanced. But there was nothing for it.

When it was high enough, she stepped into the bone-chilling water and lay down before her fears had a chance to take hold. Olgana inserted the breathing tube. Atiana stared into Olgana's eyes, hoping she hadn't promised too much. But Olgana seemed to understand, for she leaned over and kissed the crown of her head, and then lowered Atiana into the water.

"May your ancestors keep you," were the last words she heard before she was underwater.

She had difficulty at first—her mind was running wild with possibilities, with fears and emotions—but she focused on her breath, on the expansion and contraction of her ribs, the elongation of her spine, and the way the water cradled her.

And soon… Soon…

She wakes in the impenetrable darkness of the aether. Unlike the previous times, she sees little—faint overtones of midnight blue, nothing more. Slowly, as she allows herself to fall deeper, the colors coalesce: the handservant standing over the basin; the Matra herself, lying in her bed; the fire in the nearby hearth, which glows not yellow and orange but a deep, deep red.

The Matra's form is dark—almost entirely black—but there is color to her still. It might say nothing about whether or not she is truly lost to the winds, however. It may be because she has so recently passed.

The stone around the Matra's neck is dim. Atiana moves forward, opening her mind to allow the Matra's soul to touch hers, but there is nothing. No response. Not even a faint glimmer. Just the cold embers of a once-raging fire.

She touches the stone, and there is the briefest of flashes. She feels a thread leading from the stone, but she is prevented from following it.

What are you doing here, child?

It is the Duchess Polina Mirkotsk. She is not strong in the ways of the dark, but she has always been good at speaking through it, so there is little wonder that they set her as the watchdog.

I am trying to help the Matra, Saphia.

Who allowed you into her chamber?

Yvanna, now begone.

Atiana tries to drift outward, to follow the trail leading away from Saphia, but Polina stops her.

Polina speaks softly to the other Matri, bidding them to verify Atiana's words. No doubt one of the others would assume one of the palotza's rooks and ask; Atiana only hoped they didn't ask Victania.

I do not have time to wait, Atiana says. *The Matra's life depends on it.*

Nyet, Polina says.

Tell whomever you wish in Radiskoye, but do not stop me in this. You know she is close to death. I am near where you are far, too far to do anything to help her. Is it not so?

Silence.

I can feel her, Duchess. Let me go to her, please, to do what I can.

Polina is unsure of herself. One of the others—perhaps Lhudansk—advises caution, but Polina ignores her and her presence retreats.

Do not betray us, Vostroma.

Atiana says nothing in return. She turns to Saphia. She is faint, her presence distant. Atiana touches the Matra's stone once more, feeling wind and the open sea. She keeps herself within the stone, knowing this is the key to finding the Matra, but like a single note plucked from a harp, the feeling is beginning to fade.

Desperation pushes her toward haste, but this has never been the way with the aether. She keeps the sound of the note in her head, however faint, and allows it to carry her.

When she opens her eyes again, she finds herself far from any island, floating on the winds like the liberated seed of a thistle. Nearby, an Aramahn skiff floats. There are only two aboard. Ashan sits at the helm, guiding the winds into the billowing sail above him. He seems at peace—a man who has come to grips with the world around him. On deck with Ashan is the boy, Nasim, and it is to him that the connection from the Matra terminates. The thread, rather than being thin, is thick and vibrant, as if the connection originates from the *boy*, not the other way around. Nasim is sleeping, but his head and shoulders—even his legs—jerk and twitter as if he is trying to waken but cannot quite do so.

And then she sees them.

Dozens of havahezhan, wind spirits, float about the skiff. They trail about in lazy arcs, always circling back. She thinks at first it must be at Ashan's bidding, but then she realizes they are coming for the boy.

They pause for brief moments in their circling, and it is at these times that Nasim's body spasms. She cannot understand what is happening, but it seems as if they are feeding on him. Preying upon him. Does the boy realize it? Does he allow it? Has it been so all along?

This seems doubtful given the scrutiny he received at the hands of the Matra. And so it seems it must be something particular to his departure from Radiskoye or his time on the wind.

Or the tether that exists between him and the Matra.

The thought makes her go cold.

The hezhan are feeding, but it is the *Matra's* soul—not Nasim's—that they feed upon.

She moves into the path of the tether, and opens herself to it. The writhing rope leading to the boy brightens, and she realizes that she has added herself to it. She senses both Nasim and the Matra, though Saphia's terminus is very, very faint. She feels a tug at her breast as one of the havahezhan swoops in and swallows another piece of the Matra's soul.

Atiana rages against it, for it has taken a bit of her as well. She wonders how the Matra could have taken it for so long. It must have been this way ever since Nasim left the palotza five days ago.

She knows not what to do. She is helpless against such things. She feels herself becoming lost, and the more she tries to direct her awareness, the tighter the hold Nasim seems to have upon her. Soon she is forced to stop altogether for fear of losing herself to the power of this boy.

The wind spirits continue to feed. The Matra's soul is nearly extinguished, perhaps all the quicker because the hezhan somehow sensed more meat upon the bone. They swoop in, hungrier. They take larger bites, and with each one she feels weaker.

She tries to fend them off, but they only become more animated, and swoop in faster.

Her chest aches. Her *bones* ache. She screams and tries to wake, but it is not possible. Not any longer.

Nasim sleeps, and yet he appears to be screaming. Ashan attempts to wake him. He looks about the craft, over the water, perhaps sensing something, but there is nothing he can do. Either that or he chooses not to.

The bites continue, and it is clear that she is lost. She is no Matra of five decades; she is a child, and she will not be able to pull herself from this no matter what she tries.

CHAPTER 39

When the sun rose on Nikandr's fifth day on the wind, he saw near the horizon—as he had on the four previous mornings—the telltale sign of Ashan's skiff. He had come to understand that Ashan was *allowing* himself to be followed. Three times on the first day Jahalan had summoned all the winds he dared in an attempt to catch up to the skiff, but every time they closed in, the winds would push them away. They had tried again the following day, hoping Ashan was tiring, but the same thing happened, and by this time Jahalan was nearing exhaustion. Nikandr thought they would lose the skiff, but it always stayed just on the edge of sight, a dark speck on the cloudy white horizon.

"Are we to make another go, My Lord?"

This came from Viggen, a spry old sailor taking a turn at the helm. Nikandr had flown with him several times. He was an able sailor. More than able. Nikandr counted himself lucky that he'd been among those helping on the eyrie, but he hadn't counted on how superstitious the man would be. Sailors were a superstitious lot to begin with, but Viggen was worse than most. He hadn't taken the attack by the Maharraht lightly, and he considered it unlucky to take sail with so many having just died and the ship still steaming from the fire that had only just been put out.

Viggen and the crew grumbled about how bad it was the entire next day—never to Nikandr directly, but amongst themselves and within earshot. Their fears, it seemed, were confirmed near sundown. A twinkling along the eastern horizon had drawn Udra's attention.

"That is a ship," she said simply, "or I am an old gray gull."

A chill went down Nikandr's frame as Viggen and the five other men who weren't sleeping belowdecks spit downwind over the gunwale. Somehow, despite their precautions and the relative darkness, they had been spotted leaving the island. Nikandr looked up to the *Gorovna's* starward mainmast. Its sails had been burned beyond repair. Even with them gone they might have foiled the pursuit, but they were chasing Ashan, and he had kept a steady course, west by southwest. There was really no choice in direction, and the trailing ship would know this by now.

So the chase continued.

"We'll make another go," Nikandr said to Viggen, "though I doubt the outcome will be any different."

Viggen lowered his voice so that only Nikandr could hear. "Begging your pardon, My Lord Prince, but do you still think it's worth it?"

"There are grand things at work," Nikandr said just as softly, "things neither of us understand."

"As you say, My Lord."

Nikandr glanced toward the bow with purpose and waited until Viggen did the same. "That boy is at the center of them." Nikandr coughed. "Better if we find the storm before it descends upon us unannounced."

He started to cough, hoping to stem the tide that would surely follow, but just as it had at random times over the past three days, the cough devolved into a fit that gripped his chest tightly until he felt like he could give no more. Only then did it recede, leaving him exhausted for hours on end, and just when he thought he had recovered, it would happen again.

Udra did him a favor without knowing it. She said it was because of the fire, that it would soon pass, and Viggen agreed. "My brother was caught in a fire like that when he was a child. He coughed every day of his life until he died at fourteen."

Nikandr thanked him not to repeat the story. He knew, of course, that it was the wasting, but it had grown markedly worse since leaving Khalakovo. Shortly before the coughing began he would feel a constriction upon his heart. It would skip a beat, perhaps two, and the coughing would begin. As the fit progressed, he could feel the noose tightening around his heart until finally it was released. Soon after the coughing would cease.

He pulled out his soulstone and stared into its cracked, smoky depths. He knew that the progression of the disease and the state of his stone were somehow related. He had thought for a long time that the stone was merely a canvas, painted with the events of his life, but now he knew differently. The stone, more and more over the years, was becoming a part of him—little different than his heart, his stomach, his liver. He also knew that the blight was in some way related. Things had grown progressively worse over the past decade, and this phenomenon, he had no doubt, would not have been possible in years past. The world was changing. And Nasim was the key to unlocking that riddle.

On the sixth day, with the sun high but occasionally hidden by passing clouds, Nikandr sat on deck, his back to the gunwale, biting into the hardtack biscuits that were their only provisions besides weak ale. Jahalan had been summoning the winds, coaxing them into the right direction, perhaps attempting to feel for the location of the trailing ship, which had shown itself several hours ago, closer than it had been in the morning. Nikandr realized he could no longer see Ashan's skiff. He took the telescope from the helm and moved to the bowsprit. He scanned the horizon, but found nothing.

"Jahalan, where is he?"

Jahalan opened his eyes. He was nearly sleeping on his feet. He rushed to the bow and took the telescope from Nikandr. "I don't know," he said after sweeping the horizon.

They thought perhaps he was hiding among the clouds, but Ashan had never veered from his straightforward course. Had Nikandr been wrong all along? Had Ashan been toying with them in order to more easily lose them later?

Nyet. That made no sense. Ashan was arqesh; had he wanted to he could have lost them that first night.

Perhaps, then, he had changed his mind. Or perhaps he had finally realized that the *Gorovna* had been followed and it was too risky to lead Nikandr any further.

"Ship, ho!"

No sooner had the words come from the boatswain than the sound of a cannon broke across the stillness of the afternoon. Nikandr heard the whine of the grapeshot beneath the ship and a tight cluster of audible pops as it punctured one of the seaward sails. A moment later, the ship twisted counterclockwise, the telltale sign that the shot had ripped a sizable hole in the canvas.

Abaft and above, exiting a thick bank of white clouds, was the Vostroman ship. How it had gained on them so much Nikandr didn't know, but they were in for it now. Their position gave the Vostroman ship many options and the *Gorovna* few.

Nikandr took over the helm's controls. Udra was already sitting ahead of the controls, cross-legged, eyes closed and palms flat against the decking.

"Bring us down, Udra. Quickly. Viggen, prepare the cannon. Jahalan…"

"*Da*," Jahalan said as he moved to the mainmast. Once there, he opened his arms, and the alabaster gem on his brow glowed brighter. The winds gathered strength as another cannon shot rang out. This one crashed into the hull, a poor shot—they had most likely been told to take the *Gorovna* intact, along with her crew.

Nikandr tilted the ship downward. With Udra suppressing the windwood's ability to stay afloat and Jahalan's winds, they were already picking up considerable speed, but the trailing ship—Nikandr recognized it now as the *Kavda*, a swift eight-masted caravel—was already closing the distance.

Viggen and the boatswain manned the cannon at the bow. They trained it upward, and it roared to life, but even as Nikandr heard a satisfying crunch as the shot tore into their hull, two more blasts ripped into the *Gorovna's* landward mainsail.

"Give them wind, Jahalan!"

"They have two havaqiram." Jahalan's voice was calm, but his words were clipped, the muscles along his neck straining.

The wind—heading strong two points off the bow—swirled about the ship.

"I can't stop them!" Jahalan said, his face becoming red, his hands bunched now into tight fists.

The ship was slowing. The winds were too unpredictable to capture. Soon they would be dead in the wind, helpless to stop the *Kavda* as they lowered grappling hooks and took the *Gorovna* in for the kill.

Suddenly the air began to mist, and the temperature dropped from cool to frigid. In mere moments Nikandr was drenched.

"What are you doing?"

"It isn't me," Jahalan replied.

He thought at first it was the qiram aboard the *Kavda*, but their wind masters wouldn't do such a thing—the effect would be too debilitating to their line of sight.

A frigid gust cut windward across the ship, and then—as suddenly as it had come—it was gone. It blew again, and vanished. Nikandr could barely see Jahalan, who stood only four paces away, but he could still see the look of confusion on his face.

"I think we are beckoned," Nikandr said.

"Ashan?"

"Who else?"

Another cannon blast cut through the fog and tore into the decking at the stern. A man screamed, the sounds cutting through the fog like a knife.

Another shot came moments later, and Nikandr realized the *Kavda* was using the sound to target them.

"All quiet!" Nikandr shouted. "Viggen, shut that man up!"

"Aye, My Lord."

The gust came again, blowing in the same direction, as a cannon shot ripped through the landward foresail.

Nikandr stared down at the levers that allowed him to guide the bearing of the ship. He knew the situation was untenable. Even with the mist, the *Kavda* would soon correct their speed, they would close, and it would all be over.

His breath came slowly, and he felt his fingers tingle as he realized what the wind was telling him to do. He could release the ship's controls. The wind would carry them northward, toward uncharted territory. It was a decision that would wrest them from the jaws of the *Kavda*, but it was one that could ruin them just the same. If he did this, the *Gorovna* would slip free of the currents that ran between the islands, the currents that had been meticulously groomed and guided by the spires and by the delicate hand of the Matri over centuries. Outside of these shipping lanes, the aether swirled and eddied as unpredictably as it did at the base of the eyrie's cliffs. Worse—the effect was often stronger, the aether swirling into unforgiving maelstroms that would rip the ship to pieces were Nikandr to engage the ship's controls once more.

Once free of the stream that ran between the Khalakovan and Vostroman archipelagos, they would be forced to rely on the abilities of Jahalan to guide the ship like the Aramahn did in their tiny skiffs.

But really, despite his fears, there was no choice in this. If he didn't, the *Kavda* would have them.

Before he could change his mind, he pushed all three levers forward until they locked into place, and the ship began to turn and drift windward.

CHAPTER 40

The *Gorovna* twisted in the wind, and though Nikandr had not said a word, it soon became clear to any experienced sailor what was happening.

Viggen's voice cut through the mist from the stern of the ship. "Kapitan?"

"Silence on deck!" Nikandr shouted as loud as he dared.

Several more shots rang out from the *Kavda*, but they were further now and the shots went wide. A short while later, soft as a memory, Nikandr heard the order to come about. Soon the *Gorovna* would be out of reach, and it was doubtful the *Kavda* would brave the currents to chase them down. If they did, they might succeed in capturing or destroying their quarry, but more likely than not they would in the process become lost to the winds as well.

Jahalan guided them, being careful not to use too heavy a hand lest the havaqiram aboard the *Kavda* sense it. The mist began to recede. Nikandr could once again see the foremast clearly. The wounded crewman lay on his side at the stern, rolling his head from side to side while Viggen, kneeling over him, clamped his hand over the man's mouth to keep him from screaming. Udra pulled a black-and-white scarf from around her neck and began binding the man's wound. The deck around them was bloody and mangled from grapeshot.

They continued northward, a few calls from the *Kavda* coming to them from within the mist. The *Gorovna* had now completely drifted free from it, and as the distance increased, Nikandr saw how truly immense it was. It looked like a cloud the size of an island, churning as the wind pushed them onward.

"It must be Ashan," Jahalan said.

Nikandr furrowed his brow. "Or Nasim."

Jahalan laughed softly. "Or Nasim."

Nikandr studied the northern sky for any sign of the skiff, but there was none. "Is Ghayavand truly a place between worlds?"

"Who can tell? Some doubt that it exists at all. Others say it is nothing but an island where powerful qiram once lived. Others believe a doorway once existed, but that it has since closed."

"What do *you* think?"

"Me?" Jahalan's face became pensive as he too studied the horizon. "I think that something as hidden as Ghayavand is as good as a myth."

One more cannon blast interrupted the silence, but it was soft, distant, muted by the depths of the fog.

"And what if it were real? What would you do then?"

A genuine smile lit his face. "I would learn. The day we stop listening to the lessons around us…"

"Is the day we begin to die," Nikandr said, completing the proverb. "So you always say, but I have heard of the riches of Alayazhar." Jahalan, like Udra and dozens of other Aramahn, had pledged themselves to Khalakovo. They had found their place, as they say, and had dedicated themselves to teaching the Landed the ways of the world as seen through the eyes of the Aramahn.

"You mean to ask would I betray my oath. I would not, but that doesn't mean I wouldn't cry for my own loss."

"Perhaps in the next life," Nikandr said.

"Perhaps," Jahalan replied. "Do you still believe the city you saw in your visions was Alayazhar?"

Nikandr shrugged. "Who can say? Perhaps it was something Nasim saw somewhere when he was younger. But it felt real, as if *I* were the one with the memories… *Nyet*, as if I were living it, then and there."

"And what if we find this place? What then?"

"We find Ashan and we bring him back."

"What of the wasting?"

Jahalan had said the words nonchalantly, perhaps hoping to ease into the conversation, but it struck Nikandr physically. He reeled, shocked and embarrassed that Jahalan had found him out.

"Who knows?" Nikandr asked.

"Only Udra and I, but the crew suspects."

Nikandr wanted to laugh. "They consider it another ill omen, I expect."

"They do."

Nikandr arched his neck back and took a deep breath. "There is time for me yet. My only hope is to bring Nasim back home, to unlock the riddle within him."

Jahalan turned to face Nikandr. He reached out and gripped Nikandr's shoulder affectionately. "Best you take care of yourself, then. Eat, and make sure the crew sees you doing it. Throw up if you must, but do so in your own cabin."

Nikandr nodded, thankful for having someone who knew, thankful at not having to hide it, at least some of the time. "I will."

The following night, Nikandr retired to the kapitan's cabin to ride out another coughing fit. The spells were not lasting as long as they once did, but they left him feeling much more weakened when they were done. It was as if his body had had enough and his defenses were crumbling.

Viggen knocked on his door with an offer of food. He accepted, but it took him nearly an hour to force down the meager ration he'd allowed for himself and the crew. With the prevailing winds largely controlling their direction, he had chosen to stay high above the water instead of dropping to fish. It was not food, in any case, that was the issue. It was liquids. Their supply of ale was beginning to run low.

That night, he forced himself to sleep, though it was difficult with the interminable ache in his chest. When he finally did fall asleep, it was deep.

As were his dreams.

At the fluttering wings of a bird, Khamal opens his eyes. He expects a gull, but finds instead a thrush with spotted wings and a fiery red breast standing on the tower's parapet. He sees this as an ill omen. The thrush flaps down from the parapet to the wooden roof. It hops closer to Khamal's feet, and then it alights, scared by the creaking sound of the hinged door that opens nearby.

Muqallad is first, followed by Sariya, who carries a curved knife, a ceremonial khanjar. She holds it as though it would bite, but her face is resolute.

They stand before him.

"Your last chance," Muqallad says.

Khamal ignores him, giving all his attention to Sariya. She stares back, and though she acts strong, he can tell that she regrets what she has done—not enough to change her mind, but there is regret, and that is a start.

"Small consolation," he says softly.

"What?" Muqallad replies.

"You have lived centuries longer than you'd ever imagined, and you still believe that you can force upon the world its destiny."

"The fates knew well that they were ceding the world to us. They should not be surprised when a plan of their own devising bears fruit at last."

Khamal views the horizon, feeling in his heart the tear in the world that runs through the islands. "Only when this is healed can the world move on."

"Enough," Sariya says. The word is short, clipped. She is shamed at being here, and she wishes to be done with it.

Muqallad turns to her.

"He will not change his mind, and we still have much to do."

Muqallad nods, beckons her closer.

She hesitates, glancing to Khamal, but then complies.

Together, they hold the khanjar. Each reaches out to touch one of Khamal's shoulders, and for a moment, it is as it was when they worked together on this same tower, centuries ago, trying to take the world to a higher place, a higher plane.

Khamal can feel the world around him, feel the power building within the two of them. They were surprised at how easily he gave in—with barely a fight. What they didn't realize was how right it felt. They didn't realize how freeing their betrayal might be. They were all trapped on this island from the moment the rift had formed, and though he had tried to find a way to repair it, he came to learn that he would not be able to do so while here. He also knew that he could never leave.

Unless he dies.

To do so means giving himself to the fates. He has come to terms with this. It feels right.

But he cannot allow the two of them free reign while he's gone. He will die, but he will be reborn, and he will see to it that he remembers, that he returns to finish what he started.

The tip of the khanjar presses against his stomach, pierces his skin. He looks down, smiling.

"Why do you smile?" Sariya asks.

He stares into her blue eyes. "Someday I'll tell you."

"*Neh*," Muqallad says, "you will not."

Together, they thrust the khanjar home.

Khamal tips his head to the sky and screams. He feels the warmth of his own blood, already trailing down his stomach. He feels the touch of Adhiya even now. And it is in this moment that he is free.

He binds the island, binds this tower, so that neither Sariya nor Muqallad will be allowed to leave. They will be trapped. They will wait for his return, and if the fates are kind, he will return a wiser man than he is now.

Muqallad stares into Khamal's eyes. He knows. He knows, and he works to prevent what is happening.

"Help me!" through gritted teeth he shouts.

But it is too late. Khamal slips free of his mortal frame, and in doing so, cements the spell around the tower.

Nikandr woke, sweating, his chest so constricted he could hardly breathe. He could not find it in himself to cough. He was too weak, and he felt as

262 · BRADLEY P. BEAULIEU

though once he started, he would not stop until he was dead. And so he lay there holding his soulstone tightly in one hand, breathing shallowly, feeling the gentle tug of the wind upon their ship until slowly, slowly, the feeling of tightness faded.

He swallowed and took in a deeper breath. To be so caught by this spell made him feel powerless. It was something he resented. But he also felt grateful. He was alive, and so there was hope that he would weather this storm.

He kissed his soulstone and stood, testing his breath for a moment before unlatching one of the landward windows and peering into the night. Nasim's ship lay in this direction. He was sure of it. He didn't need the stars to feel where Nasim was now, some many leagues ahead of them.

Unable to sleep, he left his cabin and wandered the deck. Several men stood watch, with Viggen tending the helm. Jahalan normally slept on deck, but when Nikandr moved toward the forward patch of deck where he normally laid out his blanket, Nikandr found him sitting there, studying the sky. Nikandr waited, not wanting to interrupt, but just as unwilling to return to his cabin.

"Come," Jahalan said, making space for Nikandr to sit.

"I saw the city again," Nikandr said as he sat on the blanket. "I can feel it. We're coming closer." He studied the stars for a time as a chill wind blew abeam the ship. "Khamal died in my dream. He was murdered by the others—Muqallad and Sariya."

Jahalan was already shaking his head. "They were arqesh."

"Meaning what? That they could not have found it in themselves to commit murder?"

"Just so."

"The Maharraht murder."

"The Maharraht are not arqesh. They are selfish, thinking only of themselves."

"They claim they are doing it for you. For all of us."

"*Da*, they claim this. But what they're really doing is alleviating their own fears, their built-up hostility toward the Landed. Were they really doing it for the Aramahn, they would help. They would preach forgiveness. They would teach through kindness."

"You don't teach."

Jahalan turned his head to regard Nikandr. "I abandoned the path to vashaqiram long ago."

"And yet you feel angry over the Maharraht."

"They are an affront to our history."

"But not your future?"

"The fates lead us where they will. We are no longer the people we once were. Neither are you. Why hold on to such things? What does it gain us?"

"It gains us our legacy."

"*Da*, your *legacy*. Where would the Landed be without that?"

"Be careful, Jahalan."

Jahalan paused. "I am sorry, Nikandr. I know you put your faith in your ancestors, but even you will admit that they have helped you little these last many years."

"They see well beyond what we can see."

They were interrupted by Viggen's calls for reports from the crewmen manning the rigging.

When they were done, Jahalan continued, "I have been thinking of this chase we're on, of your dreams as well."

"And?"

"I think we should turn back while we have the chance."

"There's little enough to fear now. Ashan is leading us."

"All the more reason to abandon the chase. He's taking us for his purposes. Or perhaps the boy's. Either way, it's foolish for us to go on. Ghayavand is a place the living should no longer be. Nasim—if your dreams are right—may have a place there, and Ashan may be able to keep himself alive, but the rest of us will not be so lucky. It's a place where the worlds are torn, and believe me when I say that Adhiya will not welcome us with open arms."

"We all go to Adhiya, do we not?"

"In our own time, and in our own ways, but we go now to a place that should be left alone until the world sees fit to heal it, not before."

"Perhaps it has already healed."

"If you believe that you are a fool."

Nikandr laughed softly. "Perhaps I am. But I cannot abandon him now."

"You don't owe him anything."

"It's not him, though I do feel as though I owe him something. You must have felt it. Nasim is entangled with the future of Anuskaya, perhaps the future of the world. I cannot abandon him, not now. We are linked too closely."

"Your father needs you, as does your Duchy. If you value them, you should return home, where you can do some good."

Nikandr stood. "I have always valued your advice, Jahalan, but in this you are wrong. We will go to the island, and we will bring Nasim back if we are able."

"You do so not just at your peril, Nikandr, but mine as well. And Viggen's. And the rest of the crew."

"Then so be it."

CHAPTER 41

Atiana floats along the wind, her awareness encompassing the sea, the air, the islands hundreds of leagues away. She is no longer of her body. She is of the world, no different than the clouds or the currents of the sea.

But there is something, a scent that reminds her of who she used to be. Who she is. But how can this be? How can Nikandr be among them in the aether?

It doesn't matter. He is present, and that is enough. Through him, she can feel another. The boy. Nasim.

She is not experienced in navigating the dark, and yet she knows what she is seeing has not been noticed before—at least by the Matri. There is an imprint of Nasim in Adhiya and an echo in Erahm. He walks between worlds…

Such a thing cannot be—she knows this—and yet here it is.

And it explains much. His confusion. How else would a boy grow up when struggling to understand the very world that holds him? His pain. How could he not be torn? His attraction to Nikandr, a lodestone, a raft among the waves.

It is because of Nasim that Saphia was attacked. It is because of him that Atiana is attacked now. He has allowed the hezhan to follow—or perhaps he doesn't even realize. Either way, they feed upon her, as they do the Matra. If she could draw him closer to Adhiya, the hezhan may not be so easily able to follow.

She pushes with all her might, as she did with the babe. She has little strength, but she feels it working. The worlds, at least in this one small place, are pushed further apart. Nasim slips toward Nikandr and toward the physical world.

And then her strength is lost.

She woke once, though she was unable to open her eyes. She lay there on the edge of sleep, on the edge of waking, for a long time, and she heard people speaking—most likely of her—but try as she might she was unable to rouse herself to wakefulness.

She dreamed of storms wracking the island. At first she thought it was Kiravashya, where she had been born and raised, but she came to realize it was Khalakovo's largest island, Uyadensk. The storms were so fierce that they wiped the island clean. Gone was the city; gone was Palotza Radiskoye; gone was Iramanshah and the tiny fishing village of Izhny; everything was gone, and afterward it felt how the beginning of the world must have felt: pristine and full of hope.

As she had hours or days before, she woke several more times, and again she was unable to wake fully. She tried. She railed, but whenever she did she would slip backward into her dreams, and her screams of impotent rage would be directed toward Mileva or Ishkyna or Father for leaving her here.

And then the cycle would begin anew.

She shivered as something brushed the skin along her forearm. She had difficulty opening her eyes, but when she saw who sat next to her bed, her lethargy faded.

"Matra," Atiana said, pulling herself up in her bed. She took in the room, realizing she had been returned to her cell deep beneath the palotza.

Saphia studied her with sharp eyes. Her skin was pink and healthy. She leaned to one side in her chair, perhaps to ease her pain, but otherwise she seemed more hale than she'd been in years. "Are you well, child?" she asked. Her voice was not scratchy, an indication that she had been awake and free of the aether for some time.

"I am tired. Nothing more. May I ask what news?"

"The blockade continues. My husband has been treating with your father, to no avail."

Atiana shook her head. "He won't back down, not with Bolgravya and Dhalingrad pushing him so, but neither will he go to war over me."

"Over you, *nyet*, but there is more in the balance. The failed abduction of Nasim. The wounded and dead. But more than anything, the reasons behind your marriage. We are all of us in trouble, and I think it strikes your father worst of all."

Not wishing to admit the truth of it, Atiana didn't respond.

"You don't have to reply—I know how dire the situation is on Vostroma—but now that a wall has been erected between north and south, it will be difficult to tear down."

"Has my father asked of me?"

"Through your mother he has demanded your return, and for the death of the Grand Duke he has asked for the ships that were promised as well as the alabaster."

Atiana couldn't help but chuckle ruefully. "For the good of Bolgravya, of course."

"Of course."

She wanted to ask if her father had asked of her well-being, but she knew better. She was still—no matter how well the Khalakovos might be treating her—in the awkward position of political prisoner, and Father was not a man who would show any outward signs of concern or affection, even for his daughter, even now, and though it burned, Atiana knew he was right.

Saphia drew in a deep breath. "I came to speak with you of your time in the dark."

Atiana's memories were faint, nearly to the point of forgetting them altogether, but she was getting better at stitching her time in the dark together. She worked backward from the end, telling Saphia her story in bits and pieces. As she did, the entirety of her memories returned.

Saphia considered her words. "Nasim's hold on me seemed no harder for him than toying with a mouse. And in the end, when I was released, I don't believe he understood what he'd done. He seemed to forget me in as little time as it had taken to seize me."

Atiana paused, Saphia's words reminding her of those final moments with Nasim. "There was something more…"

Saphia's gaze sharpened. "Go on."

"I don't know whether you felt it, Matra, but Nasim… He walks between worlds."

"What do you mean?" Saphia's words were clipped.

"He lives in Erahm and Adhiya, both. I felt it when I followed the trail from you to him. It is why he is such a troubled child. I believe it is why he didn't understand what he'd done to you, and why he forgot you so quickly. He thinks you and I are as ephemeral as the hezhan."

Saphia frowned. Her gaze became distant, perhaps reliving the horror of the past week in her mind, but then she seemed to focus once more on Atiana. "How did you secure my release?"

"I pushed on the walls of the aether."

"Pushed?"

"I know no other way to explain it. I felt the walls close in around him, just like with the babe in Izhny, just like in Iramanshah when you were…"

"When I was what?"

Atiana stared, trying desperately to hide her fear.

Saphia pulled herself higher in her chair, staring down at Atiana with cold, piercing eyes. "When I was what?"

"When you were preparing to assume the boy."

As Atiana laid there, she felt as if Saphia could lay her bare with little more than her will and a cold stare. "You understand, Atiana"—she let the words fall between them like a gauntlet—"it would be unwise to repeat such a thing…"

"I do, Matra."

"The damage it could cause Khalakovo is immeasurable."

"Of course, Matra. I would never think of mentioning it."

"Yet you did, here, with me."

"Of course. It was something you needed to know."

Her voice lost some of its edge. "You were speaking of Iramanshah."

"*Da*," Atiana said, pausing to regain her composure. "I've thought on it much. The narrowing is related to all of these events. If I could take the dark once more, knowing what I know now, I'm sure I could find more."

"Knowing what you know now…"

"*Da*, Matra."

"*Nyet*. Rest. Regain your strength. When that is done, we will speak again of the dark."

She rang a bell sitting on the table next to her, a signal that Atiana's audience was at an end. Atiana knew already that Saphia, despite her promise to *speak again of the dark*, would never allow her to enter it again.

But Atiana needed to. If she was ever going to find out what was happening on Khalakovo, she would have to do so outside the walls of Radiskoye.

Olgana entered the room, preparing to take Saphia away, and Atiana realized she could not remain in this room and have any chance of escape.

"Please, Matra," Atiana said as Olgana reached Saphia's chair.

Saphia held up one hand, forestalling Olgana.

"This room weighs upon me, more than you can know." She motioned to the dark, stone walls around her. "If I am to recover, I would see the sun."

Saphia considered the room before resting her steely gaze on Atiana once more.

"Let it not be said that the Khalakovos do not repay their debts." She waved her hand, and Olgana wheeled her around and steered her toward the door. "You will have your old rooms back."

Days later, Atiana stood at the windows of the room she'd been promised—the ones her family had been given upon their arrival—and drew back the curtains to stare out into the southern gardens. The sun had yet to rise, but its light could be seen on the horizon, pale yellow against the indigo sky. The windows opened to allow air to flow in those rare days of summer, but she could easily use them to leave the confines of her room. That would only deliver her into the garden, but the garden was all she needed.

After waiting for the pair of guardsmen to pass her window, she unlatched the window and opened it. It swung open soundlessly. She had tested it the day before, and after finding a light squeak she had used the rendered fat from her dinner of roasted chicken to grease the hinges.

She swung herself outside, mindful of the river rock that sat in the flower bed beneath the window. She slipped to the nearby hedges, watching the guardsmen along the wall. Their attention was turned outward, however—after the attack, they were still wary of a threat from the outside.

Moving as quickly as she dared, she made her way to the place where Nikandr had come with his dog, Berza. She had forgotten about the path that led down from the palotza to the cliffs below, but when she had kneeled next to Nikandr that day, consoling him for what her brother had done, she had noticed the uppermost reaches of it and remembered.

She moved through two squat, gray boulders to the thin path. She turned along the first of the switchbacks, feeling the wind press her against the stone face of the cliff before turning sideways and threatening to pull her from it entirely. The wind played tricks—as much for her as for the ships that found themselves too close to it—but she continued at a fast pace, unable to believe her luck.

Don't count yourself lucky yet, Tiana, she told herself. *There's still a ways to go.*

Nearly an hour later, she came to the end of the trail. It ended some hundred feet above the surface of the waves. Years ago, it had continued on all the way down to the sea itself, but the Khalakovos had considered it not useful enough to repair when a quake had ripped away a good portion of it. That only served to help her cause; no one would think to search for her here, thinking her incapable of braving the waters below.

Indeed. As she stared downward—the water churning, white and frothing with rage—she found herself doubting. Doubting that she could jump. Doubting that she could rise to the surface. Doubting that she could make her way westward to the shore and arrive in Volgorod unseen.

This was foolish, she thought. Why risk such a thing just to speak with a woman whom she wasn't sure she could trust? Would Rehada help? Would she be *able* to help?

Perhaps, Atiana thought, and perhaps not, but she had to try, and all that stood in her way was the drop from this cliff.

The wind picked up, blowing scree against the side of her face. It bit her skin. Stung her neck.

She stared at the waves, crashing in unending rhythms. Her breath came quickly, and desperately.

She stared up, wondering if it were too late to return.

And then a bell began to ring, over and over, the alarm that she'd escaped.

She stared down, taking a full breath, releasing it slowly.

I can do this, she thought. *I am a Matra, in mind if nothing else. I have taken the dark, and I have braved the currents beyond this world to return whole. If I can do that, I can brave the waters of this world.*

"Ancients protect me," she whispered.

And she leapt.

She arced downward with increasing pace, the sound of the surf breaking against her ears.

And then she crashed against the surface of the water.

CHAPTER 42

As the sun began to rise, the bell at Rehada's door jingled. It rang again, and once more by the time she had managed to rub the sleep from her eyes and pull on her robe and make her way down the creaking stairs. When she opened the door, she stared, dumbfounded.

By the fates who live above…

Soroush had been right. No other than Atiana Radieva Vostroma stood before her, wearing a beaten woolen szubka around her shoulders and a simple cotton babushka to hide the color of her hair. She looked exhausted. The skin of her face was grimy with dirt. She was shivering from head to toe, yet she seemed hesitant to ask Rehada for entry.

"Come," Rehada said, stepping out into the quiet street and guiding her in with an arm around her shoulder. "You'll catch the hacking for sure, dressed as you are."

She guided her to the sitting room, in the center of which was a mound of pillows. There were two chairs beneath the small round windows set high into the wall, but Atiana chose to sit among the pillows instead. Rehada guessed it was a ploy to put her more at ease—few women among the Landed gentry would do what she had just done—but she still gave her a small nod of approval before moving to the cart that held the liquor.

Rehada poured two glasses of vodka and diluted them with cider. "There have been riots," Rehada said while holding the glass out.

Atiana accepted it. "I was careful." She took a healthy swallow and swished the liquid around her mouth before downing the rest in one big gulp.

Rehada sat, sipping at her own drink. "I didn't think I would ever see you again."

"You nearly didn't…"

"Why? What happened?"

Atiana shook her head, pulling the babushka off with a look that Rehada could only describe as defeated. "I—I've come because of the rift. We both know it's the cause of the deaths—the children, the babies. What I don't understand is why it's happening or how we can halt its progression."

"Why do you care? Surely at this point you could leave and summon your father's ships to save you."

"I care because what happens here could happen anywhere. Vostroma, Yrstanla, Rafsuhan. Anywhere."

Rehada looked this woman up and down, trying to weigh the truth of her words. The defeated look in Atiana's eyes was gone. She stared back resolutely, and more than that—she seemed hopeful, as if something she had long considered out of her grasp had been placed before her and was now there for the taking. She seemed, Rehada finally conceded, sincere, and so she answered in the only way she could.

"What would you have me do?"

"I need to take the dark. With Radiskoye no longer an option, Iraman-shah is all I can think of, but I'm afraid they will think me a spy and refuse me access. I need you to help."

"That seems a simple thing."

"There is more." Atiana stood and poured herself another drink—no cider this time. "Nasim…" Her words trailed off, as if she were considering whether or not the line behind which she was standing should be crossed.

"Go on," Rehada said softly.

"During the attack, he seized the Matra as easily as I would a moth and held her for days. He nearly killed her. I managed to turn his attention elsewhere, and I did it by pushing on the walls of the aether."

Rehada frowned. "Pushing?"

"The babe that died… The same thing happened then—the feeling that the walls were closing in—and it happened again when I took the dark in Iramanshah." Atiana shook her head while staring into the clear contents of her glass. "It is the key to these things—I feel it in my bones—but I need to take the dark again to unravel it."

Rehada paused. "I am not a woman trusted in the halls of Iraman-shah."

"I know," she replied, "but they will trust you in this. They must."

Rehada wondered how much of this Soroush had seen.

Probably little, but he had always been one to listen to the signs around him, to heed them when they came. He was also one to put himself in a place to hear them, and she wondered if she could ever commit to the cause the way he had.

Probably not, she realized, but she could do this at least.

"Then come, Atiana Radieva. Come with me to Iramanshah, and we shall see what we shall see."

The sound of gunfire lit the afternoon sky as they prepared to leave. Rehada had changed into sensible clothing, and Atiana already looked enough like a peasant—especially with her hair hidden—so they decided it best to leave her in the stolen, threadbare clothes she'd been wearing when she arrived. Rehada had no hezhan bound to her. She had released hers only the night before. Though she might have taken another, it would have been difficult, and she could not risk showing any propensity toward violence in front of Atiana. She could not risk revealing that she was Maharraht.

And besides, Rehada thought, it was probably best not to draw attention by wearing her circlet on a day like today. They would simply be two women, traveling out of the city toward the south of Uyadensk.

As they opened the door, two flatbed wagons trundled down the street, headed toward the center of the city, toward the sound of the fighting.

Rehada closed the door again, peering through the crack in the door to watch them. On the beds were a dozen men bearing crude weapons—long knives, scythes, pitchforks. Only a handful bore muskets, but these were the men that watched the buildings around them most closely, as if they *expected* to be attacked, or were perhaps looking for those that might run to the Boyar to report their location.

When they turned further up the street, Rehada led Atiana in the other direction, but she had been paying too much attention to the wagons. If she had been watching more closely, she would have seen the two men standing in the shadows down the street.

When she *did* see them, she already knew it was too late.

"Quickly," Rehada whispered as they turned right and began heading downhill toward the river.

Atiana said nothing. She had seen them too.

When they reached the end of the alley, Rehada dared one look back.

The men had reached the mouth of the alley. They were moving quickly now.

"Run," Rehada said.

They did, moving as quickly downhill as they dared. The stone buildings—mostly homes with small shops at the lower floors—were all two and three stories. One had a low stone wall fencing the yard and an iron gate. She leapt over the wall and grabbed a round stone. After motioning Atiana to duck down, she launched the rock across the street, down an alley that forked some twenty paces down.

She ducked down low, pulling Atiana with her, as she heard the heavy footsteps of the men approaching and the clatter of the stone as it skipped down the alley.

The soft pad of boots came nearer.

Atiana's eyes were wide, and her chest was heaving with her rapid breath, but she seemed to have her wits about her. From inside the voluminous sleeve of her szubka, Atiana pulled a rusted kindjal. It looked worn, but its edge gleamed in the late afternoon light. She stared into Rehada's eyes, making it clear she would fight if needed. Perhaps she was not so callow as she had seemed that time on the beach.

Rehada placed a hand on her wrist as the footsteps approached. In the distance, the sound of the river could be heard as the summer melt rushed toward the sea. Voices roaring in anger rose above it.

Then, without warning, the footsteps receded, and were gone altogether.

"Come," Rehada said.

They were up and off once more. They raced downhill, and reached the river in short order. They stopped at the bridge that crossed it, for further uphill there was a crowd on the bridge. They were stacking barrels beneath it, near the supports. They were stacking gunpowder, Rehada realized. They were going to destroy the bridge—one of the largest that crossed the river and the one used often by the Oprichni as they headed east to patrol the city.

Rehada whirled at the sound of men speaking in low voices. She thought it would be the streltsi, but she was wrong. It was a group of peasants hauling a hand-pulled cart. In the bed were three wooden casks containing what was most likely gunpowder.

Atiana took Rehada's hand and began walking back up the way they'd come, but they stopped once more when they saw, coming toward them, the two guardsmen.

Rehada turned and began walking swiftly across the bridge.

"Stop, there," came a voice behind her.

Rehada ran, Atiana following. Below, over the low stone wall, the Mordova coursed, creating a rush of sound.

Footsteps followed close on their heels.

A gunshot rang out. Rehada glanced behind and saw one of the guardsmen pointing a pistol at the nearby group of men, who looked on not with fear, but open hatred.

Rehada and Atiana managed to cross the river, to make it deeper into the city. The lowering sun sat behind a thick layer of clouds, casting the city in a pall, but it wasn't so dark that they could easily hide. Plus their pursuers were close behind and gaining. They were eventually caught as they reached a narrow intersection crowded on all sides by tall stone buildings. Rehada was yanked back by her arm. She tried to free herself, then to push him away with her free hand, but he shrugged off her attacks.

Atiana had pulled her kindjal, and was facing her assailant warily. "We don't wish to hurt you," Atiana said.

The strelet lunged forward, but Atiana skipped backward and slashed at his wrist. He snatched his hand back, a thread of blood marking his wrist.

"You won't be harmed," the strelet said.

Atiana shook her head. "I'm a simple woman from Izhny, come to meet with my friend. Why would you chase us?"

The man paused, stood up straighter, confused. He looked to the other, as if he were considering her words.

"Watch him!" Rehada shouted, but too late.

Quick as a mongoose he darted in, twisting away from Atiana's sharp thrust. In a blink he was inside her guard and levering her arm behind her back. Atiana screamed and the kindjal clattered against the cobbled street with a metallic ting.

"Don't do this," Atiana pleaded. "Tell them you weren't able to find us. I'll make both of you rich men."

From the shadows of the alley they'd run down, the group of men were walking forward. Two were holding pistols, another a musket, and all of them were eying the streltsi with cruel eyes that spoke of emotion that had been bottled up inside for months, years—emotion ready to burst forth now that the blight had placed its heel upon their throat.

The strelet holding Atiana turned her toward them and backed up. "By the authority of your Duke, I order you to stand down."

"Not this day," an older man with graying hair said. Rehada recognized him. His name was Kirill. He was a butcher in the poorest part of Volgorod that also ran a drug den. He was not a man Rehada would wish to be rescued by. "You'll be allowed to go unharmed, but you'll not be taking them."

"We are on the Duke's business," the strelet said, raising his pistol to point at the man. The other strelet did the same.

"One's fired," Kirill said, "leaving one shot between the two of you."

Without speaking, the two streltsi began backing up.

Kirill angled his pistol lower, toward Rehada's legs, and fired. The shot echoed in the cramped space as the strelet holding Rehada screamed. He tightened his grip around Rehada's neck, favoring his right side.

"I said you'll not be taking them."

The men behind him fanned out. The one with the musket raised his weapon to his shoulder and sighted along the length of it. Rehada was reasonably sure he was aiming at the *strelet's* head, but she was not so sure of his aim, nor of the strelet's reaction if he sensed the man was about to fire.

"That one you can have," the strelet holding Atiana said, motioning to Rehada, "but this one will be coming with us."

Kirill paused at this, studying Rehada and Atiana in turn, but then he shook his head. "*Nyet—*"

Before he'd even finished speaking, the strelet fired.

One burst of red near the crown of his head, and the man with the musket was down.

The other pistolman fired, but Atiana's man had shoved her to one side and was already rolling away. He was back up on his feet in a flash, running forward holding a short, gleaming blade he'd pulled out from a leg sheath beneath his cherkesska. The pistolman raised his arm to defend himself, but the strelet thrust beneath the other man's guard and ran him through just below the ribcage.

He pulled his weapon free as the other strelet, hampered by his bloody right leg, joined him. They fought fiercely, efficiently. Another of the peasants dropped, and another, until there were only four left to stand against them.

Rehada was about to grab for Atiana when another shot rang out, louder than the others.

Kirill was holding the smoking musket. A strelet fell to his knees, a hole in the center of his cherkesska darkening with blood. The three other men, perhaps emboldened, stormed the lone remaining strelet. Had he not been wounded, he might have won—and as it stood, he delivered a savage cut to one man's leg, and pierced another man's gut—but in the end he was taken down from a blow to the head by a fist-sized rock, thrown by the man furthest away. He fell, eyes wide, unresponsive.

The men turned toward Rehada and Atiana.

"Let us be," Rehada said.

Kirill grinned. "And what kind of fool would I be"—he pointed to Atiana—"if I let a woman of royal blood slip through my hands?"

"I am not royal," Atiana said, her eyes wild.

"Blonde hair? Fair skin and fairer hands? Promising to make the soldiers rich? *Nyet.* You're royal or I'm an old goat." He kneeled and began searching the coat of the nearest strelet. "Take them."

Rehada was nearly ready to run when she felt something press against her legs and groin and chest and neck. She felt it against her skin, along her scalp as her hair was tugged, along her whole body as the air around her seemed to shift.

And then an almighty boom shook the city. The low layer of darkening clouds glowed yellow, then orange, then red. The sound—a conflagration of unimaginable dimensions—continued. A cloud, darker and thicker than the clouds above, rose from the north, from the bridge that had been teeming with the peasant mob and barrels of gunpowder. The cloud rose higher, roiling up until it was caught in the wind. It began drifting eastward toward the sea as the sounds of the explosion finally fell away, replaced with the crackle of fire and human cries of pain and shouts for help.

"Go and see," Kirill said. "I'll meet you."

From the corner of her eye, Rehada saw a dark form filling a doorway. Standing there was a burly man with brown hair and a thick beard. Hidden as he was, only Rehada could see him. He raised one hand to his lips, and then leaned forward until he could see Kirill and the other—the youngest who had remained behind. When he saw that they weren't looking, that they were concerned with little except their men who were just now walking out of sight, he slipped quietly from the doorway, allowing a black bag to snake down from his left hand. The heft of it made it clear that it was weighted—by sand, perhaps, or small stones.

Quick as summer rain, he rushed forward and swung the bag high in the air. It came crashing down on the crown of the young man's head. He dropped to the ground immediately. Their savior spun, dodging as Kirill swung the butt of the musket at him. He slipped in around Kirill's guard and snaked the cloth bag around his neck.

Kirill's face went red. The sound of his gurgling filled air, barely discernible against the backdrop of the misery at the bridge.

Kirill slumped, and the burly man lowered him down, holding tight until there was no longer any movement coming from the old man.

When he was done, he stood and secreted the bag into his waist-length coat as if it had never existed.

"Quickly," he said, motioning to his doorway, which still stood open.

Rehada and Atiana stood their ground.

"You'll not want to be out tonight," he said, motioning toward the pillar of smoke.

Atiana stared into Rehada's eyes while shaking her head, the gesture barely noticeable.

"Not everyone sides with the mob," he said. "My wife, ancients rest her soul, was Vostroman. And I served my time in the guard." He paused as another, smaller explosion fell over the city. "But do as you wish." He turned and left, walking through his door and taking a flight of stairs upward.

Atiana looked fearful, echoing Rehada's own feelings. She had never seen a city in such turmoil, on the islands or anywhere else. The man was right,

Rehada decided. They risked death by wandering the streets, and her own home was no longer safe.

Together, they took the stairs up to a simple two-room home. The man was sitting on a rocking chair by the window. The shades were drawn, but every so often he would move one aside and peer out into the night. He appeared to be forty. His shoulders were wide, his hands huge, and with his sleeves rolled up past his elbows, showing thick forearms, he looked like he could pick either of them up with only one arm.

A low fire burned in a fireplace along one wall. Rehada relished the warmth, wishing she could bond with a spirit here and now.

"This night of all nights, what are two women like you doing out?"

Atiana sat on a stool near the hearth, warming her shaking hands, while Rehada settled herself into a creaky wooden chair. Neither answered. They couldn't. Any sort of answer would do him no good, and would probably put him in more danger if anyone were to find out where they had sheltered for the night.

"That's probably best," he said, nodding. "Sleep." He pointed to an open door. "I'll wake you before the sun's up."

"Thank you," Atiana said.

A nod was his only reply.

In the morning, he knocked on their door, and they rose and left without ever learning his name.

CHAPTER 43

"Land ahead," Udra said as she stared over the bow.

Nikandr scanned the horizon and saw an island—perhaps twenty leagues long—so green it looked like an emerald jewel against the sapphire glass of the sea.

"It is Ghayavand," Nikandr said, remembering it from his dreams.

Ashan's skiff, less than a league ahead, began to descend. The island loomed much larger now, and for a moment the skiff was lost among the darker colors of the island's forests. Nikandr felt uncomfortable following so closely. Ashan had had his way with them, but that didn't mean it had to be so now, here at the end.

"Take us around the island," he said to Jahalan and Udra. "I would have a look before we see what Ashan has in store."

Jahalan nodded and moved toward the mainmast, but before he could reach it he reeled and doubled over, grabbing his gut as he fell to the deck. The same thing happened to Udra.

Nikandr kneeled and helped Udra onto her back. "What is it?"

Jahalan was shaking his head back and forth violently, and it was then that Nikandr realized: the alabaster gem within the circlet of white gold no longer held any of the luster it had only moments ago. Somehow the bond they held with their hezhan had been cut off from them.

"My heart," Udra said, "it's been ripped from my chest."

"Worse than that," Jahalan added.

The ship began to drift downward, twisting in the wind. They were completely at the mercy of Ghayavand.

Nikandr shifted along the gunwale, keeping the island in sight.

Udra uttered a keening, a sad and empty sound in the silence of the sky. She dropped to the deck, her hands patting the surface gently. "*Neh!*" she moaned.

Nikandr didn't understand, but moments later he felt a tickle, as if insects were crawling beneath his fingers. The railing before him, its surface puckered and grayed. Small cracks ran along its length. The same was happening to the deck, to the masts, to the spars and the hull.

A cracking sound became audible. It was soft at first but soon the entire ship was alive with it. It became deafening.

An almighty snap—as if the bones of Erahm itself had just been broken—resounded through the ship. Nikandr could feel it through his boots and in his chest. Another snap came, this one just wide of his position. The *masts* were being sundered.

What in the name of the ancients was happening to his ship?

Another crack, louder than the others, was followed by the scream of a crewman. A sliver the size of a spearhead had pierced his chest. He fell, grasping it hopelessly and wailing from the pain. As something deep within the bowels of the ship gave way, sending a shudder through the ship, the man's eyes rolled up into his head and he fell unconscious.

Like a blooding, the very life of the ship was being drawn from it. It remained afloat, but it would not last. At any moment it would plummet into the waves to become lost forever among the ceaseless currents of the oceans. Even if they could somehow safely reach the shores of the island, the *Gorovna* would never fly again.

Before Nikandr could even attempt to understand what was happening, the sounds around him fell away. His breath was drawn from him as if it were his last. His heart fluttered, and his eyelids drooped.

Somewhere far ahead, the skiff they'd been chasing for over a week has touched down.

Nasim stands upon a stone perch, an eyrie crafted in the style of the ancients. He paces its length, moving onto the rocky cliff to which it is affixed and then the wide field of grass beyond. He runs his fingers over the tips of the stalks, allowing them to tickle the palms of his hands. He can feel in that moment every part of the island, every blade of grass, every chittering insect, every breath of wind, every turn of soil. It feels as though he is looking through a window that reveals the land as it was before the Grand Duchy, before the first settlers, before even the Aramahn. It feels pristine.

And still, there is imbalance. Ghayavand is one of many islands, isolated on a shelf in the sea but connected by the water, by the roots of the earth, by the ceaseless currents of the wind. It stands out in its perfection. It has withstood the blight, but the pressure is growing. In time, it too will succumb, and he finds himself saddened.

He pulls back into himself, unable to withstand the pain, but as he does, he senses the prince, the one to whom he was bonded on Hathshava, the island the Landed call Uyadensk. This connection had felt foreign then, wrong, but now it feels right, like a warm fire after days in the cold.

There is something else, as well, a feeling that he has been here before. He is of this place, though he knows not how. The memories are at the very edges of his mind, so close but still out of reach.

Above, among the clouds and the winds, a lone havahezhan dives among the drifts and eddies of the wind. And then it is gone, returned from whence it came.

He follows.

And Nikandr woke.

Someone was screaming his name.

His stomach was churning and turning as if he'd tumbled upside down without realizing it.

He was gripping the railing for support, but it crumbled at the slightest touch. He stared at the desiccated fragments still sticking to his hands, unable to comprehend *who* he was, *where* he was. His mind was reeling, not from the physical nature of what was happening around him, but the realization of what he'd just seen. It had been Nasim somewhere on Ghayavand. But the havahezhan... Nikandr knew it—or knew *of* it, at least. It had been the same hezhan that the Maharraht had summoned on the cliff below Radiskoye, the same one that had attacked him on the maiden voyage of this very ship. But how?

"Nikandr!"

How could that be?

"Nikandr, leap!"

Nikandr shook his head violently.

The ship was diving toward the sea, her nose tipped seaward, the white-capped waves high and moving fast. Jahalan was standing on the windward mainmast, ready to leap free.

Nikandr launched himself toward Jahalan. He fell only a few steps out and slid down the deck as the ship continued to rotate. Jahalan reached for him, but Nikandr shot past.

He managed to leap and grab onto the ratlines leading up to the starward mizzenmast. So brittle was the wood that the mizzen snapped, and he found himself sliding once more.

He struck the forward hull and latched onto it as the ship's starward masts tipped toward the horizon. "Go!" he commanded.

Both of them leapt just as the ship crashed into the sea.

Bitterly cold water enveloped him as he plunged beneath the waves. Hundreds of feet of rigging and yard upon yard of sail fell around him, occluding his vision. Something bit into his ribs, and began pulling him downward. He pulled himself free, feeling something scrape against his skin as he did so.

He fought for the surface. When he finally broke free of the waves, he drew on the air as if it were the liquor of life itself while wave after wave rolled over him. The spray was high, and it was difficult to see anything but the blue-white waves, but among the flotsam, he thought he saw one of the crew. He swam in that direction, using a barrel that had floated free from the ship. He was nearly exhausted by the time he reached him.

It was Viggen. He was face-down in the water, and Nikandr knew as he turned him over that he was dead.

"Jahalan!"

He screamed his name again and again.

A short while later he heard a muffled cry for help behind him. He turned in the water, seeing nothing for a moment, but then he saw a form beneath a swath of canvas that was still attached to the mast. He swam, fighting the waves with every stroke, and felt something strike his leg beneath the water. He dove under, and saw the long white tail of a serpent slither into the dark.

He regained his breath and then sucked in one last intake before heading under. He kicked beneath the rigging and reached Jahalan, who was caught beneath the sail. His movements were frantic. Nikandr could see that he was trapped in a mass of ropes and netting, and the struggling was only making things worse.

He pulled the kindjal from the sheath at his belt and with his free hand began to pull some of the ropes away. He hoped that once Jahalan realized he was here to help he would stop thrashing. He did a moment later, but Nikandr realized it was because he had fallen unconscious.

He sawed at the ropes that would not come free easily, but in his haste, he cut Jahalan's thigh. His thoughts turned to the white serpent, but the best thing he could do now was to free Jahalan and swim for the island.

Above them, the ship rolled further. The sails were pulled down on top of them, dragging them beneath the surface.

The water was dark, making it difficult to see, so he swam deeper, the only clear way to get out. He kicked away from the ship, hoping he could distance them enough that they could clear the sails.

His lungs burned. His legs and arms and chest screamed from the struggle to gain distance. But he kept going.

His breath finally gave, and he had no choice but to surface. More rigging blocked his path, but here it was sparse, and he managed to drag Jahalan through it.

He broke the surface, but not before taking in a lungful of salty water. He released long, wracking coughs. While supporting Jahalan's head to his chest, he leaned back into the water and kicked away from the ship.

"Jahalan?"

The only reply was the high wind whipping the tips of the cold white waves against his face.

"Jahalan, can you hear me?"

He wasn't breathing.

A goodly portion of a mast lay nearby. Nikandr reached it, and although it was cracking and brittle, it held well enough for him to lay Jahalan over it. He squeezed Jahalan's chest and forced the water from his lungs while trying to prevent him from slipping back beneath the waves.

"Jahalan, wake up!"

When no more water came up, he slapped Jahalan's back, slapped his cheeks, while continuing to call to him.

Suddenly Jahalan coughed and shook his head violently, then sucked in a rasping lungful of air.

Nikandr held him tight to the wood lest he take in more water. "Calm down," Nikandr said, "you're fine."

"I am"—he coughed for a long minute—"anything but fine."

Nikandr could have laughed. It felt good, even among all this madness, to have his friend with him, alive. He guided Jahalan toward shore. The majority of the ship still lay on the surface behind them, but it was breaking apart from the action of the waves and the brittle nature of the wood.

What in the name of the ancients were they going to do now? Were Ashan and Nasim—

Suddenly Jahalan was pulled beneath the water. When he resurfaced, he let out an excited shout, and Nikandr felt something cold slide along his left leg. Nikandr kicked violently, hoping to scare the serpent away, at least for a time.

"My leg!" Jahalan screamed.

"I know." Nikandr pulled his kindjal again and watched the water closely. "Just keep moving."

"I can't."

"Keep moving or these waters will see the death of us."

Jahalan moaned and grit his teeth, but he kicked, and with Nikandr's help, they made progress against the incessant waves.

The head of the serpent glided through the water toward them. He dove below and stabbed, but the serpent broke off and swam away.

When he came up, however, the image in his mind made his breath come doubly fast.

"What?" Jahalan's eyes were wide and frightened.

"Nothing," Nikandr lied. In that brief moment, he'd seen three other serpents gliding through the water, waiting for their chance to come for blood.

CHAPTER 44

"Just keep moving," Nikandr said.

They swam, Nikandr spending more time under the water than above. Jahalan knew what was happening—it was impossible not to—but he did not understand the full extent of it. There were no less than eight of them, Nikandr realized after a short while.

The waters around them were for the time being blessedly free of the serpents. He found out why only a short while later. He heard a panicked shout. Using his legs to kick as he crested a wave, he saw nearly a dozen survivors swimming together. A straggler was yanked downward. He didn't even have time to scream, but a moment later he resurfaced and his shrieks rent the air. He was tugged downward two more times, and he screamed for help the entire time. Two crewmen swam toward him, but before they could come close the man who'd been singled out by the serpents was dragged under. He was not seen again.

They moved a few hundred yards, the spray from the waves pelting their faces, when the bone-white serpents returned. Two of them shot in toward Jahalan. Nikandr dove beneath the surface and stabbed one of them, but the other slithered to one side and lunged for his arm. He tried to pull it away, but wasn't fast enough. He managed to avoid getting caught in the grips of the serpent's jaws, but the small, sharp teeth grazed his forearm, leaving bloody gashes in its wake.

"Faster!" Nikandr shouted.

Jahalan tried, but his endurance was nearly at its limit. The same was true for Nikandr, but the soul-wracking fear of seeing the creatures face-to-face was enough to keep him going a while longer.

The group ahead had reached the shallows, and many of them had already stood and begun wading toward shore when Udra screamed and was pulled under. The men shot toward her, looking down through the water, but they could not find her.

Nikandr and Jahalan reached them soon after. The serpents tried to attack them again, but there were enough now that had knives, and they stayed between the rest of the group and the serpents, protecting them when the vicious creatures came close.

Everyone dragged themselves onto the black beach, which was blessedly warm after the frigid waves. Nikandr pulled off his shirt, cut it into strips, and had one of the crewmen wrap his arm as best he could. Then he moved to Jahalan, who lay on the beach, his face nearly as pale as the serpents.

Jahalan's right leg was bleeding heavily, and Nikandr wondered how much he had lost in the water. Nikandr moved to his side, and held his arm while Pietr and Ervan worked diligently on his leg.

"It will be fine," Nikandr said.

Jahalan's eyes shut tight as the men used a belt to cut off the blood flow just below his knee. When he opened his eyes again, he was frightened, though much less than Nikandr would have been in his place. Seeming to overcome some of the pain and fear, he smiled. "My time may have come."

Nikandr shook his head. "*Nyet*. Not here, my friend. Not now."

He fell unconscious moments later.

Ervan, a thin man with curly brown hair, held the belt in place and nodded toward Jahalan's ankle. "We won't be able to staunch this wound, Kapitan. He'll die tonight if it isn't cut and sewn properly."

Nikandr swallowed. "We don't have the equipment to amputate."

"*Da*. We have nothing proper, but we can get thread easy enough, and Pietr can fashion a needle from a buckle."

"What good is a needle that large going to do him? He'll be bleeding as badly from the puncture wounds as he is right now."

Ervan shook his head violently. "*Nyet*, Kapitan. We'll need to bind it tightly for a time, but it will hold. Against this"—he tipped his head toward Jahalan's ankle—"we have no chance."

Pietr and Ervan watched him expectantly. The other men were nearby, waiting for his decision. "Do it quickly," he said finally, "and by the ancients be careful."

Nikandr was good at starting a fire without flint, but Pietr, a hard man with several deep scars running along the left side of his face, was even better. From the rough bark of the tall fern trees near the shore, he fashioned tinder and then made a bow drill from some branches and twine they liberated from some of the canvas that had washed ashore. Other men collected fresh water in huge conch shells from a tidal pool and placed it over the fire to boil. Soon they had purified water that they used to sterilize the thread and needle.

The surgery was not quick, at least not by Nikandr's recollection. He stopped by from time to time, but it was difficult seeing Jahalan losing a limb like this. He didn't know how he would tell him when he finally woke, but he knew he would be the one to do it. He owed him that much—to look at him in the face and tell him what this journey had done to him.

If only he could do the same for Udra and Viggen and the other men... But he could not, and he would have to live with the knowledge that their deaths lay at his feet.

At last the surgery was complete. Jahalan's leg was bound with strips they had boiled and let dry in the strong wind. They would make more, and hopefully in a day or two the worst would be over—for Jahalan, at least.

Nikandr and Pietr sat near the fire late that night, neither of them able to sleep. Pietr had been second mate in his haphazardly chosen crew, but he'd proven himself to be a good man. Nikandr had sailed with him several times before, but they'd never had a chance to speak at any length.

Jahalan was sleeping soundly, and though his heart seemed weak, the quick work that Ervan had made of the wound had probably saved his life.

"What are we to do?" Pietr asked while staring off toward the horizon—eastward, toward home.

Nikandr poked the fire, causing the logs to shift and sparks to drift on the brisk night wind. "Take stock of our surroundings. Build shelter."

"Forgive me, my Prince, but that is not what I meant. How will we return home? No one knows where we've gone. Even your mother, may the ancients watch over her, will not be able to find us."

"I know what you meant, but we have the men to consider first. We make shelter, we prepare defenses, and we take what the ancients provide for us."

"But with no ship..."

"I know. The man we were chasing, it seems, is now our sole source of hope. We will search for him as well. He will be headed for Alayazhr, and so shall we."

"With his ship, he'll already be there."

"Don't be so sure. This place—if legend is to be believed—is wild, untamable. Greater men than Ashan have tried over the centuries."

Pietr nodded. "If we come across his trail, Lord, I'll be able to lead you to him. Have no doubt of that."

In the morning, Nikandr waited as long as he could, hoping that Jahalan would wake so that he could speak with him, even if only for a short time, but the need to find Ashan was more pressing by far than comforting his old friend, and so he left with Pietr and two other men: Kirilai and Oleg.

They forged their way through dense growth near the shore, but this soon gave way to an ancient forest with a tall canopy high above them. The temperature soon forced them to remove their shirts. The smell of rotting wood filled the oppressive air. Small, biting insects plagued them as Pietr led the way, using a short but serviceable sword to hack a path through the undergrowth.

They came to a sharp rise and were about to follow it upward to higher ground when the earth began to shake beneath their feet. It soon became clear that it was coming closer, so they hid behind the fallen trunk of a massive, decaying tree.

Nikandr glanced to his right and saw his own fear reflected in the face of Kirilai. Ahead, a flock of white birds with long blue tails took flight and flapped noisily away. The ground thrummed. The palm fronds they were peering through fluttered in time, and soon they saw it—a hulking body made of dark earth took long strides toward them. It had four stout arms and two massive legs that looked like the ripped-up roots of trees more than they did earth. The creature—some sort of vanahezhan—slowed and finally came to a stop, as if its mass were incapable of concise movement. It scanned the forest, and Nikandr had the distinct impression it was looking for them. He knew, as did the other men, that there would be no fighting this thing. They had two pistols among them, and a fair amount of shot, but without a good deal of iron or an Aramahn qiram to protect them, their only real choices were to hide or flee.

They remained stock still as the creature lumbered forward. It lowered its bulk to its arms so that it was resting on all six appendages like some huge earthen insect. Four pits within the head twinkled like gems as it moved its head back and forth, and Nikandr wondered if this were its equivalent to smelling—akin to what Berza would do while hunting grouse.

Nikandr swallowed as it scrabbled forward, moving its head back and forth. Along the vanahezhan's soil-skin were tiny green plants with toothed leaves that opened like a clam shell. As the creature swayed, some of them clamped down, catching tiny insects in their jaws.

Next to him, Kirilai's breath was coming in short gasps. Nikandr squeezed his forearm, willing him to remain silent. But when the creature took another step forward, it became too much. Kirilai stood and sprinted away.

The vanahezhan galloped forward and leapt easily over the tall log. Kirilai, in his panic, released a long, high-pitched wail. He ran behind a tree, and Nikandr lost sight of him for a moment, but the galloping mound of earth caught up to him on the far side, downing him and stepping on his chest with one huge leg. Blood spouted from Kirilai's mouth, cutting off his scream just as the report of a pistol rang out. A puff of dirt exploded near the top of the creature's head. With one foot still pressed down onto the caved chest of Kirilai, it slowly turned its head. All four pits of glittering eyes seemed to be trained on their location.

Oleg stood next to Nikandr, staring at the beast, chest heaving.

"What have you done?" Nikandr said as he snatched the pistol away.

The creature took a step forward.

"Run!" Nikandr ordered, and he was over the log and sprinting down the far slope. "And spread out!"

He fell on the slick undergrowth and slid downward, losing the pistol he'd snatched from Oleg. He flew downhill, unable to slow his descent. He heard Pietr and Oleg behind him, but soon the sounds of their escape was replaced by the roar of a river.

Finally the ground leveled off, allowing him to come to a halt by digging his heels into the soft earth. He spared one quick glance back and saw the hezhan moving quickly, twisting through the trees like a snake.

Oleg's screams came moments later.

Nikandr stood and ran, knowing there was no longer any hope for Oleg. In the time it took him to run a hundred paces, the pounding chase of the vanahezhan picked up once more. It came louder and louder as he reached the top of a steep decline. He leapt as the sound of snapping wood came close behind him.

The ground tore at his skin as he slid downward. Above, the vanahezhan was watching him slide away. It turned to its right and followed the ridge from which Nikandr had leapt.

And then Nikandr found himself in mid-air, falling.

CHAPTER 45

Nikandr splashed into a deep and swift flowing river. He coughed, fighting to stay above the frothing water, but when he slipped down a shallow decline, the current dragged him under. He held his breath and felt himself falling again. He tumbled over stones and briefly saw the bright blue sky through the tall trees before being pulled down once more. He was turned about, and his shoulder crashed into a large, rounded rock. He fought for the surface, his lungful of air nearly exhausted, to no effect; the current was too strong.

Finally the current slowed, and he was able after several long strokes to break through to the surface. As he spluttered for breath he found himself in a wide pool. He could hear the sound of rapids ahead, but here the current was weak. He struggled for the bank, and finally, his breath coming in heaving gasps, he pulled himself up the thick grass onto firm ground.

Behind him, the booming sound of the vanahezhan was approaching. Moments later its lumbering head was visible through the trees farther up the slope.

The pounding neared his position, but he remained immobile, hoping the creature would fail to find him, but it soon became clear it was headed straight for him. He leapt into the water as the pace of the creature quickened. It roared—a sound like a growling bear and crumbling stones—and moments later the sound of wood cracking and snapping came. He turned just in time to see a tree with a trunk as thick as a ship's mainmast arcing toward him. He ducked under the water as the thing sailed overhead. Tree branches gouged his back, and he was sent tumbling deep underwater.

He swam beneath the tree and peered carefully between a cluster of vine-like branches. The vanahezhan stepped into the water and waded toward him. Its eyes glittered, and though it was silent in the water, it seemed even more menacing than when it had released its moaning call.

Nikandr was ready to dive beneath the surface to swim for the opposite shore when Pietr reached the bank of the river and began shouting and waving. The vanahezhan continued until Pietr threw a large branch, which struck it on the head. The earth spirit turned. It seemed unsure what it should do—first it stared at Nikandr behind his tree, then the screaming Pietr, then Nikandr again—but finally it began wading toward the bank.

"*Nyet!*" Nikandr screamed as he kicked his legs and began swimming away. "Over here!"

He had hoped to confuse the creature, to give himself and Pietr enough time to flee while it was caught in the water, but it didn't listen.

He didn't know what to do. He felt helpless. He wished he could control these creatures as the Aramahn did.

And then he remembered his vision of Nasim, on the ship, just before it had plummeted into the sea. He had known of their connection, their link, for some time, but it had always seemed to be at Nasim's discretion. Why, Nikandr thought, could it not work the other way?

He closed his eyes.

He reached out.

Nasim, he called. *Nasim, please hear me.*

Nothing. And the vanahezhan had nearly reached the bank. Pietr turned, ready to run.

Nikandr had become accustomed to the sensations that Nasim created when they were linked. It was one of disorientation, but also of connection to the world. That was the key, he realized.

He opened his mind to the air and its loamy scent, its kiss upon his wet skin and the clouds above. To the earth, the feel of it as it pressed against the water, and the water pressed against it, the way it held the trees in its grip, its massive presence as it rose toward the peaks of the island.

And he feels him.

He is near. So near.

He wants to ask Nasim for his help, but he cannot. He feels only the world around him, the cool touch of the water, the rippling waves and the tug of the current. He can feel the stones that lie along the riverbed, the rivulets that feed this greater body and the coursing mass of fresh water that flows out for hundreds of yards into the salty sea.

On the other side, just beyond the veil, is a jalahezhan. It watches, curious. It would be so simple to draw him across, to bring his aid. This seems wrong, somehow—a violation—but he does so anyway, for his need is great.

Nikandr shook his head, the vision that was so clear a moment ago vanishing. He watched as the massive spirit of earth gained the edge of the bank. As it began climbing out, a tendril of water snaked upward along one leg and wrapped around its waist. The vanahezhan turned and pounded four fists simultaneously into the water, sending white, frothing water high into the air. It resumed its climb up the bank, and to Nikandr its movements seemed desperate now. The thick cord of water was still around it, and the tendrils, like quickly growing vines, hungrily climbed the length of its leg. The sad cries of the creature were cut off as it was pulled backward and under the water.

The water churned as Nikandr gained the opposite shore. He ran into the forest just as the tree was grabbed by two black arms and pulled beneath the surface. The gouts of water continued to fly, and the pool was now swirling violently with the detritus of the tree and the vanahezhan. The last Nikandr saw was the tree breaking the surface in a rush and then bobbing there as the water churned and roiled.

Nikandr pointed Pietr upriver. Nasim was somewhere in that direction, he was sure. He could *feel* him.

After about half a league, they came across a shallow ford. Nikandr crossed, and they continued uphill toward a ridge they could see through the breaks in the trees. They heard movement. Someone was running ahead, hidden among the dense foliage. The tall trees were much less prevalent here, but that only meant that the going was much slower, as grass taller than men and ferns the size of a skiff now dominated the landscape.

And suddenly, the forest stopped. Ahead, a dozen paces away, was bare rock leading to the edge of a precipice.

Nasim stood there, his back to Nikandr. He turned, somehow sensing their presence, before resuming his watch of the landscape below.

"Nasim?" Nikandr said as he took a step forward. He didn't know why, but he had the distinct impression the boy was preparing to leap from the edge of the cliff.

Pietr crept forward, preparing to rush Nasim, until Nikandr grabbed his arm and shook his head.

"Nasim, can you hear me?"

Nasim turned to face Nikandr. His heels were touching the sharp edge of the rock. A wave of vertigo passed over Nikandr just watching him.

"Step away, Nasim. I want to talk to you."

The wind tugged at the simple black vest the boy wore, and played with his short brown hair.

"Where is Ashan?" Nikandr asked, taking another small step toward Nasim.

"They are near."

"Who is?"

He looked into Nikandr's eyes with a serious expression. "Sariya." He glanced back over the cliff. "And Muqallad."

"Do not be afraid, Nasim. We won't let them harm you."

Nasim shook his head. "I was meant to return here, to find them. But you know this, do you not?"

Nikandr nodded. "Where can we find them?"

Nasim pointed to the ridgeline to the north. "In Alayazhar."

Moments later, the wall of plants nearby parted, and Ashan stepped out from behind a large fern, brushing off his arms as he did so. His curly hair was tousled by the wind, and his robes were rumpled and dirty, but otherwise he looked little different from the first time they'd met on the eyrie.

As Nikandr stared at him and the calm expression on his face, all the confusion—the frustration and the rage that had built over the days since leaving Khalakovo—boiled over. He stalked forward and struck Ashan across the face.

Ashan stared at Nikandr, his eyes wild with shock and pain. Nikandr stepped in and drove a punch up and into his gut. Ashan doubled over.

Nikandr allowed him to fall to the ground. "My men died for you! Udra, a woman who has caused you no harm, is dead because of you!"

"We cannot make our way to the horizon without passing through the field of heather."

It was a common saying among the Landless—a message of focusing on the present, not the future; on the here, not the far—but it grated, and Nikandr nearly kicked him as he lay there, defenseless. "We are not heather!"

"I know this, son of Iaros," Ashan said as he came to his feet. "I only mean to say that I feel your pain, and I wish that I might have been able to prevent it."

"It was because of you that our ship crashed!"

"*Neh.*" He wiped the back of his hand across his lips, which were bleeding. He spit a wash of red to clear his mouth. And again. "It is the island you must look to, and the arqesh who still battle for its supremacy."

"My Lord Prince?" It was Pietr's voice.

Ashan looked over Nikandr's shoulder, and his eyes went wide. When Nikandr turned, he found Nasim standing at the very edge of the cliff. His arms were spread wide as the wind from far below rushed up the cliff, playing with his hair and snapping the fabric of his sleeves.

"Nasim, come," Ashan said softly. "It is not yet time."

"How can you be sure?" he asked without turning around.

"Because we haven't reached the tower."

Nasim turned and faced Ashan with a curious look on his face. "True." He walked forward as if he were taking a stroll and then took Nikandr's hand. "Then we had better find it."

As Nikandr allowed himself to be pulled along, his anger drained away. It was replaced by deep shame at attacking a man who would probably never raise a hand to defend himself. Making it worse was the realization that Ashan was also someone who had done things to protect him and his men on the journey here, a journey Nikandr himself had elected to embark on.

Ashan fell into step. Pietr followed up the rear. Part of Nikandr still wanted to be angry with Ashan, but too much of their predicament felt like *Nikandr's* fault, not Ashan's.

"I saw a tower," Nikandr said, "in my dreams."

Ashan nodded. "Nasim has spoken of it over the months I've known him. In fits and starts, he's laid out the story of his life here on Ghayavand. The tower is where he and Sariya lived, until their defenses were finally breached by Muqallad."

"I thought all three of them were warring for control of Ghayavand."

"They were, but Sariya and Nasim—or Khamal, as he was known then—were driven by need, a common cause against the other, Muqallad, who was far stronger than they."

"Even together they could not overpower him?"

"He was more ruthless than they. They would not, as he would, ravage the land nor their followers who still lived a half-life existence, caught as they were between Erahm and Adhiya."

"If this is so, then how could Sariya still live? How could there still be a struggle for this island?"

Ashan turned his gaze on Nasim, who walked ahead of them. "That is something we may find out before too long. I hoped that by bringing Nasim here he will understand the bond that lies between you, that he will be able, once and for all, to find his way fully into this world."

"Erahm."

Ashan nodded. "It is through you, his touchstone, that he has been able to make such progress. Believe me when I say he would not have been able to speak so lucidly were it not for the day you met him on the eyrie."

"That tells me little of why you came *here*."

"Then see for yourself." Ashan pointed up to the sky. They had reached the ridge. The wind was stronger here. It played along the prairie in the narrow plateau on which they found themselves. Nasim was sitting among the grass, half-hidden, staring up at the sky. Nikandr looked to where Ashan had pointed and saw a swirl of cloudstuff pull away from the larger body above it. Something in his chest began to ache as the havahezhan darted to and fro like a hummingbird, but then—as if it had just spied the humans below—it shot downward. Its form, swirling tightly as it plummeted, could only be seen because it still held the mist from the clouds.

The blood drained from Nikandr's face and he took a step forward, but he stopped when Ashan gripped his arm.

"He will not be harmed."

The havahezhan continued to plummet.

The feeling within him, bordering on pain, began to feel more and more familiar. "Tell me," he said, the thoughts still forming in his mind, "the hezhan that attacked me on Uyadensk, the one summoned by the Maharraht, could it be here, now, right before us?"

Ashan stared up at the havahezhan as it swirled and twisted, breaking away from its course toward Nasim. "Impossible."

"I can feel it"—he pressed the tips of his fingers to his soulstone—"here."

Ashan was silent as he studied the hezhan. "Do you feel as you did on the mountainside?"

He meant when Nikandr had summoned the wind to save them from the snow. "I do."

The havahezhan dropped again. A swirl of dirt was drawn upward around Nasim. Nasim dashed forward, trying to touch the wall of air, but it moved fluidly, staying just ahead. And then Nikandr realized that he had been feeling something ever since he'd seen the spirit—even *before* he'd seen it. His soulstone... He looked down and found that there was the barest iridescent quality held deep within it. His chest still hurt, and it felt nothing like what it did when he was searching for his mother, or when he touched stones with someone for the first time. Those felt like a simple warmth that suffused his chest like the remembrance of a long, warm bath while lying in bed. This felt like an absence, a loneliness, as if something he had held precious within his heart had suddenly been taken away.

"How can it be, Ashan?"

"Perhaps it became attuned to you. Perhaps your proximity to Ghayavand has drawn its attention. Who can know such things?"

Nikandr watched as the havahezhan rose into the sky and vanished. In only moments, the feeling in his chest faded and was gone.

"How could it have found me?"

"Perhaps from the qualities of this place, its similarity to Uyadensk."

Nikandr turned to regard Ashan who was staring at him calmly, with that small smile on his lips he always seemed to possess.

Ashan guessed his next question. "The rift over Uyadensk is not so different than here on Ghayavand. What began here centuries ago is now spreading."

Nikandr shook his head, confused. "The blight?"

"Can there be any doubt? I don't know how the rift that formed here remained in check for so many years. I don't know what caused it to change. But I know that it has. A chain of events has begun, and we must learn the way to reverse it, before it is too late."

Despite the warmth of this place, Nikandr shivered. "And if we do not?"

"Then I fear the entire world will become like this island. Inhospitable. Wild. The only reason Ghayavand hasn't devolved into utter madness is because of the will of Muqallad, and to a certain degree Sariya."

"What will happen when one of them dies?"

Ashan was silent as they reached the edge of the plateau they walked upon. Nikandr stopped and looked. And his mouth fell open.

The land descended quickly and reached out into the dark sea with two long and verdant arms. Nestled in the deep valley where the two arms met was a city—a city every bit as large as Volgorod. Rounded towers vaulted into the sky, and dozens—hundreds—of smaller buildings hugged the form of the mountain, creating a crescent of pale brown stone against the bright green landscape.

The size of the city was a shock, but it was the state of it that was more alarming. The towers, the buildings, even from this distance, looked like broken and empty husks, as if each had been systematically dismantled from within. It was not unlike a wasp nest would look after carrion beetles had finished devouring the interior, wasps and all.

"What happened?"

"Hubris, son of Iaros. Hubris."

CHAPTER 46

When Rehada and Atiana reached the Valley of Iramanshah, the crack of a cannon cast itself over the valley walls, echoing faintly after that first startling report. In the sky above, two ships were gliding toward an Aramahn skiff. The skiff surely could have outmaneuvered the ships, could have outraced them as well, but they would not risk the guns of the Landed ships—neither the ones on the ships chasing them nor the ones that would harry Iramanshah were they to escape.

The soldiers aboard the schooner lashed the skiff to the larger ship as they turned northward to return to the long line of ships further out to sea.

"Why do they take them?" Rehada asked Atiana, who rode nearby on a dun pony.

"As a warning to Khalakovo: no one will be allowed to land, nor to leave."

"As if a handful of Aramahn could change the balance."

"They could be spies or messengers, bringing word to Khalakovo's allies."

"Your mother would bring word to them, would she not?"

"It might be too dangerous. The other Matri could interfere with or listen to their communication. Or worse, they might attack. I have a feeling all of the Matri are taking great care while treading the dark."

"Even the Duchess Khalakovo? She is the strongest, is she not?"

"She is, but that doesn't mean she could fend off a concerted attack from the others. She runs herself ragged in peacetime." Atiana glanced up at the ships, which were small against the background of the high gray clouds. "It will be worse now."

They continued to the village in silence, and they were met by two unarmed men at the gates. As she had been instructed, Rehada asked to speak with Muwas, at which point one went to fetch him. They were led to the courtyard outside the tall doors. They waited for some time, but at last

Muwas stepped through the doors and guided Rehada away from Atiana to speak quietly by the fountain. Atiana watched them warily, with no little amount of anxiety in her eyes.

"What has happened?" Rehada asked as she motioned to the water within the fountain, which—normally a sign of life and vibrancy—lay still.

Muwas's expression was dour. "There have been deaths. One mahtar and two children were taken by the wasting. All three died early this morning."

Rehada shook her head. "You are sure?"

"There is no room for doubt."

This was unexpected. Muwas's mood was perfectly understandable now, for Rehada was feeling the same thing. She had viewed the rift and the wasting as the vengeful will of Adhiya coming to right the wrongs perpetrated against the Aramahn for these many years, but if they were taking even the chosen ones and innocent children, then what were they to think? This could no longer be viewed as a sword, ready to be taken up by the Maharraht.

Muwas stared at Atiana coldly. "As for the princess, *I* will take her to the lake."

"I was to take her."

"Soroush no longer considers that wise, and I agree. You have not been welcome inside these walls for some time, Rehada, something you should have corrected long before now."

"Speak not of what you do not know."

Muwas's expression hardened. "We all lose in this. We have known since the day we joined. Why should your anger over your daughter's death be different?"

A fury welled up inside Rehada so quickly that she nearly struck him, if only to wipe that self-righteous look off his face, but if she did she would lose her chance to accompany Atiana inside. She needed to see this through, if only because she had spared Atiana that day on the beach. She would know more. She would know all there is to know before giving Atiana up so that Soroush could have his fourth stone.

"I have come prepared," she said to him finally.

"Fahroz will see through you."

"She will not."

Muwas shook his head. "This is not what Soroush—"

"Soroush is not here. I am. And the princess will come with me."

Muwas was a stubborn man, but he knew their position here was a tenuous one. He could not raise objections—not if they wanted any hope of succeeding.

"Then you will answer to Soroush."

Rehada bowed her head and turned away. She found Fahroz walking across the courtyard toward her. An ornate, golden circlet wrapped her brow and at its center were three azurite gems. She wore an outer robe of white, an inner of yellow. Her dire expression warred with her bright clothes. "Excuse me, Muwas, I would speak with Rehada alone."

Muwas nodded and left, retreating through the tall doors to the interior of the village. Fahroz turned to Rehada, her arms crossed over her breast. "I have just come from speaking with Hilal, and there are questions you must answer, daughter of Shineshka." Before Rehada could speak, Fahroz continued. "Was Soroush one of the men you saw in Izhny?"

"*Yeh*," Rehada said without hesitation. There was no choice. Fahroz knew the answer already.

"Why did you not tell us this?"

"One Maharraht or another. It matters little to me."

"Come, Rehada. This is no *Maharraht*. You had a child with this man."

"And that child is dead."

The wrinkled skin along Fahroz's cheeks worked as she ground her jaw. "Play me not for a fool. This is more serious than you can imagine. Would you like to know Hilal's advice?" Again she continued without allowing Rehada to speak. "It was to burn you with no chance to defend yourself. Maharraht cannot be trusted with the truth, he said."

Rehada stared, refusing to answer the unspoken question.

"Are you Maharraht?"

"*Neh*," Rehada said.

Fahroz shook her head. "I would like to believe you, Rehada."

Rehada steadied herself, but she displayed what she felt was the proper amount of alarm. "I would never join them, Fahroz. You must believe me. My daughter's death was tragic. I am scarred, but I would not turn to violence to avenge something that can never be changed." Visions of the suurahezhan came to Rehada, shaming her even as she stared into Fahroz's eyes.

Fahroz weighed Rehada's words carefully as her jaw worked. "I defended you to Hilal. I told him that you would not do such a thing. Am I a fool, Rehada?"

"You are not."

"Then you will do me the favor of providing a small token of your earnestness."

Relief swept over Rehada. "Anything."

"You will confess your daughter's death, and you will do it today. Now."

She had known that this was the price to pay, but a well of fear still opened up inside Rehada. "I can't do that."

"Do this, Rehada. Do it for Ahya."

"Do not speak her name." She said the words because they must be spoken. She was completing a ruse, but she found the same reluctance seething inside her. She did not wish for her child's name to be spoken. Ahya was hers, no one else's.

"There is no harm in a name."

You lie, Rehada said to herself. If that were true, she wouldn't be feeling the burning weight at the center of her chest. She had come fully prepared to take this step, but now she wanted to leave, to flee, to return to her home and forget all about this.

But she could not. She could not afford to alienate herself from Iramanshah.

Neh. These were rationalizations. The truth was that the link to Adhiya through her stone was the only time she felt any sort of comfort, any sort of release from the pain of losing her child and her never-ending anger against the Landed. She could not bear to have it ripped from her and to go on without it as Soroush did. It would be too painful.

And so she held Fahroz's gaze and nodded.

"Say it, child."

"I will confess my daughter's death."

There was a tentative satisfaction in Fahroz's heavy, wrinkled eyes, but it was not a mocking glance. Then her gaze drifted to Atiana. "The fates can be cruel at times, daughter of Shineshka, but I think in this they are right."

Rehada turned, confused, and looked at Atiana, who was studying the massive celestia atop the nearby hill. Atiana turned then, perhaps sensing that she was being watched, and the moment their eyes met, Rehada understood exactly what Fahroz meant for her to do.

"*Neh*, Fahroz," Rehada said quietly but firmly. "Anything but that. I will confess to you, to Hilal, to the entire village. Anything. But do not make me confess to her."

Fahroz had already started shaking her head. "Those are my terms."

The pain in her hands made Rehada realize just how tightly she had been gripping them. She stared at her palms, each of which now contained four crescent-shaped marks of blood. Rather than storm away, rather than hide, Rehada laughed. Fahroz was right. The Fates had finally caught up to her, as she knew it eventually would.

She breathed deeply and released it slowly. Finally she nodded, and Fahroz returned the gesture. And then the two of them hugged.

CHAPTER 47

Rehada held her arms at her side, conscious of her posture and bearing even though Atiana—standing nearly face-to-face with her—and Fahroz—watching from a comfortable distance—were the only ones witness to it. She grew conscious of the shaking in her hands and balled them into fists to cover it, but that might be interpreted by Fahroz as disobedience or lack of acceptance and so she relaxed them and simply hoped that Atiana wouldn't notice.

She did, though. Atiana glanced down, and her face softened as if she were trying to comfort a cowardly child afraid of storm clouds and thunder. It made Rehada want to gouge her eyes from her face.

Fahroz had chosen for the confession one of the largest rooms in Iramanshah, a hall normally used for the immense meals during the solstice festivals, but this day it was entirely empty, the trestles and chairs stored away, leaving the three of them small and insignificant at its center. It was not something that would normally give Rehada pause, but this day it made her feel small, smaller than she had felt in a long, long time.

"Are you prepared to continue?" Fahroz asked in Anuskayan, her voice echoing in the immensity of the room.

"I am." Those two simple words felt foul on her tongue. She hated that she was forced to speak in their language.

"Then tell the Lady Vostroma what you are confessing."

"A hatred for the family Bolgravya."

Her voice echoed away slowly as Atiana stared and Fahroz paced a circle around them.

Fahroz stopped for a moment while she was within Rehada's periphery. "Come, Rehada…"

"A hatred for the Grand Duchy."

Fahroz resumed her pacing. "For whom?"

Rehada closed her eyes and shook her head, but she opened them again immediately. "A hatred for the Landed."

"And why do you hold hatred?"

"Because of the death of my daughter."

"Deaths happen every day, daughter of Shineshka. Why would this one, even though it was your daughter's, cause anger?"

"Because she was murdered unjustly by the streltsi of Nazakhov."

"Murdered..."

"*Da*, murdered!"

"Tell Lady Vostroma what happened."

Atiana had been prepared. She had been told, as would anyone that was to play the part of the witness, to stand still, to accept what was being told as the truth, and to speak only when spoken to. But her oh-so-sympathetic face spoke volumes, and it felt as if she were scoffing at a covenant that had been in place for eons—yet another affront the Landed would someday be held accountable for.

Rehada spoke of that day in cold terms, giving Atiana the facts, how she'd left Ahya with friends, how she'd returned to find her burning body among the wreckage of the home she'd left only hours before, but as she spoke it was not those images that played through her mind but the sights and sounds of the mountain where she had taken breath. The day had been cool, pleasant. The sky had held few clouds, but those that were present scudded across the sky, sending shadows to play over the landscape like trumpeting heralds. The wind had been brisk. It had brought a scent of Lion's Foot—the pale, late-blooming flowers that grew along the highest ranges of the southern islands. She had felt, during those hours of meditation, as though she had come to know Nazakhov deeply, as though, like the bond between mother and daughter, she was a part of it and it was a part of her. It had been exhilarating, for this had never happened to her before. It had been something that every Aramahn hoped to find but few managed in their lifetimes.

But here Rehada had discovered the weight of an island upon her shoulders. She wondered when she came down from that mountain whether any such thing could really happen. It seemed that it had all been a figment, a self-fulfilling delusion, a trick of the mind perpetrated consciously by the breath-stealing air of the tallest mountain in Bolgravya. It must be so, for what else could explain her apparent oneness with her environment and her complete inability to sense that something had gone terribly, terribly wrong with her child, her blood, her one and truest love?

As she had come to rest before that house—the one that had been burned to the ground—she had stared at the burned skeleton that had been her daughter. Her precious child had been ripped from her world by the acts of the Maharraht who had been hiding there, the prevailing attitude of the Landed for the ruthless acts committed by them, but mostly—she had no doubt in her mind—by the overriding greed of the Landed aristocracy. It was a greed that had pushed them to claw for every scrap of land in the sea, and it had done so for so long that they could no longer see that their acts would one day instill and reinforce the resistance that they hoped so fervently to root out.

Perhaps Rehada's voice contained more venom than she had realized. She had expected Atiana to soften even further, to paste a look upon her face that *would* force Rehada to claw at her, if only to remove the expression from that white skin for a moment or two. But instead Atiana was nearly emotionless, and then, in increments, her face hardened, as if she condoned the actions of the streltsi that day, as if she would have ordered the very same thing had she held the gavel of fate in her hand. Strangely, this did not upset Rehada in the least. It felt as though things had returned to balance—Atiana the oppressor, she the oppressed—and it allowed Rehada to complete her story to Fahroz's satisfaction.

"What did you do after you discovered your daughter dead?" Atiana asked. Fahroz had prepared Atiana to ask certain questions at certain times, but still, Rehada was startled by her words.

"I left that very night and traveled Erahm another full circuit before landing on Uyadensk."

"You didn't see your daughter buried?" Atiana asked.

Rehada smiled the way she would for a child. "She had gone. Her funeral pyre had already burned whether I liked it or not."

Atiana's face pursed. "I do not question your judgment—I know the ways of the Aramahn are not my own—I only wondered why you would not grieve over your child."

"I grieve as I grieve!"

Fahroz stopped near Rehada's side, her arms across her chest. "A question was posed."

Rehada shook her head. "I cannot do this."

"You cannot even speak of your child?"

"Not to her. *Nyet.*"

Fahroz stared at her for a long time, hoping Rehada would change her mind. But she would not. "You leave me no choice."

Fahroz strode toward the doors to Rehada's left. As her soft footsteps faded, a vision of Ahya leaping over the edge of a skiff came to Rehada. It had happened when they'd reached Nazakhov. Both of them had been in good spirits. Her hair trailed behind her as she ran ahead to the edge of the nearby cliff and looked down upon the ocean and the city of Bastrozna.

Rehada had come to her side and held her tight to her hip as the wind tugged at their hair and their ankle-length robes.

"Will Father meet us here?" Ahya had asked.

Rehada had smiled. "*Neh*, child. Not here."

"Where?"

"The next island. Or the one beyond that. I do not know."

"Will you teach me to touch Adhiya?"

"You are too young, yet."

Ahya had looked up at her with those bright green eyes. Her face was sad, but resigned. "You are always holding me back."

Rehada had laughed at the notion—a child of six complaining that she could not learn as an adult. Rehada had done the same to her own mother, but the difference here was how close to right Ahya was. She was very strong. Rehada had known it for several years, ever since she had noticed the spirits with which Rehada had been communing. She had *felt* them as a girl of twelve would have trouble doing, and she had been only five.

When she had come down from the mountain that day, she had decided that she would begin Ahya's training. Perhaps not that day; perhaps not in a month; but soon.

How had she forgotten such a thing? She had remembered Ahya's burgeoning abilities—that had always been a thing of pride—but she had completely forgotten, until the point where Fahroz began walking away, that she had been ready to walk with her daughter toward a higher consciousness.

The answer came almost as quickly as had the question: the pain in thinking of how her daughter's promise had been snuffed from the world had eclipsed many things. It had been too painful to consider, and so she had buried it, hoping it would never resurface again.

Suddenly she realized that she was on the ground, and that Atiana and Fahroz were kneeling next to her.

There was a keening in the room—a long wail of pain, and it took her long moments of rocking slowly back and forth to realize that it came from her. No one else. *Her*. Cries of regret for a child so pure.

"I did not grieve because it was something I could not face," she said through her sobs.

Fahroz combed her hair away from her face. "That's right, child." She helped Rehada to her feet, and when Rehada had composed herself to some small degree, she motioned for Atiana to take her place once more.

"Why did you come to Uyadensk?" Atiana asked.

"I came because I wished to know a place—another place—as well as I had known Nazakhov."

"But why Uyadensk?"

Rehada shrugged. "It is as good a place as any to know."

"By those standards, Nazakhov would be even better since you knew it so well already."

"I will never face Nazakhov again."

"You give it more meaning than it has," Fahroz interrupted. "It is only an island."

"It is a storehouse of misery."

Fahroz shook her head. "That is why you have been here for so long, is it not? You hope that Uyadensk will replace Nazakhov, that it will heal those wounds that never properly closed and have been festering ever since."

Rehada shivered. Fahroz had come extremely close to the mark, and it was less than comforting. "I wish to know a place and to move on with my life. Moving from island to island no longer held any allure."

"What is the name of your daughter's father?" Atiana asked.

"Soroush Wahad al Gatha."

"He is Maharraht, is he not?"

Rehada nodded. "He is."

"What do you feel toward Anuskaya?"

"Anger, and resentment."

Her words echoed off into the immensity of the room. When all was silence, Fahroz stopped her pacing next to Atiana and faced Rehada. "Come, daughter of Shineshka."

"I know I can never have her back, but I want in my heart for the Duchy to provide that for me. In my heart of hearts I hope to dismantle the islands, one by one. I wish to watch every single Landed man, woman, and child drown in the seas, swallowed whole, for what they have done to my child."

"Ahya will be reborn," Fahroz said.

"But what will she be then? Half of what she was? Less? She could have been great."

"She will be. As will we all one day."

Rehada wanted to stalk forward and beat the knowing look from her face. "Forgive me, daughter of Lilliah, but it is difficult at times to look beyond this life. Even more so to the one beyond that."

"Are you Maharraht?" Atiana blurted into the ensuing silence.

Her words echoed in the chamber—*aharraht, harraht, rraht.*

Everything she had said up to this point had been the truth. All of it. And she had debated with herself nearly every moment since agreeing to come here and confess: would she reveal this secret? Much rode upon this one answer, and in truth it pained her to think of lying at a time when she was speaking of her daughter so intimately. It felt too much like betrayal, a thing she could live with in almost anyone. Anyone but Ahya.

But the way Atiana had spoken those words. So sharp. So demanding. She wondered whether Fahroz had asked her to speak it thus. She doubted it now. Such traits were ingrained in the aristocracy of the islands from their birth onwards. Atiana could no more escape it than Rehada could her past. And so, though it was a betrayal, she lied.

"*Nyet.*"

"Are you Maharraht?" Fahroz repeated, perhaps displeased with the pause.

"*Nyet,*" Rehada repeated.

A time passed where Rehada refused to move her gaze from Atiana. She did not attempt to force a certain expression, as so many people do when they lie; she simply stared and allowed some small amount of the contempt she held for this woman to show through.

Fahroz seemed appeased, for she asked Atiana to step closer. When they were close enough to touch, to hug, she said, "Now forgive her."

This was the thing she had feared ever since her daughter's death. She had told herself that whatever happened, she would not forget what they had done. She would not allow the Landed to be free of their responsibility in this, and in forgiving Atiana, she was doing just that. But now that she had come this far she had no choice.

"I forgive you," Rehada said softly.

"Again."

"I forgive you."

Fahroz stood behind Atiana and regarded Rehada. "Do you feel her words, daughter of Radia?"

"I do not," Atiana replied.

"I *forgive* you," Rehada said, pouring as much feeling into her voice as she could.

"If you do not wish to forgive, Rehada, then perhaps we should stop this now."

"*I forgive you.*"

"Hold her," Fahroz replied.

Rehada stepped forward and put her arms around Atiana. She tried to hug her warmly, but it was impossible. She would rather strangle her.

"Now say it again."

Rehada did. Over and over, and she found herself tightening her hold of the Vostroman princess. As she did, as she called out those words, a memory came to her that she had not thought of for years—possibly since it had happened. Ahya, not quite six years old, was walking over a snow-swept field running her hands over the tips of the winterdead grass. Her head hung low, and her shoulders wracked rhythmically. Rehada had known all too well why she was crying. She had told Ahya a secret about her father, Soroush, who would in two months' time be taking to the winds once more. Rehada had said that he was a man that found it difficult to love and that her mother would be her guardian until her fifteenth birthday, when she would be free to take the winds as she chose.

"He doesn't love me?"

Rehada had smiled. "Of course he does, but perhaps not as much as he does his quest for understanding."

Ahya had been quiet for days after that comment, and Rehada had felt terrible about it, but she refused to leave her child unprepared for her father's departure as *she* had been when she was a child.

Ahya had confessed what she had said to Soroush, and Soroush had been deeply hurt. It became clear that he loved Ahya more than Rehada would have guessed, and her thoughts about his devotion to his daughter cut him deeply. He was a hard man, and he felt it was the best for her. It was his way of loving her, so that she would be prepared for the world to come, so that she would be ready to embrace the journey before her and move closer to vashaqiram.

Rehada had caught up to Ahya in the field and walked beside her as the bitterly cold breeze played among the stalks of grass.

Then suddenly Ahya had turned, tears streaming down her cheeks, and embraced her. "I'm sorry, Memma. I'm sorry."

As they had hugged, Rehada began to understand. Ahya thought she had driven a wedge between them by telling a secret. But in truth, there was nothing to be ashamed of. It was something she should have told Soroush herself. Her daughter had been honest where she should have been, and she was deeply embarrassed over it.

"Child, stop your tears. There is nothing to be sorry for. Nothing."

Ahya had buried her head into her shoulder and said, "Please. Please forgive me."

Rehada had leaned her head in close to Ahya's ear and whispered. "I forgive you."

Rehada came out of her dream whispering those words to Atiana. She felt her own tears creeping down her cheeks and leaking, salty and hot, into the corners of her mouth.

"I forgive you," she said one last time, to Ahya, not to Atiana.

And then she felt Fahroz's hand on her shoulder. "Enough, Rehada. It is enough."

She pulled away and found the older woman crying nearly as hard as was she. There were no tears in Atiana's eyes, but there was a certain shock there, and a faint look of apology. Rehada was not, surprisingly, angry at this. She had shed too much of that emotion already this day and so she simply nodded to her.

"Come," Fahroz said while walking toward the doors, "let us go to the lake."

CHAPTER 48

Atiana had been sure, in that small instant after Rehada had confessed that her daughter had been killed on Nazakhov, that she had somehow orchestrated the attack of the suurahezhan on Radiskoye's eyrie. But as the questioning continued, she became less convinced, and when the Aramahn beauty had begun crying upon her shoulder, she was not at all sure that Rehada could be turned to such violence… It seemed as though she had locked her emotions away for so long that it would be inconceivable for her to perform murder and still hold such feelings inside. Surely, if that had been so, they would have been released like vapors from a bottle.

Still, the entire experience had been jarring. She hadn't known that Rehada had been a mother, and certainly hadn't known what sort of pain she had gone through. It was strange, once again, to be faced with a different reality than the one she had pictured for Nikandr's lover.

One thing bothered her about this, though. Clearly Rehada had harbored resentment for the Landed since her daughter's regrettable death. Why, then, would she remain here in Uyadensk and flirt with the aristocracy? Why wouldn't she simply take to the winds or stay with her own kind? Perhaps what she said was true: that she wished to know a place as she had Nazakhov. But that didn't explain her attraction to Nikandr. It may be that she wanted to use him, to place herself in a position of power that she could achieve in no other way.

The thoughts fled as they moved deeper into the village toward the lake. It had not been long since Atiana had taken the dark, but as always, a churning in her gut began to rise as the ritual approached.

The lake, once they reached it, felt different. The first time, it had been a unique experience. She had known about the lakes in the villages, but she had had no idea what sort of power they held. She wondered if the Matri knew that they could be used in the same way as the drowning chambers. Surely they must, but who would use them? Only a handful of Aramahn in all the world could do such a thing; Fahroz was perhaps their most adept and still she was like a child to Atiana, who in turn was like a child to the longstanding Matri.

Despite these assurances, the lake seemed like a weakness, something that should be dealt with. In time, if she had any say over it, she would.

Fahroz and Rehada led the way to the shoreline. They waited as Atiana disrobed, at which point they worked together to rub the rendered goat's fat over her body.

She lay back in the freezing water and with the other two women's arms holding her, floated free. She fought against the urge to shiver, to stiffen, and found that this time it was much easier than any of the others had been. She wondered if, in time, she would begin to yearn for the aether as Saphia did.

She relaxed and fell deeper into the embrace of the water as the constricting tube through which she breathed became less and less of a hindrance. And soon… Soon…

Her mind expands to fill the lake and the cavern that holds it. It is an easy thing to do, and for the first time there is pleasure—a release that occurs at the moment of crossing—and she thinks immediately to Saphia and her constant desire to wander the aether. Is this the first sign that the same will happen to her?

The transition occurs faster than in times past, but it is no less easy. The winds seems more turbulent, and she wonders if that is due to her lack of mastery or the state of the island.

She moves beyond the lake, hoping to find a frame of reference from which she can view the rift. She failed to find it the last time, but she is not so inexperienced as she was then. She thinks about her past failures, but she is convinced that things will be different now.

As she searches, she feels the presence of another. It is not like the feeling of communing with one of the Matri. Instead, it is the feeling of a soulstone, one she has touched in recent weeks, and she realizes with a start that it is Nikandr's. As the winds of the aether rage around her, beckoning her to give of herself more fully, she allows herself to be drawn toward the stone. It is dangerous, what she does. She is not so experienced yet that she can take this shift lightly. She knows that if she does not maintain awareness of herself in Iramanshah, she might be lost forever, but she is well grounded in the lake, and Nikandr's light is bright. It will make, she hopes, the return journey easier; her body in the lake and his stone will act like spires for a windship, anchoring the ley lines so that she might traverse them home.

She finds herself hovering above an island, not unlike any of the dozens of others sprinkled around the Great Sea, but she soon realizes that this is vastly different. Worlds different.

She can feel with the lightest touch the hezhan that inhabit the island. They are spread thinly in most places except for one location—a city nestled between two arms of a mountain that travel down to the sea. The city is large, but it is also bereft of life. Gone from its houses are roofs and walls. Stone fences lay shattered. The taller buildings closer to the center are broken and torn; some are mere husks.

The hezhan move about the city, perhaps searching—for what she does not know. As she approaches, she realizes she was wrong. These are not hezhan. They are of Adhiya, but they are also of Erahm. Their colors—blue mixed with tendrils of red—remind her of the babe she saw, the one that had been ... assumed by the vanahezhan. She has not thought of it before, but the act of assuming a bird like the rooks is eerily similar to what she sees here, only it is a hezhan assuming a human instead of a human assuming an animal, and it forces her to rethink the very nature of the hezhan.

One of the creatures moves faster, and she is drawn toward it because nearby there are four men, and one is Nikandr. They hide in a building as the creature stalks toward the open doorway. It sniffs the air and appears ready to step inside. She knows that if this happens it could mean the life of all four of them, but she does not know how to prevent it. She moves around one side and tries to call its attention toward her. If it notices her efforts, it does not show it.

A moment later it opens its darkened mouth and calls soundlessly to the sky, and when it does, there is a subtle shift in the aether. She feels, in that one small moment, a lattice of connections that span the entire city. It starts near the water—at a tall tower that is strangely intact—and spreads outward like the shattering impact of a stone upon a pane of leaded glass.

She was ready to search for the rift on Khalakovo, but here is something so much larger, so much more dangerous. She wonders, staring at it, whether this could happen to Khalakovo. Could something spread so far? Or would it take intervention of some sort?

As she studies the faint but powerful lines of the web covering the city, she realizes that there are telltale signs she might look for on Khalakovo. The aether lies between worlds; it is neither of Erahm nor Adhiya, and yet of both, for it stands between them, separating them, binding them. When she rides the aether, she remains at its center—the safest place. But these tendrils that spread from one world to the other are in fact easier to discern near the edges. If she can expand her awareness, as dangerous as that is for a novice, she might be able to find it more easily.

She returns her attention to Nikandr and the men, she sees that the creature has left. It pains her to leave, but she knows that she must.

Ancients keep you, my love, she whispers, and allows herself to be drawn back toward Iramanshah.

As she nears the island the presence of others become known to her. It is the other Matri, but like a blind woman grasping ineffectually for an intruder she is unable to find them.

Mother, she wills. *Saphia*.

They do not answer, but the sense that she is being watched grows. She wonders whether having gone to Ghayavand has anything to do with it. It feels no different than the times she had been in Radiskoye or Galostina, but that doesn't mean that there is not some primal shift in perspective that occurs when drifting through the aether from within the confines of Iramanshah.

She tries to relax her mind further while keeping tight rein on the aether. Again the winds buffet her, and she uses this to attempt to locate the source of the disturbance. She tries for long moments, refusing to think about the time she has already spent. She must act quickly, but not recklessly, and she cannot allow her thoughts of the material world to affect her or she will be thrown from the aether in moments.

As she had in Ghayavand, she allows her vision to expand as she navigates the currents. At the edge of her vision, she sees it, and though it is impossible to look upon it directly she can perceive a white line as thin and bright as a distant lightning strike running the length of the island. By and large it runs beneath the ground, trailing, perhaps, the hidden inner workings of stone. There are several places, however, where it rises to the surface, and even one where it swirls above ground like a dust demon.

She approaches, and as she does, faint thoughts come to her. She is sure that it is the Matri communing with one another, but she is again unable to discern their thoughts to any coherent degree, so she focuses on the swirling energy before her.

It is here that the suurahezhan crossed over. She knows because of Nikandr's description of the place and also because of the tinge of red that remains on the ground beneath the swirling storm of energy. This is the rift that spans the aether and binds Adhiya to Erahm. It is why the spirits have been crossing, and surely the presence of such a thing would cause other effects—the imbalance of the two worlds touching might cause poor crops, might it not, as well as the erratic behavior on fishing grounds?

She places herself in the locus of the crossing, hoping to sense more than she can while spread so thinly. It is a difficult thing, for the aether is wide and lends itself naturally to a widening of one's self, to a thinning of the senses, and as she focuses, she feels the pull of the aether upon her. She becomes disoriented. She can feel not just this island—Duzol and Grakhosk and Yfa are the strongest—but others as well: Kravozhny and Yrlanda and even little Ishal far to the east. Beyond these she can feel the pull of the other archipelagos. Mirkotsk and Rhavanki and her motherland, Vostroma.

She takes hold of the aether before she is pulled too far, before her mind snaps over the immensity of it all. Experiencing so much is beyond her. It is beyond even the Matri, she is sure.

She realizes, as she moves away from the location and considers it from a safe distance, that it was the rift that had pulled her so. She had known that it had spread among the islands, but she had no idea how interconnected it was. The sense that she has found something truly important is breathtaking, but it is also unnerving. She has found it, yet it is completely foreign. It is an act of nature. How can she hope to combat this? How can any of them?

As she considers moving closer to the swirl of light, she hears the voices once more. She is surprised, however, to feel the mind of her mother.

Daughter, is that you?

Her first instinct is to hide, but she does not know how to do such a thing, and after thinking about it for a moment it seems cowardly.

It is I, she says.

The feeling of her mother intensifies, and as it does, so do four other presences. She has not spoken with any of them in some time, but she knows them to be the other Matri, the ones currently aligned against Khalakovo: Dhalingrad, Khazabyirsk, Nodhvyansk, and Bolgravya. She wonders why their presences feel so near when Saphia and the other Matri might be able to sense them. But then she feels a disturbance in the aether, an echo of life crossing over. It feels distant, but only because her mind is so focused on the rift. As she expands to encompass more of the island, she feels them. Deaths. Many of them. It is centered on Volgorod's eyrie, but there is more coming from Radiskoye.

It can mean only one thing: her father has lost his patience and the blockade has progressed to all-out war.

Child, where are you? A moment later, she feels her mother's surprise—she knows that Atiana lies within the lake in Iramanshah. *What are you doing there?*

She debates whether to reveal her true purpose, but in the end she realizes it would do more harm than good. Whether she likes it or not, Mother is too loyal to Father, and the chance that she would betray her confidence is too great.

She portrays a sense of indignance that she hopes is enough to fool her mother. *I have been trying to find a way to reach you since I left Radiskoye.*

She feels a probing as her mother attempts to read the truth in her thoughts, but Atiana is not so young as she once was. She is able to harden the walls around her, enough to make her mother back away.

Remain where you are, was her mother's terse reply.

Her presence recedes. The others remain, little more than watchdogs ready to bark.

She no longer cares. She attempts to flee, to return to her form, but the Matri stand in her way. They hold her in place, preventing her from moving.

Release me, she shouts, but they do not listen.

The time is long past, Bolgravya says, *for you to be chained.*

This can mean only one thing: someone will be sent to Iramanshah to fetch her. She tries to widen her awareness, but the Matri push back. They tighten their grip. They press.

Nyet, Atiana realizes. It is not the Matri. It is something in Iramanshah...

Her shell. Her body, floating in the lake...

Something is wrong.

She attempts to return, but there is a presence that surrounds her. It is cold, fluid. As she tries to pin it down, to *understand* it, it slips free, always pressing, always bearing down.

She cannot breathe.

The air releases from her lungs, and she finds herself unable to draw even the smallest of breaths through the simple wooden tube that touches her lips.

She can feel her body though she still rides the currents, and she marvels at the feeling of being in both worlds at once. It is in this moment that she realizes that the veil to Adhiya has been pulled aside.

It is a glimpse of pure beauty.

Pure pain.

Pure madness.

She knows that a hezhan has found her. It preys upon her as the vanahezhan preyed upon the babe.

She rails against it. Thrashing in her terror.

And she wakes.

Seeing, towering above her, the liquid form of a jalahezhan.

CHAPTER 49

Atiana fell back into the water.

Her skin was numb, her muscles slow to respond, but her fear helped her to put distance between her and the beast.

As she did, she could still feel the presences around her—not only the hezhan, but Rehada in the water behind her, Fahroz on the stony beach, and a man, further in the recesses of the lake.

She remembered him, the one Rehada had been speaking to before they'd entered the village. Muwas. He was controlling the spirit. She could feel, even now, the connection that snaked between them, a cord of aether that allowed him to force his will upon it.

She could feel as well a concentration of aether below her—something that lay on the lake bed—though what it was she couldn't guess.

Then Rehada was at her side, pulling her up by her arm. "In the lake!" Rehada shouted.

A blast of water struck Atiana in the chest, sending her beneath the surface. Something slick grabbed her ankle and pulled her, dragged her down against the rough surface of the lake bed. Her legs and back were scraped by sharp stone. She screamed, losing what little air she had in her lungs.

A hand gripped hers.

She slipped free as the rush of the water pulled her deeper.

She kicked and thrashed and fought. She gained the surface and drew breath, managing only a whisper of air before she was pulled under. Water invaded her throat, her lungs.

She coughed reflexively, which did nothing but draw in more water.

She kicked, but the hezhan had her.

She was pressed down against stone. The pressure built. What little air she had in her lungs escaped, bubbling upward, barely visible against the orange glint of the siraj lamps along the shore.

She could still feel the hezhan. Could still feel Muwas. Could still feel the stone on the lake bed and the walls of the aether closing in. They were drawn in tight, much as they were with the babe and Nasim.

Desperate, she pushed against them, as hard as she could manage.

The aether widened. Adhiya and Erahm were distanced. And she felt in her mind the cord between Muwas and the hezhan snap.

Immediately the pressure against her chest eased. The water stilled.

She was disoriented, but she followed the light. Stars blossomed in her vision, and the world began to fade.

A warm hand gripped her wrist, pulled her up and out of the water. She was thrown over someone's shoulder, which pressed into her stomach with each ungainly step forward. Water expelled from her lungs and splashed into the surface of the lake below her. As they reached the shallows, she began spluttering, spitting the last of the water from her lungs, and then a coughing fit overcame her. It seemed to last forever, her body wracking painfully from the force of it.

But then at last it faded. Above her, a stout Aramahn man stood. Next to him was Rehada and Fahroz.

"Muwas," Atiana said, her voice hoarse. "He lies deeper in the lake. There. It was he that summoned the hezhan."

The burly quram moved to the edge of the water. He closed his eyes and opened his palms to the water. As his head tilted back, a wind began to blow. It was cold, but not so cold as Atiana had been in the water, and to her it felt good in the darkness of this place.

After a moment, the prow of a boat could be seen approaching. It turned lazily as it was pushed by the wind to the shore. When it finally arrived, the Aramahn man stepped to its side and hoisted from its confines the unconscious form of Muwas.

Atiana stood upon a grassy hill high on the mountain that held the village of Iramanshah. Ahead, the ground sloped upward until it reached a ridge where a dozen obsidian stones stood sentinel. Only paces away, a crowd of Aramahn stood in a circle around Muwas. He kneeled in the center of this tribunal of the village elders, staring at them defiantly as the light of the glowing stones lit his face in ghastly relief.

Rehada stood nearby, the wind tugging at her robes—this day as much an outsider as Atiana.

Atiana had watched far below in the darkness near the lake as the village elders had gathered and discussed what had happened in hushed voices. They had granted Muwas a chance to defend himself, but he had refused to do so. He had merely stared at them, claiming it was for them that he was doing this. "You should be on your knees," he'd said. "You should hail me as a martyr, not seek to dim the brightness of my flame." The elders had looked upon him with sadness, which had only emboldened him.

In little time, they had made their decision. Muwas would be burned—his ability to bond with spirits taken from him—and shortly after, they had all trekked up to the mountain to perform the ritual.

Muwas had come without argument, but when he'd reached the light of the sun, his outlook had changed. He became unsure of himself, and though some of his defiance remained in his eyes, it seemed more an act, whereas before it had been heartfelt.

The village elders gathered in a circle around him. Muwas stared at two of the Aramahn in particular. One was a young woman, not much older than Atiana. She wore a stone of tourmaline. A suuraqiram. The other, a man whose knees were so bad he was barely able to walk without help, wore a stone of opal. A dhoshaqiram. Together, they represented the opposed elements to water, and together, they would burn Muwas's abilities from him, even though, in doing so, they would be giving up their own.

"Why?" Atiana asked in nearly a whisper. "Why sacrifice two, who can do so much good, so that one can no longer do harm?"

Rehada glanced over, perhaps judging whether or not the question was serious. "He cannot be allowed to commune with spirits—not in this life, in any case. Perhaps in another he will turn to the path of peace."

"What do the hezhan care of peace?"

"You would rather we let him go?"

Atiana could feel the weight of the lake all over again, the burn as the water slipped hungrily down her throat. "He would have killed me, and he will kill again given the chance."

"He may," Rehada said.

"And you care so little for that?"

"I care that he is given a chance to learn."

"The Maharraht will never learn. More turn to their cause every day."

Rehada's silence made Atiana turn.

"They will learn," Rehada said, almost too soft to hear.

"You're deceiving yourself if you believe that."

Rehada turned, a mournful expression on her face as she met Atiana's gaze. "What are we to do?"

Atiana was about to snap back a reply, but she held her tongue. Nearby, the tribunal clasped hands until the circle was complete. Muwas looked up at the ones who would lose their ability to bond, and Atiana saw in him not anger, not contempt, but a sadness she would never have predicted. She thought at first it was an act, a gesture meant to garner sympathy, but as the ritual continued, the expression deepened, became so palpable that

Atiana could feel it in her chest.

"Please," he said in Mahndi, glancing between the two of them. "Do not do this."

The ritual continued. Atiana thought that he would show some outward sign of pain, that he would cry out, but he did not. He exhaled and fell to his hands and knees. The exhalation continued until surely there was nothing left in his lungs.

Then, all was silence.

The two Aramahn that had given of themselves bent over. The old man had to be held up by the two on either side of him. One by one, they dispersed, leaving Muwas alone with his past.

Atiana watched him closely. His legs were folded beneath him. His eyes were distant, searching.

What would it be like to lose such a thing? Like losing a limb? Losing a loved one? Would the memory of it fade with time or would it burn forever, a constant reminder of what he'd once had?

"Will he return to the Maharraht?" Atiana asked.

"That is what the village hopes."

"So he can tell them of his pain…"

Rehada nodded as a tear slipped down her cheek. Muwas was studying Rehada now, and there was a strange look in his eyes. One of regret, perhaps, or a keen yearning—why, she couldn't guess.

"Why do you cry?" Atiana asked.

"That should be obvious."

"I want to hear it from you. Your words."

Rehada turned impatiently. "We've all lost much this day, Atiana Radieva, even you."

Atiana turned back to Muwas. She nearly began crying herself. "I believe you, daughter of Shineshka."

The boom of a cannon brought Atiana out of her reverie. She looked up, the memories of her time in the aether returning in a flash. She recalled her fight with the jalahezhan. She knew that she had caused Muwas to release his bond with that spirit. What she had forgotten was her mother's promise to find her.

Against the solid white cloud cover, sails rose above the ridge. It was a smaller ship, only six masts, but it mattered little. She had already been seen by the men on deck. Their commander shouted, and only then—as the words washed faintly over her—did Atiana realize that it was her brother who had given the command. His beard was fuller, and he seemed to have become more gaunt in the weeks since she'd seen him, but there was no doubt.

Four ropes snaked down from the ship. Eight streltsi slipped along them quickly and efficiently to the ground. They swung their muskets off their shoulders and advanced through the circle of obsidian stones.

Rehada watched the streltsi, the muscle along her jaw working feverishly. Her fists were bunched, and her eyes were filled with more hate than she had ever seen among the peace-loving Aramahn.

Atiana touched her arm.

Rehada jumped and looked down upon Atiana with a look not unlike the one she had favored the streltsi with, but then she seemed to recognize Atiana, and her face relaxed.

"Don't do anything foolish," Atiana whispered.

Before Rehada could respond, one of the streltsi shouted for them to lie down.

"*Nyet.*" Borund's voice. "There is no need for any such thing. They will come quietly, won't you, sister? You and the woman, both…"

"Rehada Ulan al Shineshka will go nowhere." Fahroz placed herself in Borund's path. "She has done nothing, nor has Atiana Radieva Vostroma."

Borund motioned for his men to stop.

Fahroz's face was red and her eyes were fierce. "You come bearing weapons into an Aramahn village."

"Atiana is a daughter of Vostroma, and she will come with us."

"Atiana can do as she will, as can Rehada, but if they wish to stay, they will both be allowed to do so."

Borund took one step forward. Atiana could tell by his posture alone that he was tense as catgut and might be pushed too far if Fahroz didn't back down. "Their presence is requested by the Duke and Duchess of Vostroma."

A handful more Aramahn stepped out of the tunnel, their faces angry. Upon seeing them, several streltsi trained their weapons upon them. Borund had a look of desperation about him, though why that was Atiana couldn't guess.

There was no clean way out of this. Borund would not leave this place without her. She had no choice but to go with him.

"I will go," she said simply, hoping to jar Borund out of his state of mind.

"Of course you will, sister," he said, his attention fixed on Fahroz.

Atiana ignored him. "Fahroz, I would go with my brother."

Fahroz nodded and waited for Rehada to give her own answer.

Rather than reply directly, Rehada moved in and embraced Atiana. "Forgive me," she whispered, and then she stepped back to Fahroz's side.

Atiana stared, confused. When they had hugged, she had felt, just as she had felt in the cold water of the lake, the locus of aether. It was now in Rehada's robes, secreted away.

Perhaps Rehada saw her watching, staring at the precise location of whatever it was she had hidden. She looked uncomfortable, and she crossed her arms in front of her, feigning a chill.

It was Atiana who shivered, however. Rehada had lied to her. She knew now that whatever it was—stone or jewel or some unearthly remnant of the jalahezhan—Rehada had wanted it all along. She had wanted it before coming to the village. Before stepping into the chamber for her confession. Before lying to Atiana so completely.

She knew now what she should have known from the beginning.

She knew that Rehada was Maharraht.

CHAPTER 50

Nikandr watched as Nasim walked forward several more steps over the rubble littering the streets. His eyes were closed, as they had been since entering the city over an hour ago, but he had so far unfailingly led them deeper toward the center of Alayazhar.

Nikandr glanced up at the sun, which had already begun to descend. "We're taking too long," Nikandr said when Nasim had remained in the same place for an interminable amount of time.

Ashan held his hand up and whispered, "I asked for silence."

"That was three hours ago. We are past high sun already. We will have little enough time in this tower of yours, and even less to get ourselves outside the city before the sun goes down."

"That is something I am prepared to face."

"And take us with you?" Pietr asked.

Ashan frowned at Pietr. "Give Nasim the time he needs." He took two steps forward, following Nasim's movement. "And by the fates, be silent."

Pietr looked back the way they'd come. "My Prince, it will take us some time to regain the forest…"

"How much longer?" Nikandr asked Ashan.

"As long as it takes."

Nasim shambled forward. They hadn't known when they'd entered the city where they were headed, but Nikandr knew it was toward the tower, the one he'd seen in his dreams. The only trouble was they didn't know what might lay in wait.

"They must know of our presence," Nikandr had said when they'd first entered the city.

"Were that true," Ashan had replied, "we would have been met long before now. As I approached this island, it felt as if it were asleep."

"But our ship…"

Ashan had nodded. "There is no doubt that the island began to wake when we arrived. I hope that we can find Sariya before Muqallad himself rises from his slumber. We must trust to Nasim, let his memories return. He will find the way."

Beyond the shattered husks of a nearby building, a column of smoke rose—a thin black trail weaving against a clear blue sky. Surely it was a suurahezhan, yet when Nikandr grabbed Ashan's arm to make him aware of it, the arqesh merely glanced up and brushed his hand away.

Nasim came to a halt in the intersection of two wide streets. The trail of black smoke was shifting, coming closer. Soon the hezhan would cross their path, and Ashan was just standing there, studying Nasim, while Nikandr's heart pounded in his chest.

"Enough," Nikandr said. They'd already been attacked by one hezhan this day; he wasn't about to stand idly by and allow another to find them. He threw Nasim over his shoulder and ran as quickly as he could manage down one street, out of the suurahezhan's path.

Pietr grabbed Ashan's arm, twisted it behind him, and forced him to follow. They hid behind a half-collapsed wall of stone. Nikandr set Nasim down and peered around the corner. The smoke, two streets up, had ceased moving. Nasim breathed rapidly, nostrils flaring, eyes closed. Somehow the boy was communing with the suurahezhan—Nikandr was sure of it.

Ashan tried to approach, but Pietr made it clear that to do so would be unwise.

Nikandr returned his attention to the street.

And his breath caught.

Standing beyond the remnants of an ornate stone fountain was not a suurahezhan, but a boy—a boy who appeared to be a few years older than Nasim. His lips were pulled back in a rictus grin, and his lips were coal black. He had no hair, nor clothes, and he was crouched like a feral animal, penis and scrotum hanging beneath the jaundiced skin of his backside. Though taut skin smoothed the valleys where his eyes once were, his head swiveled back and forth, back and forth, all the while the telltale wavering of intense heat rising from his form.

This was an akhoz, Nikandr remembered, one of the children that remained, twisted and haunted, after the sundering of Alayazhar.

The akhoz crouched lower, head twisting and turning, but ever closer to their position.

Something deep inside Nikandr—the part that fears the wild things of the night—told him how foolish it would be to draw this twisted creature's attention.

Nasim, who had been squirming restlessly ever since they'd seen the akhoz, released a strangled cry and fought to pull away.

The akhoz snapped its head in their direction.

Nikandr picked Nasim up and sprinted way, Pietr and Ashan close behind. Weakened from the ordeals of the last several days, Nikandr had trouble moving with any great pace until a sound like the bleat of a diseased and dying goat spurred him onward.

They ducked into an open doorway halfway up the block. Inside was a room that was largely intact. The ceiling had crumbled in one corner, and the wooden floorboards had partially rotted away. Near the center of the room were the remains of two skeletons—one larger, one smaller. Immediately, an image came to Nikandr of a woman holding her child that was so vivid he began to believe he was seeing an echo of the past.

Nasim had stopped crying. Nikandr held him tight against his chest just inside the interior wall, largely out of sight. Were he to lean forward he would have a good view of the street, but he refused to do so. He refused to do anything but breathe, and when he realized that his breath was coming altogether too quickly, he forced himself to slow its pace.

Outside, footsteps approached. They scuffed against the stone. Closer and closer. His heart thumped madly. He was terrified Nasim would scream again, so he held him tight and rubbed his hair tenderly, hoping it lent the boy some sense of calm, some sense that things would be all right.

A smell like burning wool drifted into the room. It heightened sharply as the footsteps reached the doorway. Sounds of sniffing came, like a hound snuffling for truffles. The air in the room became warmer, and there was a sound, amplified in the enclosed space, of a crackling, like a pine cone thrown into the embers, a dying fire.

The thing bleated—a lonely, heartless thing, as if it were calling out to more of its kind.

Nikandr prayed it wasn't so.

A noise came, like whispering. Nikandr looked down when he realized it was coming from Nasim. He held him close and shushed quietly in his ear, but Nasim wouldn't stop, and Nikandr couldn't find it in himself to take a step any more drastic than this.

Nasim's whispered words sounded like Mahndi, but the cadence sounded different, as if it were some other dialect than what was used among the islands today.

The creature at the doorway spoke, perhaps in reply. It sounded like the voice of a dying man, ragged and harsh, and it had the same cadence that Nasim had used.

Nasim responded—a bare whisper—and the akhoz spoke again.

Then the sounds of its footsteps retreated, softened, and finally were gone.

Pietr crept to the doorway and dared a look outside. "Empty, My Prince."

Ashan pulled Nasim away from Nikandr and kneeled in front of him. While holding Nasim's shoulders, he stared deeply into the boy's eyes. Nasim's face was tight. Sweat rolled down his forehead. He whispered words soundlessly, perhaps coaxing the akhoz away from them.

Nikandr shivered as he watched. He cared for Nasim—cared for him deeply—but there was something about him that shook Nikandr to his very core.

"My Prince," Pietr said, taking his eyes off of the street only long enough to send him a serious and worried look. "We should leave."

"Pietr's right," Nikandr said. "We would be wiser to leave and study the city more closely."

Ashan stood, apparently satisfied that Nasim had not been unduly affected. "If we give Nasim the time he needs now, he will find the way to the tower, and it will be at a time of our choosing." He stared at Nikandr severely. "If we leave, Muqallad will wake. We will never get back in, and we will be hunted and killed if they find a way beyond the protection Nasim is providing us. Our best chance to get what we need, to learn more, is to go on. Now."

The last thing Nikandr wanted was to remain, especially not without knowing more of the city and its dangers, but they had come this far, and Ashan's words rang true. This may be their last, best chance to learn more of Nasim's past life and to unlock his potential. There was something to be said for surprise, and the quicker they finished their business here, the quicker they could find a way off this island.

They continued, and Nasim moved faster. Before the akhoz the city had been a study in silence, but as they treaded lower into Alayazhar—closer to the waterfront—they began hearing long, wailing bleats that tainted the cool air. Each one sent shivers running down Nikandr's frame. Pietr seemed worse. He was constantly scanning the avenues around them, even when Nikandr whispered for him to stop. Even Ashan seemed uncomfortable with the sounds which were at times far away and at times very close—perhaps only a block or less away.

Over the next few hours, despite the wretched cries, they did not see another akhoz.

They came to a section of the city older than the rest. Tall, rounded buildings dominated here. The traceries carved into the surface of the pink stone were intricate and weatherworn. Far ahead stood an ivory tower with two sprawling wings spreading out from its base. The tower was nestled between other hulking structures, many of which looked like they were mere shells.

Nikandr had seen such buildings on his first and only trip to the Yrstanlan island of Galahesh. One of its oldest cities, Baressa, was the site of the final battle between the Empire and the islands. Much of the old city had been gutted by cannon fire, both from the armada that the fledgling state of Anuskaya had amassed, and from the sizable army that had landed. Though Nikandr was sure there had been no cannons on Alayazhar when the rift had formed, the buildings looked much the same as those in Baressa had—walls stripped away, revealing gutted interiors. They were skeletons more than they were buildings. But the tower was different. It appeared to be whole and untouched, and Nikandr knew that it was the tower from his dreams, the one where Khamal had been killed.

Nikandr's stomach felt rank, and the closer he came to the tower, the more pronounced it became. He couldn't shake the feeling that within the walls of that tower lay his doom. By the time they had reached its tall, wrought-iron fence, the feeling had become so pronounced that he was forced to grit his teeth against the pain.

He reached out and grabbed one of the rusted bars of the fence.

And the moment he does, he feels a change, as if the world has shifted from underneath him. The pain in his gut is no less painful, but he straightens and takes in the surrounding buildings, which are now complete, whole, pristine. The wind is hot and stifling where only moments ago it was cool, and there hangs in the air a sense of change, of coiled intent, like a lion in the moments before it leaps.

He pulls himself upright.

And only then does he realize that he is alone.

CHAPTER 51

He pulls open the gate. It swings soundlessly. The black iron is dark with a freshly oiled luster and not a single trace of rust.

Lining the stone path are dried bushes with bare branches and parched earth beneath. As he walks, leaves sprout and fill until the bushes are full and vibrant. The wooden door buried into the deep stone walls of the tower lays open, and he walks in without another thought. When he steps inside, he realizes something is different. Whether it has been this way since the destruction of Alayazhar or when he stepped into the tower, he is not sure, but he can now for the first time since leaving Khalakovo sense his soulstone. It feels much the same as it always has—a warmth within his chest not unlike the feeling of deep-seated contentment. It should provide comfort, but does not. The feelings ring false, another illusion in this ancient and ruined place.

Inside is a circular room that occupies the entirety of the lowest level. A set of stairs with an ornate stone banister hugs the interior curve of the wall. He takes this, feeling more and more uncomfortable the higher he rises. He climbs level after level, finding nothing but empty rooms and lonely thoughts, but there is always a yearning that urges him to go on like that final and inevitable march toward death.

The stairs lead to a room on the highest level. An ornate bed lies at its center. The bedding is pooled to one side, as if its owner had only just risen.

Like the cardinal directions of the compass rose, four windows are set into the stone walls; at one of these stands a woman. She has long golden hair that runs down past the small of her back and she wears not the robes of the Aramahn, nor the dresses of the Grand Duchy, but a simple yet elegant gown of roughspun silk. He notes that she is gazing north, the direction of winter, of water, indicating, perhaps, that she is a woman who owns a cool temperament. It could also mean that she hides her feelings, that her intentions would be difficult to discern.

She turns her head to look upon him. Golden hair and bright blue eyes. She is timeless. Ageless. She is beauty itself.

She returns her attention to the city. If she is concerned over his arrival she does not show it.

"Come," she says.

He sees no gem upon her brow, though such things feel meaningless here. Gems are for the Aramahn. They are used to create a bond between human and hezhan, a link from Erahm to Adhiya. Who would say what such a thing would look like here? He was not even convinced he was still *in* Erahm.

Seeing no reason to deny her command, he joins her at the window. Through the clear but imperfect glass he can see the sprawling city as it climbs the long slope toward the valley walls. Wide thoroughfares as straight as arrows run from the tower outward, and they are lined by buildings that vary in style and color but add to the aesthetic appeal of the layout. Beyond the tower itself and the nearest of the buildings, the city is as broken as he knew it to be.

When she speaks again, she sounds as old as the island itself. "You have come from Hathshava," she says.

It was the ancient name for Khalakovo—the island of Uyadensk in particular—and it was discarded once the Aramahn ceded the archipelago to the Landed. Suddenly, he feels conscious of his family's role in displacing so many—he does not feel ashamed, only aware of the history as never before.

"I have," he replies.

"And before that?" She looks upon him with a familiarity that cannot be explained until he realizes who she thinks he is. She believes she is looking upon the face of Khamal—or at least who Khamal had become when he was reborn.

"Before that... Alastra."

"And before that?"

He shrugs. "I cannot remember."

She turns to him, face pinched in annoyance. "You cannot?"

Outside, more of the buildings have become whole. It is as if she is waking and as she does more and more of the city is granted its previous glory. He wonders whether her memories, her perceptions, include the people who once lived here. Perhaps they will emerge from their homes, on their way to the shore or the hills to meditate upon their lives. Then again, perhaps when the city is complete she will remember what happened. Perhaps he will be lost here with her, caught within the trap Khamal had laid for her upon his death.

"Why have you come?" she asks.

"I've come for Nasim."

She looks down, and though he can see nothing in the pristine courtyard below he wonders whether she is seeing something completely different, whether in her eyes Nasim and Ashan and Pietr were in that decrepit courtyard, searching for him.

When she speaks again, there is curiosity in her voice, and longing. "He is strange, this one."

"He is."

She turns suddenly, and stares fiercely at his stone.

Nikandr holds it in one hand, more conscious of it than he's been since it cracked on the deck of his ship. "Nasim dimmed it on Hathshava."

She smiles. For the life of him he cannot remember seeing a more beautiful face. "It was not dimmed at all."

"It was."

She looks up at him. Her eyes are the blue of the ocean deeps. "It became brighter than you could know. He did not spurn you that day. He did not harm you. He *chose* you."

"Chose me for what?"

She reaches out, her fingers stopping just short of touching the smooth surface of the stone. "Perhaps he senses what is to come. Perhaps he feels you kindred. Perhaps he wishes to ground himself deeper in Erahm, so lost is he on the other side."

"I am no more kindred to him than I am to you."

This seems to startle her. She looks up, a frown complicating her features. "Then perhaps you did *not* come for him. Perhaps you came for me."

"I did not know you existed before today."

She smiles. "The fates care little about what you know. What matters is that you are here now, and that I have awoken. You wish for something. You hope to find a way to this boy. And I? I wish for something as well."

"Tell me."

"I wish to live… If you can answer me five questions, you can have the solution to your problem."

"What sort of questions?"

"The sort you can answer, to be sure, but it will take insight, Hathshava. It will take insight."

"And if I can't answer them?"

She smiles. Her beauty, despite the peril, stirs fires deep within. "Then you will stay."

"And if I refuse?"

She shrugs. "You know the way out."

Doubt runs thick within him. He does not know what sort of questions she might ask, and he worries that she will trick him. But what is there to do? If he leaves, they might never get a chance to learn the true nature of Nasim. They might never learn how to heal the blight that is destroying the islands. The gains, he decides, outweigh the risks many times over.

"I will need a way off this island as well."

She shakes her head. "The fates saw fit to bring you here; they can see your way home."

He tightens his jaw, takes a deep breath, and nods. "Ask."

She steps back from the window and motions to it. "What draws near?"

Outside, the city has completed itself. Down one of the main thoroughfares comes a man wearing an ornate robe of bright blue cloth with a ragged hem. He has a limp, and it grows worse as he approaches the tower.

Eventually he stops and looks down at his feet, or perhaps at his ankles, and then behind, as if confused at how this could have come to pass.

The Aramahn enjoy games of words, and it is clear that this will follow those ancient traditions. The question was not what can be seen by the naked eye, but what the scene represents. They stood at the northern window, the same window at which the woman was standing when he arrived, and so he thinks these must all be related to the nature of the directions. The Aramahn equate north with water, but also with winter. And the man, though still hale, appears to have his best days behind him.

"Winter," he answers. "Winter draws near."

She smiles a smile that says how much she is enjoying their game. He notices for the first time wrinkles at the corners of her eyes; they lend her a sagacious quality but also a sense of mortality he hadn't expected. Perhaps she notices, for her smile fades and she slips to the eastern window.

"What will she reap?"

The scene in the window is not of the city at all. It is of an open field with a girl running across it. A boy chases after, and together they drop among the tall stalks of grass and begin pulling the clothes from their bodies, kissing one another fiercely. Soon they are naked and making love, the boy on top thrusting as she holds him close.

Surely they are sowing the seeds of a child. That must be the answer, and it hangs on his lips for long seconds, but east is the direction of autumn, and autumn is a time of dying, of preparation for the long winter ahead. The answer cannot be so simple.

When they are done, the boy pulls on his clothes and leaves. The girl, after he is gone, puts her head between her knees and begins to cry. Making love had been a ploy—an attempt, perhaps, to make him love her when she knows that he will not.

What else can such a thing reap? Whether she has a child or not, she will never be happy until she lets him go.

"Misery," he says, which he realizes belatedly is another meaning of east for the Aramahn.

The woman smiles again, but this time it seems forced, as if she has underestimated him and has now vowed to correct her mistake. She moves to the southern window and motions to it.

"When will he find what he seeks?"

The scene outside the window is of an old Landed man in a boat. His grizzled and pockmarked face holds an expression of savage concentration as he uses scarred hands to secure an ebony-skinned cod onto a hook. He throws the fish—now attached to a line which in turn is attached to a pole resting in a sleeve on the gunwale—into the water and repeats the process on another line, and another, until he has four lines in. And then he waits, staring at the sea as he rests his chin upon his hands. Every so often he touches the tips of his fingers to one of the poles, perhaps praying to his fathers for a catch that might never come.

The window faces south, the direction of summer, of heat, of willfulness. That he uses such large bait gives clue to what he is searching for—a large catch. Too large. It speaks of a man who will not give up even though what he searches for is clearly beyond his means. This man has pride and a lifetime on the water to guide him, but he also has a desperation that says he will never get what he wants, that even if he does it will not be enough.

"Never," comes the answer from his mouth, though it is with a sense of sadness, for he has known men like this.

She looks into his eyes with respect and a touch of anger. Her jaw is set grimly, as if she wishes this game to be over and done with. When she moves to the western window, she crosses her arms over her chest.

"Who will she become?"

The image—Nikandr draws in breath without meaning to—is of Rehada. She is younger than when they had first met, perhaps only twenty years old. She is standing before the burnt, smoking remains of a house, and she is staring at a blackened skeleton, its posture locked in the rigor of what must surely have been a very gruesome and painful death.

Others talk around her, and *to* her, but she pays them no mind. She has eyes only for the body, and he suddenly realizes the ironic joke that is being played on him. Here is he, gazing through the window of spring, of birth and growth, as Rehada looks upon what must surely have been her child. The look upon her face is one of cold surety, of ruthless calculation, and it wars with what he knows of her. She has always been warm, has in fact been open about her life around the islands and her decision to live upon

Uyadensk… But she has never once mentioned a child.

What else, then, has she lied about?

Who will she become?

He has seen such looks before, upon the faces of the enemy, of those who will not rest until the Landed have been pushed from the islands, and it suddenly strikes him the meaning of the word Maharraht. Its primary meaning is *the forgotten, the shunned,* but it stems from a beautiful desert flower that only blooms in spring, and in the ancient language of Kalhani—a language that the woman questioning him surely knows—it is akin to spring and rebirth.

"I know who she becomes," he finally answers, a knot forming in his throat.

"Then say it."

He swallows. Once. Twice. "Do not make me."

"What is in a word?"

"A word can weigh heavier than stone."

"Say it," she says, her voice hard.

"Maharraht."

Her smile is one of pleasure, as though a grand plan has just come together. She walks to the center of the room and stands near the bed. She spreads her arms wide and the views through all four windows change. He does not look, however. His mind is preoccupied with a woman he thought he loved, but he is forced to focus himself once more when she speaks her final question.

"How are they related?"

The scenes in the window show different people at different times in their lives. Two men, one woman, and a girl. There is nothing he can see that connects them—not their clothes, not their surroundings, not their mannerisms. He inspects each one closely, watching for any sign that might give him a clue, but he finds nothing, and his heart begins to beat heavily. He has come so far… He cannot come this close only to fail.

There is nothing of the smile Sariya had when this game first began. In fact, she seems sad as she watches him. Sad and lonely.

He realizes that she stands near the bed in the center of the room. The center for the Aramahn is no *one* direction; it is *all* directions. It is the cycle of life; it is rebirth. It is what has come before and what has yet to come. These images can be no other than her previous lives, and suddenly he realizes that she misses them. Somehow she has become trapped in this place. She is Ghayavand—part and parcel of this island—but it was not always so. She wants to be free from it, and if that cannot happen, she wants him to join her.

"They are you," he says.

She runs her fingers over the sheets on the bed while stepping closer to him. She is stunning. The curve of her jaw, the line of her neck, skin soft and smooth, arms that might hold him forever.

"The things you might see." The very words from her lips sing. "They would astound you. I will share all of it if you would remain."

When he doesn't open his mouth—he cannot for fear of acceding—she deems it a refusal and steps away from the bed. She approaches him with graceful steps until they are chest to chest. He feels the warmth coming from her, the swell of her breasts pressing against his ribs, the tickle of her hair as she leans in and nestles against his neck. The faint smell of jasmine taints the air as she places one warm kiss at the base of his neck, and as her arms wrap around him and caress his back, he feels himself harden.

"We would be one. Forever."

He realizes as she speaks these words that he would not mind such a thing. He is young, but life on the islands has been hard. They would rule this place and no one would stand against them. No one.

CHAPTER 52

He leans down and kisses her. Her lips are moist and hot. He takes her in his arms and holds her tight as their kiss deepens, and soon he realizes that they are moving toward the bed. He removes his clothes as she slips the dress from her shoulders and allows it to pool about her feet. He picks her up and together they fall into the bed. He runs down the length of her, pressing kiss after kiss against her neck, her breasts, her stomach, and finally her thighs. She spreads her legs at the merest touch, and when he runs his tongue near her lips, she sucks in breath.

When he can stand it no more, he runs his chest along her stomach and breasts and kisses her once more, ready to enter her.

As he waits, prolonging the pleasure to the point of ache, something strikes him—he cannot feel her heartbeat. He can feel his own, which is beating madly, but he cannot feel hers. He leans down and kisses her cheek and ear, if only to gain a bit more time.

He knows not how, but it is true—no blood runs through her veins. And he realizes with a start where he is, who this woman is, his purpose here.

Where, he wonders with a growing sense of desperation, are Ashan and Nasim and Pietr?

"Come," she whispers, reaching between her legs and stroking him with her hand.

He resists, and feels her tense beneath him.

Her grip tightens. "Come."

He tries to pull away but she grabs the back of his neck and with a strength that belies her frame pulls him down until their lips are once again locked.

He twists away and falls from the bed. "*Nyet!*"

She pauses, her expression no longer one of anger, but shock. She slips from the bed and stands over him. "What did you say?"

"I said, *nyet.*"

Her eyes thin. "Khamal?"

"I am Nikandr Iaroslov Khalakovo. Khamal is the man you betrayed for Muqallad."

She stands taller, but somehow it only makes her seem frail. She draws her arms in, glances through the nearby windows. "Has it been so long?"

"It has, and Nasim has done nothing to you. Give me the knowledge to reach him. To make him whole."

She tries to smile, and fails, but her eyes regain their sharpness. "The answer is there," she says, motioning with one hand toward his chest.

His stone is glowing as brightly as it had in the donjon below Radiskoye. He shakes his head. "I don't understand."

"He calls to you."

"What can I do?"

Outside, the sky has gone deep red. "Accept him. Give of yourself to him."

"How?"

She motions to the windows. "Muqallad has awoken. He will come for Khamal, and for you."

"Tell me how to reach him!"

She shakes her head.

Nikandr feels something deep within his chest, akin to the ache of the havahezhan. It has become familiar now, and more than that, it feels proper, even with the pain.

Sariya gazes at his chest. She reaches out, as if to touch his stone, but he pulls away.

"It has been with you for a long time."

Nikandr nods, feeling something important in her words. "Since it crossed on Hathshava."

She glances toward the windows. They have darkened further, leaving only the deepest of reds. The light coming from Nikandr's stone casts Sariya in ghastly relief.

"It was with you well before then."

Nikandr stares at her, confused. She must be confused, he thinks, but there is a depth of understanding in those beautiful blue eyes, an understanding that comes not in a fleeting handful of years on this mortal plane, but lifetimes, centuries. He knows that she is right. The hezhan *has* been with him since before Soroush summoned it. It had been with him since he'd had the wasting. *Nyet*. It was the *cause* of the wasting. It had been feeding on him, draining him through the aether, always there, always drawing from him like a reservoir no matter how meager its gain might be.

"I can rid you of it."

"How?"

She steps forward. "You need but ask."

He takes a step of his own, ready to accept. "Please."

She smiles and places her hand over his heart, over his stone. "There is a cost. Your bond with Nasim will be broken."

He shakes his head, confused.

"It is how he has come to find you, Hathshava. It is how your bond has remained intact over all this time, over all these leagues."

Like a flower closing as dusk approaches, the elation inside him diminishes. He stares down at her hand. All he need do is ask. He can still find Nasim, can still find a way to reach him and to help Ashan heal the blight over Khalakovo...

A vision of Nasim comes to him. That young boy holding himself tightly about the chest, rocking himself from the pain. There are times when Nikandr is able to take that away, and if Sariya is right, he might be able to heal him completely.

He cannot accept her offer, not if it means abandoning Nasim.

He takes her wrist and pulls it away from his chest.

Sariya nods, a rueful smile on her face. "You must hurry," Sariya says. She turns and walks toward the nearest window, toward winter.

And then she is gone.

He starts toward the far side of the room, ready to take the stairs down, to find Nasim and to run, to digest what Sariya has told him, but there are no stairs.

"Sariya!"

Winds tear at the tower. The windows rattle. A low rumbling thrums through the structure and up through his feet.

He stares at his stone again, knowing the only way out now is to listen to her words. *Accept him. Give of yourself.*

He holds the stone tight in his hand and closes his eyes. He casts himself outward, as he does with his mother.

I am here! I am here, Nasim!

A stone breaks from the wall and falls to the floor. Fine powder sifts downward from the ancient wooden planks above. A presence forms beyond the walls of the tower. It approaches, more curious than anything, but soon a sense of anger and revenge is palpable.

Accept him.

"Please, Nasim," he whispers.

He opens his heart to this boy who seems lost among the world, but who also is at the center of the storm. So much depends on him, and yet he is nearly incapable of action, given only to those rare moments of lucidity.

Doubts begin to form as a crack is torn in the wall. The tower shifts and groans.

This cannot be what Sariya meant. He must accept Nasim for who he was. Must welcome him.

He does so, giving merely love, nothing else.

He feels the most tentative of touches, as he does before his mother finds him.

And his world goes dark.

Nikandr woke, lying on the ground with Pietr just next to him on the moss-covered cobbles. Nasim, kneeling between them, had one hand over Nikandr's heart, the other over Pietr's. Moments after Nikandr began to stir, he pulled his hands away and hugged himself tightly—a more familiar position. He refused to meet Nikandr's eye. He only rocked back and forth while staring at Pietr with a grieved expression on his young face. Tears fell from his clenched eyes, and finally he fell forward across Pietr's chest. "Forgive me!" he cried. "I'm so sorry! Please, forgive me!"

Nikandr stood, failing to understand why Pietr had been lying next to him until he realized Pietr's chest was not rising with breath.

"He asked Nasim to do it."

Nikandr looked up to find Ashan standing nearby. He had a look of pity on his face.

Ashan pointed to Nikandr's chest. "He knew, at least a little, what that meant."

Nikandr looked down and saw his soulstone. Under the bright light of sunset, the chalcedony stone glowed as brilliantly as it had inside the tower, but the feelings of ache, of being drawn slowly outward, remained. The havahezhan, the creature bound to him on the far side of the aether, was still there, preying upon him.

Nikandr kneeled next to Pietr. He stared into the older man's face, at the light scars that ran though the black stubble on his chin and cheeks. He was unmoving, breathless, and yet in that moment he seemed full of life, so much had he granted to Nikandr. "Go safely," he whispered, "and may the ancients protect you." He leaned forward and kissed his cheeks, and then, knowing time was growing short, he stood. "We must hurry. Muqallad has awoken, and we have precious little time."

Ashan glanced at the tower, a look of worry and recognition on his face, as if he saw for the first time what it might mean to confront Muqallad directly.

Then they were running through the streets, Nasim in tow. The boy was silent, his face streaked with tears.

"Nasim, can you hear me?" Nikandr asked.

Nasim didn't respond. Other than his outburst of emotion over Pietr he seemed little different than before. Nikandr had hoped there would be some sort of catharsis, an awakening. Surely Nikandr would feel something as well—were they not linked, after all?—but Nasim, despite allowing them to rush him through the streets, seemed to have the same distant expression, the same lack of awareness of his surroundings, the same inability to communicate. It hadn't been Nikandr's appeal, then, that had saved him from the tower. It had been Pietr's sacrifice.

All this way, all this time, lost lives and injury, and they'd failed.

They took the same path from the city they'd taken on their way in. Before they'd gone halfway toward the outskirts, however, the animal sounds of the akhoz rent the chill air. The call of one was echoed by many others, several chillingly close.

The sounds of their footsteps slapping the stone streets came nearer. Their panting—akin to that of a winded horse, heavy and long and wet—came louder.

Nikandr held Nasim's hand, trying to force him to run faster, but he would not. In fact, his pace was beginning to slow. His tears were gone, but his look of regret remained.

And then he tripped.

Nikandr lost his grip, and Nasim fell heavily to the ground.

Nikandr stopped, looking at his soulstone and then Nasim. He could *feel* him now, through the stone, as surely as he'd ever felt anything.

And then movement caught his attention. Beyond Nasim, from behind a broken building of blond stone, came the misshapen form of a girl. She was naked and thin. The air above her wavered with heat. She appeared to be no older than twelve, though she had the same blackened lips as the other akhoz.

Another came, behind her. And another, to her right. Soon, they were all around, cutting off all hopes of escape. They closed in, drawing closer with a restrained gait and an intensity that Nikandr could only describe as hunger.

Nikandr crept toward Nasim, sure that the akhoz would charge and devour them if he moved too quickly. Then he felt a blinding pain in his chest, a pain so sharp it brought him to his knees. Ashan was at his side in moments, but he stopped when he realized that the akhoz were no longer advancing.

It was then—as the pain continued to burn inside him—that Nikandr noticed a man pacing up the street toward them. He was taller than Nikandr, with curly black hair that trailed down to his shoulders and rings of gold that were woven into his long black beard. He wore sandals of the finest leather. His outer robe was white with embroidery of silver threads woven through the cuffs and hem. His inner robe was the blue of the sky.

The akhoz parted as he approached.

Muqallad came to a halt near Nasim, who was writhing in pain with an expression of shock and wonder. He kneeled, and as he did the world around them slowed. The akhoz ceased moving. Ashan, turning toward Nikandr, froze. The few clouds in the sky continued to drift, and the air above the akhoz continued to waver—

—but all else is silent. All else is still.

The pain in Nikandr's chest vanishes. He feels complete, whole, more than he has ever felt before. He remembers the lives behind him. Senses those that lie before. He feels… another life. One that crosses his at the junction in which he now finds himself—on the island that holds centuries of his past life. The one from Hathshava.

"You have come," Muqallad says to Nasim.

"*Yeh*," Nasim replies, though it is through the other's lips.

Muqallad raises his head, surprised. "Khamal."

Nasim shakes his head. "No more."

Muqallad's dark eyes narrow. "*Neh*. You are different now, aren't you?"

"I am."

Muqallad smiles. "Reborn. As you had planned."

"As I had planned…"

He stares into Nikandr's eyes. His gaze is piercing, precise. "Why return?"

"We cannot escape our past," Nasim replies.

"*Neh*, but we can forge our future."

The confusion inside Nikandr swells. He feels as though he is both participant and bystander to this conversation, both actor and audience.

The air shimmers as Muqallad stands. It is clear, just as with Sariya, that he is slowly gaining control—over himself and his surroundings. He is entering Erahm once more, after having been banished since the moment of Khamal's death. Fear wells up inside Nikandr. Nasim, as lucid as he is now, must know this. Why does he allow it?

But then he understands. Nasim is not merely allowing it. He *wants* Muqallad to enter the material world. He needs him to do so to regain himself and the pieces he left behind.

Perhaps Muqallad recognizes this, for there is a shift in the air, a sense that everything in this small space between worlds has stopped.

"That has always been your way," Nikandr says, hoping to draw Muqallad's attention. "Hasn't it?"

Muqallad stares into Nikandr's eyes, seems to grow as he does so. "Should we trust to the ancients, as you do?" From the corner of his eye, Nikandr sees the akhoz moving, ever so slowly. "Should we bury our dead"—Muqallad points to Nikandr's chest—"with the stones that guided them through life? Or should we strive to better ourselves and pave the way for those who have yet to come?"

"We should honor ourselves, our families, and strive to understand those who are not the same."

"As your family did with Nasim?"

"We are not perfect."

"*Neh*, you are not."

"Nor are the Maharraht," Nikandr continues. "I used to think them an invention of my time. But now I wonder if the very seeds of their arrival weren't sown on this island."

Muqallad's face goes red. He takes a step forward, and when he does, Nikandr rushes forward and takes him into a deep embrace.

Muqallad struggles. He is strong, but Nikandr holds tight, hoping that the mere contact will complete the process.

They fall to the ground. Muqallad screams in rage—perhaps also in pain—and then Nasim is standing over them both. His eyes are sharp and piercing. His face is angry.

"Not now," Nasim says as he reaches down and touches Muqallad's forehead.

Muqallad rears back. His whole body stiffens as his eyes roll back. His skin begins to wrinkle, and Nikandr releases him from the sheer terror of it. As he scrabbles away, Muqallad continues to wither. His arms curl around his waist, and his legs pull up toward his chest. He looks, in these last moments, like Nasim, pained and ignorant of the world around him.

His skin dries, turns gray, begins to flake. And then, as the wind picks up, it falls away as if he is so much sand being blown across the desert floor.

"Come," Nasim says, holding his hand out to Nikandr. He tips his head toward the akhoz. "They will wake soon."

The world is already speeding up. The akhoz shamble forward. Ashan is spreading his arms wide, his chest open to the sky.

Nikandr allows Nasim to pull him to his feet, and together they pull Ashan out through the akhoz.

By the time they have passed the circle of the akhoz, the world continues as it always has.

They ran, and with the akhoz slowed by the fall of their master, they quickly added distance between them. But Nikandr knew this was temporary at best. The akhoz were already gaining speed, and if anything, their anger rose to new heights as they howled in their pursuit.

They reached the edges of the city, where the buildings were more sparse. The road led to the trail that would take them higher toward the island's central ridge and toward the remains of Nikandr's crew, but before they had passed the last of the ruined stone buildings, a call came from behind—higher-pitched, more insistent.

An akhoz, the same girl as before, was frenzied in her pursuit and was now much closer than the pack further behind. She would be on them in moments.

Nikandr pulled his kindjal, not knowing what else to do. Ashan, the jasper gem upon his wrist glowing faintly, turned and raised his hands up high. The ground rose in a mound before the akhoz. They squealed as they were flung backward. A vanahezhan stood, fully formed, sidestepping to place itself in the path of the akhoz as she attempted to circumvent it to reach Nasim.

Nikandr had not expected even an arqesh like Ashan to be able to summon a hezhan—he should have only been able to use its powers on this plane—but surely it had something to do with the particulars of Ghayavand.

The akhoz's blackened eyes widened and her lips pulled back, revealing the shattered remains of teeth, as the hezhan charged forward. The akhoz darted to one side and gripped the hezhan's massive arm. A sizzling sound filled the air as the hezhan moaned and reared backward. Its arm dried in an instant and powdered to dust as the akhoz retreated once more.

She was not quick enough, however. The other arm of the hezhan pounded her across the head. It sounded like a hammer that butchers use to fell pigs before the slaughter. The akhoz flew through the air and landed in a heap, her head bent backward under her body.

She lay there, lifeless, as the other akhoz approached, and when Nikandr looked beyond to the city, he saw three more shamble from the streets—then another pair—all of them heading their way. They had only minutes to defeat the nearest of them and flee before they were overwhelmed.

The older akhoz leapt when it neared the vanahezhan. The beast was not ready for it, and the akhoz landed on its chest. The akhoz remained in place as it hugged the chest of the earth spirit and released a hoarse cry into the air. The hezhan moaned as the heat intensified to the point that Nikandr had to retreat.

Moments later, the hezhan's body powdered just as its arm had, and parts of it began to ablate in a way that was eerily similar to Muqallad's death.

Nikandr tried to advance with his kindjal, but the heat was too intense. However, when the hezhan finally fell to the ground, the heat dropped to almost normal levels. The akhoz was bent over, perhaps recovering itself after expending so much energy.

Nikandr did not hesitate. He advanced and struck, driving the knife deep into the exposed back of the akhoz.

The creature turned and knocked Nikandr away with a vicious swipe of its arm. The heat from the akhoz's skin was not nearly as formidable as it had been moments ago, but it was still enough to burn Nikandr's forearm. He fell away, and rolled back to his feet.

The akhoz screamed as he tried to reach the knife in his back, but each time he grabbed the hilt of the weapon, he screamed louder and pulled his hand away as if the *kindjal* were burning *him*.

Ashan was kneeling, his arms spaced wide and his hands flat against the ground. He was whispering and rocking rhythmically back and forth. There was a pool of water collecting before him, and it was starting to trickle downhill. Before it could go far, however, it rose up and took form. It looked vaguely childlike—reaching only Nikandr's waist—but it was twice as wide as he was.

The jalahezhan rolled forward and struck the akhoz's legs. A sizzling sound accompanied the water spirit's efforts as it slipped higher and higher along the akhoz's body. The akhoz screamed, still trying to rid himself of the knife while bearing down to create more heat. A white gout of steam rose as the two creatures fought for control.

The jalahezhan seemed to be holding its own—the akhoz had been forced to the ground and water was gurgling into his mouth—but then the trailing akhoz reached it, and soon they had surrounded the water spirit. Moments later, the jalahezhan lost form and the water splashed to the ground. Steam rose. Their feet sizzled as they collectively turned and began moving up the trail.

Nikandr and Ashan and Nasim fled, but they were exhausted, and Ashan had already summoned two hezhan, something that must have sapped his strength sorely.

Finally, Ashan stopped, his breath coming in great gasps. He turned and faced the akhoz, opening his arms wide and tilting his head back to the sky while whispering words of prayer or perhaps commands in Mahndi. In the air before him the telltale signs of a dhoshahezhan formed. A crackling sound rent the air, which smelled suddenly acrid. Its shape—more elusive than when they were seen playing among lightning storms—was fluid, like an air spirit, but also more angular as the faint sparks of light brought on by its energy defined its boundaries.

Nikandr kneeled next to Nasim and turned the boy to face him. "Please. You must do something."

But Nasim didn't seem to hear him. His eyes were clamped shut and his face held a look of supreme discomfort, as if what he were doing was already taking too much. What effect it might be having, Nikandr had no idea. Perhaps without Nasim's efforts they would be facing a score of akhoz and not just six.

Still, six, twenty, it mattered little if the dhoshahezhan could not save them, and Nikandr didn't see how it could.

The akhoz once again surrounded the hezhan, preferring to deal with the thing that might harm them before dispatching their true prey. This was not so easy as the last, however. Blue-white lightning arced from the hezhan, through three of them, and back to the source. Two of them spasmed and dropped to the ground, unconscious or dead; the third fell to hands and knees, its torso convulsing as it fought to regain control of its body.

The other akhoz reared backward—a posture reminiscent of what Ashan had just done—and exhaled gouts of flame from their mouths. The muscles along their necks tightened like bowstrings, and their arms flayed backward as they released every remaining bit of breath within their lungs.

The shimmering signs of the dhoshahezhan seemed to elongate as the fire pulled the air upward. More lightning shot downward, arcing between two of the akhoz, but it was noticeably weaker than the previous, and the akhoz were only momentarily fazed. Together the four remaining breathed once more, and the death throes of the hezhan were evidenced by a faint crackle and the barest winking of light.

The two wounded akhoz had just begun lifting themselves from the ground when a great boom rent the air. The skin of three of the akhoz lifted in random places about their bodies as grape shot tore into them.

Nikandr looked up and saw a ship—the *Kavda*—floating not a hundred paces above them in the sky, and standing at the gunwale, his face unreadable, was Grigory Stasayev Bolgravya.

The fore cannon bucked as it coughed its own shot, and another of the akhoz was taken. The gun crew worked feverishly to reload as a rope ladder snaked downward.

Nikandr guided Nasim as Ashan limped toward the ladder. The akhoz screamed and gave chase, but they seemed hesitant. They released their fiery breath up toward the ship, but it didn't travel high enough to do damage.

One of the akhoz shook its head and sprinted forward, but its left arm was taken off by another blast from the rear cannon. It fell to the ground, moaning and reaching for the dismembered arm that now lay far out of reach.

The ship descended far enough that Nikandr could lift Nasim up to the ladder. Ashan followed and Nikandr brought up the rear as the ship lifted.

Nikandr's legs and feet were burned by one last blast from two more akhoz, but he would count himself lucky if he had only blisters.

When he reached the deck, he found Grigory waiting. Five streltsi stood behind him—two held Ashan and Nasim; the other three held pistols at the ready.

Grigory jutted his chin toward the ladder. "If I hadn't been given orders to bring you back, Iaroslov, I would have left you to them."

Nikandr held his eye. "Spoken like a hound well trained."

Grigory waved one hand, at which point two of the streltsi came forward and bound Nikandr's hands behind his back. "We'll see if your tongue is so loose when you return to a Khalakovo that finds itself in Bolgravyan hands."

"Never."

Grigory smiled. "By now Vostroma will have ordered the attack." Grigory shook his head sadly. "The eyrie will be taken first. Radiskoye will be saved for last, and it will be torn apart unless your father agrees to cede his islands to us."

"He would die first."

The smile on Grigory's face was one of pure pleasure. "We can only hope, Nischka. And do not worry for your former bride. She has been promised to me, to reforge the southern alliance that has been, shall we say, *lacking* these last twenty years. I care little for that, but I will admit that I won't mind sharing a bed with Atiana Radieva."

Grigory paused, waiting for Nikandr to speak, and then his face lit into a smile and he released a full-chested laugh. "Your bride has just been stolen, Nischka. Can it be the vaunted Son of the North has no words?"

"She was never my bride," Nikandr said, feeling his face burn. "She was a woman chosen by my mother, a woman as replaceable as your own mother."

It was Grigory's turn to burn red. His mother, Alesya, had been spurned by the Duke of Mirkotsk when he discovered just how homely she was. It had led to a small skirmish between the two duchies and had nearly led to civil war. Stasa had taken her as his bride, cementing his relationship with Dhalingrad, and he had refused to allow anyone to speak of the matter after they had been married.

Grigory stepped forward and struck Nikandr across the face. It stung, but Nikandr refused to bend.

"I'll be sure to write to tell you how she tastes." Nikandr could smell vodka on Grigory's breath.

They were brought belowdecks—Ashan without his bracelets and circlet—and thrown into a small, windowless room near the center of the ship.

Nasim was taken elsewhere, no doubt so Grigory could turn his attentions on the boy before they reached the blockade. Nikandr started to think better of raising Grigory's ire. He sincerely hoped the man didn't do something eminently foolish with Nasim.

Like make him angry.

CHAPTER 53

Borund sat within the kapitan's cabin, eying Atiana like a prisoner of war—like some Motherless wretch he was ready to drag before his father for questioning. On a silver perch fixed to the wall sat an old black rook with a chipped beak. Its eyes were not sharp, and it was preening its feathers, so Atiana did not think her mother or any of the other Matri were inhabiting its form. Considering what was happening on Khalakovo the possibility was even more remote. Still, she reminded herself to watch her tongue.

"Mother said you were glad to be there," Borund said.

"I was not *glad*," Atiana said.

"Then what were you?"

"Relieved to be out of the village."

"And what were you doing there in the first place?"

"I told you. I had escaped from Radiskoye."

"But why go to a Motherless village?"

"There were riots in the streets, Bora. You would rather I returned to Radiskoye?"

Borund shrugged his shoulders, which were not as round as she remembered them. No doubt he had not been eating well, rations being what they were. "You could have hidden in Izhny, or anywhere else for that matter. You could have stayed in one place until Mother found you."

"You assume Mother was even looking for me. I practically tripped over her before she noticed me. I managed to get myself to a place where she could find me. That should be enough for you." Borund opened his mouth to speak, but Atiana talked over him. "Enough, brother. You act like I *wanted* to be left there, when it was you and Father who abandoned me."

"You were not abandoned."

"Then what happened?" The feeling of betrayal she had felt on the eyrie—the ship pulling away, taking Borund and Father with it, while the barrel of a gun was being held to her head—all came back in a rush. "How could you have forgotten me?"

"I checked on the three of you before I left. Ishkyna said you had already boarded the yacht."

"And you believed her?"

"Mileva said the same thing. Why would they lie?"

Atiana wanted to grab the brass seal sitting at the edge of Borund's desk and throw it at him, but Borund had changed. He was harder, and she couldn't act like she had years ago. He was being groomed to take Father's place, and the last thing she could afford was to give him a reason to scrutinize her further. "Because it *suits* them, Bora. Do you even know what your sisters are like anymore?"

"Why were you gone?" he asked, ignoring her question. "Why did it suit them to lie for you?"

She knew she had to give him an element of the truth, but she did not trust him enough to give him the complete story. "I left to investigate the crossing of the suurahezhan."

"When your father told everyone explicitly they were to do no such thing."

Atiana shrugged. "Why shouldn't I have? The Khalakovos had all but ceased their investigations."

"I would think by now the reason for that was clear. They already had the ones who did it and were protecting them."

"Perhaps, but if it were that cut-and-dry, why would they not simply hand them over?"

Borund smiled, the patronizing one he saved for his sisters when he thought they were being foolish. "Come, Tiana. You're not so naïve as that."

"What? You still think they hired a Landless qiram and a witless boy to summon an elder spirit to kill Bolgravya? *Nyet*, Borund, it's not so obvious as you think."

He stared at her doubtfully.

"The spirits are not easily bound," she continued. "It might as easily have attacked them."

His face pinched into a look of annoyance. "There are things we will never know about the Aramahn. The man, Ashan, was arqesh, and the boy clearly had powers that can only be guessed at."

"And what if they *had* summoned it? It is a dangerous thing to banish them once they've come. We know this. Why did it slip back through the aether if it had been consciously summoned?"

"Times change. In our lifetimes alone, the world has begun remaking itself. Who knows how the spirits might have changed in that same time or over the course of centuries?"

"You're trying to give the crossing more meaning than it has."

"Spoken like a true bride of Khalakovo."

"They are the words of a woman who doesn't like seeing lives wasted"— she pointed south, toward Volgorod's eyrie—"which is exactly what's happening now."

"They brought it upon themselves."

"*Nyet, Father* brought it upon them."

"And he was right to do so!" Borund's face was turning red. "Khalakovo has been lording their gems and windwood over us for two decades. And for you—a daughter of Vostroma—they give us three windworn ships and a handful of gems? Did you know I told Father to throw their offer to the winds? He refused because we needed those ships, but then Iaros murders the Grand Duke himself so that he can have the mantle he's been lusting after for years… It's too much, Atiana. Too much. I don't know how you can expect us to stand idly by when we were there to witness it. I thought your blood ran thicker than that."

"Perhaps that's the difference between us, Borund. I don't look at the surface of a thing and make judgment."

"*Nyet*, you pitter and patter like your sisters, pretending to play at games where you hardly know the players much less the rules." Borund waved a hand at the cabin door. "Go. I can't stomach to look at you. Get belowdecks and stay there until we meet with the *Fierga*."

The *Fierga* was an old warship that had been relegated to patrol duty around Vostroma. Atiana was surprised it had been sent, and even more surprised it had made the journey across the Neck. Still, it made it clear that Mother had ordered her home, and this was something she could not allow.

Summoning all the authority she could muster, Atiana stood and stared at Borund squarely. "I would stay, Borund. I wish to remain until the conflict is over."

"And I might have allowed it if our Matra hadn't already spoken. You will return home, Atiana."

"Let me stay until I can speak with her."

He shook his head. "Mother has been awake for nearly a week preparing for this day. Her hands are full, and as soon as the violence has eased—which should be soon—she will sleep."

"A few days will matter little, Bora."

"I have given my word." Borund stood and pointed at the door again. "Now go."

Atiana stood, her shoulders square, refusing to move.

"Go!"

She knew that to stay and argue would only harden his stance, so she bowed her head and left the cabin, hoping she could speak with him once more before she left, though she already knew that if she did his answer would be the same.

When Atiana reached the *Fierga*, the kapitan of the ship escorted her to an empty cabin, a spare place that smelled of garlic and windsmen. It was a room that was meant to sleep four, but with only a skeleton crew aboard, there was plenty of room to spare.

She sat there for a long while, wondering how she was going to escape, when she heard a scratching at the oval window. She opened it to find a black rook flapping its wings to remain standing on the narrow sill. It was Zoya, Mother's favorite. It hopped down to the floor and then flapped its wings to sit upon one of the top bunks.

Atiana bowed her head. "Matra."

The old rook cawed. "I see you made it back alive. Perhaps next time you won't be so quick to ignore our warnings."

After a moment of confusion, Atiana recognized Ishkyna's biting tone, even through the raw voice of the rook.

"You said you'd never take the dark again."

"And leave my poor sister alone in the world? Never."

Atiana scoffed. "I should burn this old rook while you writhe inside it."

The rook craned its neck and cawed. "Why, because we gave you more time to do what you needed to do?"

"You *left me* on Khalakovo."

"A place you clearly wanted to remain."

"The Duke nearly *murdered* me."

"But he did not. It would have been an utterly foolish thing to do."

"*Da*, and men think so clearly when their blood has risen."

"The Duke of Khalakovo, no matter how much you might admire him, dear sister, is nothing if not calm of heart. He might have tried to scare Father—he might have even meant in his heart to kill you—but his tender soul would not allow it." By *tender*, she meant weak, something she had said while referring to Atiana, as if tenderness were a vice to be rooted out as quickly and efficiently as one could. The rook stretched its chipped beak wide, shook its head furiously, and continued. "Now that I think of it, it was a terribly apt union Mother had arranged. Too bad it will never happen now."

Atiana reached up and grasped the body of the rook, pinning the wings tight. "If you've only come to chide me"—she moved toward the open window—"then I'd rather be alone."

The bird pecked at her hand. Atiana ignored it until blood was drawn from her knuckle, at which point she flung the rook away. It flapped to the floor and hopped back up to its previous position on the uppermost bunk. "So defensive, sister. I'd have thought you'd be glad to have company aboard a ship like this."

"Not if all you're offering are barbs."

The rook cawed. "Barbs aside, I did want to make sure you were healthy and hale. We were worried."

Atiana laughed. It was as close to an apology as she was going to get from Ishkyna. "You can see well enough I've made it through the war alive."

"War… This is hardly more than posturing, Tiana. A rustling of feathers."

"Says the woman speaking from the depths of Galostina."

"Well, since you're in the thick of it, why don't you share with your dear sister what you were about? Surely the need for secrecy has passed—or are those pretty lips still sealed?"

Atiana could ill afford to give her sister too much, so she gave bits and pieces: her time in Radiskoye, her escape through the sea, the mad dash through Volgorod and the explosion at the bridge—only enough of what really happened to appease her and only because she had to give information in order to get it.

"And what now?" Atiana asked when she was done. "What has happened to the eyrie?"

"If you couldn't guess by my presence, the eyrie is ours."

"And Radiskoye?"

"It has been left intact for the time being. The attack on the eyrie was largely symbolic. The true threats are the ships massing near Mirkotsk."

"Then why take it now?"

"To pressure Khalakovo to step down peaceably. Father has said that he would accept a written declaration of fault, a ceding of his seat to Ranos, and a grant of a dozen ships."

"Iaros will never agree to that."

"Don't be so sure. No one wants war, least of all the most remote of the Duchies. Rhavanki and Khazabyirsk have been even harder struck by the blight than we have, and Lhudansk practically begged Khalakovo to settle this before Father left. The only Duchy that has any strength of will and the canvas to back it up is Mirkotsk, but even they would stop beating the drums of war if an opportunity for peace presented itself. Khalakovo knows this, and even if he *does* urge for an attack, he knows it may push Lhudansk to step down, and if one goes, all will follow."

"You underestimate Saphia. She is a persuasive woman."

The rook bobbed its head up and down, releasing a ragged call. It sounded more than a little like Ishkyna's grating laugh. "You have not seen much of her since the attack, Tiana. She is feeble now, both in heart and in mind. She can hardly take the dark for more than a few hours at a time."

This was surprising and unsettling news. Atiana had thought Saphia a woman who would never weaken, never break. But perhaps her ordeal with Nasim had been more taxing than she would have guessed.

"Shkyna, I need your help."

The bird flapped its wings, a small loss of control by the inexperienced Ishkyna at this sudden and perhaps unexpected request for help. "What could a young bride need from an old matron like me?"

"Do not jest. My need is great."

The rook stared at her for a long time. Its eyes blinked, as if Ishkyna were trying to measure the truth in her words but was having difficulty through the foreign eyes of the rook. It reminded Atiana of Ishkyna so much that she felt suddenly homesick, and the cumulative weight of the events since she had arrived on Khalakovo threatened to bury her. She nearly cried, but this was not a time for such a thing. She needed now more than ever to keep her mind to the task at hand.

"I need you to speak with the kapitan. I need you to tell him that we are to return to Duzol and for him to leave me there."

"And why would the kapitan believe…"

The rook stopped. Ishkyna had realized what Atiana meant for her to do. She wanted Ishkyna to present herself not as the *daughter* of the Matra, but as the Matra herself. The old kapitan had worn a soulstone around his neck, but he was a lesser officer, a man relegated not just to the rear of the blockade, but to transport duty—hardly a position of importance—and so the Matra would hardly know him and he would hardly know her.

"He will see through it," Ishkyna said.

"You know better, Shkyna. Have you even *heard* of Kapitan Malorov?"

"I am not the Matra."

Atiana was surprised. There was fear in her sister's voice. She would have to be careful. "Mother keeps as much track of the military as you or I do. You have little to worry about there."

"What if she touched stones with all of them before they left?"

"As quickly as the blockade was cobbled together? Unlikely, and I'm surprised at you. I thought you'd be eager to spread dissent in this—how did you put it?—farce of a war…"

"Farce or not, Mother would find out soon enough what I'd done."

"And you'll simply tell her the truth, that I asked to go."

"For what purpose?"

"Unfinished affairs."

"Nikandr?"

"I'll reveal everything when I return to Vostroma."

The rook flapped over to the open window and clucked. "I'm afraid, sister, that this is something I cannot do. I may like to pull at loose strings, but this is too much."

"Shkyna, please! It will work."

"I know it will work. I'm worried about my hide once it has."

"Mother won't do a thing."

"*Nyet*, but Father will. He has changed as much as Borund. It's too much to ask. When you reach the island, we'll play trump—you and I and Mileva, like we always have. You'll be a world away from your troubles, and in no time you'll forget Nikandr and his stubborn family."

"Ishkyna!"

The rook had already flapped out of the window. Atiana watched it wing through the rigging and climb higher into the overcast sky until it was lost in the white canvas of the landward sails.

CHAPTER 54

Rehada entered the mouth of the cave at dusk. The height of it was so low that she had to bend over to reach the interior. She could smell wood burning, and when she turned a corner she found the source. In the center of the natural cavern burned a meager fire. The smoke trailed upward and was lost through a long crack in the stone ceiling. Soroush kneeled on the far side, pointedly ignoring her approach as he stirred the fire with a partially burnt switch. When his brother, Bersuq, saw her, he stood and motioned for the two others sitting next to him to follow. They were forced to hunch over, making them look like a line of the walking wounded.

Rehada kneeled on the opposite side of the fire and watched as the orange light played across Soroush's dark skin. His turban lay on top of his folded outer robe. His long black hair was pulled over one shoulder.

"Where is Muwas?" Soroush asked without looking up.

"Taken. Burned."

The silence between them lengthened, deepened. Soroush had been burned himself five years ago. Rehada could only imagine what it must feel like, to be cut off from touching Adhiya, to never again feel the bond with a hezhan. It would be an empty life. At least for a while. Perhaps forever.

Rehada reached into the pouch at her waist and retrieved the azurite gemstone. It was smooth, no larger than a thrush's egg, and even though she wasn't aligned with water, she could feel the power emanating from within it.

"At least he was able to find this for us." She set it down near the fire, close enough for Soroush to reach.

He picked it up, turned it in his fingers as the firelight played against the silken surface. "You witnessed it, the burning?"

"I did."

"You did nothing to protect him?"

"I—there was nothing I could have done."

"Nothing?"

"You were not there, Soroush. He was caught with blood upon his hands."

After setting the stone down next to the fire, Soroush regarded Rehada. "The woman I knew—the woman I sent to this island seven years ago— would have fought for his freedom."

"You would prefer that I had? That I were dead like Ahya?"

Anger flared in his gray-green eyes. "I've never told you, Rehada, but the men who murdered Ahya… Nearly all of them are dead, most by my hand. It took years, and by the time you left for Khalakovo, I had begun to feel thin, worn down, as I do now. Like a hawk no longer hungry for prey, my thirst for revenge faded."

She glanced toward the cave's entrance, making sure the other men had truly left. She had never heard Soroush speak this way. His anger was fading before her very eyes.

"And if my own thirst is thus," he continued, "I wonder what it must be like for you."

"You think I don't have the stomach for it any longer?"

"Our minds are not made for such things."

"My mind is as filled with hate as it has ever been."

Soroush shook his head. "I doubt that, daughter of Shineshka."

"You doubt that I would wipe them from the islands if I could?"

"If it were so easy as that, neh, I think you would. But it is not easy. It is harder than I ever thought it would be. And I have seen the same struggle within you—don't think I haven't. The Aramahn are a clean people, are we not? But it is impossible to lie in the mud and not have it cling to you when at last you rise."

"What of you?" Rehada shot back. "How can you go on if your will has left?"

Soroush was silent for a time. The fire had begun to die, but he stoked it back to life. "There was an attack years ago on Nodhvyansk. Lohram and Bersuq and I had just landed on the island, and we heard of a group of our people being chased by a Landed warship. We didn't find the windship in time, but we found the six who had fallen to their deaths when their skiff was blown to bits by the ship's cannons.

"One of them, a woman who had seen eighty years, had nearly saved herself. We found her lying in the tall grasses, the gem within her circlet dim, her body broken. She took my hand as I knelt next to her and looked into my eyes. She could barely take breath, but she forced these words out before she died: 'Forgive them… Please, child, forgive them. Do not take revenge on my account.' I asked her how she could say such things when those men had caused the deaths of so many she had loved, and she said: 'Because I love them as much as I love you.'" Soroush took in a deep, halting breath. "She loved *them* as much as she loved *me*. I stayed by her side until she died, but I will not lie and say that I comforted her. I hated her. I hated the words she had spoken, not because she could find it within herself to love those that deserve none of it, but because the Landed have forced us to this, squabbling amongst ourselves while they take everything.

"It is easy for me to sustain myself now. I admit that I do not think of Ahya as often as I should, but I think of that woman every day. I think of her and reflect on what has become of us. I long for the day we can move freely among the winds, as we once did, but I no longer believe it will happen in this lifetime."

Rehada watched Soroush with a mixture of sadness and regret and anger. She wished the same determination ran through her veins, but she had to admit—to herself if no one else—that it no longer did. Something had been burned out of her by the lake when she had asked Atiana for forgiveness. She saw—for the first time in a very long time—some of the promise that her mother had spoken of when she was young. She had believed that the Landed would eventually reconcile with the Aramahn. It may take lifetimes, she'd told Rehada, but it would happen.

Without saying another word, Rehada stood and held her hand out to Soroush. He stared, the fire and the shadows warring against his face, and then he dropped the blackened switch into the fire and followed her to the blankets that lay on the far side of the cave.

With slow deliberation they pulled the clothes from their bodies until it was just the two of them, skin-on-skin, embracing and kissing, then exploring and finally groping. Rehada lay down, pulling Soroush with her. When he entered her she arched her back both in pleasure and in pain. Soroush had always been a gentle lover, but he thrust into her powerfully now. It felt as though he was filled with anger—or perhaps regret—that they might never see each other again.

The same emotions took hold of her. She pulled him tight against her chest and ran her nails down his back. He thrust harder. She pulled his hair and bit his neck. Each thrust felt like an accusation. She cried out, knowing in her heart it was true. She had strayed from the path they had started on together, and after this night, they would walk on paths that would never converge, only cross.

As he spent himself inside her, releasing an urgent groan through clenched teeth, she held him tight and gripped his waist with her legs and pulled him deep inside her and surrendered a muffled cry of her own into his long black hair.

Slowly, they fell from the heights to which they had risen, and soon they had fallen asleep in each other's arms.

When Rehada woke in the early morning hours, Soroush was snoring softly next to her. There was no light coming into the cavern, and the fire had gone cold, so she lit the darkness with the gem held within her circlet. Soroush's face was filled with worry; she could tell from his eyes that he was dreaming.

As softly as she could, she pulled on her clothes and left the cave. The wind outside was cold. The ephemeral summer of the islands was coming to a close once more, and soon the winds of autumn would descend upon them, a harbinger of the bitter winds yet to come. The eastern horizon was awash in indigo, and it would soon be light. She had to be far away from here by the time he woke.

She had just started down the trail leading toward the lowland forest below her when she caught movement from the corner of her eye.

Soroush stood naked at the mouth of the cave.

She had been sure last night that he had decided to let her go, but as he stood there, his eyes judgmental and his stance rigid, she wondered whether he had changed his mind. She wondered whether, once she had given him what he wanted, he would kill her as he had done to so many traitors to the cause.

She realized that she didn't care. If he would kill her, then it would be so. And yet, another part of her hoped that he would succeed. It was why, despite her better judgment, she had given him the azurite stone.

She turned and began walking away.

"I know where he is," Soroush said. "I can feel him. We will have him before the day is out."

She stopped in her tracks. She did not turn around, however. She couldn't find it in herself to look at him—whether it was from fear of what he would do or a doubt that she lacked conviction to leave him she didn't know. She realized in those small moments of silence just how lonely Soroush must be if he would call to her, even now, hoping that she might return.

"You need only one stone, then," she said.

"*Neh.*"

A chill ran down her spine. She turned, slowly, to find Soroush holding a rounded opal, beautiful to behold even in the thin morning light.

"How long have you had it?"

"Months," he said simply. "I liberated it on Rhavanki when the first of the hezhan was summoned."

The pieces began forming quickly within Rehada's mind. "When will it happen?"

"Tomorrow."

One day, then. One day was all that stood between Soroush and the culmination of his plans.

She turned away from him, knowing she must leave now. As she continued down the rocky trail, she could feel him watching her. She could feel the bond they once shared fading, slipping through her fingers like sand, and she was not at all sure that this was what she wanted.

But she had chosen, and so had he.

She headed south among the leafy trees as the sun touched the horizon. She had thoughts of returning to Iramanshah, but the truth was that she had no idea how she might be received. There was no telling what Muwas might have told them. It was ironic—though not surprising—that the people from whom she had worked so hard to distance herself, her *own* people, were not the ones she could turn to in this time of desperate need.

Her thoughts turned to Ashan and Nasim and Nikandr. Everything now rested with them, and she had learned practically nothing of them since they'd left Volgorod. It was with this dire need for information that her destination was resolved.

Radiskoye.

It was the last place she'd ever thought to find herself turning for help. It was a place she once, given the chance, would have burned to the ground. But times had changed. *She* had changed. And everything now rode on her ability to reach them.

CHAPTER 55

As Nikandr sat within one of the holds aboard the *Kavda*, the ship dipped and rose, dipped and rose. His stomach heaved. A pewter pot of water hung from a hook on the ceiling, but he didn't have the heart to drink any more of it. It would only fuel his nausea.

They had been caught in a windstorm for over a day, but it felt like weeks. He had long since emptied his stomach onto the floorboards. He had thought himself a stout windsman, but he had always taken to the deck when things got bad. Never had he remained belowdecks—unable to gauge the winds—for more than a few hours at a time, and now that he had it had gotten to him.

Someone coughed. Nikandr looked up at Ervan and two of his men who were bracing themselves in the corner of the hold. They looked as sick as Nikandr felt. Other than Jahalan, Ashan, and Nasim—who were being kept in another hold somewhere on the ship—they were all that remained of the crew that he had brought with him on the *Gorovna*. He looked away, unable to hold Ervan's gaze.

So many had died, but it was Pietr that occupied his mind the most. The others had died trying to save themselves, but Pietr—if Ashan was to be believed—had given himself willingly that Nikandr might live.

"Where do you think they're taking us?" Ervan asked, his voice a croak.

It took Nikandr some time before he could reply, for his stomach always grew queasy with words. "I doubt—I doubt they would bring us to Vostroma. Grigory will—want to flaunt his prize"—he coughed—"in front of the dukes. And Vostroma, no doubt, will want to use me as a bargaining chip."

Through the floorboards Nikandr could feel and hear wooden gears turning. Finally there came a heavy thud. Immediately the ship began to turn, to right itself so that it was once again aligned with the ley lines running from Vostroma to Khalakovo. They had reached the currents where the ship's keel could once again be used to maneuver the ship—as it was meant to be—and even though this meant they were close to being handed over to the traitor dukes, Nikandr didn't care. He would give almost anything for a break from the incessant movement.

Eventually, the ship began to glide more surely on the wind, and Nikandr took heart, taking it as a good omen despite their circumstances.

A short while later, a muffled cawing filtered down into the bowels of the ship. The rooks often called this way when landing on a ship, but the sounds kept going and going. It was ragged and raw and desperate, and he wondered whether someone was trying to kill the thing. Yelling could be heard over the bird's caws, and though it was difficult to tell for certain, it sounded like Grigory. It continued for some time, the voice becoming higher in pitch and urgency.

Footsteps rushed down the hallway a short time later. Three streltsi opened the door and ordered Nikandr and Ervan up to the deck. They were led to the rear of the ship where standing over Nasim was Grigory holding a cocked pistol.

An old rook was flapping around the deck like a fish. After a moment, Nikandr recognized the old, miserable thing. It was missing one foot and had been with the Bolgravyas for more than two decades. Brunhald was its name, and it had seemed old when he had first laid eyes on it as a boy, now it seemed positively ancient—its feathers ragged, a bald patch on the back of its head, its beak chipped and misshapen.

Grigory, who was more used to the wasting than most, stared at Nikandr with a faint look of disgust, as if he didn't dare step too close lest the wasting take him as well. He pointed the pistol at Nikandr's chest. "What has he done?"

Nikandr shook his head, confused.

"Tell me! What has this Motherless wretch done?"

Nasim had done something similar to Nikandr's mother when she'd attempted to assume him, and he wondered whether Alesya had just attempted the same thing. He debated on whether or not to tell Grigory, but before he could say anything, Grigory stepped over to Ervan and pulled him by the arm to the gunwale.

When he stepped back and pointed the pistol at Ervan's chest, Nikandr raised his hands in submission and said, "*Nyet*, Grigory! All right! My mother suffered something similar when I left Radiskoye!"

"What had the boy done?"

Nikandr tried to convey his confusion as best he could, if only to get Grigory to lower the weapon. "She had been studying him"—Nikandr could not, with the Aramahn close by, admit that his mother had tried to assume the boy—"and Nasim found her. He fought her and struck her dumb just before Borund took me away."

The rook continued to flap and caw and scratch its stump of a leg against the deck.

"How?" Grigory's voice was practically hysterical. "How can he do this? The Landless do not ride the aether."

"I don't know."

Grigory's face hardened. "You *do* know!" He shook the pistol at Ervan's chest. "Now tell me!"

Nikandr tried to find an explanation that would appease him, but the truth was he didn't know the nature of the bond himself. Had he been able to speak with his mother or Atiana or even Victania he might have been able to understand it more fully, but other than the dream he had had on the *Gorovna*, he had not given it much thought. He hadn't had the time.

In his loss for words he could see the decision in Grigory as he turned his gaze upon Ervan.

The muscles along his forearm tightened.

"*Nyet*!" Nikandr screamed.

The gun roared.

Grigory's wrist recoiled.

A burst of red appeared at the center of Ervan's chest and he fell backward over the gunwale, his eyes wide with shock.

The smell of gunpowder laced the air, and then was gone like so much dust upon the wind.

The following moments passed with the sounds of cawing and the wind whipping over the ship. Nikandr stared into Grigory's eyes and found smugness there, as if to say Nikandr had been asking for this ever since Stasa Bolgravya had been murdered.

But then something caught Nikandr's attention, and it drew him back from the urge to rush Grigory if only to strike him once before being shot. Above Grigory's shoulders, slipping from one bright cloud to another, was a ship. It was far off, but it was using the clouds to hide its approach. He refused to look at it directly, not wanting to draw attention, but he dearly hoped it was a ship allied to his father's cause. And so, in an instant, he made a decision. He had to delay. He had to give the ship time so that he and the rest of the crew might still be saved.

Grigory, perhaps nervous now that he had no weapon with which to defend himself, held out his hand and received from a nearby strelet a loaded pistol to replace the one he'd just fired. As soon as he had the weapon in hand he stared down at the deck. The old rook was no longer cawing, nor was it moving.

Grigory's face went white as he stared at the bird.

"The same happened to Higald, my mother's strongest and most prized rook," Nikandr lied. "No doubt the bond was severed when the rook died."

"You lie," Grigory said, his red face examining Nikandr's for any reason to raise the weapon and fire it on either him or Nasim.

Nikandr went on, "I would not lie about a thing such as this. The Matri are above all." The sentiment for the Matri was generally the same all over the islands, but he chose the phrasing that ruled in the south, hoping the note of familiarity would draw Grigory down from his perch.

"How do you know she recovered?"

"She found me, on the way to Ghayavand, and we spoke for a short time."

As if just remembering his own soulstone, Grigory pulled it out from his shirt and held it in his hand.

"I cannot feel her."

"It was the same with me." This was true, but it had been because the power in his soulstone had been all but extinguished at the time.

Incredibly, the bird raised its head and scratched at the deck. A moment later it pulled in its wings and lay there, its chest expanding and contracting slowly. It looked sickly, as though it could just as easily die as pull in another breath.

"You see," Nikandr said, "if the bird lives, then your mother surely does too."

"We will see. If I find you have lied to me—"

His next words were cut short by an explosion of wood at the bow. A moment later, the boom of a cannon rent the still air. Another volley of grape shot tore into the ship. Two more rang out in succession, cutting huge holes into the starward sails. One sailor screamed as he fell from a yardarm. He missed the deck and continued to plummet toward open sea.

Grigory spun and fell to the deck, grimacing in pain and holding his left arm tightly. In moments his shoulder was swathed in red.

A bell rang out over and over as the crew rushed to their stations. The streltsi manned the fore and aft gun positions, preparing the stout iron cannons to fire upon the two ships that were bearing down on them from above.

Nikandr's heart sank as he took them in. They were not Khalakovan, nor Bolgravyan. They weren't from any the Grand Duchies.

They were Maharraht.

They were small, fast-moving ships with two small gun emplacements, fore and aft. With superior numbers they were a good match for the *Kavda* and her three guns, but with the *Kavda* now hampered by the damage, it was going to be a slaughter.

Though he didn't know for certain why the Maharraht had come, it was too much of a coincidence to ignore the fact that they were attacking the very ship that held Nasim. They would probably want the boy alive, perhaps Ashan as well, but the rest would be put to death.

Seeing that he was all but forgotten, a rough plan formed in his mind. He grabbed Nasim and pulled him to the ladder leading belowdecks. The ship was already listing aftward. With so many holes already cut into the starward sails the seaward winds were pushing the ship off balance. If Grigory were not both very careful and very lucky, this was going to be a short battle indeed.

"Wait here," he told Nasim and then he sprinted down the passageway beyond where his men were being kept. Common men such as they would not be harmed and there was little they could provide in the way of information that Grigory didn't already know. In order to give the *Kavda* time to escape, it was crucial that the Maharraht see Nasim escaping, but they also needed to be highly mobile in order to move fast enough to evade pursuit.

He reached a door secured by an iron padlock. He kicked the door in and found Ashan kneeling on the floor next to Jahalan, who was unconscious but breathing evenly.

"Come," Nikandr said, knowing that if Jahalan were not able to move on his own he would have to be left behind.

"Where is Nasim?"

Nikandr pointed up the passageway as another volley struck the deck above them. "He is close. Now come, unless you want to give him up to the Maharraht after all we've been through."

Ashan frowned, but stood and followed Nikandr to the ladder. Nasim was cowering there, holding the ladder tightly. He left him to Ashan and climbed to the top of the ladder as another volley tore into the *Kavda*. One man's screams were cut short as sporadic musket fire began falling on them from above.

Grigory, holding his bloody shoulder tightly, was standing below the helm as a fat sailor maneuvered the three stout steering levers.

"Descend!" Grigory yelled. "Descend!"

Nikandr ducked out of sight as Grigory turned and ran toward the fore of the ship.

Clearly he hoped to gain speed by dropping down near sea level, but if he wasn't careful, they would end up *in* the sea, not riding the currents above it.

As the ship began its descent, another volley howled in from the attacking ships. A series of groans and cracks rent the air. The starward mainmast was tilting to port. Some of the rigging snapped and the mast fell to the deck, shattering the wooden railing. Without the mast connected to the bulk of the ship, the windwood had lost its buoyancy quickly but was still acting as weight upon the ship.

Nasim, two rungs lower, began to whimper. Ashan held him close, shushing into his ear.

"Prepare yourself," Nikandr said to Ashan. "On the next volley, we will move quickly and quietly to the kapitan's cabin."

The next volley crashed into ship moments later. Nikandr climbed out and ran aft to the ship's rear cabin as another shot struck the yardarm and sails just above him.

Ashan followed with Nasim in tow. The door was not locked, and they ducked inside as quickly as they could. No alarms were raised, so it appeared they were safe for the moment.

Chopping sounds rang throughout the ship—the crew attempting to hack the rigging lines. It wouldn't work, Nikandr thought to himself. They were going to fall into the sea and then he would die in this cabin. It was possible Grigory and some of his crew would be captured by the Maharraht and be held for ransom, but it was just as likely that once they had found Nasim—dead or alive—the rest would be left to the sea.

As Nikandr began searching the cabin for his soulstone and for Ashan's gems, the ship's descent began to slow—the workings of Grigory's two havaqiram, no doubt, but it would be too late.

Then a sound of cracking wood and whipping ropes and the hollow thud of tackle was heard. All three of them were thrown against the floorboards as a ragged cheer rose on the deck. Their deceleration slowed, but Nikandr could no longer tell whether they had leveled or had started to climb again.

He found what he was looking for in a small, unlocked chest in the lowest drawer of the kapitan's desk. He pulled his soulstone on and gave the bracelets, anklets, and circlet to Ashan.

Ashan stared at them. "What can we hope to do now?"

"You can summon the winds as you did on Zhabyn's ship. We'll take a skiff and escape."

Ashan was already shaking his head. "I released the bond to my havahezhan on Ghayavand. It is not so easy to forge another."

"You must try, Ashan. It is our only hope."

"There is much you must do before you can—"

"If you cannot, then we must submit to the Maharraht."

"You may not realize it, Nikandr Iaroslov, but you cannot bond a hezhan simply by willing it so."

Nikandr's heart began to sink, but it quickly turned to horror when he realized Nasim had opened the door to the cabin and was walking out onto the deck.

"Nasim," he whispered harshly, "come back!"

They rushed forward just as a huge gust of wind blew across the deck. One moment, Nasim was framed within the cabin doorway, his hair and clothes whipping about, and the next he was whisked upward and away like a withered leaf by a brisk autumn wind. Nikandr ran to the doorway and was blown off his feet as the wind shrieked. He slipped along the decking and struck the gunwale, but he saw Nasim tumbling up into the sky.

"Nasim!"

He continued to fly higher in the sky toward one of the Maharraht ships.

The forward guns shot upward at the ship, but Nikandr screamed at them to cease firing. "Do not harm the boy!"

Grigory, standing near the center of the ship, looked at him, dumbfounded, and then stared upward as Nasim slipped over the top of the ship and was lost from sight. Immediately the ship turned to port and set a southward course to follow in the wake of its sister ship.

CHAPTER 56

When Atiana woke, it was to the sound of her door opening. By the light of early dawn she saw Kapitan Malorov standing there, his stubbled face grim, his eyes judgmental. "Come," he said gruffly.

The air on deck was crisp, and the wind was strong. Summer had nearly ended, and soon the skies would be filled with high clouds and terrible winds in preparation for the long winter. Below the ship was an island. Atiana was confused at first—it should have taken days to reach Vostroma—but as she looked at the island she began to understand. This was Duzol, the smaller island south of Uyadensk. The shape of it was unmistakable, as was the small spire that rested in Oshtoyets, a keep standing on the edge of a broad set of white cliffs.

She turned and saw the larger island in the distance. She also saw a handful of circling windships—they looked like little more than insects from this distance.

She was ushered into a skiff, where an Aramahn woman, no older than Atiana, waited. Once she was aboard, the skiff's mooring ropes were released and it drifted away from the body of the old warship. The journey was silent as the woman fought with the ropes and the single sail to guide the ship landward. They reached the grassy flatland of Duzol's coast in short order, and soon Atiana was left alone, watching the skiff as it floated up toward the ship.

Her attention was taken by the flapping wings of the old rook, Zoya. It winged down from beneath the ship and glided in an ungraceful arc as it fought the stiff wind every bit of the way. It beat the air as it landed, and then studied Atiana with something akin to amusement.

"Enough, Ishkyna. What have you done?"

"You give her too much credit," said the rook.

"Mileva?"

The rook cawed. "Ishkyna and I spoke upon her return, and I must say

I was so taken by your plight that I felt forced to help."

"*Nyet*, sister. You felt guilty."

"And why would I feel guilt?"

"For abandoning me," Atiana said.

The rook clucked and bobbed its head. "Very well. Perhaps I felt you were owed something for what might have happened in Radiskoye. But perhaps one day you'll thank me when you discover the new arrangements that Mother has made for you."

"What arrangements?"

"I'm surprised our dear brother hasn't told you."

"Must you always play games?"

The caw it released was so loud it made Atiana cringe. "Your new husband, Tiana. Mother has decided it with Alesya."

Alesya was Stasa Bolgravya's wife and the Matra of Bolgravya. If Mother had made arrangements with *her*, it could only mean that Atiana's marriage to Nikandr had been cast aside in favor of one of Alesya's brood, and that, of course, meant that her hand had been promised to Grigory.

"Never," Atiana said, and she meant it, more than she thought she might at such a thing. She had taken her marriage to Nikandr lightly, almost as more of a jest than anything else, but she had come to see a side of Nikandr that she never thought she would: he was a good man, an honest man, a man she could be proud of.

"Perhaps so, sister, but you had better begin to work magic if you hope to change your fate."

"Why?"

"Because Nikandr is being held at the top of the cliff, in the donjon of Oshtoyets."

"It cannot be."

"He was found and captured by Grigory on Ghayavand."

"And the boy?" If Nasim had been found, too, then there was a chance that they might be able to step away from the edge of war. They might be able to repair the damage caused by her father and the other headstrong dukes.

"The *Kavda* was attacked by the Maharraht. They took him."

Atiana's heart sank, more for the implications than the loss. The fact that the Maharraht had taken the boy would make it look like a rescue—as if the boy had been a tool of theirs from the beginning—and in truth she wondered if that might not be the case.

"Go," the rook said. "Find a way to save your husband if you can, and I, in turn, will consider my debt paid. Oh, and give my regards to Grigory..."

With that the ebony bird flapped away, up toward the ship that was already a half-league distant.

Atiana turned and regarded the formidable hill. Only the tip of the spire could be seen from her vantage. It was all serious climbing, unless she wanted to head further up the beach, but that would take too long, and her gut told her there was little time to spare.

Atiana stood in the courtyard of the small, stone-walled fort as the po-lupolkovnik left to inform Grigory of her arrival. Given its inhospitable nature, the dukes would no doubt have taken refuge in a large manor house a few leagues south, but she was sure that if Nikandr was being kept here that Grigory would remain as well. Even as a boy, he had always been one to gloat, and now, even though he was older, he felt the need to make a name for himself, to do things that would attract notice no matter how overreaching they might seem.

Grigory arrived a few minutes later, still buttoning a coat that had once been fine but was now sullied by dirt and stains. It was clear that one arm was wounded, for he was using only one arm to button the coat while the other hung limp at his side.

"My dear Atiana. I was given no warning of your arrival."

Atiana smiled. "As was my wish."

"I don't understand. Your father told me of your rescue only last night. He said that you were being brought back to Vostroma."

"*Da*, that is what he believed."

"Then forgive me, but how have you come to be here?"

"My dear Grigory, have you been informed of our pending marriage?"

Grigory's awkward smile warred with the confusion in his eyes. "Of course."

"And so have I, and if you think that I would allow myself to be carted away to safety before speaking with you, then you are sadly mistaken."

His smile grew more confident. "I thought you would not approve."

Atiana returned his smile, but she took care not to let things go too far—if her plan was to have any chance of success Grigory had to be convinced of her lies. "I don't *know* if I approve, which is exactly the point."

He laughed. "Do tell."

Atiana shrugged and took a half-step closer so that she was just within arm's reach. "There was a wisdom of sorts in the alliance with Khalakovo, but I had always thought that a marriage within the southern duchies would be wiser."

The look on Grigory's face was composed, but he was disappointed.

"And," she continued, smiling briefly, "I have always thought that we were cut from the same cloth. Haven't you?"

"I…" He swallowed. "I will admit that I have, but I must also admit that

I never imagined you thought the same way. You have always seemed so...
distant."

"Out of necessity, Grigory. My mother told me when I was fifteen that I
would one day be married to a man from the north. How could I reveal my
true feelings knowing that? Now please, are you going to keep me in this
infernal wind the entire day or are you going to invite me in for a drink?"

"Please"—he motioned toward the keep—"forgive me. Manners are the
first thing to go in times of war."

As they walked side by side toward the iron-studded door to the keep
proper, Atiana said, "I had no idea we were at war."

"Do you smell peace in the air?"

Atiana held her tongue as they headed inside. She had thought at first that
Grigory was merely boasting for her benefit, but he seemed too proud of
his words. "There will be little bloodshed in the days to come. Khalakovo
will see reason."

They walked down the short, cold corridor to a room that held little more
than a table and an unkempt bed in one corner. If Grigory had been the one
to capture Nikandr, then no doubt he would also have his soulstone, and
she doubted that there would be any place that he would keep it other than
here in his chambers—however temporary they may be. She did not see,
however, an obvious place where it might be kept other than the wardrobe
in one corner or the stout chest that sat at the foot of the bed.

Grigory closed the door and motioned her to the table. She took her own
chair since Grigory didn't seem willing to pull it out for her.

"If all there was to this story was Khalakovo you might well have been
right." From a small table behind the door Grigory retrieved a dark blue
bottle of vodka and two glazed mugs. "But there is much more that we
might gain."

He poured two drinks, grimacing as his wounded shoulder was put to
work, and handed one to her. As he sat, he downed half his drink, swishing
it around noisily before swallowing.

Atiana sipped at hers, being careful not to raise her nose at the sour bite
from the liquor. "If you attack, the other dukes will come to his aid."

Grigory smiled. "When you wish to kill a wolf, you do not go stumbling
through the forest after it. You set out meat and wait for the scent of it to
drive the wolf beyond caution."

"The dukes are no pack of wolves, Grigory, nor are their Matri."

"They'll have no choice. They cannot allow Khalakovo to fall."

"But Borund said you have given Iaros a choice. If he steps down, you
will not attack."

"First, Iaros would never do such a thing." He downed the last of his vodka and slapped the mug down onto the table. "Never. Second, your brother has left out an important detail. We demanded the boy as proof of their sincerity."

"They don't *have* the boy."

The grin that Grigory pasted onto his face was one that Atiana dearly wished she could wipe from it. "Just so."

"So our fathers and the other dukes would tear down the north so they can what? Install their own men in their stead?"

"Is there any other choice?"

"It cannot hold."

"Neither can the status quo. Did you know, Atiana, that while you were holed up in Radiskoye, there were food riots on Nodhvyansk and Bolgravya?"

Atiana tried to hide her surprise. "I did not."

"One of them on Tolvodyen lasted four days. And while it is clear that the Maharraht are focusing their attention on Khalakovo—ancients only know why—they still have enough strength to stage a crippling raid on a keep in Dhalingrad."

"Times are hard."

"This is my point." The vein along the side of Grigory's forehead pulsed heavily. "There is no room for error in the seasons to come. If we do not do something, there will be nothing left. For anyone."

"So why not take what we want…"

"*Da!* Why not? You may not have noticed while playing trump with your sisters, but Khalakovo has been lording their advantage over your father and the rest of us for decades. It is time that came to an end. It is time for the balance to shift."

As he reached forward to pour himself another drink, Atiana was drawn by something shifting within his shirt. She had seen his chain when he had walked out to meet her, but she had paid no attention. Nearly all the men in the Grand Duchy wore their soulstones on stout chains such as his, but she realized now that he didn't wear just one chain; he wore two.

One held Grigory's stone, of course, but she knew now that the other held Nikandr's. It only made sense. He was in an unfamiliar place in a dangerous time. He would want such a prize close at all times. Plus, it would feed his fragile ego, lording Nikandr's stone like a prize. It was not normally done, as the stone, despite its long affiliation to Nikandr, would be imprinted with some of Grigory's soul, his thoughts. When Nikandr was reunited with it, it would have a stain, a scent that would taint Nikandr's life for years to come.

Atiana quickly finished the last of her drink and placed the mug next to his. He paused, looking up at her with a harsh expression, but then he relaxed and filled both mugs a healthy amount.

Atiana shrugged as she accepted hers from him. "It's true. Khalakovo has been unrelenting in his diplomacy."

"You have a gift for understatement."

She allowed a smile to warm her face. "Well, then—how can I say this?— it's good to be in a place where I'm wanted." She held his gaze. "Assuming, of course, that I *am* wanted."

"Of you, I could say nothing else."

She glanced at the bed in the corner, utterly unsure of how she was going to get the necklace away from him. "It feels like years since I've been in a proper bed."

He stood, a token of gentlemanly behavior. "Do you wish to rest?"

"I am more tired than I have ever been, Bolgravya." She downed the last of her second glass of liquor, willing it to fill her so that she might be numb to at least a portion of what was to come. "But in all sincerity"—she stood, moving toward him until they were face to face; she set the mug down, allowing her free hand to run along the front of his shirt—"that is the furthest thing from my mind."

Nearly an hour later, they lay naked in his bed, Grigory snoring softly and Atiana fighting to stay awake. He had refused, even through their lovemaking, to remove his necklace. She had not forced the issue, for she hadn't wished to draw attention to it, but the time was nearing where either she would be sent inland or he would be called away for further duty.

She nuzzled closer, laying her hand on his hairless white chest, far away from the bandages that were wrapped around his right shoulder. When he did not stir, she picked up the soulstone that she had known to be deadened. She had seen it in the shattered hallway in Radiskoye just before Nikandr had left. How, then, had it regained life? Had it been that it had never been truly lifeless? Had it merely been a temporary effect? Nikandr had been so certain—surely if it had held even a single spark of life, he would have sensed it.

She placed her hand on the stone and lifted it. She was careful not to let the chain tickle his skin, though given the amount of liquor he had imbued, she doubted he would feel something so subtle.

She examined the chain and the setting. It was sound—as all such chains were made to be. She might be able to slip it over his head, but she would much rather remove only the stone, perhaps the setting as well, so that he would still feel the two chains around his neck and hopefully not notice the missing gem until it was too late.

Seeing no real alternative, she slipped out from underneath the covers and stood next to the bed, holding it for a moment to steady herself from the haze of alcohol running through her. She searched the room for anything that might help her, but it was so spare. There was a well-stocked liquor cabinet, clothes, two fish oil lanterns, some simple pottery, several leather-bound books... There was also a stack of orders containing the signature of her father, Zhabyn Olegov Vostroma. She paged through them, intrigued, but they were mundane—all of them detailing the supplies that were to be given to Grigory and his ship from the hastily constructed supply house here on Duzol.

Her heart jumped as Grigory shifted onto his side, both his stone and Nikandr's slipping down into the soft bedding. And then she spied his clothes lying on the floor next to the bed. On his black leather belt was a sheath that held his ceremonial kindjal. Her eyes darted between the blade and the stones, then she padded forward and slipped the kindjal free of its pristine leather sheath. Holding it behind her, she slipped back under the covers. She eyed the stones, pulling Nikandr's far enough away from Grigory's so that she would have enough room to do what she needed to do. Once she was satisfied with its position, she placed the tip of the knife onto the heavy link that connected the stone's setting to the chain itself. She held it with both hands and bore down on it with all her weight.

Either the knife was not sharp enough or the metal was too strong, for all that happened was that it pulled the bedding far enough that it roused Grigory. He lifted his arm and scratched his neck, but then he drifted back to sleep.

After counting slowly to thirty, she repositioned the stone and leaned on the knife again. She raised herself up higher and pressed her weight downward, hoping it would be enough to break the link. She tried again and again. On the fourth try, the link broke with an audible but muffled clink.

And then she looked up as Grigory sharply drew breath.

By the ancients, he was staring straight at her.

CHAPTER 57

Atiana was certain that Grigory would snatch the kindjal from her and plunge it into her chest—just as she had done with the necklace's link—but when she realized he was staring into her *eyes* she knew that he didn't yet understand what had woken him.

The kindjal had plunged down into the mattress so that by and large it was hidden. She shot forward, onto his chest, covering the knife with her belly as she kissed him passionately. She slid the knife up and underneath her now-vacant pillow as she climbed higher, allowing her breasts to brush against his arm and then his naked chest.

He grimaced in pain and pulled away, looking at her, not unkindly, but certainly not with the fervor of their one and only time between the sheets. He closed his eyes tightly and shook them open. "How long have I been asleep?"

She smiled the smile of the love-struck while searching delicately but with a growing sense of urgency for Nikandr's stone, which had slipped away in her attempts to divert Grigory's attention. "Who cares?"

"Atiana, please. Your father's men should be arriving sometime today to transfer your one-time fiancé to a manor house down the hill."

"Nikandr is *here*?"

He pulled the covers away and sat up, looming over her as she lay there. From the corner of her eye she saw the stone slip down into the depression his right knee was creating. She reached up and scratched his stomach to keep his attention riveted to her.

He nearly doubled over—a ticklish man—and climbed over her to reach the floor. Immediately she released her hold of the knife, trusting that a man like Grigory wouldn't adjust the pillows, and placed herself squarely on top of the stone.

"Would that interest you?"

Now that he was gone from the bed and pulling his clothes on, she allowed the expression upon her face to slip to one of concern, and then to anger. "Perhaps you didn't hear what happened on Radiskoye's eyrie, Griga, but a gun was held to my head, and Nikandr's father had his finger on the trigger. I know in my heart the craven nearly ended a woman's life because his son had been taken from him. I have words for his son—words about his father, words about Nikandr himself—that I would say to him before all of this is over."

"Then come, and we will visit him—"

"They are words for Nikandr alone…"

Grigory stopped as he was pulling on his belt. She thought he had noticed his knife missing, but he was staring directly at her. "*Nyet,*" he said with a satisfied smile. "Anything you wish to say to Nikandr you can say in front of your future husband."

She slipped from the bed as he was pulling his shirt over his head. In one smooth motion she positioned the stone beneath the pillow and pulled the knife out from underneath it. She embraced Grigory before he could fully pull the shirt on and slipped the kindjal into its sheath while hugging him tightly. "Fair enough," she said, kissing him on the mouth as his head emerged from the confines of his shirt.

"Enough." He pulled away, favoring his wounded shoulder. "I have much to do. Get yourself dressed and meet me outside."

As he opened the door, two streltsi further up the hall looked in their direction. Grigory didn't make an attempt to block their view of the room—or more importantly, Atiana standing naked within it. He closed the door behind him like a wolf who had just won his bitch… *Nyet,* she thought, like a young, impudent aristocrat who'd claimed the prize no one thought him capable of winning.

She turned to the bed and spit upon it.

And then she retrieved Nikandr's stone before pulling on her clothes.

The door before her clanked as the gaoler turned the keys. The immense door—after a hard shove from the gaoler—opened with a horrible groan. Atiana stepped inside. Dim light came from small windows worked into the stone walls.

There were four cells in the tight space with a wide aisleway between them. All four were occupied, and in the dimness, Atiana was having trouble discerning where Nikandr was being held. Two crewmen occupied the leftmost cells. In the first cell on the right was an Aramahn man with a mop of curly brown hair and a short, ragged beard.

In the final cell, lying on the straw layering the cell floor, was Nikandr, but he did not rise as she approached.

"Stand, Khalakovo," Atiana said.

He jumped as she spoke. Her stomach churned as he rolled slowly over. Grigory had not mentioned that he was in such a state, and she realized that the information had been withheld for a purpose—Grigory had wanted to see her reaction as she laid eyes on him. Beyond her initial shock—which she hoped Grigory had not been able to see so well in the darkness—she hid her emotions well. She kept a steely gaze on Nikandr as he made it first to all fours, then to his knees. He breathed deeply, coughing painfully several times, before summoning the energy to pull himself up to his feet.

His face was a mass of black and purple bruises. His lip was swollen and cut, and the blood that had leaked from a gash along the bridge of his nose ran down his face and into the stubble along his lip and chin and neck. She found it impossible not to let some emotion show while staring at him. She wondered how long it had taken them, how much it had hurt.

But more than this, Nikandr looked frail, sunken. His eyes were dark, and his cheeks had started to draw inward. The wasting had progressed quickly in the time since she'd last seen him. He had looked, not whole, but vibrant still, in that hallway of Radiskoye before he'd left on his ship. She had still harbored visions of their future together, but now,,, How could anyone envision a future with a man that looked like he would be dead in the span of months, perhaps weeks?

And yet she found, as she stared placidly into his eyes, that the feelings *hadn't* diminished. They'd *grown* in strength. There was a certain fire within him, not unlike Victania, that one had to admire.

"I see there is little enough left for me to do."

Nikandr staggered forward and grabbed the iron bars of the cell. He glared at her, then Grigory, without speaking.

"Come, Nischka," Grigory said. "Don't tell me you aren't going to wish us a fruitful marriage…"

Atiana turned to Grigory. "I was under the impression that *I* was the one who would speak with him."

Grigory smiled and then laughed, showing the imperfect canines that hung high above his otherwise flawless teeth. He bowed his head and flourished a hand toward Nikandr, clamping his mouth in an exaggerated fashion.

Atiana turned back to Nikandr and stepped up to the bars. Had she wanted to, she could have leaned forward and kissed his hands. "I had at one time thought our arrangement necessary."

Nikandr stared, perhaps confused.

Atiana continued, "Perhaps in time I could have grown to stomach it, but after seeing how low your father will stoop, I have no doubt you're already on your way to following in his footsteps. Grigory knew the day of the Grand Duke's murder how gutless you were, but I had convinced myself it was otherwise."

When Nikandr spoke, it was with a scratchy voice that sounded like it hadn't been used in weeks. "Grigory, it seems, is very wise."

"Do not jest, Khalakovo. As far as this war has come, there is little time left for such things."

"I wasn't aware we were at war."

"Well you should have! It was inevitable, and you should have foreseen it—you as well as your mother and father."

The look of betrayal and hurt on his face drove a spike of regret through her heart. "Perhaps we should have murdered all of you in your sleep as your father and brother tried to do to us."

"If that had been his plan, Nischka, you would not be alive today." She took a step forward and took his hand. He allowed her to take it, and she was glad, for it was the only thing she could think to do. She spit upon his hand, and, using a quick move, slipped the stone into his palm and closed his fingers around it.

Nikandr stared at his fist, confusion plain on his face.

"Surprised?" Atiana said. "Perhaps now you'll run to your mother like you used to when we were children." She turned and headed for the door. "I should have known even then, seeing how quick you were to beg for her help."

Grigory's eyes were full of amusement and deep satisfaction, but she didn't spare him more than a glance for fear she would spit in his face.

She walked out, hoping Nikandr had the sense to keep the stone hidden until they were gone. Thankfully, Grigory followed, his lust for gloating apparently sated.

She was moved within the hour to a manor house far down the hill near a small village called Laksova. Her father and the other dukes were supposed to have arrived before evening meal, but they were late. She wondered, late at night while listening to the cannon fire coming from Oshtoyets, whether it was because there was movement afoot on the part of the Khalakovos. She worried for Nikandr—many things could go wrong in any attempt to free him from his prison.

Long after the sounds of cannon and musket fire had ceased, she lay awake, unable to find sleep. The morning sun began to brighten the window of the bedroom. She went down for a breakfast of cheese and apples, and though the cheese was sour and the apples withered, she wolfed them down, ravenous after how little she had eaten over the past few days. Borund and Grigory entered the narrow eating hall as she was finishing her still-steaming cup of tea.

Borund stood across the table from her, staring down at her as if she were still a little girl. "You should have been safe on Vostroma by now."

"I will not be told where to go, Bora. Not any longer."

"We are at *war*, Tiana. This is no time for your obstinate ways."

"It seems to me the *men* are the obstinate ones. If the Matri had been allowed to discuss this before Father sanctioned this foolish plan, we would all be having tea in Radiskoye, laughing at our foolishness."

Borund looked furious. "Is that what you think?"

"Can there be any doubt?"

"Perhaps, dear sister, you are thinking with your loins."

Both Borund and Grigory were staring at her with judgmental looks. Clearly they were waiting for her to confess.

"If there's something you wish to say, Borund, you ought to come out and say it."

"Did you arrange for Nikandr's rescue?"

With nonchalance, she raised her eyebrows and took a bite from the browned flesh of her half-eaten apple. "I wasn't aware that he had been."

"You surely were," Grigory said. His face was red now, and it took all the concentration Atiana possessed not to stare at his neck, at the chain that had not so long ago held Nikandr's soulstone.

"I most surely was not. It seems to me that he was in *your* charge, Grigory, not mine."

He was desperate to accuse her, but he could not—to admit that she had taken Nikandr's stone would be admitting his own failure, and he would not do so before Borund, so he set his jaw and remained silent, pointedly keeping his eyes fixed downward.

Borund noticed and nodded to the door. "I would speak with my sister alone, Griga."

Grigory stared at Borund as if he'd been betrayed, but then he nodded and left, his boots echoing sharply against the cold stone floors.

"I can no longer arrange for you to be shipped home," Borund said when the sounds had faded.

"Good. I don't *wish* to go home."

"But you will remain here until the hostilities have ended."

"Hostilities?"

Borund paused, shifting his weight to the other leg. "We will attack today. There is no choice left to us."

"It seems that things are well in hand."

"*Nyet*, Atiana, they are not *in hand*. All of our rooks have been driven mad or have flown off."

"All of them?"

"All. Clearly the other Matri are crippling us so that we are blind. Now promise me that you won't cause any more trouble."

She was about to chide him, but this was the most serious she had seen Borund in a very long time. "Dear brother, I do believe you care for me."

"I care little, Tiana. There are two more should some unforeseen fate befall you. It's only that it would be difficult afterward to explain things to Mother." He took one step back, glancing toward the door. "And poor Grigory will be heartbroken. You wouldn't want to disappoint him, would you?"

"Never," she said, though in truth part of her was terrified to be left alone with Grigory now that he knew what she'd done. Still, she was willing to risk it; it was the only way she could find her way back to Nikandr—back to Volgorod—so she could help.

"Keep well," Borund said as he strode away.

Grigory was gone for some time, escorting Borund back to his windship, perhaps requesting that he—as the sole remaining voice of Bolgravya—be allowed to join the battle. Part of her wished that he *would* leave, but he returned shortly after midday.

An unseasonable snowfall had begun outside, a terrible omen for the day ahead. Grigory had a dusting of it on his hair and long gray cherkesska when he came into the sitting room. He ordered the skinny old peasant woman who was cleaning the mantel around the fireplace from the room. When she was gone, he rounded on Atiana, who sat in a chair holding a book of poems, more to give him the illusion that she was at ease than for any form of entertainment. She hadn't read a single word since she'd picked up the book an hour before.

From around his neck Grigory pulled the chain that had once held Nikandr's soulstone. He held it out for her to see, waiting for her to respond.

"Whatever is that?" she asked, holding the book upright as if she were ready to return to it the moment Grigory proved himself dull.

Grigory stepped forward and stood over her. "Why would you give him his stone?"

She knew it was unwise, she knew Grigory's penchant for lashing out, but she couldn't help but allow a broad smile to spread across her face. "What stone?"

He snatched the book from her grip and backhanded her before she had a chance to react. The sound—wood striking stone—played loudly in her ears as pain blossomed across the left side of her face. Grigory, shaking his hand as if it had been unexpectedly painful, looked for a moment as if he regretted what he had done, but then his eyes hardened. "Why would you betray all of us for *him*, a man who's done nothing but work to undermine your father since the moment he landed?"

She could not speak. He was still standing over her, his breath coming rapidly, his face red and the pulse of his neck beating strongly. The look in his eye made it clear that he would simply strike her again no matter what she said.

When he did raise his hand, she cowered. "I owed him, Grigory. I owed him. That is why I gave him the stone."

"What could you *owe* him?"

"I owed him his life, as his father had granted me mine."

"Iaros nearly slew you in cold blood!"

"Dozens of his men had died, Grigory. That is hardly cold blood."

"But the daughter of a duke..."

"Is just as legitimate a target as a son. Had the same thing happened in Galostina, I would not have thought twice about putting a gun to Victania's pretty little head—and I tell you this, *I* would have pulled the trigger."

Grigory's face was still red, his forehead still pinched with emotion, but he was watching her with a calculating eye now. "You would have me believe that you gave Nikandr his stone in repayment for Iaros choosing to spare your life."

"I don't care what you believe—"

He slapped her again before she could say more. She held her cheek, unable to see the room clearly now through the tears forming in her eyes. When she had once again summoned the courage to look up, his face was not filled with rage, as she had thought it would be. Rather, he appeared proud, perhaps vindicated.

"Bolgravya is too good for a woman like you." He turned and walked to the door. He opened it and nodded to someone outside her field of vision. A moment later a tapping came against the polished wooden floor. An old rook limped into the room. She recognized it immediately as Brunhald, the oldest of Bolgravya's rooks and the one that Alesya preferred above all others—ancestors only knew why. One of its legs ended in a stump instead of a clawed foot, and it was this leg that tapped as it walked.

Borund had said that all of the rooks had been chased away. She wondered if he had known then about Brunhald. Most likely not. Most likely Alesya had told Grigory to keep this secret to himself. All the better to keep her precious child safe, to enact her plans as she saw fit—regardless of whatever agreement the men had made amongst themselves. It was with this realization that Atiana understood, for the first time, the position in which Alesya had found herself when her husband the Grand Duke had been killed. She was a thousand leagues from her son, the only voice of her family now that Stasa was gone. She would feel rudderless, adrift on the winds that had so quickly risen with the death of her husband. It was no surprise, then, that she would take steps to protect not only her son—the rightful heir of their Duchy—but also to position their interests for maximum gain, or, more accurately, minimum loss, with the mantle of Grand Duke sure to pass to one of the other duchies.

Brunhald opened her crooked beak and released a long, ragged caw. "Do not fret, child. My son has spoken with rashness. With haste. There may yet be room for a union."

"I fear," Atiana said, still holding her cheek tenderly against the pain of speaking, "that when my father discovers what your son has done, it will be difficult for him to keep his head."

The old rook arched her neck far back and then pecked the floor three times. "We shall see, Atiana Radieva. We shall see."

She pecked twice more, and Atiana felt herself go dizzy. She could feel, as she had in the aether from time to time, Alesya's presence, but unlike the aether, where the Matri felt distant, it now felt as if Alesya were staring down upon Atiana with a hand upon her throat, refusing to allow her to move.

"What are you doing?"

This is what comes of betrayal such as yours, girl.

The intensity of the feelings grew, as did the sensation that she was being choked. She began to sense Alesya's emotions—a seething anger at Atiana's allegiance to Khalakovo and pure satisfaction that she would now be forced to pay for it.

Then the pain quickly became too much, and Atiana's world went dark.

CHAPTER 58

When Rehada neared the cliffs that housed Volgorod's massive eyrie, she heard the boom of cannon fire. It blasted the air as she spurred her pony onward along the plateau that would lead her past the eyrie and on toward Volgorod. A dozen windships crisscrossed the island in an attempt to intimidate and to search for signs of organized resistance. She knew she had been seen along her journey from the northwestern part of the island—it was impossible not to be—but she had stopped in a house she kept in Izhny to retrieve a set of peasant clothes for her ride east. She hoped that the men in the windships would consider one lone woman riding on a sickly pony beneath their notice, and so far that had held true.

From Izhny she had made a calculated choice: take the slower northern route and avoid any potential conflict or take the more navigable southern one and put herself within reach of the forces of the traitor dukes that held the eyrie. She knew that the eyrie had been taken, knew that their men would be stationed there in force to protect the jewel they had seized, and yet she still did not consider it an unwise decision until she was surprised by the sound of hoof beats coming fast behind her. She was on a slow decline, the wind driving the tall grasses around her like waves upon the sea, and she could see from this vantage neither the eyrie ahead nor the decline toward Izhny behind. It was the blindest part of the journey, and her assailants must have known this as well.

There were five of them—mounted men bearing muskets and black cherkesskas and brown kolpak hats cut in the shorter style of the southern Duchies. They had tall, strong ponies, which were probably fresh. One of the streltsi raised his weapon and waved it back and forth above his head, a signal for her to stop.

Stopping was not something she could afford. They would undoubtedly take her to the eyrie for questioning.

She spurred her pony to a full gallop. Her loosely tied babushka was pulled from her head by the wind, revealing the circlet upon her brow. The men shouted as she summoned the spirit bonded to her through the tourmaline gem. She felt the warmth upon her brow first, then through her cheeks and scalp and neck. It quickly suffused her frame as her pony—already breathing heavily—galloped on.

The thrill of her bond ran through her from the pit of her stomach to the knot in her throat. She turned in her saddle and cast her hand over the landscape. In a tight line over the grass that lay between her and her pursuers, fire blazed.

The men were well trained. The flames had jumped over the well-traveled trail, allowing the streltsi a path through the fire. They continued on with little drop in pace and leveled their muskets once they were beyond the wall of flame. The first of them fired a moment later. A musket ball struck the earth ahead of her. Another shot whizzed by. The next struck her pony in the chest.

It fell to the ground, throwing Rehada from its back.

She had been prepared for this, and had slowed the pony's gait. She rolled away and came to her feet, standing her ground as the ponies charged and another musket shot struck the earth to her right.

She drew from the suurahezhan again, giving some part of herself to the spirit as she did so. It was no small amount, and she had not drawn such energy from Adhiya in a very long time. She felt her knees buckle as a ball of fire formed between her arms. The heat of it was painful and beautiful and exhilarating in the same breath, and when she released it, it was with a sense of longing and loss.

The ball of bright orange flame shot forth, striking the lead pony and its rider. Both fell to the ground, the pony screaming, the rider diving away and rolling on the grasses in an attempt at snuffing the flames.

The fire had sprayed against another strelet. Rehada fed this from the suurahezhan, pulling as much as she could manage. It was more than she had ever drawn from a single spirit, and she was already weakening to the point that her heart began to skip beats, her world began to close in around her, her vision was invaded by bright sparks of light.

Despite this she reveled in the feeling of touching Adhiya, of communing with the spirit. She nearly allowed the hezhan to take her, and she realized—almost too late—that this must be yet another result of the rift that ran through Volgorod. She bore down, cutting herself off from the suurahezhan. It fought her, but she was not so young in the craft to be taken in this manner, and the spirit was not so old that it was overly powerful.

Still, as she released the connection, her vision blackened and the world was lost from view.

When she opened her eyes, she was staring up at the sky. The sound of licking flames could be heard, so it could not have been long. She propped herself up on her elbows and took in the scene as the sickening smell of roasted flesh swept over her.

All five of the ponymen were dead. Four of the ponies were as well, and her own was dying, its blood still leaking from just below its ribs as it took breath in a rapid and shallow manner.

One of the ponies was still alive, and she remembered—now that she had achieved some distance—preventing the fire from striking it, though at the time the notion had been nearly drowned by her thirst for more contact with the suurahezhan.

She walked to the pony, knowing the streltsi at the eyrie and the ships in the sky—even the host of Matri who patrolled the island—would soon come to investigate.

"Come," she said to the pony as she ran her hand down its neck. "We have a ways to go, you and I."

With her circlet hidden away in the pouch at her belt, Rehada walked alone, her arms in clear sight, on the cobbled road leading up to the Boyar's mansion. A guard of a dozen streltsi stood along a low stone wall ahead. Beyond them stood the walls of the mansion itself. The stout walls held an imposing iron gate at its two entry points, and there were now several hastily constructed barricades of stone along the road leading up to the gates, forcing anyone who wanted to enter to veer back and forth before reaching the gates themselves.

A sotnik raised his hand as she approached.

"I wish to see the Boyar," Rehada said.

He stood taller. "And what would he want with you?"

"I bring news of Atiana Vostroma, who escaped Radiskoye only days ago."

His expression turned grim, and he glanced back at the mansion before speaking again. "You can give the message to me."

She was already shaking her head. "I have just come from Iramanshah," she lied. "I bear a message from Fahroz Bashar al Lilliah herself, meant for the Boyar's ears only."

"That is impossible," he said flatly.

"It concerns a threat posed by the Maharraht." This much, at least, was true.

"Then tell me and it will be relayed through proper channels."

"I will not."

He looked uncomfortable, glancing back toward the mansion several more times. In the end he frowned and said, "Wait here."

And wait she did. She had known that the eyrie had been taken. She had known that the blockade had been circling the island and Radiskoye ceaselessly since the duke of Vostroma had staged his revolt. What she hadn't known was that ground troops had moved in around the palotza. She had discovered this upon reaching Volgorod.

The traitor Dukes had landed Polkovnik Andreya Antonov, the head of Vostroma's military, as well as two thousand streltsi. They had positioned themselves on the shallow plain that lay between Volgorod and Palotza Radiskoye, securing footholds close to each of the prized locations.

Ranos Khalakovo, as Boyar of the Island of Uyadensk and sitting Posadnik of the City, had responded in kind, organizing his not-inconsiderable number of troops to the edges of the city, ready to respond should Andreya issue the order to attack.

Rehada had no idea how she was going to reach Radiskoye. Attempting to take a windship, even a skiff, would be foolish to say the least. Her passage would be sensed and a ship would cut off her approach well before she reached the palotza. Travel by water would not work either, as the palotza—even though it was near the water's edge—rested atop tall, unscalable cliffs. Travel by land, given the position of Andreya's forces, had also been taken from her.

And so she found herself making a decision that at first seemed foolish, but felt wiser in increments in light of the fact that her eventual goal was to reach the Duke of Khalakovo.

The noon hour passed, and she grew worried that this was taking too long. Soroush had said that they would move tomorrow, meaning she had little enough time in which to find Iaros, to convince him of her earnestness, and to give them time to prevent what was about to happen. What could be done at this point she wasn't sure—Zhabyn Vostroma had a stranglehold on the island—but she was certain she didn't stand a chance by herself. Only Iaros had the wherewithal to negotiate a cessation of hostilities or organize an outright attack to buy them time to deal with Soroush.

When the sotnik stepped out of the mansion and began walking over the expanse of stone leading to the gates, he was accompanied by Nikandr's sister, Victania. She wore a blue dress, extravagant for a peasant woman but clearly plain for the Princess. Two braids wrapped around her head and tied her long brown hair back like an Aramahn circlet. Her face was grim as she came closer and finally stopped several paces away.

"I was told you wish to speak to my brother."

"I do."

"That you have some knowledge of the Maharraht? A threat?"

Rehada nodded.

Victania's serious eyes thinned. "You are Nikandr's lover, are you not?"

Rehada nearly shook her head, ready to deny it in order to reach Ranos, but Victania knew too much. Rehada had been with Nikandr for years, and she had attended several high-profile dinners hosted by various Landed families in Volgorod, and even one in Radiskoye when the Duke had been away. It was too likely that Victania knew a lot more about Rehada than she would have originally guessed, and so she nodded.

"Do you have news of him?" Victania asked. Her voice had softened. Rehada knew how close the two of them were.

"I'm sorry, but I haven't."

At this, Victania's face hardened. "My brother is away. I'm afraid he is not able to see you."

"But I have come from Iramanshah, from—"

"*Da*, from Fahroz herself, but let me tell you, Rehada, if Fahroz has something she wishes to tell us, she can come herself so we can weigh her words properly." Victania turned and began striding back toward the mansion, but she stopped momentarily and turned her head halfway around. "Run back, won't you? And tell her not to send a woman of the sheets to do her talking for her."

She resumed her walk, but stopped at the growing sound of ponies clomping along the cobbled street. A handful of military men dressed in black cherkesskas were riding toward the mansion. At their head were two men: an imposing but graying polkovnik...

And Ranos.

His thin mustache and beard were still in place, but stubble was growing in around his cheeks and neck, making him look haggard and wild.

The nearby sotnik clapped his heels together and saluted the incoming men who had no doubt come from surveying the preparations for Andreya's attack.

Ranos saluted in turn, but then noticed Rehada. His face frowned as recognition dawned on him, and then he looked up and found Victania standing just inside the gates. He spoke quickly to the polkovnik with the hanging white beard, and immediately all of the cavalry rode in through the gates, leaving Ranos alone with Rehada.

Victania strode forward as Ranos heeled his pony closer. "Why have you come?" he asked plainly.

"I need to speak with your father."

He laughed. "The Duke, if you haven't noticed, is occupied."

"All the more reason he should speak with me."

Victania stepped past Rehada to reach Ranos's side. "Don't listen to her. She's already lied to get this close to you."

"Tell me what you're after," Ranos said to Rehada, "or I'll ask you to leave."

She could tell by the tone of his voice that he was weary, that he would simply leave if her rationale wasn't convincing enough, so she poured all of the emotion bottled up inside her into one simple statement: "If you wish for your precious Duchy to see another day, son of Iaros, then you'll listen to what I have to say."

"Ridiculous," Victania snapped.

Ranos looked down at his sister and then to Rehada, perhaps weighing her words.

"Go on," he said.

The mask over Rehada's eyes and the rope binding her hands were the least of her worries. The boat in which she sat was tumbling over the tall waves in merciless cycles, and without her sight, she was completely unable to anticipate any of it. She had already heaved up the contents of her stomach four times, and as another tall wave struck, she found herself dry heaving between her legs.

"Please," she said to the sotnik sitting on the next thwart forward, "I only need a small amount of time to recover."

"You heard my orders," the strelet said.

Six oars struck the water in synchronized time as the spray pelted her face. The wind was high, and the weather had turned bitterly cold toward the end of the day, and despite the fact that Rehada wore a heavily oiled canvas coat, she was soaked from head to foot and almost completely numb.

Though Victania had tried diligently to get him to cast her out, Ranos had agreed to Rehada's demands. There was a significant problem, however—communication with the Matra had been sporadic at best. They hadn't been able to speak with her in several days. Of the three rooks that were kept permanently at the mansion, two had apparently been killed by the third, which had flown out of its cage when their keeper had come to investigate the swath of blood and black feathers that lay inside their cage. Three days prior, another rook had flown down from the palotza, but the moment it had landed it began rolling on the ground, cawing, and then it flew back into the air and was never seen again. Clearly the other Matri were in league, working to prevent effective communication between Radiskoye and Volgorod, which presented Ranos with a difficult task: he agreed that his father needed to hear what Rehada had to say, but he saw no easy way to make that happen.

In the end, he had arranged for her to be ferried away by a hand-selected crew of oarsmen. Their mission was to take her to the cliffs below Radiskoye and to guide her into the cavern that held a passage leading up to the palotza. The only issue was that Rehada could not be allowed to see the route. She argued that it would be night, that she would be able to see very little in any case, but Ranos would not budge.

And so she found herself fighting to keep herself from sliding along the thwart, fighting to stay warm, fighting to prevent herself from heaving again, an action that brought only pain.

"How much longer?" she asked between waves of nausea.

"You know I cannot tell."

"Please."

"Knowing won't make it any shorter or longer. Just sit and breathe deeply."

As he spoke, something thudded against the boat. She thought at first they had struck bottom, but it happened again a moment later, and the boat began to slip sideways.

She heard the thump and clatter of wood, and the sotnik sitting ahead of her stood. "Pull, men, pull!"

"What is it?" she asked as a cold spike of fear slid deep inside her chest. The boat slid further and was tugged downward momentarily. "*What is it?*"

"Be quiet!"

A moment later the crack of a musket went off just above her head, making her cringe with fear.

The boat was pulled sharply to port, and something splashed into the water just over the starboard gunwale.

"*Kozyol!*" the sotnik swore. "Pull harder!"

Then something heavy and wet fell across Rehada's lap.

CHAPTER 59

Sharp pain shot through Rehada's thighs. She placed her hands over the cold, slimy tentacle, knowing immediately what sort of creature had attacked the boat. There were several types of squid that wandered the oceans, but only one of them, the goedrun, was large enough and aggressive enough to attack ships. A smaller ship such as theirs was particularly attractive, as it could be tipped over, instantly turning its inhabitants into prey. Given the diameter of the tentacle, she guessed the goedrun was still young, but it was more than a match for the ship if it could get enough tentacles around to capsize it.

"Cut them!" the sotnik shouted, and she heard two of the men moments later sawing at the tentacle as the ship tilted sharply to port.

"Let me free," Rehada shouted, putting as much command into her voice as she could muster.

She was ignored as another tentacle slipped over the crown of her head and into the laps of the streltsi behind her. The two men screamed and she could hear them sawing at this tentacle as well.

"My circlet!" Rehada screamed.

"Give it to her, Goran!" one of the soldiers behind her shouted.

After a moment's pause, she could feel the sotnik's kindjal against the rope at her wrist. An instant later, her hands were free. She pulled the mask off of her face and by the dim light of the quarter moon found the grim-faced sotnik rummaging through a burlap sack at his feet. He pulled her circlet out, but it dropped as the boat tilted sharply upward and he grabbed the gunwales for balance.

Rehada snatched up her circlet, but had already noticed that the stone was dark. Even before she placed it upon her head she knew the truth of it: the suurahezhan she had bonded with had abandoned her, leaving her utterly defenseless. It may have been because of the trip over the water, it may have simply been its time, but something told her it was yet another

384

manifestation of the rift, the rift that Soroush was ready to rip wide open if given the chance.

The streltsi shifted aft, ready to hack at the massive tentacle that had grabbed the boat. As they searched the water, shashkas raised, an arm of the goedrun whipped up out of the water and wrapped around two of them before they had a chance to duck out of its path.

One was able to pull away, but the other was wrapped up tight and was pulled off the boat in a blink, splashing into the dark waves before the shock could even register upon his face.

"Give me your gunpowder," Rehada said to the sotnik.

He complied without question, unfastening and handing her one of the wooden cartridges hanging from leather cords along the front of his bandolier.

"All of them," she said while pouring the contents into her lap.

He handed the cartridges as quickly as he could, and Rehada added their contents—ten cartridges' worth—to the one in her lap, hoping it would be enough.

"A spark," Rehada said.

From a small leather bag on his bandolier he pulled out a piece of flint and held out his kindjal. "Run the knife—"

"I know," she snapped, snatching both of them away as the boat tipped upward. There were no tentacles above the water, but by the silver light of the moon she could see many—two dozen or more—floating alongside the boat.

"Behind me, quickly."

The sotnik complied as Rehada closed her eyes and focused her mind upon the stone set within her circlet. Through it she could feel, barely, Adhiya, though she could not yet feel a hezhan waiting for her. She began to chant, forcing away the danger of the moment, the closeness of the streltsi, utter strangers to this ritual. She forced away the cold, the wind, the spray of the water against her face and instead focused on herself and the stone. She willed herself into it, asking a spirit to hear her plea, asking it to bond with her.

She promised it life, a view of the world it had left, the world it would one day return to. She promised it a bond that would last as long as it wished. She would feed it as she could, and it in turn would feed her.

The rocking of the boat, the screaming of the men, invaded her senses for a moment, but she blocked them out once more.

Take me, she called. *Take me, and you will be rewarded.*

And she felt it. The barest touch of a suurahezhan, the only form of spirit—ever since she was young—she had ever been able to bond with.

She called it closer, allowing it to see her more clearly, to hear, to touch.

And when it did, she ran the knife, hard and quick, down the length of the flint.

Her world went white.

She heard a sound like a hurricane blowing through a forest. She smelled burnt wool. She felt heat, though it was not, she knew, the heat from the gunpowder; it was the heat of the suurahezhan filling her. It suffused every pore, every bit of bone and muscle, every drop of blood. She was aflame. She was fire itself.

It felt good and true, and when she opened her eyes there was a strange moment of reorientation—along with the realization that she was in the material world and not, sadly, the land beyond.

The circlet upon her brow was lit with a pale orange flame. She willed fire to course from her hand to the tentacles wrapped around the ship and two of the soldiers. One whipped up and arced back into the water, splashing loudly. The other had been wrapped around the thigh of a strelet, and when it pulled back, the man came with him, falling hard against the bottom of the boat and then pulled sharply out and away. A heavy thud was accompanied by a sharp crack as the man's head snapped backward as it struck the gunwale. He did not shout as he flew limply through the air. Then the tentacle shot under the surface of the dark water, and he was gone.

Over a dozen dark cords flew into the night sky, and Rehada could see in the water a bare silhouette of the white creature lying only a few paces beneath the surface of the water. She could see its body shaped like the head of a spear; she could see the darkened and moving orb that must be its eye.

As the tentacles descended she focused all of her energy tightly, and like the gunpowder she had used to attract the suurahezhan, released it upward and outward in a spray of bright white fire that burned emerald green at the edges. Many of the tentacles were burned outright, their withered ends falling into the ship, twitching and curling, the pincers underneath still biting the streltsi.

The tentacles slapped below the water. In a great heave the beast drew them inward while shooting downward. In moments it was lost from sight.

The sotnik ordered the boat cleared as he moved toward the fore of the boat and pulled off his bandolier and then his cherkesska. As the men began removing tentacles and flicking them overboard with booted feet or the tips of their knives, the sotnik offered Rehada his coat, turning his eyes away as he did so. Only then did she realize that her clothes had been burned away. Only some scraps at her wrists remained, and some cloth—her skirt—that had pooled around her feet. She took the coat and pulled it on quickly, suddenly feeling very exposed out on the sea among these men. Soon the boat was clear, and all of them were breathing heavily as the wind howled over the waves.

The sotnik returned to his previous position, looking up at Rehada with a look of relief and gratitude. He motioned to the thwart in front of him and waited patiently as Rehada sat.

"My thanks go to you—all of our thanks—but I must have your circlet if we're to continue."

Rehada stared at him levelly. "You will not have it." She was still full with the feeling of the suurahezhan running through her; she would not give up the spirit so shortly after summoning it.

"I have my orders."

"I saved your lives."

He bowed his head. "And I am grateful, but there was no question as to how you'd be entering the palotza."

"You will take me as I am…"

He looked at her, then to the men behind her, who had taken up the oars once more—now four strong instead of six—and were waiting for orders. "Turn 'round, men. Turn 'round."

The streltsi did as they were ordered, dipping the starboard oars into the water and pulling hard.

"Stop," Rehada said, but they did not listen. "Stop!" Only when she had pulled off the circlet did the sotnik nod and the streltsi pull their oars from the water. It felt like betrayal—another in a long list of them—but she could not abandon her cause. Not now. She handed the circlet to the sotnik and waited as he tied the blindfold around her head.

The boat turned and began moving steadily. The rocking had never ceased, but it was more marked now, and Rehada once again found herself fighting off nausea as they continued through the night.

They reached a cave of some kind. She could tell because the wind dropped, as did the waves, and the sound of the oars slapping in the water—as well as the grunting of the men—began to echo. The effect deepened the further they went, and eventually they ran aground.

Rehada was led out of the boat and along a short, sandy stretch. The sand turned to stone, and then Rehada was pulled to a stop. Footsteps receded, a low conversation was held somewhere up ahead, too soft to hear and too difficult to understand with the echoing.

Rehada was transferred to another man, who gripped her elbow forcefully.

Rehada felt someone's hand reaching inside the large pocket of the cherkesska she still wore. "Your circlet will remain here," the sotnik said. She guessed it was as much for the other man's benefit as it was hers. "May the fates guide your way," he said, offering her an ancient Aramahn saying at their parting. He kissed her forehead, quickly, tenderly, and then his footsteps receded and she was led deeper into the cave.

They came upon an incline and eventually stairs. She was terribly cold now, though she didn't know why it had taken so long to register. The wind upon the open sea had been much colder, but the memories of the goedrun and the threat of dry heaving were the foremost in her mind. Now there was time to think. And feel.

She tripped several times, for the man said little while guiding her upward.

"It would go faster if I could see."

"The blindfold remains," he said gruffly.

The climb upward was interminably long. Sweat tickled her scalp. It ran down her forehead and the small of her back. Her legs burned terribly, to the point where she had to ask to rest several times on the ascent, until finally they came to a place that felt warmer.

"Wait here," the gruff man told her. His heavy footsteps receded and another hushed conversation was held. Then a door opened and closed with a heavy and echoing thud.

She waited, standing, not knowing where the man had gone, not knowing where she was, though she assumed she now stood in the bowels of Radiskoye.

Now that she was still she realized it was not warm at all. It had merely been the exertion and the relative increase in temperature that had given her that impression. The sweat on her body was drying and the cool air of the room was beginning to sink deep beneath her skin, so she found herself shivering horribly, an impression she did not want to give.

She began to wonder why she was being left alone for so long. Though her hands were tied she could easily have taken the rope off, but she did not want to be found with it off after she had been told to keep it on, despite how foolish it seemed now that they had come so far. She had felt like this many times before—being placed in a position of subservience to the Landed. They seemed to revel in it—keeping the Aramahn beneath them—and she found some of her old hatred returning. She wondered if she had made a mistake by coming here, whether she should fabricate a story and let Soroush do what he would. Let fate take its natural course.

But she could not. This was not about her, or Soroush, or the guard who took enjoyment from stepping on her pride. This was about the world, Erahm, and her sister, Adhiya, and the course that the two of them would take from this point forward. If there was anything more important, she didn't know what it might be.

The door ahead of her opened, and she heard only one set of footsteps enter the room. She thought at first it was the man who had led her up, but she smelled on the air the scent of myrrh, which the aristocracy of the Grand Duchy had seemed to favor in recent years, so she knew it must be someone of import, and since the footsteps had sounded heavy, like a man's, she could only assume it would be one in particular.

"I hope you are well, Iaros son of Aleksi."

There came a soft chuckle. Footsteps approached and finally the blindfold was pulled away.

She squinted momentarily, even though the only light was from a small copper lamp sitting on a nearby bench. There was a wooden rack with pegs that held several woolen sweaters and oiled canvas coats. Thick leather boots sat jumbled in one corner.

Iaros, strangely enough, wore a wool cherkesska, and not of the sort a duke would wear. It was simple and weatherworn, the kind of no-nonsense garb a traveling merchant might use. He looked the same as he had several years before, the only time she had seen him up close. He had a gray beard with a sprinkling of brown still remaining, trimmed so that it hung partway down his chest. He was balding, but there were tufts of hair on the very top of his head.

The strange thing was how composed he looked, how free of care even after everything that had happened. His palotza was besieged, his Duchy at grave risk and had been for weeks, but one would wonder whether he was going out for a ride in the countryside as little as he seemed to show it.

There were two doors. From behind the one Iaros had used to enter the room she could hear men gathering and talking softly.

"You were my son's lover," Iaros said, pulling her attention back to him.

She smiled, wondering whether he was trying to put her off balance. "I was not aware that our relationship had ended."

"I'll have to remember that," he said, raising his eyebrows, "and discuss it with Nikandr when I see him again."

"And when might that be?"

She hoped that if he had any information about Nikandr that he would share it, but instead he simply frowned and shrugged his shoulders. "When the ancestors see fit to reunite us. Now you've come a terribly long way and through more than a little bit of danger to speak with me. What is it you want?"

She was hesitant at first—it felt like speaking with the enemy—but once she started, she found the floodgates opening wide. She told him of her knowledge of Nasim and how he had come to land on Khalakovo, how Ashan had stolen him away from the Maharraht, how he had summoned the suurahezhan and her assumptions as to why it had happened. She told him that Nasim would now have been recovered by the Maharraht. She told him of the grave danger Khalakovo was now in, and the ritual that Soroush would perform this very day at sunset. She knew that she was giving up more information than a woman like her should have, but she didn't care.

Iaros's expression changed little during the entire exchange, and when she was done, he combed his beard with his fingers, studying her face as the silence lengthened.

"You are Maharraht?" he asked plainly.

So conditioned was she to hide the truth that a denial nearly came from her lips before she could prevent it, but instead she took a deep breath and looked him in the eye and replied, "*Da.*"

"Then tell me, why should I believe a word of this? Why shouldn't I stand the gibbet in the courtyard above and let you hang from it?"

This was the moment she had feared the most—the point at which Iaros would have to decide if she was telling the truth. She had thought long and hard on how to convince him, but she knew that any profession of honesty would fall upon deaf ears. So she said the only thing she could.

"Because I love your son."

Iaros's head jerked back and his eyes widened momentarily. "Pardon me?"

"Perhaps such a thing is hard for you to believe, but it is so."

"Does he return your love?"

"*Nyet,*" she said flatly. "I do not think he does."

"Then why? Why risk everything for a man who cares less for you than you care for him?"

She shook her head. "You don't understand. Nikandr was a bridge. A bridge I needed to return to myself. Strangely enough, Atiana served in much the same manner. I can no longer follow the path of revenge and hatred. I must follow the path of healing, for Nikandr, for my daughter, even for you."

"So kind of you."

"I don't care whether you appreciate it or not."

"Well, forgive me if I find this all difficult to believe, but perhaps there is a way to determine whether you're telling the truth."

"How?"

"We'll ask Nikandr about it when we see him."

She glanced at the door, hearing more men gathering behind it. "And how will we do that?"

Iaros nodded toward the door that would lead back down to the caverns. "Why, the same way you entered."

CHAPTER 60

Nikandr knew that a soulstone had been placed into his palm—there was no mistaking the feeling of a stone once it touches the skin—but he had to admit that it didn't feel like his. He knew enough to keep it hidden until Atiana and Grigory had left, though in an attempt to appear nonchalant, and after the beating he'd received from the streltsi, he nearly dropped it. His hands didn't completely betray him, however, and soon, thankfully, they had left.

He waited for what felt like an interminable period of time, convinced that the moment he looked at what he now held in his hand the gaoler would peer inside the room and discover it the very same moment he did.

He did not speak. That had been the excuse the gaoler had needed the last time to enter the room and beat him senseless with two Bolgravyan streltsi. Ashan had pleaded for them to stop, but the only thing that had done was to shift some of their attention to him. They had exercised some restraint with the older man, and for that Nikandr was glad.

As the minutes passed he realized that the stone was indeed his, but it had been tainted, and it didn't take much to figure out why. Grigory, that baseless spawn of a goat, had *worn* it. He had done it so that Nikandr could feel his presence, so that he would *always* feel it. It would fade with time, as the memories would, but there would always be a part of Grigory imprinted upon the stone.

He could feel something else as well. Nasim… He was not imprinted upon the stone as Grigory was. Rather, it was more like Victania described the aether, how she could feel others at a distance though they were hundreds of leagues apart. This was how it felt with Nasim—as though he could call out and Nasim would answer. The only trouble was that he had no idea how to do such a thing.

He turned his back toward the door and opened his palm carefully. And there it lay. His stone. As alive as it had been after Nasim had somehow reawakened it. He wondered where the boy was now. The Maharraht wanted to use him to widen the rift, to create a gap that would lay waste to Uyadensk and perhaps the entire archipelago.

He could not risk speaking with Ashan. Not now. The only real course of action was the one that Atiana had given him: he had to reach his mother. *You should have foreseen it*, she had said, *as well as your mother and father.* She had clearly been referring to the attack that would be launched against Radiskoye. Her words were a warning to get out of this fort tonight, not only because they were apparently ready to move him but because an attack was imminent.

He gripped the stone tightly and closed his eyes, calling out to his mother. As always, he felt nothing in return. He never knew whether his calls had been heard until a rook found him or she told him so later. It was the nature of the aether, and there was more than a small chance that she would not hear him at all. The blockade had surely taken its toll. She had most likely been riding the winds for days by now, and her attention might be completely absorbed by other tasks. He also had no idea how strong she was after Nasim had attacked her. It was possible she was no longer as sharp as she once was.

But she was also the most gifted Matri of her generation. If anyone could overcome such odds, she could.

The gaoler entered the room nearly an hour later. It took Nikandr a moment to orient himself, so engrossed in concentration was he. The sunlight coming in through the small, high windows had started to dim.

The gaoler brought cold bowls of cabbage stew, though there was barely more than a handful with a small crust of bread soaking up what small amount of liquid there was. Still, after the meager meals he'd been given the last several days, he was glad to have anything to fill his stomach.

The gaoler left, closing the door behind him, and still Nikandr was silent. He dearly wanted to speak with Ashan, but he couldn't risk it.

The sunlight dimmed until early dusk reigned. He began to despair. If Mother had heard him she most likely would have sent a ship to rescue him near dusk when it was still light enough to fly and when their arrival might be masked. If it became too dark, particularly with the overcast sky, it would be nearly impossible to mount a rescue. When full night finally arrived, and he began to accept that he would not be saved.

He was startled some time later by the sound of the gaoler's outer door opening. Two men talked, the door opened again, and then all was silence.

"Ashan," Nikandr whispered, knowing they were finally alone.

Ashan was sitting in the corner of his cell furthest away from Nikandr.

His head was resting on his forearms, which were propped up against his bent knees. At Nikandr's words he lifted his head and peered through the gloom. "Do not risk another beating, Nikandr."

"I need to understand what happened on Ghayavand." He held up his soulstone for Ashan to see. It glinted softly in the darkness.

"How did you?"

"Atiana. Now tell me, what does it mean? The stone was dead before I entered the tower, and now the life of it has returned, brighter than before. And I can feel Nasim... I can feel him just by touching the stone."

"Sariya did nothing?"

"She was holding Muqallad back, preventing him from finding us."

"Not us. Nasim."

"Nasim, then."

"And you said you had opened yourself to Nasim. Accepted him..."

"You know this. I've told you."

Ashan frowned in concentration. "Pietr..."

Nikandr waited for him to go on, but he didn't. He merely stared straight ahead, picking at his lips with thumb and forefinger.

"What about Pietr?"

Ashan shivered as he turned and looked at Nikandr. "In essence, Nasim sacrificed him."

Nikandr coughed, trying and failing to understand the significance. "What of it?"

"He gave a life to draw you forth, creating a small rift in the aether which he used to draw you back. I wonder if the same could be done for Nasim."

Nikandr coughed again, longer this time. The wasting seemed stronger here in Oshtoyets—either that or the disease was progressing faster. "I don't understand."

They were interrupted by the sound of the outer door opening once more. The gaoler was speaking with several men in his antechamber. Nikandr recognized one of them, and his blood went cold.

It was Borund.

They had come to take him away, and now it would be impossible to escape. Impossible.

Keys clanked in the door and Borund stepped in, followed by Grigory. Borund looked much thinner than he had weeks ago, though he had retained a certain heft. His dark beard was thicker as well, making him look more than a little like a wet bear.

"War doesn't suit you, Bora."

Borund laughed. The sound of it brought a host of fond memories from simpler times, but the look in his eye was the same as many—fear and distrust of those with the wasting. "I could say the same of you, Nischka."

Nikandr shrugged. "I *do* like flying more than fighting."

Borund waved at Ashan's cell door, and then Nikandr's.

"I beg of you, Borund, listen to reason. Surely Grigory has told you that the Maharraht have stolen the boy. They're planning something. They're going to widen the rift that runs through Uyadensk. Let me go to my father and warn him. It's not too late to bring this to a close before the very course of our lives change forever."

Grigory began to speak, but Borund raised his hand, giving Nikandr a clear indication that Zhabyn Vostroma was still very much in command. "Too late, Nischka. It was too late the moment you refused to hand over that boy, and to claim now that he is an enemy of Khalakovo reeks of desperation."

Two streltsi picked Ashan up and led him out of the donjon as the gaoler unlocked Nikandr's door.

Nikandr did not try to argue. Anything he said now would only cement Borund's opinion. The only hope he had now was to speak with Zhabyn, to convince him that a trade with his father was in his best interests. Perhaps he would agree to give Nikandr over if Father agreed to give up Radiskoye. The decision could not be allowed to stand, but it would give Nikandr the time he needed to locate the Maharraht and stop them.

Waiting in the crisp evening air of the fort's courtyard were a dozen mounts and a flatbed wagon. Borund and Grigory mounted ponies as the streltsi guided Ashan and Nikandr up to the rear of the wagon and chained them to heavy iron loops bolted through the bed.

They left, tack jingling, hooves clomping, with Borund and Grigory at the fore, followed by four mounted streltsi, the wagon, and four soldiers at the rear. Flying as a captive to Grigory on the *Kavda* had felt strange, but it had been a relatively private affair. Here, being dragged in the open on the bed of a wagon like a criminal being taken to the gallows was much more personal, much more public. Grigory turned in his seat several times to look at him though the sun had long since set and there was only a faint amount of light in the western sky.

The trail leading down toward the manor house was not in disrepair, but neither was it often used, and so the ride was rough.

They were only minutes away from the fort when, in the brush to the right of the trail, a light flashed, followed immediately by the crack of a musket.

A split-second later, the strelet riding furthest ahead dropped from his saddle and thumped to the ground.

CHAPTER 61

Shouts were raised as more flashes sparked in the darkness. Each shot il-luminated, for one split second, the man who had fired the weapon—prone bodies facing the trail, eyes sighting along the length of a barrel. There were at least a dozen, and based on the rate of fire, Nikandr assumed they had each brought two loaded muskets with them.

Five streltsi, and one of the soldiers driving the wagon, dropped in the opening volley. Two of the remaining men returned fire. The other kicked his pony with a "Yah!" and was off after Grigory and Borund, who had also given their ponies free rein.

One more of the soldiers was shot before the remaining two dropped their weapons and raised their hands above their heads.

Nikandr heard a man's voice call from the darkness. "Quickly," he said. Soldiers were now approaching the wagon. "Prince Nikandr Iaroslov…" the voice called.

"I am here," Nikandr said.

Up the hill, a large bell began clanging within the walls of Oshtoyets. It would be only moments before the soldiers in the fort were on them.

The soldier, bearing the stars of a desyatnik, hopped up to the wagon, stepping past Ashan to take a key from the driver. He used it to unlock the chains that secured Nikandr and Ashan to the iron rings. "Where is the other?" he said, referring to the key that would release their manacles.

"I don't have it," the driver said quickly. "Prince Grigory kept them for himself."

Using his pistol, and that of his second-in-command, he shot first Nikandr's and then Ashan's manacles free.

"Quickly, My Lord," the desyatnik said, motioning Nikandr to the steep downward slope to the northwest.

Nikandr needed no reminder of how little time they had before the pur-suit was on them. He leapt down and then he and Ashan and the soldiers were off, running down the mountain at a speed that made Nikandr fear he would break an ankle at any moment. Ashan, despite his age, held up well, and all of them made it down to a plateau before the sound of galloping ponies could be heard from the trail behind them. The sound of barking dogs came as well.

"Halt," the desyatnik called. "Reload, one musket only."

They did, and they were as quick, even in the darkness, as Nikandr had ever seen. In less than twenty seconds, they were done, and as a group they descended along the next slope.

The barking dogs, perhaps eight or nine of them, were gaining on them quickly. When it was clear they would not be able to outrun them, the desyatnik called for another halt and for the men to line up their shots. In fits and starts, a dozen shots rang out, and a good many of the dogs were felled; but three made it through, leaping upon the men, who defended themselves with muskets at the ready.

Two soldiers cried out, but the others pulled long knives from the sheaths strapped to their thighs and stabbed the dogs until all of them lay dead or dying. They continued without pause, though it was with no small amount of regret since most of the dogs—perhaps all—had been Khalakovo's. It was a terrible betrayal to kill beasts that had been raised to protect his father's land.

The pursuit was gaining on them. Nikandr spared a quick glance, seeing only silhouettes—perhaps a dozen of them—with more following on foot.

The first shots rang out as they reached a gently sloping land that led down to the seashore. A waterborne ship waited in the distance. More shots were fired, and one of the men to Nikandr's right was struck. He grunted—no more than this—and on they went. Another shot struck the ground near Nikandr's feet. He cringed reflexively as a spray of loose gravel pelted his legs and chest and face.

The ponies had reached open land behind them, and they were now galloping wide, clearly hoping to cut them off before they could reach the ship.

They had not counted on the men from the ship.

A half-dozen shots rang out, accompanied by flashes of white. Three ponies fell. The enemy reined in and fired into Nikandr's group—ignoring the ship—as their reinforcements on foot began to close in. One soldier screamed and fell. Immediately two others shouldered their weapons and lifted him up, supporting him while moving as quickly as they could manage.

"Reload," the desyatnik called as more shots came in from the ship. They did so on the run, and as they finally neared the water's edge, the desyatnik ordered them to fire. Most did so, the others continuing into the surf.

Two rowboats waited. The soldiers levered themselves in as return fire came from the shore. They rowed furiously as the men on the ship attempted to suppress the fire of the men in pursuit. Another soldier was shot through the chest, but finally they rowed beyond the far side of the ship so that it would shield them from any more incoming fire. Immediately, the firing from the deck ceased as well—the men taking cover as the ship, which had already put on a good amount of sail, headed westward toward open sea.

"All quiet," came a voice that was soft but nonetheless carried over the entire ship.

By the time they reached the deck, the men on the shore had given up. Minutes later, nearly a league out to sea, Nikandr saw the barest form of a windship scouring the waves. Their ship had veered from their initial course, however, and was now heading in a northerly direction.

Minutes passed, and slowly it became clear that the pursuing ship would not find them. And finally, Nikandr breathed a sigh of relief he'd been holding since the first shot had been fired outside the keep.

Nikandr couldn't sleep, partly because of his wounds, partly because of his inherent distaste for waterborne craft, and partly because he was so unsure about what the coming day would bring. Kapitan Lidan would tell him little except that he had been ordered to take the desyatnik and his men to the coast of Duzol and to bring him southeast when they returned.

"But there is nothing to the southeast," Nikandr said.

"The Matra said you'd be transferred."

"To what?"

"I'm sorry, My Lord Prince, she didn't say."

Most likely there hadn't been time to arrange anything more complex. It was probably wise, as well, not to tell the man too much in case they were caught. There would probably be a windship sent to pick him up. He only hoped it came sooner rather than later, for his stomach's sake if nothing else.

He abandoned his cabin well before dawn. The air was bitterly cold and blustery. As the sky brightened in the east, the black wings of a bird could be seen heading toward them from the south. It became clear that it was a rook, but it did not land. It only turned and flew southward again, a sign that they should follow. If Nikandr had judged their speed correctly, they were heading toward the Shallows, an area directly south of Uyadensk that had a mass of sandbars spread over an area nearly as large as Duzol.

As the sun rose, a high layer of clouds rushed in from the west. Not long after, snowflakes began to fall—an ill omen for the day to come.

Two airships were spotted off the port bow flying low over the sea. At first he thought they belonged to one of the traitor dukes, but then he recognized a ship he had sailed on three different occasions—a massive four-masted galleon known as the *Hawk of Rhavanki*. Then he saw where they were headed: a mass of seven windships anchored in the sandbars.

Clearly an important gathering had been called, and it made a certain sort of sense—the traitor dukes would be scouring the islands, all of them, in search of Nikandr and in hopes of suppressing any incoming resistance. Father's only hope for surprise was to avoid such places and to have the allied Matri mask their presence from the others.

Ashan stood on deck, watching. He had a concerned look on his face, as if this was the last thing he had hoped for.

Nikandr stepped close to him and spoke softly, even though he was among allies. "In the cell last night, you said that Nasim would be healed if I drew him across."

"That is what I believe."

"Why? What does the rift have to do with it?"

"It is only at the rift, Nikandr, the deepest part, that we will have any hope of success." Ashan glanced around the deck, then up to the rigging, making sure no one was close enough to hear.

"And my stone?"

"That is what will draw him. He will see it and you will draw him to our world."

They fell silent as Kapitan Lidan joined them. He pointed up to the sky, to a skiff that was headed their way. "Best you get ready."

Soon they were on the skiff and headed toward the *Zhabek*, a ship of Mirkotsk nearly as large as the *Hawk*. The snow had begun to fall more heavily, though it was still only a light snowfall. On deck, Nikandr was surprised to see several dukes: Andreyo Rhavanki, Heodor Lhudansk, and Aleg Khazabyirsk were speaking beneath the helm, and they were not dressed in their rich coats of office, but the long, dark cherkesskas cut in the style of the windsmen. Each had the designs of their Duchy and other badges of honor upon their left breast.

"What is happening?" Ashan asked. His face was tight, the wind whipping his curly hair about his forehead and cheeks.

"We'll find out soon enough."

"But Nasim…"

"I'll do what I can, Ashan. For now you must trust me."

Father stepped out from the kapitan's cabin along with Yevgeny Mirkotsk. He came to a standstill, however, when he noticed the incoming skiff.

Nikandr couldn't help but notice his reaction. It was one of anger, of disappointment, as if it were Nikandr who was to blame for everything that had happened.

The skiff dropped its sails and was reeled in at the stern of the ship, and when Nikandr disembarked onto the aftcastle, Father was there waiting for him. He pulled him to the landward side. As Ashan stepped calmly onto deck, he was met by several streltsi, who led him amidships.

Father studied Nikandr with a cross look on his face, hands clasped behind his back as the chill wind tugged at his beard and hair. "Do you realize what might have happened, leaving as you did?"

"I know what it *did* cost, Father, and I still believe it was the right thing to do."

"Because of the blight…"

Nikandr had been ready to argue against his father's position. To hear him leap to the very reason for Nikandr's flight from Radiskoye those weeks ago made him feel as if he'd slipped on a rain-slick deck.

"*Da*, because of the blight."

"And what have you found?"

"I believe it can be healed."

"Through the boy?"

Nikandr cocked his head, confused. "How did you know?"

Father looked to the stairs leading down from the aftcastle and made a beckoning motion with one hand. The soldier standing there immediately bowed and left.

"What is it?"

Father did not reply, but a moment later the strelet returned with Rehada in tow. Snow fell across the ship. White snowflakes landed on her black hair before melting away. When the strelet had brought her to their side and left, Rehada met Nikandr's eyes only for a moment, as if she were embarrassed to acknowledge his presence in front of his father.

"What has happened?" Nikandr asked, sure that Rehada's presence meant something momentous was about to happen.

Father looked up to the sun, which lay behind a large gray cloud limned in white. "When the sun strikes noon, a battle will begin such as the islands haven't seen since the War of Seven Seas."

Nikandr still hoped, perhaps foolishly, that bloodshed could be avoided. "We could speak with them. They might—"

Father held up his hand, forestalling him. "They will not listen to reason. Not now. Not when their advantage has been pressed so far. We will attack, for truly there is no choice left to us."

"The Matri…"

"Are as prepared as they will ever be. Everything has been arranged, Nischka. Now, there is something I would very much like for you to discuss with your dear friend, Rehada."

"And what would that be?"

"She has confessed to me that she is Maharraht."

Nikandr's blood rushed to his face. He had known this since Ghayavand, but some small part of him had still held hope that it had been a lie. He looked to Rehada, but she refused to meet his eye.

"For years she has been plying from you secrets that should have remained safely within the walls of Radiskoye. Yet she came to me through no small amount of danger to tell me of Nasim and the plans the Maharraht have drawn.

"So, I put it to you, Nischka. Weigh the truth in her words. If you think she can be believed, then so be it. Take her to find the boy and bring him back if you can. But if you believe she is lying, that she works for our enemy still, then you will tell me so, and we will settle this before the hour is out."

With that Father walked away, his bootsteps heavy on the deck, leaving Nikandr alone with a woman he had come to love—a woman he loved still. It pained him to see her cowed, a woman who had always burned brightly from within, but then it occurred to him just how gifted she was at acting.

"Is it true?"

She finally raised her head and looked him in the eye. "*Yeh.*"

"All that time?"

She nodded. "I was Maharraht well before I landed on Khalakovo."

"How, Rehada? Why?"

She shook her head. "I will not repeat the litany of reasons here. Some day, if the time is right, I may do so. But I won't defend myself."

"You had better."

"I won't." She stood taller, her eyes fierce. "When you see your wife again, ask *her* of my history."

"Atiana?"

Rehada's long black hair played in the wind as she stared at him with dark, pained eyes.

Nikandr felt his heart hardening. "My father was deadly serious."

She leaned over and spat at his feet. "Kill me if you will, son of Iaros. I have no fear of dying."

Nikandr felt himself gritting his jaw, felt the tightness in his chest and stomach. He forced himself to breathe deeply and release it. He waited until the tightness eased before speaking again. "Tell me at the least why you changed your mind."

She stared at him, as hard as ever, but then her look softened ever so slightly. "Because there are things greater than the Maharraht, greater than the Grand Duchy."

"No grand words, Rehada. Not now."

"We stand on a precipice. Soroush would push us over the edge—all of us—if only to begin the world anew. I no longer believe there is wisdom in such a course, no matter how much I might once have wished to do the same. There is something in Nasim, something precious, something Soroush would use against you. If he's allowed to go through with his plans, it will be destroyed. I have no doubt of this, and it's something I would see saved. That is why I have come. Not for you. Not for Khalakovo. Not even for the Aramahn. It is for Nasim and the worlds he walks between."

Nikandr stood still, breathing, weighing her words. There was truth in her words, but he realized that he should not be allowed such judgment. She had been Maharraht since before the day they had met and he had failed to uncover the truth of it. He was the wrong person to be standing here, determining if she should live or die. She may very well be orchestrating a trap for the Maharraht that might lead to something worse. With the wrong decision he might give the Maharraht exactly what they wanted.

But he also knew, as he stood there looking into her defiant eyes, that he was trapped. She had pulled him into her net long ago, and he could no more order her death than he could his father's—not when everything rang so true—and he realized that his father must have known this as well.

Father *wanted* to believe her words.

And with that, he knew what he must do, and he left Rehada to render his decision.

CHAPTER 62

Nikandr watched as the first of the ships far ahead were lost from view in the snowstorm that had progressed steadily from a dusting to an outright blizzard. He had been too brash earlier. He had declared the storm an ill omen without considering its ability to hide them as their ships descended on Volgorod.

Behind the swiftest ships—which had been placed at the vanguard of the attack—were nearly five dozen more. It represented the entirety of their resources. Some were warships, more than ready for battle. Some had been hastily fitted with cannons in order to play a role in the battle—Nikandr could locate these easily by the way they listed to one side, the cannons not having been aligned properly with the masts. Other ships were decoys that had been fitted with *cannons* that were no more than mast poles painted black and affixed to cannon mounts. They would fool no one if they came close, but that was not their goal. They were there to provide cover so that Nikandr and Ashan and Rehada would have enough time to do what was needed.

Nikandr stood at the helm of the *Adnon*, a twelve-masted brigantine. Rehada was nearby, peering into the gray clouds as snow fell upon her dark robes and hair. She looked grim, as opposed to Ashan, who stood in the center of the deck near the mainmast, as calm as ever.

The first of the cannon shots came before they had closed to within several leagues of the shores of Uyadensk. It was not long after midday, but the sky was a leaden gray, the snow splashing across it in vast, eddying swaths. A return volley sounded. It was impossible to tell who was the attacker and who the defender. The return shot had been fired quickly, which pointed to a prepared crew—a state that would probably not describe the enemy. Then again, they might have been more prepared than he had guessed—they would be expecting *some* sort of attack, after all—or the Matri may have sensed their approach.

As agreed, their ship and two others assigned as escorts lowered their altitude. Only minutes later a twelve-masted brigantine appeared in the air ahead of them, on a near collision course with the ship to their landward side. It fired its forward cannon even before it had begun to tail off its original course, but when it did, it began to veer across the *Adnon's* path.

"Fire!" Nikandr shouted, "And dive, men! Dive!"

After an adjustment to the fore cannon's aim, the gunner holding the firing brand lowered the glowing red tip to the touch hole. A tail of white blasted forth from the mouth. Nikandr could feel it in his feet as the shot tore into the seaward foresail of the oncoming ship.

"Dive!" Nikandr repeated.

Their dhoshaqiram was a man no older than Nikandr. He was very gifted, the Duke of Mirkotsk had said, and so had been assigned to Nikandr's ship, but he was not working fast enough. The oncoming ship's hull would sail past—barely—but the ships' rigging was going to tear both ships apart.

Nikandr pulled hard on the levers of the helm, causing the *Adnon* to tilt counterclockwise. The ship responded, but slowly. It wasn't going to turn in time.

Nikandr pulled harder than was wise—too often the workings of the keel would bend or snap outright if the steersman pulled too hard—and at the last moment the two forward masts passed one another. The two seaward mainmasts, however—longer than the foremasts—caught one another, and the *Adnon's*—a single length of windwood—snapped a third of the way down. The other ship lost a spar and dozens of yards of sail and rope as it was ripped away by the *Adnon's* wounded mast.

Rigging and sails were ripped away as the ships cleared one another. A sailor was slipping along a rope, hoping to avoid the debris, but he was caught by a large wooden block across his back. He fell to the deck with a meaty thump.

"Fire aft!" Nikandr shouted.

The other ship's kapitan called out the same command. The two cannons fired nearly simultaneously. Several of the *Adnon's* crew, less than ten paces from where Nikandr stood at the helm, were ripped apart by the incoming grape shot. All three men fell to the deck, little more than bloody masses of flesh and lead.

The chained shot his own men had fired a scant moment before they had died whipped outward, the two balls twirling before catching the starward mizzenmast halfway along its length. A huge crack rent the air, and the mast tilted forward noticeably, the three white sails flapping like sheets. The mast tilted to one side as the ship's nose tipped higher than its rear.

The *Adnon* continued on, Nikandr righting its heading and adjusting for the wounded mast. The other ship was soon lost from sight, swallowed whole by the howling storm.

Nikandr released his breath slowly. At the very least there was no need to worry about that ship. With yards and yards of canvas gone or ineffective, the entire characteristics of the ship would be thrown off. In this wind, in the low visibility, it would not rejoin the battle. It would in fact be just as likely to crash into land or sea as regain the eyrie.

Before they had gone another quarter-league, a crewman shouted, "Ship, aft!"

Behind them, in the blowing snow, a small, eight-masted caravel resolved against the background of the dark gray clouds. Moments later, another came clear—a huge, sixteen-masted clipper.

"Sound the bell," Nikandr called.

Nearby, the boatswain rang a brass bell three times, just loudly enough for the ship on either side of them to hear. Moments later, the two ships began tailing away as Nikandr ordered the ship to climb. He felt himself grow heavy as the ship obeyed. The landward ship dropped and trailed away. The other ship began slipping windward, maintaining altitude.

Two shots came from the clipper, but they had been directed toward the starward ship. The other trailing ship, however, was ascending, hungry on the tail of the *Adnon*.

Now that it was closer and the ship could be seen more clearly through the snow, Nikandr realized whose ship it was. To the confused looks of his men, he laughed—even Rehada stared at him with a dour expression—but he ignored them all while staring at the trailing ship. With dozens of ships sailing the winds, the ancients had seen fit for Grigory to have found him.

"Get the gunners to the rear, boatswain," Nikandr said, "and have them fire at will."

The boatswain clapped his heels and shouted for the men to move aft. They hauled their equipment with them, and several crewmen came behind, hefting sacks of powder and the wooden trays that held the burlap bags of shot.

A rook flapped in and landed on the deck near Nikandr's feet. It wore the device of Mirkotsk around its ankle.

"Swiftly, Iaroslov," the rook said.

"What's happened?"

"The Maharraht have secured an area near Radiskoye. Vostroma's men have either not noticed or are choosing to ignore them."

"Ranos?"

"Has begun the attack on the eyrie."

"Then we'll be alone?"

The rook tilted its head backward and cawed as grape shot whizzed through the air above them. "It appears so, Khalakovo, but it may not hold." It flapped its wings and took to the air. "It may not hold," it repeated as it flew over the edge of the ship and dropped from view.

Ashan, who hadn't moved during the fighting, woke himself and climbed the stairs to reach the aftcastle. "We have reached land," he said to Nikandr.

"After the next cannon shot, drift down as we agreed," Nikandr called, "and prepare the skiffs."

At the calls from the ship's master, two dozen streltsi stormed up from belowdecks and moved themselves into the two skiffs waiting on either side of the deck.

The aft cannon fired, but its aim was too low and it tore a meaningless hole into the hull of the *Kavda*. As soon as the shot had been fired, everyone—the crew and Rehada and Ashan—grabbed onto whatever they could. The next moment, the dhoshaqiram allowed much of the buoyancy to leave the windwood, and the *Adnon* plummeted.

As soon as the *Kavda* was lost from view, the waiting streltsi filed into the skiffs. Ashan, Rehada, and Nikandr moved to the one on the landward side. Once they were seated, the crewmen above began cranking the windlass like madmen, letting out the stout ropes that held the skiff secure. The other skiff followed suit, and soon they were floating free of the ship's seaward sails.

The wind was strong. It threatened to swing them into the sails, but these men were seasoned. They raised the skiff's sails quickly and released the catches on the two steel clamps securing the ropes.

Ashan, working alone, used the two ropes attached to the lower corners of the sail to guide the ship. He was their lone havaqiram, but he was exceptional, and he guided the ship forward and downward smoothly and quickly. The other skiff, steered by a younger havaqiram, was having trouble with the wind, but he was a man Father had sworn by, and he seemed to be holding his own.

The *Adnon*, now far above and ahead of them, was nearly lost from sight, but the *Kavda* had lowered further—perhaps overcompensating for the sudden drop of the *Adnon*. Nikandr was sure that they would launch skiffs of their own, but they continued doggedly. Nikandr was watching the deck closely when a silhouette stepped to the gunwales and looked downward through the swirling snow.

He could not be sure—he could see no clear details—but something inside him knew that it was Atiana. He nearly called out to her, but it was a foolish notion, quickly discarded. She would not hear him, and if she could, so could the others on the ship. Above all, it was pointless. He could do nothing to help her—assuming help was needed at all.

Their ship was drawn downward into a thickening curtain of white. They landed without incident, though as soon as they did they heard a long, ragged line of musket fire come to them through the swirling snow. The shouting of men—a battle cry—and cannon fire sounded in reply. From a further distance—muted by the weather—were more cannon shots. The nearer conflict must be the battle for Volgorod, and the farther was surely Ranos's desperate attempt to wrest back the eyrie. With those two loci and their relative distances judged by the cannon fire, it didn't take long for Nikandr to determine where they were. He had judged the distance well. They were no more than a half-league from the site of the suurahezhan's crossing, the event that had started all of them on this long and winding path.

As the streltsi gathered their equipment and readied themselves, Nikandr beckoned Rehada and Ashan and the two Aramahn from the second skiff.

"Can you do anything about the snow?" Nikandr asked Ashan.

"You wish me to stop it?"

"*Nyet*, I'd like *more* to cover our approach."

Ashan nodded. "I'll see what can be done."

Atiana felt her legs move, felt them lead her about the ship. She tried to stop, to simply stand still, but when she did her muscles, her very bones, screamed in pain, and she was forced to relent. She tried to speak, and once even managed a guttural sound, but then Grigory's mother exerted her control once more, relegating Atiana to watching as *she* decided what Atiana would do.

Atiana should have been able to protect herself from the Matra's attack, but Alesya had hidden her intentions well. It made Atiana wonder how many times Alesya had done this before. Plenty, she thought, and there was a growing certainty within her that Alesya would not allow her to pass this information along to anyone. When the need for her had passed she would take an unfortunate fall, she would tumble into the sea, and Grigory would deliver grave apologies to Vostroma for their loss.

Alesya had rooted from her mind the location of the rift and had bid Grigory to set sail for it. She wanted him to prevent whatever it was that Khalakovo was planning with the Maharraht. She wanted for him to return the hero, to set up Bolgravya as the savior in this conflict.

As the ship flew through the snow toward Volgorod, the sounds of cannon fire broke. A massive clipper came abaft of the *Kavda*. The boatswain issued a recognition signal, receiving the correct answer in reply. The clipper, a battle-tested ship flying the colors of Nodhvyansk, settled into line with the

Kavda. As it did, Atiana could feel the presence of a soulstone.

Nikandr's soulstone.

Atiana was confused. This was a phenomenon spoken of in the annals of the Grand Duchy, but not in recent years. To feel someone, *anyone*, outside the bounds of the aether was extremely rare, and Atiana assumed it was related to her proximity to the rift—or perhaps the weather, which, after hours on deck, had left her numb, much as she would be while taking the dark. Whatever the reason, she knew with certainty that Nikandr was aboard a ship off the windward bow. She desperately tried to hide this from Alesya, but it was not something she had learned how to do. To think about hiding something was to think about the thing itself, and that was all it took for Alesya to sense what she had learned.

Alesya forced Atiana to turn from the gunwale and address Grigory, who stood near the helm. "Nikandr is nearby." She pointed. "Just there."

"How can you be sure?"

Alesya raised Atiana's arm and touched her breast, where her soulstone lay. "There is more of a bond between Atiana and Nikandr than I would have guessed."

Grigory frowned, but then he threw his arm toward the pilot and pointed in the same direction that Atiana had. "Change course."

"*Da*, Kapitan."

And so they followed.

Cannon fire broke out, and a wounded Vostroman ship took shape from within the thick of the white snow and sped past them. Not long after, three ships could be seen, heading in the same direction as the *Kavda.*

Three more ships appeared, and soon after they were spotted all three broke off in different directions.

"Which?" Grigory asked Atiana.

Again she tried to hide the information by focusing on other things: the cold, the snow, her anger at being held prisoner within her own skin, but it was useless.

"The center," Alesya said, pointing.

They followed the brigantine as the clipper behind them angled starward to pursue one of the other ships. Cannon fire tore into the hull. Surprisingly, Alesya's fear stood out strongly. She ducked down, putting her hands over her head as the concussion traveled along the deck.

For a moment, Atiana could move again. She crawled forward of her own free will, but the next moment found herself trapped once more. Alesya forced her to stand. She composed herself, anger and embarrassment emanating from her.

In the confusion, Nikandr's ship was lost in the drifting snow. Grigory called out for the *Kavda* to drop in pursuit. One moment everyone was grabbing onto ropes or railings or rigging, and the next moment Atiana's stomach was in her throat. She held onto the rope of a nearby deadeye and held on for dear life, sure the ship would crash to the ground.

"She's ahead, Kapitan," a crewman shouted, pointing off the windward bow.

The ship leveled off, and Alesya was able to restore control once more.

She could see through the snow the barest hint of the ship's form, but she could also feel Nikandr somewhere below. The feeling was beginning to fade, though she didn't understand why.

Alesya forced her to the gunwale. Far below, there were two skiffs, barely visible. They were lost among the currents of snow a moment later.

"Nikandr is on one of the skiffs, along with a score of streltsi."

"Prepare the skiffs!" Grigory shouted. "Quickly."

"*Nyet*. Let them go." Alesya stared downward, into the swirling snow. "Allow Nikandr to think that he hasn't been seen." She turned back to Grigory. "*Then* we'll fill our skiffs and send them hunting."

Nikandr watched as the streltsi spread out in rows of four and began marching forward, muskets at the ready. The snow was falling so heavily he could see little more than white. The snow was already a foot deep and getting deeper by the moment, making the going slow and arduous.

The site of the suurahezhan's crossing was less than a mile ahead. So far there had been no sign of the Maharraht, but the sounds of the battle for the eyrie and Radiskoye had shown no signs of letting up.

Then he heard it. Chanting, from a single voice. He signaled to the sotnik to slow the men, and to spread them out. They obeyed silently, all except the sotnik and his two desyatni.

The snowfall had eased. They could see dozens of yards ahead of them. The ground was white except for the blackened face of a small outcropping of rock and the handful of scrub brush that dotted the terrain.

Nikandr turned to Ashan, whose forehead was pinched in concentration. He looked to Nikandr and shook his head. There was nothing, apparently, he could do to help.

If Ashan were powerless, Nikandr wondered if it had more to do with the rift than the Maharraht.

He waved for the men to lower themselves to the ground. They did so, crawling through the deep snow until they saw a depression in the terrain. A man sat in the middle of it. His eyes were closed, and he was chanting softly. He wore a black turban dusted with snow. Upon his brow was a brown gem of jasper, sparkling brightly despite the relatively dim light.

The sotnik turned to Nikandr and pointed his finger at the Maharraht, cocking his thumb like a musket.

Nikandr shook his head. He didn't want to do anything rash. They had no idea where Nasim might be, and he refused to jeopardize him needlessly. He turned to Rehada, who was studying the man with a piercing stare. She was conflicted—sadness and doubt clearly warring within her.

Nikandr moved to her side and whispered to her, "Who is he?"

He never heard her response.

A series of sharp cracks resonated beneath him. He could feel it running along his hands and knees.

"Back up!" he shouted.

Before any of them could react, the ground erupted.

Nikandr felt himself lifted and thrown through the air like dust on the wind. He fell softly onto his back in the deep snow, his knee burning from the awkward angle at which he'd landed. Several yards away, standing tall as two men, was a mound of snow-covered earth not unlike the vanahezhan he had seen on Ghayavand. It stalked toward Ashan as the sotnik fired his musket. The flash from the pan was dimmed by the burlap sack protecting it against the snow. The musket ball struck the beast's head as two more shots tore into it. Nearly all of the streltsi discharged their firearms into the hezhan.

Mere moments later, a cry rose up behind them.

Nikandr turned, recognizing the trap well too late.

It was the Maharraht—at least a score of them—advancing through the drifts. They trained their muskets as they advanced. A split second later, they stopped and released a clatter of musket fire.

Nikandr's men cried out in pain as musket shots tore into them. Four dropped to the snow. Ashan spread his arms wide, and gazed to the sky. A musket shot pierced his pale yellow robes just below one arm, tugging at the fabric like a child trying to gain his attention.

"Ashan, beware!" Nikandr shouted as he backed away, but Ashan didn't listen.

The vanahezhan pounded through the snow, but before it could come within striking distance its feet were caught as if it had stepped into deep, sucking mud. Its momentum carried it forward. Loud snaps broke above the din of battle. The beast's body tumbled to the ground, and though its arms caught it, they were held by the same effect. The thing struggled like a collared wolf against the restraints holding it.

As one, the streltsi began retreating toward the depression where the vanaqiram had been only moments ago.

The Maharraht pressed their advantage, but then several of their muskets discharged before they were ready. Rehada's doing.

"Something is wrong," Rehada told Nikandr as she knelt down beside him.

"You noticed?"

Rehada shook her head. "I mean this doesn't feel right. Soroush should be here, and so should Nasim."

"Behind!" the sotnik yelled.

Nikandr glanced back while reloading his own musket. Several dozen yards up, firing from the top of a small knoll, were more Maharraht. Another strelet and the burly desyatnik were felled as the sotnik ordered half of them to return fire.

After one volley, as his men were reloading their weapons, the Maharraht charged.

Nikandr stared at them, knowing they were severely outnumbered, knowing they would most likely die whatever they did.

That may be true, Nikandr thought, but he would not go easily.

He drew his shashka and held it high over his head. "Charge!" he yelled as he sprinted forward.

Atiana watched in horror as Bolgravya's streltsi unloaded from the skiffs. They marched forward, muskets at the ready. She could feel Alesya's growing desire to have this done with and to rid herself of Atiana—she was growing increasingly disgusted by her nearness to Atiana's emotions and thoughts.

Meanwhile, Atiana's awareness of the rift had been growing like the coming light of dawn. There was a distinct feeling of familiarity to it that she could only attribute to her discovery of it within the aether. It lay wide open, a gaping maw in the fabric of the world, and through it she could feel the touch of Adhiya. She could feel warmth and earth and water, even air.

And running through it all was the scent of life.

But there was something else, the feeling that this place—the rift—was like one of any number of threads that ran through the fabric of Erahm—as if the filaments of Adhiya were spread throughout the world like thistledown. The nearest was the one on Duzol, all the more familiar since she had just come from there, and it felt—as it had within the aether—ripe.

Alesya paid little attention to these thoughts because the sounds of battle had broken out. And it was close.

Very close.

The shouts of Duchy men could be heard, as well as the high calls of the Maharraht. The crack of musket fire pattered like the first heavy raindrops of a terrible summer storm. Flashes of white were seen through the curtain of snow.

Grigory raised his fist, a signal that was quickly passed down the line. The men halted.

"Can you feel the boy?" Grigory asked.

Alesya forced Atiana to shake her head. "*Nyet*. There is nothing."

"Where is he?"

"She does not know."

And then Nikandr's voice filtered through the cries.

Grigory's face hardened.

He motioned for the men to fan out to his left, to converge on the sounds of the musket fire that lay between them and Nikandr. They stalked forward, but one of the Maharraht called out a warning. Many of them turned and fired, as Grigory's men laid into them.

It was then, with several Maharraht dropping their muskets and charging with wickedly curved shamshirs drawn, that Atiana realized why Duzol felt so near. Why it felt *ripe*.

The rift here on Uyadensk was not the place where Nasim could be used. It never had been. Ashan had been wrong in the beginning, and she had been wrong in the end. Like a jeweler calculating the perfect angle with which to strike the uncut stone, the Maharraht had understood that the key was not the rift on Uyadensk, but the one on Duzol—not because it was the largest, but because by ripping it wider it would cause a chain of events that would lead to the destruction they hoped to wreak.

"Grigory, stop!" Alesya yelled through Atiana's voice. "Stop!"

Grigory didn't listen. He couldn't. He was locked in swordplay, parrying the fierce slashes from a tall Maharraht warrior.

That was when it struck.

A musket ball.

Without warning.

Straight through Atiana's chest.

The enemy on the knoll had inexplicably pulled away, leaving Nikandr's men free to face the Maharraht to the rear. The two forces crashed together. Men shouted as steel fell upon steel. In moments, their line was complete chaos. Blood fell upon the snow as soldiers dropped on both sides.

Nikandr parried the attacks of a warrior with a long black mustache. He retreated, keeping his parries slow, baiting the other man. When he finally overextended his advantage, Nikandr sidestepped quickly and drove his shashka through the man's gut. He withdrew quickly and slashed the man across the throat before he could attempt a dying stroke.

His men were in disarray. There were less than a dozen left against twenty

Maharraht. It would be over in moments.

But then a cry rose from beyond the knoll. Nearly two dozen streltsi came running over the hill.

"Hold, men! Hold!"

They did, and soon after the other group of streltsi fell upon the Maharraht. None of the enemy withdrew, however. None turned to run. They fought to the death, the last cutting four streltsi down before he took a musket shot at point-blank range through his chest, and even then he grabbed the end of the unfortunate soldier's musket and swung his shamshir high over his head and swept it across the other man's neck. The strelet's head fell against the beaten and bloody snow, emitting a sound like a fallen gourd.

The Maharraht tried to fight on, but he fell to his knees while stumbling against the uneven, blood-matted snow. He blinked several times before the streltsi nearby fell upon him, unleashing their fury, their swords rising and falling and cutting him into barely recognizable pieces.

And then Nikandr saw the commander of the streltsi.

It was Grigory.

And he was pointing a musket directly at Nikandr's chest. "Lay down arms, Khalakovo."

Nikandr stood there, blood trickling across his elbow and along his forearm. He shook his head and allowed his shashka to fall to the trampled snow at his feet. They were in no position to disobey, and he would not sacrifice his men for one last, meaningless gasp. "Lower your arms."

"My Lord Prince," a Bolgravyan desyatnik called from the top of the knoll. "It's Lady Vostroma. She says we are not in the right place."

"I can spare no time for her now."

"She is calling for you. She's been shot."

Nikandr's breath fell away.

Grigory's face went white. He turned and with two of his men and a havaqiram ran toward the top of the rise.

Nikandr tried to follow but was stopped by Grigory's men. He railed against them. "Let me pass!" he shouted. But they would not.

Grigory turned, pausing to stare at Nikandr with a look on his face like he was considering allowing him to come. He looked—in that one brief moment—like a boy who was having trouble with the mantle that had fallen into his lap. It looked like he desperately *wanted* help, even from a man he called an enemy. But then his expression hardened, and he motioned for the streltsi to lead Nikandr back toward his men.

Rehada was being held closely, her circlet gone. Of Nikandr's men less than twenty remained. They stood there, haggard, and it was then that Nikandr realized that Ashan was missing. He scanned the bodies of the fallen, becoming frantic when he didn't see Ashan among them, but when the wind began to blow across the battlefield, he knew that the arqesh had managed to slip away.

The wind gained in intensity, lifting new waves of snow from the ground and pushing men back who were unprepared. It ebbed for one moment, giving everyone a chance to regain their footing, but then, as if the brief pause had been an inhalation, the wind howled with the force of a gale. It sounded like a great, ravenous beast ready to devour them all.

Nikandr fell to the ground as men were swept from their feet. Their kolpak hats flew off their heads as wet snow and dirt pelted them. One man even fired his musket in the direction of the wind, perhaps seeing something he thought was the enemy. The next moment, he toppled backwards and was lost in a rain of white.

The wind cut fiercely against the Vostroman soldiers, pushing them from the lip of the knoll, and Nikandr understood what Ashan was trying to do.

"This way!" he shouted from hands and knees. He dare not stand up lest he be blown about like the men standing only a few paces away. In fact, the intensity increased even more, forcing him to drop to the ground and lay prone.

He didn't know if his men had heard his order, but when he was able to rise, the sotnik was at his elbow, pulling him up and helping him stumble toward the opposite side of the hill.

Rehada and Ashan caught up with the group just as they reached the place where Grigory's men had huddled. There was a wide swath of matted snow and a fair amount of blood, but it was otherwise empty.

They quickly chased after using the trail they had left behind. They found a skiff, its sails cut to shreds, and an imprint in the snow of another that had recently left.

"What do we do, My Lord?" the sotnik asked.

"I don't know," Nikandr said listlessly. "I have no idea where they would go."

"I know," Rehada said. "They go to Duzol."

CHAPTER 63

Atiana realized she was in the air again. She felt light, not only because she was flying through the stormy weather in the bottom of a skiff but because she felt wholly unencumbered by her mortal frame. She felt, in fact, like a havahezhan must: free and ethereal.

She fell unconscious. When she woke again, it was to a jostling of the skiff. They had landed, and someone was standing over her, asking her where they needed to go. He looked familiar, but for the life of her she couldn't place him.

"The spire on the fort," she said weakly.

"You are sure?" he asked.

It was a man she didn't care for—she knew this much—but she saw no reason to withhold the information.

"I am." It felt like each word weighed ten stone.

He looked down on her, ungracious.

"We go," he said, though she understood it was not to her.

"And the Lady Princess?"

A pause.

"Leave her."

Flakes of snow fell upon her face, soft touches of ice upon deadened skin.

The sound of footsteps through snow were all around her, but then they faded, leaving only the nearby waves and the wind as it whistled through the trees. She could see neither of these things, but she realized with a growing certainty that she could *feel* them. The snow beneath her fingers, the grass beneath the snow, the earth through which the grass extended its roots, and the bedrock of the island beneath the soft, pliable earth. She felt all of this and more.

And soon… Soon…

She hears the call of a lonely heron, hears its mate over a mile away. She feels the weight of a nearby copse of trees upon the earth, small in comparison to its larger sister to the south. She feels the wind as it brushes against the evergreen branches, the pine cones as they are tugged free to fall against the snow, the rabbits as they huddle in their warrens, waiting for the storm to pass.

Her awareness spreads to the entire island, and there is one thing that is glaringly out of place.

The rift.

It glows against her senses like a brand, though it does not feel warm. Nor does it feel cold. It feels … wrong. It feels like an insult to this place, an injustice that must be righted, for surely it is a wound that will never heal on its own. The festering must be purged. Only then can the land begin to heal.

She moves in toward the strongest presence of the rift on the island. The spire. It is a mere branch in comparison to the massive trunk that towers above Radiskoye. She is certain that it is the weakest link on the archipelago. Tear it down and Radiskoye's goes with it, and if Radiskoye's goes, then so will all the others—the entire chain will devolve into little more than a gaping maw that leads directly to Adhiya. And then the spirits will avail themselves of anything they wish.

Like a ship in a gale, she finds it difficult to navigate. Her mind is thrown about by the aether, the currents as unpredictable as a cornered lynx. They pull at her, drawing her attention not to one place, but to everything. Duzol—and the entire archipelago beyond it—feels more alive and also closer to death than she had thought possible.

It is the taint of the world beyond, she knows, yet still she finds it difficult to focus her attention, until she senses him.

Nasim.

He is chained to the spire. A spike has been driven into it. From this, manacles hang down and entrap his wrists. The spire itself is bright white against the backdrop of satin black. Most would be a dark blue, even against the spire, but Nasim is nearly as white. He does not fight; he does not scream. Every so often a shiver runs the length of his body, and his eyes move spasmodically beneath closed lids.

Men in ragged lengths of robes circle the spire, which stands in the courtyard of the keep. There are no men of the Duchy to be seen. She assumes they have been killed or are being kept in the donjon of Oshtoyets.

She recognizes two of the Maharraht—Bersuq and Soroush—the same two that raised the vanahezhan on the beach near Izhny.

Soroush approaches Nasim. In his hands he holds five stones, one for each of the aspects: jasper for earth, alabaster for air, tourmaline for fire, azurite for water, and opal for the raw stuff of life. All of them glow as brightly as the spire and Nasim.

The Maharraht are chanting, though she can hear no words. Soroush steps close to Nasim and presses the gem of tourmaline into his mouth. Water is forced down Nasim's throat, and soon it is clear he has swallowed it, for he glows brighter.

Near Bersuq stands a brazier. From it stems a tuft of fire, the fire of Adhiya. In moments it has grown to the size of a man.

This is a crossing, happening as she watches, and in a blink it begins to burn her as if she's been thrown into a blacksmith's forge. She screams from the pain, and it intensifies until she no longer knows who she is.

And then, suddenly, it stops.

In the silence it is jarring to hear Nasim's breathing. It comes softly at first—little more than a telltale sigh like a breeze blowing through the springtime grasses—but it intensifies, and there comes from him a tendril of gossamer light. It flows outward and reaches for Adhiya.

In the aether it is easy to forget that there are not only the dimensions of the physical world; there is another: a length of measure toward Adhiya that is so subliminal that it is often missed by even the most gifted Matra. She learned of such things from her mother, and she had long thought the information useless. But now she finds it invaluable. Essential.

She can sense where the tendril is headed: to a shadow on the other side that is shaped just like the bright imprint of Nasim on the mortal plane. As Soroush places the alabaster stone in Nasim's mouth, the link grows stronger, and it is clear what they are attempting to do. An echo of Nasim lives beyond the aether. He is of Erahm and Adhiya, both, and they are attempting to draw the two together. She does not know what will happen should they succeed; she only knows that it must be stopped.

Something familiar draws her attention. A soulstone. She pulls her attention away from the ritual and turns northward. A skiff comes, and within it sits Nikandr, but his mind is free of his body. He floats as the Matri do, and he is drawn toward the boy, Nasim.

There is something holding him back, however. The Maharraht within the courtyard—Soroush and Bersuq and the others—they are chanting; they are drawing about them energy that will keep Nikandr from reaching Nasim, and she knows that this cannot be allowed. She must break their hold on the keep. After that, it will be up to Nikandr and the ancients.

Then the suurahezhan shifts. It lifts its head and turns toward the skiff, its attention focused on Rehada in particular.

And there is nothing Atiana can do to stop it.

When Nikandr and his companions returned to their own skiffs, they found that one of its sails had been slashed, just as Grigory's had. The other skiff, however, was still intact, and they discovered why a moment later.

The loud crack of a pistol rose above the distant sounds of the windship battle still raging to the south. The ball zipped past Nikandr and with a meaty thud bit deep into the chest of the strelet marching double-time behind him. A strelet in a gray cherkesska leapt into the boat, shashka in hand. He attempted to slash its sail, but Nikandr fired his pistol and the man crumpled, his sword slipping from his hand.

They took to the skiff, loading sixteen men. It was unwise, Nikandr knew, but he felt the risk was necessary. He needed to reach Duzol before Soroush could complete his plans, and he would need the men to help stop him once they arrived.

Ashan took the sail and raced them southwest. The storm was beginning to abate, but there was snow falling still. They came closer to the eyrie than Nikandr was comfortable with, but the risk of being spotted and fired upon was one they would have to live with.

As they passed the eyrie, two large ships passed above them. They were firing upon one another, but Nikandr could not tell which ships were aligned with which sides. They were a goodly distance away and the snow was thick enough to obscure details.

Soon they were over open water and rushing toward Duzol. Long minutes passed, without either island in sight, but then from the canvas of white ahead came the darkening mass of Duzol, and soon they could make out the cliffs, upon which sat Oshtoyets, the small keep where Rehada had said the Maharraht and Nasim would be found.

"Straight in, men!" Nikandr ordered, knowing this was no time for subtlety and hoping that at the very least surprise would be with them.

The keep came into view, its gray walls dappled in white. The spire in the courtyard, however, was quite different. Not a flake of white marred its smooth black surface. Wisps of steam rose along its sides.

"Turn away," Rehada said.

"*Nyet*, stay on course."

"Turn away!" Rehada yelled.

Ashan, manning the skiff's sails, responded, drawing the wind from the north and shifting his stance to accommodate the way it pulled at the sails. But it was too late. From within the courtyard, Nikandr could see what Rehada had been worried about. The bright and burning form of a suurahezhan resolved there, and it was larger than the one that had killed Stasa Bolgravya. Its head was as high as the wall itself. Its form was ephemeral—shifting and sliding hypnotically—but it was still quite clear when it turned and focused its attention on their skiff.

On the walls stood many men—the remains of the Maharraht. They had muskets held at the ready, but they did not raise them to their shoulders. In fact they made no move to fire.

Within the courtyard stood Soroush.

And Nasim.

Nikandr could feel him. He was scared and lonely and in pain, but most of all he was worried; he was being used—he knew this—and there was nothing he could do to prevent it.

Soroush leaned over and placed something in Nasim's mouth. Nasim accepted it. It tasted metallic. Of the earth. It was smooth and cool to the touch.

"Stop, Nischka," Rehada shouted.

He felt it slip down his throat and fall heavily into the pit of his stomach.

Rehada slapped him across the cheek.

He felt the pain, but it was nothing compared to the feeling of ecstasy as another spirit, a havahezhan, was drawn from Adhiya into the mortal realm. She slapped him again and again, and finally his men had to hold her back. As he saw Rehada screaming in pain from their attempts to prevent her from striking him again, he was drawn back from the edge.

At that moment, Ashan released his hold on the ropes. The sail flew upward and flapped in the wind as he opened his arms wide and stared up to the sky. A heavy mist formed between them and the suurahezhan, which now stood less than a hundred paces away. Nikandr heard the beast moan as a fireball flew from the palm of the beast's raised hand. As it sped toward them, the mist continued to coalesce. It formed into sleet and snow and ice, and the wind held it in place, pulling it together tightly.

"Hold on!" Nikandr shouted. He could still feel Nasim, could feel the havahezhan forming within the courtyard, but he was, for now, in control of his feelings and thoughts.

When the ball of flame struck the forming cloud a hiss was released as loud as lava pouring into the sea. The ball of fire was weakened, but not extinguished. It was off course, but then it curved sharply, guided by the suurahezhan, and struck the underside of the skiff.

The skiff rotated around the keel, nearly to the point of overturning. Nikandr lost his grip and slipped free from the confines of the skiff. He was saved when he grabbed onto the gunwale, but five others slipped from the sides and fell screaming to the waves below.

But then the skiff righted itself, and the hull struck him in the chest. He lost his grip. Two streltsi grabbed his wrists, but the palms of their hands were slick, and they could not hold on.

Nikandr fell, the skiff above him falling away.

As he plummeted, he could feel the havahezhan, not the elder that had been summoned moments ago, but the one that had been with him since before the attack on the *Gorovna*.

Help me, he called to it.

Please help.

It did not, and the wind whipped by him faster.

The words of Sariya came to him then. *Give yourself to him.*

She'd meant the words for Nasim, but he knew that it applied to the qiram as they gave themselves to the spirits.

He did so now.

He turned as he fell so he was facing the frothing water below. He spread his arms wide and closed his eyes as he had seen Jahalan do so many times before. He felt the wind whip past him, felt the pressure of it on his chest. He opened himself to the spirit, to do what it would with him.

Atiana knows she is dying. She can feel her body failing as it lies upon the snow on the coast of Duzol. Oddly, she is much more in tune with it now that it is broken and nearly useless than she had ever been able to do when she was healthy and whole. Her lifeblood spills, but it has so far done little to stifle her ability to walk among the winds of the aether.

She studies the tendril that flows from Nasim to the ghost of his self in Adhiya. Nasim in the material world is solid and stable, a white brand against the darkness of the keep. Nasim in the spirit world is impossible to define. His form shifts abruptly, as do the colors that he contains.

As the third stone is placed upon his tongue, the tendril thickens. She can feel him, his pain, his desire to stop what is happening but also his utter inability to do so. She tries to strengthen him, to support him so that he might make it through this trial alive and fight those that are trying to use him, but it is no use. Though she can feel him and his emotions, she is powerless to affect him.

Nikandr is still near, but he is not so focused on Nasim as he once was. She must change this, and Bersuq is the key. Soroush is too intent on what he is doing, whereas Bersuq is allowing his mind to float as he chants. He is ripe for the picking, and if she can assume him, then it would loosen the hold they had upon the keep.

She moves closer to the men. Fear grows within her, for she has never assumed another. She can feel upon Bersuq his gem. He is bonded to a spirit, and it glows in the aether like a bright, piercing star. She steps toward him, careful to avoid the spirit.

And then she enters Bersuq.

Immediately he rails against her. She maintains the tenuous hold she has upon him, but by the barest of margins. She can sense his fear—fear that the Matri have found him—and she presses her advantage.

Dozens of ships are on their way, she tells him. *In moments, a horde the likes of which you've never seen will descend upon Oshtoyets.*

But he is emboldened. He knows that even with a thousand men the Grand Duchy will have difficulty holding against such beasts. And they are not like the first elder that had been summoned those weeks ago. These would not willingly dissipate and return from whence they'd come. These would batter the Landed until their masters gave them leave to stop.

Only if you can keep the boy alive, she says.

It is their only weakness, and it gives Bersuq pause.

It is enough. She storms through him, forcing him into the deepest corners of his mind to the point that he can no longer comprehend the possibility of regaining himself.

The world comes alive through Bersuq's senses: the smell of a peat fire; the heat from the suurahezhan against his skin; the touch of Bersuq's tongue as she forces him to continue to chant, mimicking his low, rhythmic sounds.

The other Maharraht do not appear to have noticed, so lost in their actions are they. She watches closely as Soroush takes another gem: jasper. He reaches out to Nasim, and she nearly stops him, nearly throws herself against him so that Nasim will not be forced to summon another elder to the mortal plane. As she watches Nasim's mouth open, watches Soroush place the milky stone upon his tongue, she realizes that there is a sense of satisfaction within Bersuq. He is still buried in the corners of his mind, but it is unmistakable. He is pleased.

Nasim swallows the stone, his head bobbing as he does so, and she believes at first that Bersuq's satisfaction comes from what Nasim is doing. Four stones have been swallowed. The earth begins to crack as the vanahezhan takes shape in the courtyard. It is a mass of cracked brick and dark, packed earth. It stands and pounds the earth with its four massive arms.

And then Soroush's chanting stops. "Did you think," he says while turning his head to look at her, "that we would be taken so easily?"

Bersuq's fingers go cold and tingly.

She cannot respond, for she suddenly realizes why Bersuq is satisfied—not because of Nasim, but because of *her*. He is pleased that she has assumed him, that her soul now rests within the constraints of his physical shell. And she knows that she must escape.

She attempts to but finds herself trapped. She claws toward the aether, scrabbles away, hoping that by throwing everything into this one last gasp that he will lose hold.

But it's no good. She is bound.

Very faintly, but perfectly clear, she hears Bersuq laughing.

Soroush is smiling as well. "Settle yourself, Matra." He picks up the final stone—an opal, the stone of life. "You're going nowhere."

CHAPTER 64

Rehada watched numbly as the streltsi leapt over the gunwales. As they moved in formation up the hill toward the keep, Rehada remained in the skiff. She had watched and had been able to do nothing as Nikandr fell from the ship, lost to the winds and the sea. She swallowed, fighting back tears, fighting back the rage that was boiling within her.

Ashan stood just outside the skiff, holding his hand out to her. "Come," he said. "There is work to do yet."

She wanted to tell him to go on without her, that she would be useless, a danger to the soldiers who were there to protect her. But far up the hill, the havahezhan was already cresting the wall and flying toward them. It drew snow up from the ground, which whirled around it, making plain something that was normally difficult to see.

She knew she couldn't abandon them. There was still Nasim to think of. A part of her wished that her heart was filled with revenge, but it was not. Too much of those emotions had been burned from her. But there was still a desire to set things right. With or without Nikandr, she would do what she set out to do.

The streltsi gained, trekking up the steep ground that led to the keep, but they halted when they realized the hezhan was heading straight for them.

The air had already begun to thin. At first Rehada could only feel it as a drawing of her breath, but as the wind began to howl, it became more marked, and soon it was nearly impossible to breathe. Ashan had prepared them for this. Many of the streltsi did as he had commanded and held their breath. Two, however, did not; they quickly fell to their knees, gasping for air.

The streltsi held their muskets up in a warding gesture, using the iron to ward against the hezhan. They knew it would do little more than give it pause, but they knew it was necessary for Ashan and Rehada to fight as they could.

Ashan was already using his stone of alabaster to dampen the wind, but in comparison to the elder his spirit was weak and was having little effect.

Rehada closed her eyes and opened herself to her suurahezhan. She willed flame into being, deep within the body of the havahezhan.

One of the streltsi tilted forward and fell into the muddy snow, unconscious. Another joined him moments later, his nose breaking and spouting blood over the trampled earth.

Rehada redoubled her efforts, imploring her bonded spirit to help. She felt it feeding from her, pulling from the stuff of life to sustain itself in this world. She pushed harder than she ever had, and the flame burned brightly within the havahezhan.

Ashan was communing with his vanahezhan as well, sending mounds of earth against the wind spirit. It would not be harmed by such things directly, but the presence of earth sapped its strength, and soon Rehada could feel the wind returning to her lungs. She took a deep breath, preparing for the next attack, but as she did the earth lifted beneath her and threw her a dozen feet through the air.

She landed on her back with a woof. She heard ringing in her ears as all other sound fell away. Her breath came in shallow gasps. She stared up at the blanket of gray clouds in the sky, wondering how she had come to be here.

The ringing peaked and then began to ebb. She heard an almighty crash, followed by a pounding that she could feel in the earth beneath her.

She raised her head and stared toward the keep. The vanahezhan—as tall as the keep itself—had burst through the wooden gates and was stalking toward them. Within the walls, the frothing form of a jalahezhan was pulling itself to full height. It looked like a water funnel, but then it too slipped over the wall and began to slide and glide over the snow toward them.

The presence of the jalahezhan could be felt, even at a distance. Coupled with the havahezhan, the elements opposed to fire, it was too much to fight, and Rehada could feel her control slipping away.

She stood and drew upon her suurahezhan, hoping it wasn't too late. "Now, Ashan!"

Together they burned the spirit of air. She could feel the intensity, but she knew it wouldn't be enough. Her energy was already flagging. Mere moments later, she collapsed. Her head hung low as pain rippled through her. The havahezhan had done something that had never happened before. It had torn her bonded spirit, leaving her soul bare. The only thing that had come close was those rare cases when her circlet had been taken from her unwillingly, but this felt infinitely worse. It felt as if a part of her had been ripped away, leaving her bloody and raw inside.

Ashan stood nearby, holding his own against the elder, but the tide had already begun to turn. He shook, his gentle face locked in a grimace.

And then he fell. The grass smoked as it was touched by his skin. He lay there, his chest unmoving, while the havahezhan descended upon the soldiers. Some screamed, but the sounds of their pain was swallowed by the thundering gale that now enveloped them.

One by one the streltsi dropped. One lay a few paces away from Rehada, his eyes already vacant. Small rocks and ice cut into his lifeless face, leaving small trails of red against his snow-white skin.

Rehada turned to see the elder suurahezhan slipping over the walls of Oshtoyets. She could no longer feel her bonded hezhan, but she could feel the elder, and it occurred to her how akin it felt to her. It was hundreds of yards away, but there was a purity about it that she could not help but admire. She wondered who it might have been in another life, how great it might be in the next.

Perhaps it had been her mother. Perhaps Ahya.

She stood, knowing what she was about to do was not wise, but knowing also that she would do it even if the hezhan claimed her. "To me!" she cried, rallying the few remaining soldiers. "To me, men of Khalakovo!"

They heard something in her voice, some small amount of hope, and five of them formed a guard in front of her. Two were sucked away by the raging wind, but the rest were able to escort her up toward the keep.

The jalahezhan had slithered down the hill, but the suurahezhan had moved faster. Rehada stood in its path, motioning the streltsi to stop and allow her to proceed.

The suurahezhan, wavering heat rising above the dark red surface of its skin, came to a halt before Rehada. It recognized her, and for the moment did not attack. Rehada threw aside her circlet—knowing this was no spirit to be enticed by mere stones—and spread her arms wide. "I am yours," she said simply. Her mind was as resolute as it ever would be. There was no fear, only purpose and a willingness to give of herself.

The elder did not need her—it had already entered the world and had no need of a bridge—but it was intrigued, and it felt a kinship, the same kinship that Rehada felt with every bit of her heart.

Rehada stepped forward.

And felt the fire of the world.

It consumed her, gave light to the innermost recesses of her mind, those places she hadn't wanted to visit, hadn't wanted to uncover. But she had been ready for this—there was no longer anything left for her to hide.

The spirit felt this. It accepted her, and for the time being, granted her a bond.

She turned toward the havahezhan, which had sensed this new threat and was now twisting toward her. The Landed soldiers scrambled away, watching her with crazed eyes. They feared her, which was as it should be. She was flame. She was fire itself.

Her clothes burned away. She stood naked in the snow, pouring herself into one last effort as the havahezhan raged against her, hoping to knock her from her feet. But she was no mere candle to be snuffed by an errant breeze.

She could feel the pain of the wind spirit, could feel it slipping away toward Adhiya. Had it not been weakened already, it might have fought longer, but as it was, the suurahezhan was too strong, and soon the spirit of wind was lost, the last remnant of its existence a buffet of wind against the snow.

The vanahezhan was closing in, its earthen form looming large. Ashan had regained his feet. He seemed pained with exertion as he drew water up from beneath the earth, using the snow to infuse the earth spirit as it approached. More and more of its form was softened by the water, ablating it as the thing stalked forward.

The hezhan paused, however, and replenished itself with the muddy earth at its feet. It was slowed, but it would not be defeated. Not like this.

The jalahezhan reached two of the soldiers who were holding up their guns. It bore down on them, splitting around their simple defense and drowning them in moments.

The shot of a cannon brought Rehada's attention toward the keep. A passing ship unleashed another cannon shot into the courtyard. Several more ships followed, each of them loosing blasts of their own.

The jalahezhan, perhaps sensing they were a greater threat, turned toward the oncoming ships. Droplets of water flew off of its body and up toward the nearest of them. More and more of it flowed like rain up and against the oncoming galleon, its body shrinking as it did so. It fell against the sails and the deck of the ship as the crewmen working frantically to prepare their dousing rods.

And then it reformed.

Musket fire snapped across the ship. Men shouted as the water spirit slipped around the men holding the dousing rods and attacked those that had yet to fire.

The vanahezhan had finished with the forward streltsi. Only two streltsi and the sotnik remained. Ashan was still trying to slow the approach of the vanahezhan. Rehada summoned the power of the suurahezhan once more, focusing a blast of heat against the spirit of earth.

The vanahezhan stopped. It seemed to gather its strength. A moment later the earth rolled before it like a wave upon the water. It traveled outward—tight and focused on Rehada and Ashan.

It struck, sending her flying. She landed with a thud as the wave of earth thundered onward and was lost among the sloping hills behind her.

She looked toward Ashan. He lay unmoving, unconscious or dead. The vanahezhan lumbered forward, mere moments from reaching him.

She poured everything she had left, but she had already given too much. She managed a gout of flame that lasted no longer than a breath, and then the suurahezhan released her, knowing she was now little more than a mere husk. The moment it did, however, it slipped back through the aether to Adhiya. The vanahezhan's attack had weakened it—that and the demands Rehada had placed on it—and when it had released her, it had also released a critical bond that was keeping it squarely grounded to this world.

In a way she was glad, for she could no longer have controlled it, but in another it made her desperate, for she had been left utterly powerless to prevent the vanahezhan from reaching Ashan.

CHAPTER 65

The wind whipped around Nikandr, pushed harder and harder against his frame as he rushed toward the sea. His descent was slowing, but it seemed impossible to prevent himself from plummeting into the waves. Strangely, that only deepened his commitment to the hezhan. He released all of his worries, all of his hopes, and drew strength from the hezhan, asking—not demanding—that it help him.

The winds blew harder. It rushed up and around him, whipping his clothes and his hair. He slowed and halted in midair—only seconds from the water—and then he was flying upward along the cliff. The walls of Oshtoyets were high above him. He urged the winds to push him faster, knowing there was little time left. He had to reach Nasim to protect him somehow.

The wind roared in his ears as he crested the wall. In the center of the courtyard was the black spire towering five stories high, and at its base was Nasim, chained to a spike set into the obsidian stone. The Maharraht stood around the spire in a circle, chanting, but as Nikandr moved toward the battlements, one of them spotted him. Nikandr could not hear above the noise, but the Maharraht summoned another, who had an alabaster stone set into the circlet on his brow. He raised his hands, and immediately the winds shifted, pushing Nikandr over the courtyard.

And then the wind was utterly, inexplicably gone. He fell nearly two stories and crashed onto the stone, striking his head as he did so.

Pain resounded through him—especially along the back of his skull—as he woke to a low and rhythmic chanting. He tried to move, but cold metal held his wrists in place. His arms were pulled painfully above his head.

Soroush stood before him, his eyes serious, his long black beard blowing in the wind. "It is true that the fates are kind." He did not seem smug, but rather grateful, as if he truly felt that the fates had smiled upon him.

"The day is not yet done," Nikandr replied.

"But it is, Nikandr Iaroslov. It is." He held the stone of opal between his fingers. "This was the first of the stones—I found it on Rhavanki—but did you know that you granted me the second?"

Nikandr shivered, knowing it was true.

"Rehada gave me the third. My brother the fourth. And your betrothed gave me the fifth. We are linked, you and I, through more than this struggle." He paused, waiting for this all to sink in. "I wonder if we were not brothers in another life."

An acid taste formed in Nikandr's mouth. He spit to clear it.

Soroush smiled, not unkindly. "You may think not, but how can you not see what has become of the two of us and not wonder why we have been brought together? Or perhaps you think your ancestors have been watching over you. Have they, son of Iaros? Have they brought this into being?"

"The ancients cannot see all there is to see."

"*Neh?*" He regarded the glimmering jewel held between his thumb and forefinger. "But they must see what is coming now."

"Nikandr?"

It was Nasim's voice. Nikandr turned. He was unable to see Nasim, but he knew he was there. He could *feel* him—chained to another face of the spire.

"Please help me."

Soroush seemed bothered by these words, but he quickly regained his composure. "He cannot, child."

Soroush may have spoken more—Nikandr isn't sure, because his awareness expands. He loses touch with the reality around him. His eyes roll back into his head, and he can no longer feel his body, but he can feel the granite cutting down through the cliff and the rivers running through the hills of Duzol.

He stands on the shores of Adhiya. He feels the heat of white fire, the cold of eternally shifting waters, the touch of wind and the solidity of earth and stone—through it all runs the essence of life. Like thread along a seam these elements draw Nasim tighter—the part of him that walks the lands of the spirits is bit by bit being drawn closer to his self in the mortal plane. This is by design—it is what Soroush has been planning to do ever since landing on Khalakovo.

The scene in the courtyard is shown through Nasim's senses. The stone of opal—the last of the stones—glitters between Soroush's fingers, inches from Nasim's mouth.

Nasim dearly wishes to take it.

Do not, Nasim.

He hears Nikandr's words, but the lure is simply too strong. This stone is part of him, just as the other four now are. It is with this realization that thoughts crystallize in Nikandr's mind, thoughts that had been eluding him since the ritual started—these spirits, these elders, are aspects of Nasim, perhaps former lives, perhaps future ones.

Accept him, Sariya said. He must. He must do this, or all will be lost. He has been trying to remain grounded—trying to remain *himself*—while still helping Nasim, but this is not the way. He must give of himself that Nasim might live.

So he releases completely. He is a rock among the waters that Nasim might swim to, and Nasim finds that he is able to resist the call of the stone being offered to him, to resist that final aspect of himself, no matter how enticing it might be. In this small victory he finds courage.

A look of confusion plays across Soroush's face. He strokes Nasim's hair. "There is nothing to fear, child."

Still Nasim disobeys. There is a light that sparks within him that has not been present until now.

Soroush's face becomes not angry, but filled with intent. He presses a forearm against Nasim's throat and with his other hand tries to force the stone into Nasim's mouth.

Nasim resists, shaking his head back and forth.

Soroush strikes again and again.

It takes only one small slip, and the stone is inside.

Spit it out, Nikandr says.

There is a pause. Nasim stares up at the layer of clouds. Nikandr can taste the stone, taste the call of Adhiya. He can feel Nasim's other half—the half he has been separated from since birth—resolve itself. It is now clearer than it has ever been, and there is an undeniable attraction to it.

Nasim forgets Soroush, forgets about the hezhan that have been summoned and the one that awaits.

Forgets Nikandr.

Nyet! Nikandr pleads. *Please, Nasim, do not do this.*

He can think of nothing save this rift—this gulf—that has defined his existence, that has caused him so much pain.

Nasim!

Ever so briefly, he glances over to Nikandr.

And then he swallows the stone.

A release of pleasure and ecstasy follows. Nasim has been fractured for so long that he doesn't know what to do with himself now that he's been made whole.

So he screams.

The earth beneath him buckles. With a sound like rolling thunder, the curtain wall cracks. The remaining door at the gate splinters with an audible snap, sending shards of wood flying. The dhoshahezhan—the final spirit—begins to resolve on the far side of the courtyard.

Nikandr feels the world slow, or rather, feels the gears of this world and of the world beyond move as he has never felt them before. Nasim was made whole when he swallowed the final stone, but he was also granted something beyond any Aramahn before him, beyond even the hezhan themselves.

He regards the courtyard anew. He sees the dhoshahezhan fully formed as the telltale sparks of lightning arc over its frame. It feels akin to another, and the realization of this brings Nikandr's presence to the fore of his mind.

A bright white flash of pain runs through Nikandr. It feels as though he has been thrown into the forge of life, to be recast as the fates see fit.

Nearby, Soroush kneels. He clasps his hands behind his back, and raises his head to the sky while his brother, Bersuq, pulls a curved khanjar from a sheath at his belt. Nikandr is confused, but as Bersuq steps forward, knife held tightly with both hands, he begins to see.

Bersuq is preparing to kill his brother. Just as Nasim sacrificed Pietr to open a channel for Nikandr's return to Erahm, Soroush's death will open a channel for Nasim to return to Adhiya. It will complete the cycle, tearing open the rift that runs through Duzol, and with it the neighboring rifts over Khalakovo and perhaps beyond.

Nikandr draws back into his own form. He hears gunfire, the shouts of men, the shots of cannons—but it is distant, as if from a dream. He rails against his bonds, screaming for Bersuq to stop. Bersuq pauses, staring into Nikandr's eyes, and in that one small moment, Nikandr feels her.

Atiana.

She is near. He knows this to be true. And can it be? She is within Bersuq. She has assumed him.

The next moment, Bersuq has resumed his march toward Soroush, preparing to lay the blade across his exposed throat.

Atiana! Do not let him do this!

A moment later, in an explosion of stone and dust, the blast of a cannon shatters the center of the courtyard. Nikandr turns away, shielding his face, coughing uncontrollably, and when he turns back he can see nothing. The entire courtyard has been reduced to a thick haze of pale yellow dust.

Atiana watches through Bersuq's eyes as a windship drifts over the keep. In the distance, two more float free of the clouds. The Maharraht have been idle, with orders to allow the ritual to proceed without interference, but now that the enemy has discovered them, they burst into action, raising their weapons and firing the keep's four large cannons on the nearest of the windships.

Though she is held within Bersuq's frame, trapped, she touches the aether still, and she can feel the shift well before the dhoshahezhan appears in the courtyard. The aether swells, pressing itself against the world as a spark of lightning materializes several paces away. The hair on Bersuq's neck and arms rise as the spirit steps fully into the world. It is a gathering of lightning, balled up into a writhing form no taller than a man, but more powerful for it.

Soroush kneels, baring his throat. Bersuq turns to him, pulling a khanjar from his belt. She doesn't understand what is happening until she hears Nikandr's voice. *Atiana! Do not let him do this!*

A moment later a cannon shot gouges the earth, and Bersuq is thrown to the ground. His ears ring, and he coughs uncontrollably as dust fills his lungs.

Nearby, the bright sparks of the dhoshahezhan shift. A white bolt of lightning flies upward and strikes one of the crewmen in the ship flying low above the keep. Through the haze, she can see it continue through one, two, three more before arcing sharply upward into the clouds. All four men fall from their perches, lifeless, two falling wide of the ship and plummeting toward the sea's cold embrace.

The ship's rear cannon belches flame and the shot passes through the hezhan. The iron fouls the spirit's next bolt, which charges through several of the Maharraht on the walls. All of them fall—one jerking spasmodically before coming to a rest.

As Bersuq's coughing begins to subside, he searches frantically for his knife. Knowing she has little time, Atiana exerts her influence over him once more. He fights, but there is little left within him that can withstand her frantic assault. He fights her every command, but still she forces him to walk to the spire. Nikandr is chained there. The muscles along Bersuq's arms are tight as harp strings, but they obey.

Nikandr collapses to the ground, but he fails to see Soroush storming up behind him.

Atiana forces Bersuq to launch himself at Soroush. As she does the presence of the Matri coalesce around her. Her mother is chief among them.

Bersuq rails against the bonds within his mind as Atiana struggles to regain her composure. *Help me,* she pleads.

But they do not. They begin instead to pull her away.

Nyet! You know not what you do!

Atiana claws at them, tries to fend them off, but there are simply too many, and soon she loses her hold.

Nikandr coughed as he fell to the broken stones of the courtyard. Bersuq stood before him, his face a mixture of pain and rage and confusion.

Nikandr shielded his eyes as a bolt of lightning cracked through the air, striking the chain holding Nasim to the spire. The chains that held Nasim in place clanked as they fell to his sides.

The air was ripe with possibility, with hope. The rift was present—it was in Nikandr's gut, in his chest—and he could feel how Nasim struggled with the place he was in, standing squarely at a fork in the path of both worlds. His face was in more pain that Nikandr had ever seen, but he did not cower. He did not flinch.

Nikandr looked down at his soulstone. It was as bright as it had been in the tower in Alayazhar. *Accept him*, Sariya had said. *Give of yourself.*

He had not known what that meant. But he understood now.

He wrenched the stone downward, breaking the chain. With Nasim watching, he held it out. It glowed brilliantly now, brighter than it ever had.

"You are sure?" Nasim asked.

"I am," Nikandr replied, knowing that he was giving Nasim more than just a simple piece of chalcedony. This was part of him, as much as his father, his mother. His sister and brother. It was not an easy thing to surrender, but he did so gladly.

Nasim took it in his hands, staring at it for a good long moment. And then he placed it in his mouth.

But nothing happened.

Nothing.

By the ancients, what had gone wrong?

Atiana watches as Nasim consumes Nikandr's stone. He glows whiter than he had before, but that is the only difference she can see. She can feel his pain even from this distance, even without trying to—so great has it become. How he is managing to contain it all she cannot imagine.

Soroush is raging, perhaps demanding that the Maharraht fire upon him, but Nasim raises a finger, issues a thought, and the dhoshahezhan sends a bolt of lightning through him.

The keep's gates are shattered and ruined. Through them file a dozen streltsi led by Grigory. Several train their weapons on the Maharraht, but their weapons do not fire. A moment later they drop them as if they've been burned.

The Maharraht smile—Nasim, they believe, has joined them—but moments later the same happens to them, leaving everyone weaponless with an elder spirit standing in their midst.

Atiana is loosely connected to the Matri, but her mother begins to slip from her consciousness. She realizes too late that she is attempting to assume Nasim.

Nyet! Atiana pleads.

She knows what she is about, the other Matri tell her.

She does not! Atiana shouts. *Do not allow her to do this.*

We cannot abide this boy—

Atiana does not listen. Something else has drawn her attention. She has realized how present the walls of the aether are—they are close, as they were along the rift on Uyadensk, but they are not close enough. What Nikandr has done will not complete the cycle. The walls are still too far apart for him to bridge the gap.

She calms herself.

As she did with the babe, as she did with Nasim before, she touches the walls, but unlike those other times she does not push them away. Instead she draws them inward.

And they obey.

Moments later a surge of energy courses through her.

Nasim collapses as a storm is unleashed upon the aether. She can feel the emotions of the other Matri, but also of the Maharraht, of the streltsi, of Grigory, of Rehada somewhere outside the walls. And Nikandr.

But she cannot feel Nasim's.

Or Mother's.

The pain grows within her until it reaches beyond the heights of the clouds, beyond even the stars.

And she woke.

Woke to the sound of the cold, bitter wind, her heart barely beating, her skin numb to the world.

This cannot be, she thought sadly as she lay there, listening once again to the sad sound of the shore, to the soft breeze playing among the boughs of the pine.

She turned her head and looked upon the trees—tall and green and proud. She stared at them a good long while, wondering where the world might take her.

This was a good place to die, she decided—whether she was taken into the house of her ancestors or returned to Adhiya in preparation for the next life, she could be proud of what she had done.

CHAPTER 66

The musket shots around Rehada had stopped. The streltsi—only the sotnik and two others remained—were out of ammunition. They limped forward and placed themselves between her and the lumbering vanahezhan, protecting her, but they made no move to do the same for Ashan, who lay unconscious a dozen yards away.

"Please," Rehada said, "save him."

The sotnik, blood streaming along the side of his eye and down his cheek from a vicious cut to his forehead, looked down at her with dispassionate eyes. "I'll not waste more lives."

The vanahezhan was now only a handful of strides away from Ashan.

"He's done his best to save you."

"There's nothing we can do."

The vanahezhan had reached Ashan. Rehada ran forward, crying out and waving her arms, hoping to distract it, even if only for a moment. The hezhan, however, was of a singular mind. It stared down—perhaps curious over an arqesh like Ashan—but then reared up and raised its arms over its head.

But then the ground it stood upon broke, crumbling beneath its feet. It stumbled, trying to regain its footing as more and more earth gave way. A sinkhole had opened up like some great, gaping mouth. And then, as quick and deadly as a landslide, the edges of it snapped closed with a resounding boom.

Rehada scanned the horizon, knowing Ashan could not have done such a thing. The clouds were beginning to break apart, revealing here and there the dark blue sky. Skiffs were slipping down between them—not just a few, but dozens, then hundreds.

The Landed caravel was still under attack. All three topsails were fluttering loose. Another broke free of the ship completely and floated on the unseen currents. She could not see the jalahezhan, but the ship suddenly began to tilt. Then the nose dipped landward. It was already low in the sky, nearing the ground, and the tilting of the forward portions of the ship caused the bowsprit to gouge a long trench into the earth.

Rehada watched in horror as the twelve-masted ship crumbled while rolling onto its side—masts snapping and cracking in the cold wind. It slid against the snow and muddy earth for a hundred paces before finally coming to a halt.

The jalahezhan emerged from the bowels of the ship. Perhaps sensing the newest threat, it sprayed itself against the incoming skiffs. A dozen were weighted down, and they dropped like kingfishers. Several twisted in the air like maple seeds, throwing the Aramahn within them to the fate of the winds. They plummeted and struck the earth not far from the ruined windship.

The qiram reacted quickly. Wind was pulled from the sky to mingle with the elder. It was difficult to follow with the naked eye, but there were telltale signs of motion—sprays of blue water flowing between skiffs. A sound like the sigh of the surf drifted down from the unassuming battle, but it grew in volume until it resounded like the mighty crash of water against the cliffs below Radiskoye.

And then, in the span of a heartbeat, the sound was gone.

She felt someone at her shoulder. It was the younger of the two remaining streltsi, holding a cherkesska for her to wear over her naked form. She took it gladly. Even had she a bonded spirit, she was in no state to summon even a meager amount of warmth.

She waved to the sotnik. "We must go to the keep. Quickly."

The sotnik paused only to retrieve a musket and to load it with ammunition retrieved from the dead. His two streltsi did likewise, and then they were off, moving as quickly as they could toward the keep.

Off to the northwest, four large ships of the Grand Duchy had moved in and were holding position. Nearly a dozen skiffs were launched, each bearing a score of soldiers, but before they could move more than a dozen yards, they were blown back by a fierce wind.

Rehada shaded her eyes and stared southward. This was the Aramahn's doing. They would not allow the Landed to approach the keep—not while things were still tenuous.

Dozens upon dozens of Aramahn skiffs were now heading toward their position. Without speaking, Rehada and Ashan and the soldiers picked up their pace—they were all eager to reach the keep's interior before the Aramahn could do anything to prevent it.

Inside, the fallen lay everywhere. Grigory's men stood just inside the gates. The Maharraht were atop the wall and at the base of it. Some were clearly dead, but many were alive—lying down, eyes closed, breathing shallowly.

"Check them," Ashan said to the sotnik.

The sotnik pointed for his men to check the Maharraht upon the wall. As they moved to obey, Rehada saw the sotnik pause and level a severe expression on Nasim. He seemed angry, this man, but in the end Rehada wrote it off as curiosity over the boy who had been at the center of this raging storm.

She gave it little thought as she moved toward the spire, where Nasim lay. Nasim watched her approach, but he said nothing. She might have thought he was still in the state he'd always seemed to be in, but she knew better. His expression of pain—a nearly constant companion—had been replaced with a look of serenity. It looked strange upon him, though she was glad that he had somehow—even if it lasted only for a short time—found peace.

Ashan looked down upon Nasim, and then to Soroush and Bersuq, who lay next to one another. Ashan seemed confused as he studied them, perhaps wondering what had come to pass within these walls.

"Rehada?"

She turned.

And her breath caught.

For long moments, she could only stare. Nikandr was standing in a doorway leading into the keep proper.

"How?" she asked.

He did not answer. He merely strode forward and took her into a deep embrace. It was warm, and tender, and though she felt many eyes upon them, she did nothing to stop it.

Finally she pulled away, though it was with great reluctance. She walked with him back toward the spire and kneeled to get a closer look at Nasim. She brushed a stray lock of hair away from his eyes. "Are you here with us?"

Nasim studied her intently with his bright brown eyes. "Atiana lies upon the beach." He turned to look at Nikandr. "There is time yet to save her."

Nikandr smiled and nodded. "We will, Nasim."

And then Rehada heard a click.

She spun toward the gates and found the sotnik sighting along the length of his musket. For a split second she thought he was aiming at her.

But then she understood.

She began moving, already knowing it would be too late. He had all the time in the world.

She fell across Nasim as the gun roared. She felt something bite the small of her back. It burned bright white and she spasmed while holding tight to Nasim.

"*Neh!*" Nasim shouted as Nikandr screamed in rage.

Another musket was fired. Was it right above her? She could no longer tell.

Her thigh felt warm. It had been so cold for so long she didn't realize how badly it would tingle. She felt it along her shin as well, and then the pain became so great that she was forced to roll off Nasim and onto her back.

She stared up at the sky. The swiftly moving clouds were continuing to break. Bits of blue could be seen, and the sun, lowering to the west, shone down upon her for the first time that day.

Nikandr kneeled over her. He was speaking but she couldn't tell what he was saying. Nasim was there as well. His face was not full of sorrow, as she had expected, but instead hope. She knew somewhere within herself that he was being brave for her—just as Malekh had been those many weeks ago. He had stood upon the gallows and smiled upon her. How could she not do the same for Nasim?

She smiled as her body grew heavy. She reached up and brushed Nasim's cheek. "Go well," she tried to say, but the sounds were so soft she could barely hear them.

She turned to Nikandr, who looked down on her not with a smile but with an expression of deep regret.

"Do not be sad, Nischka," she whispered. "We will meet again."

"You don't know that," he said.

She managed to nod despite the pain that came with it. "We will."

And then, she could do no more than look upon the sky.

She was ready.

At last, the world, as it had before, as it would again, folded her into its sweet embrace.

CHAPTER 67

"Come."

Nikandr heard the words, but he couldn't manage to turn away. Rehada stared unmoving at the sky. Her face had gone slack and she looked nothing like the woman he had—however imperfectly—come to know these past several years. It was painful to see her like this, but he could no more turn his gaze away than he could turn back the sands of time.

"Come," Ashan said, more forcefully. "There is another to attend to."

Finally, Nikandr complied, but before they could move from where they stood, the gates were pushed open and a dozen Aramahn men and women stepped inside. They took in the scene around them, looking to Nikandr like a tribunal ready to mete both judgment and punishment.

"There is a woman," Nikandr began.

"She has been found." It was Fahroz. But she looked so different. It felt as if he'd been gone from Khalakovo for years.

She pointed toward the far side of the courtyard. Three score of Aramahn filed into the keep and began picking up the fallen Maharraht.

Nikandr shook his head. "Leave them. The Duke, my father—"

"Your father has no say in this." The tone of her voice was emotionless, but her eyes were bright with anger. "These are our own, and will be treated as such." She held out her hand, and Nikandr realized that she was motioning for Nasim.

Nasim looked up at Nikandr, his eyes wide.

Ashan stepped forward. "Do not do this, daughter of Lilliah. The boy has been through much."

"You have never known when you were wasting words, son of Ahrumea, but I tell you that you are doing so now. The boy comes with us."

Several qiram were there, their circlets aflame with the hezhan that were bonded to them. They were prepared to resist, if that was what it came to, but none of them appeared ready to welcome it.

Ashan touched Nasim's shoulders. "All will be well, Nasim. You must go with them."

"I will not."

Tension laced Nasim's words. Nikandr knew what he could do—the evidence lay all around them—but something told him that the time had passed. Fahroz may have known this, but more likely she didn't care. The Aramahn had risked much and were willing to risk more to ensure that Nasim was taken into proper care.

Ashan kneeled next to Nasim until they were face to face. "You will be at home with them. And there is little left that I can teach you."

A tear leaked from Nasim's eye and traveled down his cheek. It was followed quickly by another. "Do not lie, Ashan. Not to me."

Ashan smiled. "Lying is a thing with which I have become all too familiar. Better for us to be parted if only for that." Nasim opened his mouth to speak, but Ashan talked over him. "We will see each other again—do not fear—but for now, you must go with Fahroz."

Nasim swallowed several times, and then turned to Nikandr. "We are one, you and I."

Nikandr knew this to be true. He could feel Nasim more strongly than ever before. Nikandr suspected it was due to the fact that Nasim now stood firmly in Erahm, but it was also because the rift had been healed. It was still there—like a fresh and aching wound—but it was no longer festering. Soon it would scar over and the healing of Khalakovo would begin.

Nikandr kneeled to look Nasim in the eye. "We are, Nasim. We are one."

For a moment Nasim looked fragile, as if he wanted nothing more than to simply be held, to embrace someone that he loved, but then he turned on his heels and strode from the courtyard, never once looking back.

The suddenness of it made Nikandr feel lost. "I would see him again," Nikandr said to Fahroz.

As the last of the Maharraht were carried out of the keep, Fahroz's expression was deadly serious. "Do not place your hopes on such a thing, son of Saphia. As long as we are able, your paths will never again cross."

Two Aramahn entered the courtyard carrying a length of canvas between them. They laid it down gently near the spire, and Fahroz motioned for Nikandr to approach. "Take care of her." With that, she left, the rest of the Aramahn filing out behind her.

He had known Atiana was among the folds of heavy white cloth, but it was a vast relief when he kneeled and saw her face. Her clothes were beyond bloody, but her dress had been ripped away at her side, and a bolt of white cloth had been wrapped around her to stanch the bleeding. She was extremely pale, but her eyes were open, and she seemed more alert than he could have hoped for.

"It's all right," Nikandr said softly.

Atiana blinked and focused on him. A soft smile came to her lips, but then her head turned to one side and all trace of relief fled. She had spotted Rehada.

A tear leaked down Atiana's face.

She seemed grieved. Truly, deeply grieved.

Nikandr understood it not at all, but he gripped Atiana's shoulder and whispered into her ear that everything would be all right.

A strelet opened one of the stout iron gates of the Boyar's mansion, and Nikandr rode out and into the streets of the old city. He passed the circle where the gibbets lay, the place that he had seen Rehada while those boys were being hanged. He had checked the court records and had come to suspect that the Aramahn boy that had been hung with the urchins was innocent of the charges—as he had claimed all along. He was not innocent of all things, however. He had been working for Rehada, Nikandr was sure; he had been her servant, running messages between Volgorod and Izhny, perhaps since Rehada had arrived on the island.

Nikandr shook his head as he reined his pony northward, toward Eyrie Road. He had been such a fool. He should have suspected Rehada shortly after they'd met. He had been wracking his brain for the last week, trying to piece together the clues that should have been apparent from the start, but he had so far been almost completely unsuccessful. Only in Malekh had he found any small link from Rehada to the Maharraht. She had covered her tracks well—either that or Nikandr had convinced himself that because of her beauty, because of how different her world was from his, that she could not possibly mean him harm.

He had been a fool, but he would not change any of it. He had loved her—he was man enough to admit that now—and had things gone differently, he might never have come to know her as he had.

"Nikandr!" The sound of another pony trotting came to him, muffled by the thin layer of snow upon the ground.

Nikandr slowed his pony, but did not turn around.

Ranos pulled alongside him and matched his black mare to Nikandr's cream-colored gelding. "Where are you headed?"

"None of your business, brother."

They continued to ride in silence for a time, moving from the older section of the city to one that was newer, with smaller, half-timber frames and small yards behind stout stone walls.

"I don't blame you for being reticent—there is much for you to consider, I'll admit—but when the sun sets on this day, it must end. I need you."

"I am not a bookkeeper, Ranos."

"You will be running the shipping of our family."

"I would do this family a greater service by *flying* a ship."

"As you've made perfectly clear, but we can take no chances, not with Father being taken to Vostroma, not with Borund sitting on the throne of Radiskoye."

Nikandr's face burned as their ponies climbed up a curving stone bridge and down the other side. "Borund may find his seat difficult to keep."

Ranos shook his head. "I will not discuss this again. Borund will be our liege for the next two years, and if anything happens to him—be it death from the plague or a fall from a height—Father's life will be forfeit."

Nikandr could still remember how the blood had drained from his face when he had learned what had happened. The battle for the eyrie had gone well, but Mother was horribly weakened. She had been the reason they could overpower the other Matri in the first place, but she had been left permanently crippled by her time with Nasim. With their communications restored, Zhabyn had been able to make better use of his superior numbers.

In little time they turned the tide, and Father had been caught off guard. His ship had been captured as well as that of Yevgeny Mirkotsk. Mirkotsk was offered his rightful place in the Grand Duchy if only Iaros would step down and allow Borund to take his place. It would be an arrangement that would last two years, during which time Iaros would become thrall to Vostroma. Mother would be forced to step down as well, though Nikandr knew that this was a much worse punishment than the one that awaited Father. Mother had been too close to the aether for too long to be separated from it now. She would die—Nikandr knew this—but there was no persuading Vostroma to allow anything different. They would kill her before they allowed her to take the dark again.

If there were no uprisings and if Khalakovo produced as they should, further sanctions would not be levied and Father's title would be restored to him at the end of the two years.

A meeting had been held that very night in Radiskoye and Zhabyn had been selected as Grand Duke. He had accepted the newly made crown on Father's throne.

Though his presence had been requested by Zhabyn himself, Father had not attended. He had elected to stay among the rooms on the lower levels that had such a short time ago been home to Nasim and Ashan, and later Atiana.

And now he was boarding a ship, ready to sail for Palotza Galostina.

Nikandr and Ranos continued their ride through the outskirts of Volgorod and up the slope toward the island's central ridge. The wind was clearer here, unobstructed, and it cut through their heavy cherkesskas mercilessly, but neither of them spurred their ponies to move any faster. They were men of the Grand Duchy. The wind was a part of their bones.

They finally reached the ridge, at which point both of them stopped.

To the east stood Verodnaya. A third of the way down from the snowy peak was Radiskoye, a crystalline jewel among the hard black rock of the mountain. They could not see the palotza's eyrie from this vantage, but they didn't need to. The ship they were here to watch had already drifted upward from its perch and was now cutting westward. It was Vostroma's largest ship. All sixteen of its masts took on sail, but Nikandr saw, even from this distance, the signs of battle upon the hull and the hastily repaired canvas. His father lay on board that ship, a prisoner to the man that had betrayed him.

It continued west, and though it was too distant for Nikandr to identify any individuals standing on the deck, there was, near the stern, someone holding a red bolt of cloth. It fluttered in the wind, and then it was released. It floated lazily behind the ship, making its way toward solid ground.

"And what pray tell is that?" Ranos asked.

"That, dear brother, is none of your business."

Ranos studied Nikandr for a time. They had discussed Atiana many times over the past week, Ranos each time advising him to forget about her, but he knew as well as Nikandr that the cloth had been held by Atiana, that it had been sent as a sign of her love, and if Nikandr felt he should reserve some special place for her, then perhaps, after all of this, he deserved the right to do so.

"Farewell," Ranos said softly.

This was not spoken to Nikandr, nor Atiana, but to their father.

"Farewell," Nikandr repeated, for Father and Atiana, both.

When the ship had become no more than a mark on the horizon, Ranos pulled his reins over and began heading back toward the city. "Coming?" he said.

"I have business to attend to," Nikandr said, and he spurred his pony in the other direction, toward Iramanshah.

Ranos said nothing in return. They had discussed how often he should visit the village, but on this particular day he was going to give him all the leeway he needed.

It took Nikandr three hours to reach Iramanshah. He was pressing to make it in such a short time, but it was necessary to get there by midday.

Ashan met him at the edge of the village.

"Come," he said simply.

They continued through the narrow pass that led to the village and the valley that housed it.

"I leave tomorrow," Ashan said simply.

Nikandr knew the day had been fast approaching. There were so many partings today that he was having trouble conceiving of just how much he would miss them all. Better for it to happen now, quickly. There was much for him to do in the days ahead, and it was best that he start it with a fresh mind.

"You go to look for Nasim?"

"*Da*. He was spirited away three nights ago."

Nikandr knew this already. He had felt it. The bond they shared lingered for days after, but then it began to fade, and he had known that they were taking him far, far away to a place where no one could manipulate him, to a place where he could be taught by the Aramahn mahtar in a way that they saw fit. The feeling had diminished over the course of the next day, and then, last night, it had simply vanished.

He didn't know whether the feelings would reawaken when Nasim came near—perhaps they would cease altogether once they had been apart long enough—but Nikandr suspected that their bond would remain until one of them was dead.

"I would thank you, son of Iaros."

Nikandr shook his head, ready to put off such compliments, but he stopped when Ashan raised his hand and smiled.

"Not for saving us," Ashan continued, "though there is that too. It is for befriending him, for leading him here. It is a greater gift than I had ever hoped for, and I'm sure Nasim feels the same way."

Nikandr couldn't respond. He still wasn't sure how he felt toward Nasim. As a friend. A father. A disciple. It was an uncomfortable mixture, one he was not ready to discuss.

When they reached the large stone plaza before the entrance to the village, they found hundreds of Aramahn standing near the fountain, which for the first time in Nikandr's memory was dry.

Fahroz, holding a lit torch, stood by a small, shallow-sided skiff. Within it, wrapped completely by white cloth, was Rehada. The torch burned black smoke as Fahroz spoke words of hope, words that asked the fates for kindness to this child of the world, and hope that she had learned enough in this life to resume her path toward vashaqiram.

Nikandr listened at first, but his mind began to drift to Rehada, their memories, and it was enough for him to simply wish her well.

"It is fire that granted her," Fahroz said, "and it was fire that took her."

She touched the torch to the bottom of the skiff. In moments a healthy flame had spread along the wood that had been stacked beneath Rehada's white, bound form. Another qiram with a glowing opal held within the circlet upon his brow stepped forward and gently touched the hull of the skiff. Immediately the craft began to rise. It had no sail, and so was taken by the wind. It was slow, gentle at first, but the wind was stronger higher up, and it began to tug at the craft, making it bob as it slid eastward.

It was not lost upon Nikandr that Atiana had traveled on another ship mere hours ago—though in the opposite direction. Ironic, but apropos.

"Farewell," Nikandr said as black smoke wafted ahead of the ship and across the blue sky.

The Aramahn began to separate—first alone, then in pairs and in groups. Fahroz joined Ashan and Nikandr.

There was an uncomfortable silence until Ashan finally bowed his head and said, "You have business to attend to." He stepped forward and kissed Nikandr's cheeks. "Keep well, Nikandr, son of Iaros.

"And you, Ashan, son of Ahrumea."

Soon, Nikandr was left alone with Fahroz. She made no form of greeting. She simply turned and headed into the village. "You should not come often."

"I won't once I'm sure that she is well."

"She is as well as she will ever be."

Nikandr let the comment go.

She led him deep into the bowels of Iramanshah, past the formed tunnels to the raw passageways that had been forged by Erahm herself. Finally, they came to a massive cavern with a black lake crowding a small stone beach. A pier lit brightly by siraj lanterns led a short way out into the water. Upon the pier stood Victania and Olgana, talking softly with one another, both of them peering down into the water.

A rook, standing on a silver perch just next to them, flapped its wings as Nikandr approached. Then it stilled and was silent.

When Victania noticed him, she spoke softly to Olgana, and Olgana left, bowing her head to Nikandr as she passed. Nikandr waited, hoping that Fahroz would leave as well, but she did not. She ruled here, and she would no longer stand by as the Aramahn were used, so she stood and watched as Nikandr made his way out along the pier.

He stopped when he saw his mother resting below the surface of the dark water, a breathing tube rising above the surface. "Is she well?" he asked Victania.

"Not well, but better than we had hoped."

Victania was watching Nikandr closely. He waited for her to speak, and grew uncomfortable when she did not. "Out with it," he said.

She placed a tender hand on his shoulder, waiting for him to look her in the eye. He obliged, and was surprised to find a look of regret in her eyes.

"I am sorry, Nischka."

"Whatever for?"

"There was more to them both than I would have guessed."

He didn't really wish to speak of them—not so soon after saying good-bye—but this was a compassionate gesture from a sister who was not often given to them. "Thank you."

She pulled him into an embrace. "And thank *you*." She was shivering, and he realized it was not from the cold.

She was referring to her condition. The wasting. The rift had begun to heal. All but those worst affected had already begun to show signs of health—Victania more than most—but Nikandr felt, as did Ashan, that few would be healed completely and that someday the rift would return, or a new one would form, and the disease would begin its steady march once more.

"Look at me," Victania said.

Nikandr realized his eyes were unfocused; he was staring down into the depths of the lake. He regarded Victania and held her gaze.

"You should feel proud, dear Nischka. You have given us all a gift."

"Would that I could switch places."

"But you cannot." Victania smiled, softening the severe lines of her face and exposing her true beauty. "You have been healed, thank the ancients." She glanced to one side, toward Mother. "Now is the time to look to our future, not our past. We have been given a reprieve. Best we use it wisely."

Nikandr nodded as he regarded their mother. He took in a deep breath of the frigid air and motioned for Victania to leave. "I would sit with her awhile."

Victania nodded, giving him one last quick kiss on the cheek before following Olgana up the long flight of stairs and into the village proper.

Below the surface of the water, Mother's form was lit in ghostly relief. He had come three times since she'd been moved from Radiskoye. Despite the threats from Zhabyn and Borund, there had been no choice in the matter. He was only thankful that Fahroz had agreed. *Enough have died,* she had said.

Mere moments from thinking these thoughts, the rook cawed, making Nikandr jump. "*Privyet,* Nischka."

"*Privyet,* Mother."

The rook raised its head and cawed again. A laugh. "Not so glum, my son.

Things could have turned out far, far worse."

"They could have also turned out far, far better."

"Look not to what might have been. This is a time of healing. A time of preparation. The Khalakovos are not dead."

"I know that well."

"Then act like it. Your brother needs you, and even in times like this, we must prepare. The Vostromas will not hold these islands forever, and when we return to the seat of our power, we will rise higher than we ever have before."

Empty words, Nikandr thought—Mother might not live the two years the Vostromas had agreed to, much less the years beyond that it would take them to actually relinquish control of Khalakovo. But more than this, there was something within him that Nasim and the conflict with the Maharraht had awoken. The rift had closed—everyone agreed—but this was not the end of it. Someday, another rift would form, perhaps worse than this one, and they might not have Nasim to save them when it did. The rifts must be studied, and that was where Nikandr felt he must be.

There was nothing to do about it now—his family needed him, so he would stay—but some day, some day not far from now, he would leave to discover what he could.

The rook flapped its wings. "Tell me how you summoned the boy."

"I've told you that three times already."

"It is important," the rook cawed. "Tell me again."

And so Nikandr did.

ACKNOWLEDGMENTS

The Winds of Khalakovo was years in the making, and there are many people to thank. As I was thinking about who, exactly, should be included in this note, there was a strong urge to add as many people as I could—friends and family who supported me, fellow writers who critiqued not this book, but the earliest of my scribblings, instructors at the various workshops I've attended, writers who've influenced my work, and so on and so on—but it occurs to me that I have a few books in which to thank everyone, so for the time being I'm going to set aside this page for those who directly influenced this book.

There were several people that read very early versions of the novel—a handful of chapters only—and though I feel that I inflicted upon them something that wasn't ready to read, their feedback helped to crystallize my thoughts, and for that I am grateful. Thank you Paul Genesse, Sarah Kelly, Kelly Swails, and Ian Tregillis for those quick but crucial reads.

The gang from Starry Heaven 2009 was of immense (immense!) help in taking this novel to the next level. Many exuberant thank yous go to Sarah Kelly (again), Rob Ziegler, Bill Shunn, Greg Van Eekhout, Sandra McDonald, Sarah Prineas, Jon Hansen, and Gary Shockley. Very special shout outs go to Debbie Daughetee and Deb Coates for reading the entirety of Part I, and to Eugene Myers, bless his soul, for reading not only the first fifty pages at Starry Heaven, but the entire manuscript after I completed it later that year.

There are many people to thank at Night Shade Books. Thanks to Jeremy Lassen for taking a chance on this not-quite-traditional epic fantasy. Thanks to Ross Lockhart, my editor, who championed this story and combed the manuscript countless times, looking for the hobgoblins that plagued it. Thanks to Holliann Russell, who copy-edited *Winds* with a deft hand, indeed. Thanks to John Joseph Adams for working so hard to get the word out. To Adam Paquette, a standing ovation for a cover piece that seemed to spring straight from my own imagination. And thank you to the rest of the crew at Night Shade, who do some things I'm aware of but many more that I'm not. You all deserve a healthy round of applause (and more beer).

Thanks to my agent, Russell Galen, and the fine folks at Scovil, Galen, and Ghosh. Like publishers, agents do a million things that I'm never even aware of, all with my future in mind. Though I see but little, I know that I'm in good hands, now and in the future, and for this I thank you all.

The biggest thank you of all, saved for last, goes to my good friend and brother writer, Paul Genesse. Thank you, Paul, for reading and critiquing so many versions of the manuscript and for talking with me at length about the ins and outs of this story. *Winds* would not be what it is today without your help.

ABOUT THE AUTHOR

Bradley P. Beaulieu fell in love with fantasy the moment he started reading *The Hobbit* in third grade. From that point on, though he tried reading many other things, fantasy became his touchstone. He always came back to it, and when he started to dabble in writing, fantasy—epic fantasy especially—was the type of story he most dearly wished to share. In 2006, his story, "In the Eyes of the Empress's Cat", was voted a Million Writers Award notable story, and in 2004, he became a winner in the Writers of the Future 20 contest. Other stories have appeared in *Realms of Fantasy*, *Intergalactic Medicine Show*, *Beneath Ceaseless Skies*, and several DAW anthologies.

Brad lives in Racine, Wisconsin with his wife and two children. By day, Brad is a software engineer, wrangling code into something resembling usefulness. He is also an amateur cook. He loves to cook spicy dishes, particularly Mexican and southwestern. As time goes on, Brad finds that his interests are slowly being whittled down to these two things: family and writing. In that order.

For more, please visit www.quillings.com.